Praise for Linda Winfree's *Hold On to Me*

"...a thrilling journey through danger and suspense."
~ *Sheryl, Sensual Ecataromance*

"...a welcome addition to Ms. Winfree's HEARTS OF THE SOUTH series...as engaging and gritty as its predecessors and has a depth that is undeniable...Tick's ability to forgive and his innate sexiness are hard to resist and when Caitlin finally surrenders the sex is explosive and caring in one brilliantly written love story."
~ *Jenn, Romance Junkies*

"Tick is everything you'd want in a wounded hero...Spectacular, handsome, just the right amount of Alpha male...Caitlin is a pro and she's out to prove it, but she can't quite shut the door firmly and permanently on Tick...A great read that I will keep to read again. If you like romantic suspense with as much romance as suspense...it's more than well worth your time and money."
~ *Shara, My Book Cravings*

"I couldn't stop reading it...Tick has some interrogation techniques you will not want to miss!"
~ *Tina, Two Lips Reviews*

"I like Tick. He isn't all sunshine and cheer, but he is not some self-absorbed angst-ridden fellow...Instead, he is just a man trying his best to be Captain America when it comes to his job and I have to adore him for that."
~ *Mrs. Giggles*

Look for these titles by *Linda Winfree*

Now Available:

What Mattered Most

Hearts of the South Series:
Truth and Consequences (Book 1)
His Ordinary Life (Book 2)
Hold On to Me (Book 3)
Anything But Mine (Book 4)
Memories of Us (Book 5)
Hearts Awakened (Book 6)

Coming Soon:

Hearts of the South Series:
Fall Into Me (Book 7)
Facing It (Book 8)

Hold On to Me

Linda Winfree

A SAMHAIN PUBLISHING, LTD. publication.

Samhain Publishing, Ltd.
577 Mulberry Street, Suite 1520
Macon, GA 31201
www.samhainpublishing.com

Editing by Anne Scott
Cover by Dawn Seewer

First Samhain Publishing, Ltd. electronic publication: December 2007
First Samhain Publishing, Ltd. print publication: October 2008

Dedication

For my sweetheart—you know who you are.

Chapter One

"My life is shit lately." Tick Calvert tossed another dead chicken in the pail and surveyed the floor. Squawking birds jostled for room in the sea of poultry surging through the massive state-of-the-art building. He rubbed a wrist over his sweaty forehead.

Ash pitched two feathered corpses into a bucket and chuckled. "Maybe if you thought about something other than work, it wouldn't be."

"I've got three dead girls, another missing and no leads. What should I be thinking about?" Tick hefted the five-gallon bucket of carcasses and carried it to the door. One lifeless pullet tumbled to the grass. How had he gotten roped into doing this anyway? He'd stopped by to check out a witness's story and here he was, helping Ash Hardison clear a chicken house. Fine, he owned a hefty portion of the no-waste farming operation, but none of his assignments when he'd been with the FBI had ever involved dead poultry.

"When was the last time you did something non-work related?"

"I took Mama to church Sunday." Tick stepped into the glaring oppressive sunlight of a June afternoon in Georgia. The putrid scent of death and manure lingered in his nostrils, and he dragged in deep breaths of the hot, still air. "At least I date. I haven't turned into a hermit chicken farmer like you."

"You don't date. You browse."

"Shut up, Hardison." Tick tugged off his gloves and shoved them in the back pocket of his jeans. Sweat trickled down his spine, T-shirt clinging to his skin. Today was supposed to be one of his rare days off, but he'd spent most of it verifying details from the witness statements spread across his desk at the Chandler County Sheriff's Office. It simply didn't feel right, taking a day off with those cases quickly growing cold.

Ash laughed, undisturbed. "Go home and shower. We'll get a beer later, and you can cry in it."

"Sorry, too much to do. Now tell me about Nate Holton. He says he was out here the night Sharon Ingler disappeared."

"He was." Ash shrugged. "For about an hour. Picked up a load of chickens for McGee's."

"Remember what time he arrived? When he left?"

"You're kidding, right?" Ash lifted an eyebrow at him and Tick suppressed a frustrated sigh. "It was still light when he got here, and dark when he left. I guess he arrived around eight thirty or so. Probably left at nine thirty."

Exactly the story Nate had given him. "Anything else?"

"He was sober."

Yeah, with Nate Holton, that would be unusual. To be honest, Nate wasn't really on his radar as a suspect, but checking the veracity of any witness's statement was standard procedure. "I'm out of here. Thanks for the information."

"Anytime." Ash rested a shoulder on the chicken house door. "And if you change your mind about that beer, give me a call. We hermits have to get out every once in a while."

Tick waved in acknowledgement and headed for his truck. Behind him, the door squeaked closed. A water spigot stood at a crooked angle by the driveway and he stopped to wash up. After splashing icy water on his face, he pushed his hair back and tried to ignore the annoyed dejection dogging him. Damn it, he needed a lead on this case.

A beige Chevy sedan pulled into the driveway and Tick paused by his dusty 4x4, a hand raised against the glare off the car's windshield. Another lost insurance salesperson who hadn't figured out Long Lonesome Road turned into Old Lonely Road two intersections back.

The car door opened and a pair of black, high-heeled loafers kicked up tiny puffs of dust. No-nonsense shoes, but nice ankles. If she was blonde, maybe he'd have his life insurance coverage reevaluated. The woman stepped from the car and sunlight glinted off glossy black hair. Recognition slammed through him, stopping the breath in his throat.

She walked toward him, a black suit and ivory blouse hugging her slim, athletic body. His gaze dropped to long runner's legs, made to wrap around a man's waist, and he couldn't help remembering having them around his. Arousal jolted him, hard, and fury rushed through him, even harder. He jerked his attention back to her face, the deep green eyes he knew so well hidden from him by dark sunglasses.

"Hello, Calvert."

He'd always loved hearing her say his name, the way her husky voice with its hint of a cultured Texas drawl wound around the syllables. He still had dreams about that voice. Holy hell. This was really happening. Caitlin Falconetti stood before him in all her Bureau glory, and he was dirty, wet, and smelled of dead chicken. He swallowed and pushed all the relentless anger into his voice.

"Falconetti. What brings you to the wilds and badlands of Georgia?"

"Looking for you. Your dispatcher told me where to find you when I called." She frowned and her mouth thinned. "You weren't expecting me."

Thumbs hitched in his back pockets, he looked down at her. "No, I wasn't."

But he could guess why she was here, and he was pretty sure it had more to do with Amy Gillabeaux than with wanting to see him again. The hungry rage tried to grab him once more. Fat chance she'd look him up after using the threat of a sexual harassment charge to get rid of him in the first place.

Lord, when Stanton found out Caitlin was here, he'd bust a gut. Her frown disappeared, but as a gusty breeze washed hot air laden with the smell of chicken manure over them, she wrinkled her nose.

He forced himself to relax and adopt a false nonchalance. She couldn't have turned up yesterday, when he'd just gotten out of court and was wearing a suit. He tugged a hand through his hair, oft-washed T-shirt riding up with the motion. "Let me guess. Tommy Gillabeaux called the FBI."

"It seems Senator Gillabeaux and my assistant director

were college fraternity brothers. He wants you to have the complete resources of the bureau at your disposal while you're investigating his daughter's death." A cynical sneer twisted her full mouth. "Including the services of a CASKU profiler and the ERT if needed."

He was looking at the profiler from the FBI's Child Abduction and Serial Killer Unit. Guess he was just lucky the Evidence Response Team hadn't appeared in full force as well. His pride struggled to lift its battered head. So local law enforcement wasn't good enough for Tommy, and his own ten years' experience with the FBI wasn't sufficient. Now he understood why so many local cops hated seeing the FBI show up.

His pride called in stubbornness for reinforcement. He crossed his arms over his chest. "We're not sure it's a serial. The deaths could be unrelated."

"I know that, Calvert, and I'm well aware you can handle a multiple-murder investigation." Her cool professional smile made his skin crawl. The distant expression was one she'd used on him before—when she'd made it clear his ass was out of her life. Now more than anything, he wanted the sunglasses gone so he could see her eyes, see if any of the real Caitlin remained.

With a rough sigh, he rubbed at his nape and forced his pride into a deep, dark hole. Professionalism and practicality. "I don't need you here."

"Like I want to be here, Calvert. Neither of us has a choice."

Oh, he had a choice, all right. At the first chance, he'd be on the phone, screaming for her to be on the next plane back to Quantico. If they wanted to send him another profiler, the ERT, hell, the entire Behavioral Sciences Unit, fine. But no way in hell was he working a case with Caitlin Falconetti. Not now, not ever.

His cell, lying on the dashboard, buzzed to life, a Gary Allan tune splitting the tension.

Thankful for the interruption, Tick spun away to snatch up the phone. "Calvert."

"Tick." Cookie's familiar voice, usually filled with wicked and tasteless humor, vibrated with strain, and Tick straightened, senses alert. He and the other man went way back, and if Cookie was serious, something was *seriously* wrong. "We've got another body. Pulled her out of the river. You might want to take a look. We're right off the boat ramp at Plant Chandler."

The tense note in Cookie's voice lifted the hair on Tick's nape. "What aren't you telling me?"

A rough sigh rumbled over the line. "I'm pretty sure it's Vontressa King."

"Oh, hell." He rubbed his temples. The ache that had plagued him since he'd rolled out of bed after yet another mostly sleepless night increased. He glanced at Caitlin, her incisive gaze trained on him. "I'll be right there."

Vontressa. Damn it. While filling out the missing persons report for her mother, he'd hoped...he'd prayed over this, that the nineteen-year-old wouldn't turn out to be another victim. Three already—their Jane Doe, college students Sharon Ingler and Amy Gillabeaux. Now, less than two days after Amy's body had been discovered, there was another one.

Holy hell, this was going to kill Miss Lauree.

Breaking the connection, he tossed the phone on the truck seat. "Our discussion is going to have to wait."

"You have another one, don't you."

He ignored her quiet statement and pulled the spare department polo shirt from behind the truck seat. He jerked his damp T-shirt over his head and flung it in the floorboard. His jeans and work boots would have to do; he didn't have time to go home and change. He yanked on the clean shirt and tucked it in with terse movements.

"I'm coming with you."

Lord, had he ever had that trace of Fed arrogance in his voice? He turned a glare on her and settled his department cap on his head. "No, hell, you're not."

She wasn't going to walk in here and take over. Over his freakin' dead body.

"You might as well face it, Calvert." Her mouth thinned. "The politics won this time. I'm here and I can help you. Do you really want me to have to report back that you refused the bureau's services?"

He stalked to the passenger side, opened the door and moved his tackle box to the bed. "Get in."

Her tiny triumphant smile sent resentment burning under his skin. Once she was in the seat, he slammed the door and strode to the driver's side.

She slipped her suit jacket off, folding it neatly across her lap. Her hair shifted over her shoulders and he fought off an insane urge to separate the thick strands he knew felt like cool silk.

As he backed out of the driveway, he glanced her way. A black suit. Very FBI. He still had a closet full of dark somber suits—black, navy, charcoal.

She stared out the window, lips pursed in concentration. Her fitted skirt rode up along her upper thigh. The fabric parted at a short side slit, affording him a glimpse of her leanly muscled leg. He knew what that soft skin felt like, too.

First her hair, now her skin. He pulled his attention back to the road. He would never survive this investigation. Damn it, he shouldn't still be attracted to her. The fact he was pissed him off to no end.

She shifted in the seat, tugging her skirt closer to her knee in an absent movement. His gaze wandered her way again. Her wrap-style blouse gapped a scant inch, exposing the upper edge of a fancy, lacy bra the soft color of a camellia bloom.

The bra she'd worn the last night they'd shared had been almost the same color. They hadn't even made it to the bed in his hotel room the first time—he'd taken her against the wall just inside the door. She'd been anything but coolly professional then, her tongue invading his mouth as he'd driven into her body.

The right front wheel dropped off the pavement, bumping on the rough shoulder. He resisted the instinct to jerk the wheel and eased the truck back onto the road.

She looked around, arching one perfect eyebrow. "Problem?"

Yeah. She was here, making him crazy, and he had to act like a seasoned investigator. With Caitlin there, Stanton would be watching him like a bird dog anyway, and Cookie had the sharpest eyes he'd ever seen. Sounded like a problem to him.

"No. Just zoned for a second."

She flicked a hand toward the whirling blue lights in the distance. "Looks like this is it."

The crime scene lay mere feet from the county line and patrol units lined the blacktop on either side. One car sat with its engine running, windows cracked, and in the backseat, the department's German Shepherd waited, watching the commotion with eager eyes.

They left Tick's truck parked along the narrow two-lane highway and hiked the hundred feet to the site boundary. He was grateful for the walk, using the opportunity to get his thoughts back under control.

He held the yellow crime scene tape for Caitlin to duck under. The officers had stopped at the barrier. Several greeted Tick and eyed Caitlin with open curiosity, a couple with a hint of resentment. In this part of the state, law enforcement remained very much a man's game, and he tried to view her through their eyes. Her aloof authority screamed Fed and her impeccable grooming whispered old money.

He started to take her arm as they picked their way down the steep incline of the riverbank, but pulled his hand back. A few yards from the water's edge, Stanton Reed and Jeff Schaefer, their newest investigator, gestured toward what looked like a huddled mass of wet rags.

Tick knew better. Caitlin damn sure did.

"Stan." At his greeting, Stanton straightened to his full height of six feet six inches. He glanced at Tick's companion and grimaced, angry surprise flaring in his eyes. Caitlin caught his gaze for a moment and looked away, scanning the scene.

"Tick." The lines by Stanton's mouth betrayed a tense weariness. "Schaefer, go tell Cookie to quit shooting the bull and get down here."

Jeff, in full uniform and professional demeanor, tapped the rim of his campaign hat. "Yes, sir."

Tick jerked a thumb in Caitlin's direction. "Stan, you remember Agent Falconetti, right?"

Dislike twisted Stanton's lean face. "I remember her. Come on, let's go talk to Cookie. He can fill you in. Falconetti? Don't touch anything."

"Don't worry, Reed. I passed crime scene protocol with flying colors. I'll just stand right here with my hands in my pockets and be a good little girl while you big boys play your whodunit games."

Tick ignored Stanton's scowl. Stanton had been his partner during his years with the FBI, and as long as Tick could remember, Stanton and Caitlin had clashed like fire and gasoline, due to a shared and equal need for control. Tick followed his friend up the bank, matching his long stride despite the three-inch difference in height.

Stanton glanced sideways at him. "What the hell is she doing here? Tell me it's in an official capacity and that she's not with you."

Tick shrugged, refusing to let the hostility get to him. He had enough crap to deal with where Caitlin was concerned; he didn't need Stanton's, too. "She's the profiler the bureau sent at Tommy's request."

"Shit." Stanton ran a hand over his mouth. "Fucking fantastic. Four dead bodies, no leads, and Falconetti on top of that."

"Hey, Lamar Eugene, about time you got here, boy!" Cookie shouted, the earlier tension gone from his voice.

Tick winced at the investigator's enthusiasm. Unlike Stanton, nothing much bothered Cookie, and not even two bodies in two days could tone him down for long. Stanton shook his head. "Fill him in, Cookie. I'm going to radio and see what's keeping the coroner."

"Why do I have nonessential personnel on my scene? Damn rookies act like it's a freakin' carnival sideshow." Cookie stopped at the crime scene tape. His hunter green polo shirt bore impressive sweat stains under muscular arms. He glanced down the rise at the river's edge and whistled softly. "Hey, who's the chick?"

"She's not a chick. That's Falconetti, the Fed rent-a-goon Tommy Gillabeaux wanted."

"Hey, I'd rent her anytime." Cookie examined Caitlin, male appreciation lighting his gray eyes. True to her word, she was standing quite still, looking at the body from a distance, hands tucked under her elbows. "She's hot. Damn fine pair of legs."

Frustration jerked along Tick's skin. Yeah, she was hot, but he'd rather Cookie hadn't noticed. And he wished the other man would stop looking at her like she was his favorite meal, just waiting to be savored. Besides, what the hell did Tick care who looked at her anymore? She wasn't his.

"She's not hot. She's, oh, hell, I don't know...she's professional."

"Yeah." Cookie nudged Tick's shoulder. "That's what makes her so hot."

"Damn it, she's not one of your little playmates, okay? Leave her alone."

"I haven't even spoken to her." Cookie managed to look offended, although a grin twitched at his lips. "I'm not doing anything."

"You're looking at her. Like she's just another piece of ass."

"Sounds to me like you're jealous. I think you want her for yourself."

He poked Tick in the chest, and Tick brushed his finger away. He wouldn't kill him. Killing him would be bad for department morale, even if it would make him feel better. "Tell me what the hell is going on."

They ducked under the tape and navigated the incline again. "Georgia Power guy doing routine maintenance check on the hydraulics found her. She's young, late teens, maybe early twenties. African American, five-five or so, probably a hundred pounds sopping wet."

"You're a sick bastard."

"Yeah, I know." Cookie heaved an unrepentant sigh as they reached the water's edge. "Looks like Vontressa King to me. Anyway, appears she's been in the water several days."

That sounded about right. Two days before, Vontressa's mama had shown up at the sheriff's department, panic-stricken because her daughter hadn't called home in two days. Her new apartment had been empty, her car missing, and there was no sign of the girl. Tick's stomach dropped. He'd really hoped she'd simply taken a spur-of-the-moment trip.

Tick stopped behind Caitlin. The spiced fruit scent of her shampoo filled his nostrils, but couldn't override the smell of damp riverbank, bedding fish and decomposing flesh.

"She was strangled." Caitlin glanced at him over her shoulder. "Look at the bruising on her neck."

Tick squinted at the corpse, but didn't move closer. They'd need official verification, but he was looking at Vontressa King's face. Her body was bloated and blue, making it difficult to tell if the marks were bruises or just normal discoloration for a body submerged in the water for an extended time. His attention zeroed in on a distinctive mark among the bruising—a perfectly round contusion, about an inch in diameter.

The same damn thing they'd seen on Jane Doe's remains, on Amy and Sharon's bodies.

He didn't need Caitlin Falconetti to tell him he had a freakin' serial killer on his hands.

"Well, shit," Cookie said, stretching the curse into two syllables. "Guess we can't put it down as an accidental drowning."

Caitlin glanced at him, and moving to her side, Tick read the beginnings of active dislike in her eyes before she lowered her gaze. He cleared his throat and gave Cookie a non-verbal warning sure to be ignored. "Cait, this is Investigator Mark Cook. Cookie, Agent Caitlin Falconetti."

Caitlin stared at the girl in the water. "Tell me more about the others."

Cookie exchanged a look with Tick. At Tick's nod, he shrugged. "Sure thing. Let's get this one tagged and bagged, and I'll go over my notes with you."

Still eyeing the body, Caitlin tilted her head. "Do you process your own scenes?"

"We're capable, but the GBI has a crime scene unit out of Moultrie. They're on the way." Cookie jerked a thumb in Tick's direction. "Bureau Boy here likes to have a specialist on his murder scenes."

"It keeps the chain of evidence clear," Tick explained.

"Good," Caitlin said, and the unexpected approval in her face warmed Tick more than he wanted to admit. That was the Caitlin he remembered, the one who made him forget everything but her.

Oh, Lord. He was in major trouble.

CR

"Cait." Tick's deep voice slid over her, and Caitlin glanced up from the rough diagram she'd sketched in her notebook. The crime scene unit had come and gone, the coroner had removed the deceased, and all of the deputies but the K-9 officer had returned to duty.

She tucked her hair behind her ear and tried to ignore the fine trickle of sweat between her breasts. "Yes?"

"I know you wanted to go over everything with us, but I have to notify the family." He looked like hell, tired, worn out, the faint lines by his eyes deeper than she remembered. He'd lost weight, a fact his jeans and shirt camouflaged, except she'd seen the changes in his waist and torso when he'd stripped the faded T-shirt off earlier. "I can get Cookie or Jeff to run you to the station."

Atop the incline, the two investigators stood on the other side of the crime scene tape. The thought of getting in a car with either of them, with any unknown man, cop or not, sent unease running down her spine. "I'd rather go with you."

He lifted a brow, his eyes dark and serious, a little mocking. "Really."

Heat touched her face and neck. She knew what he was remembering, the desperate way she'd used the only weapon she had left to get him out of her office, out of her life. "Yes. Really."

"So you're okay being alone in a vehicle with me? Not afraid I'll make any unwanted advances?"

The barb hit home, her cheeks burning hotter. She turned her attention to the river, watching the slow slide of the brown water in the wide channel. Anything to keep from having to meet the censure in his deep gaze.

"Falconetti." Exasperation saturated his rough exhale. "I need to go. I'm not looking forward to this."

Although her job usually involved dealing with the victims in an abstract sense, weeks, months or even years after the crime, she could imagine. She closed the notebook with a small snap. "I'm ready."

He had an easier time navigating the slope than she did, the mud sucking at her sturdy heels. She sighed. Just being with him made her feel discombobulated. Focused on him, she'd left the flats she kept just for these types of situations in her rental car. Damn it, these had been her favorite pair of Ferragamos, too.

As he moved ahead to lift the crime scene tape for her, she glowered at the back of his head. If she could just drum up enough anger, even over a pair of shoes, she'd stop being so aware of him. She didn't want to feel sympathy for him as he prepared to tell a family their daughter was dead. She didn't want to feel anything where he was concerned.

Cold-hearted bitch.

She shivered under the hot sun as the ever-present, unwanted voice slithered through her brain. She sucked in a deep breath, trying to keep the sudden memories and the edge of panic at bay.

Damn it, she'd known coming down here was a bad idea.

The familiar chill set in around her heart. She could do this. Get in, do the job, get out, just like always.

Except "always" had been her life before. "Always" had never involved an angry Tick Calvert either.

Ducking under the tape, she didn't look at him. A faint trace of clean, male sweat tickled her nose, and sensory memories flashed through her. Hot, bare skin sliding against hers, the rasp of stubble on her breasts and stomach, his dark whisper in her ear. Heat flushed her face, a sharp ache piercing low in her belly.

More memories followed, the loss and emptiness that had come later. The bite of remembered desire disappeared, washed away by another icy chill.

Her heel caught on an exposed root, and she faltered. His hand closed around her upper arm, every finger imprinted on her skin through her silk blouse.

"Thanks." She stepped away, still unable to look at him. She glanced up and straight into Cookie's keen gray eyes. He shifted his gaze from her to Tick and back again, then ran a finger over his mouth, eyebrows raised. She kept her face carefully schooled, shoving down the irritation and embarrassment.

Tick let the tape fall back into place. "We're going to the Kings', then we'll meet y'all at the office."

Cookie's smirk widened to a grin. "Don't get lost, now."

She sensed the stiffening of Tick's entire body. Schaefer turned his head, mouth pinched in a disgusted expression.

"Let's go." His voice tight, Tick gestured toward his truck.

As they moved away, Schaefer's words carried to them. "Cookie, do you just not think before you open your big mouth or what?"

Tick wrenched the passenger door open and waited for her to climb in before closing the door with more than necessary force. Behind the steering wheel, he blew out a long breath. "I should have warned you that Cookie's entire purpose in life is to make me miserable. I'm sorry if he embarrassed you."

She stared at her mud-encrusted shoes and forced a laugh. "I've heard worse."

He turned the key in the ignition and the engine rumbled to life. Without another word, he executed a three-point turn and drove back toward town.

She kept her gaze fixed on the passing scenery, pecan groves and small stands of scrubby oaks flying by. She didn't watch his long-fingered hands on the steering wheel, afraid of the memories that would arouse. Those memories, and the what-ifs they always dredged up, were the last thing she needed right now. Maintaining her distance and objectivity was crucial.

She cast a quick glance at the tight, set line of his jaw, shadowed with a hint of stubble. Why was he making this notification? It was obvious he didn't want to, just as obvious he had the authority to delegate it elsewhere.

"Why didn't you send someone else?" She regretted the words as soon as she uttered them.

He tensed further. "Because it's my place."

"How so?" *God, Caitlin, just shut up and leave it alone, would you? Keep it cool and professional.*

"Because." The word sounded as if he were grinding glass between his teeth. "Miss Lauree is like family. She's a nurse's

21

aide and she took care of my grandmother for years after the first stroke. I grew up with her oldest boy, David; we played football and baseball together all through school. You don't send someone else to do a job that belongs to you by rights."

Honor and duty. He was all about those things, always had been. It was part of what she admired most about him.

But she'd be damned before she'd be his *duty*.

He made a couple of left-hand turns, driving deeper into a neighborhood of small houses, each painted a bright color—robin's-egg blue, neon seafoam, Pepto-Bismol pink. He parked in front of the sole white house on the street, its shutters a deep hunter green. The fence was plain field wire, but the yard held a riot of blooming plants and every concrete yard decoration imaginable. Red geraniums and lacy ferns marched up the steps to a tiny stoop. Yellow ribbons fluttered on the gate.

Tick dropped his head, taking an audible deep breath. He pushed open his door and she didn't wait for him to come around the truck. Down the street, music pulsed from a box Chevy, the bass vibrating the air. Three teenagers gathered around the car, washing and polishing. One lifted a hand in greeting and Tick returned the wave. On the porch next door, an elderly woman fanned herself with a funeral home fan and watched with open curiosity.

The gate opened smoothly and Tick let her precede him before he fell in beside her. Tension radiated from him. Caitlin eyed the rigid line of his shoulders and fought a ridiculous urge to take his hand. The wooden front door stood open, the aroma of frying chicken flowing out the screen door. The laugh track of a sitcom filtered out as well. Caitlin stopped on the stoop, Tick one step below. The ordinariness of the scene, the horror of what they were about to do churned in her stomach.

He leaned forward to rap on the doorframe. Caitlin shifted, minimizing their proximity. A small boy appeared at the screen door, his wide eyes a beautiful, luminous ebony. He stared at them a moment and ran down the hall. "Grandma! The po-po's here!"

Caitlin glanced at Tick. "The po-po?"

A mirthless smile flirted with his mouth and disappeared. "Yeah. I've gone from being a Fibbie to being the local po-po. Smart career move, huh?"

He wasn't sure of himself, of his decision to leave the bureau. The hint of vulnerability increased his appeal and she shored up her defenses. Fine. She found him appealing. She craved Ben and Jerry's Phish Food, too, but she turned it down when common sense required her to do so. Same concept.

A woman approached the door, her steps slow and measured. She dried her hands on the red apron she wore over a dress patterned with bees and hives. Resigned fear lurked in her eyes and she clutched the edges of her apron. "Lamar?"

"Miss Lauree. Could we come in for a little while?"

Lauree King placed one hand over her heart and reached for the screen door with the other, pushing it open. "You found my Vontressa, didn't you?"

His lashes fell, and he swallowed, his Adam's apple moving. He looked up at Miss Lauree. "Yes, ma'am, we did."

A horrified "oh" rushed out of the older woman, and her hand fanned over her heart. She sagged, aging further in seconds, and Tick stepped forward into the house, reaching to support her. She hung on to him, tears spilling with her harsh sobs. A wail rent the air.

Caitlin eased into the cool dimness of the hallway, guiding the screen door closed. Miss Lauree clutched at Tick, her grief like a horrible, living thing. Caitlin clenched her hands, nails biting her palms, her eyes burning with empathy. Oh, God, how did he do this?

"Where...where is she?" Miss Lauree gasped, her hands grasping his arms like wrinkled talons.

"The crime lab in Moultrie," Tick said, his voice gentle. "It'll be a few days before we can release her. I need someone to make an official identification. Do you think David can do that?"

Miss Lauree was shaking her head, mouth working, nothing but rough moans escaping. She crumpled, and Tick went with her, kneeling on the worn linoleum. He murmured reassuring condolences.

His deep voice curled around Caitlin's heart. She swallowed hard. Oh, damn it, the sooner they found this killer, the better. Or she just might go and do something really stupid, like forget the limitations of her new reality and fall for Tick Calvert all over again.

♋

The administrative office of the Chandler County Sheriff's Department turned out to be a literal hole in the wall. The squatty two-story building behind the local courthouse was undergoing renovations, and the door and part of the wall had been detached at the office entrance. At the top of the wide concrete steps, Caitlin removed her sunglasses, the memory of Lauree King's sobs still ringing in her head.

Tick held the thick piece of construction plastic flapping in the rough opening, allowing her to precede him into the chaos. A new glass door leaned against the wall, waiting to be installed. The whine of a circular saw carried up the stairwell at the end of the hall. Deputies milled, passing good-natured insults as first shift prepared to go home and second shift got ready for duty.

"I need to grab the case files." Tick bypassed the front desk with a curt nod at the young officer there and ushered Caitlin into the hall with a gesture. He disappeared through the open door of a closet masquerading as an office adjacent to the squad room. Somewhere downstairs, a board crashed to the floor.

Caitlin surveyed the squad room, a tight, drab area with a smattering of desks. A long counter along one wall held officer mailboxes and a coffee station. A door on the opposite side of the room mirrored Tick's other than the six-pointed sheriff's star stenciled on it. Reed's office, obviously. Beside the coffee counter stood a third door, open to the hidden room beyond.

"Damn it." Tick stalked from his office, grimacing. He ran a hand through his hair, and Caitlin suppressed a surge of affection. How often had she seen him do that over the years, when he was tense or frustrated? He needed a haircut, the black strands falling onto his forehead in tousled disarray. Her fingers itched to touch them and see if they were as thick and soft as she remembered.

Enthusiastic hammering echoed up the stairs. Tick strode to the doorway by the counter and she trailed him into a makeshift conference room. Mismatched office chairs flanked a scarred wooden table, and on the wall, a dingy whiteboard and buckling cork bulletin board hung next to a large map of the area. Ancient water stains marred the ceiling tiles.

"Cookie, did you take the folders off my desk?"

At Tick's voice, Cookie and Jeff Schaefer both looked up, Jeff from the crime scene report he was writing, Cookie from the file he was perusing. He blinked, obviously trying for an innocent expression, although the impish light in his eyes killed the attempt cold. "Yeah. Why?"

Tick opened his mouth, closed it and shook his head, jaw clenched. Caitlin leaned a shoulder against the doorjamb. Cook knew Tick well enough to be aware of his territorial tendencies. This was the second time today she'd witnessed the investigator pushing Tick's buttons, although the aggravation hinted more at good-natured male teasing than any real malice. Definite history there, she realized, her curiosity aroused.

Jeff dropped his gaze to his report again. His pen scratched across the paper. Tick stepped forward to lay out the remaining case dossiers on the table. His lean body was tense, his movements jerky. Caitlin folded her arms over her midriff. The last time she'd seen him that uptight had been during the Reese rape case, more personal to him than anything he'd ever worked before.

How much of that taut, vibrating stiffness was because of her? She'd hurt him badly, she knew that, but she'd had a damn good reason. And it had been months. Surely, this was case-related stress...

A different awareness prickled over her skin. Apprehension gripping her stomach, she glanced to her left and found Cookie watching her.

Watching her watch Tick.

Discomfited, she held his gaze but he didn't look away. He studied her, his gray eyes sharp and assessing, openly interested. Oh, God. How much of her emotions had been on her face?

She lifted her chin and tried staring him down with her coldest bureau expression, the one that had reduced plenty of other officers to flustered incoherence. Unperturbed, he grinned, rubbing at his chin with thumb and forefinger, still examining her like she was a particularly fascinating specimen.

The sudden silence sank into her consciousness. Jeff's pen had stopped moving and paper no longer shuffled under Tick's edgy movements. She was sure the visual power struggle between her and Cook had both men's attention.

Damned if she'd break first, though.

With a deliberate movement, Cookie turned his head, leaving her with the impression he was merely shifting his attention somewhere more interesting rather than conceding. He met Tick's narrowed gaze, his grin morphing to a smirk. Tick's face darkened with a scowl, nostrils flaring slightly as he looked from Cookie to her.

Stepping forward, she flipped open the file folder labeled Jane Doe. She winced. A stark crime scene photo stared up at her and her gaze traced over the crumpled form of the young woman's body. Long hair blew across the face but didn't disguise the staring eyes, wide open in death.

She cleared her throat. "Any idea who she might be?"

Cookie kicked back in his chair, picking at his teeth with a thumbnail. "Nope. We pulled nationwide missing person reports, but didn't turn up anything yet."

Sadness shivered over her. This never got any easier, seeing the anonymous victims, wondering if anyone missed them, loved them, looked for them. "She had to come from somewhere."

Schaefer pointed at the bulletin board outside Tick's office, just visible through the open door. Missing fliers covered every inch. "Lots of runaways move through here on their way to Atlanta. They all think they're going to make it big up there."

She flipped the photo over, glancing at the officer's report underneath. Deputy Chris Parker, first on scene. The girl's nude body discovered in thick underbrush. No trace evidence recovered from the scene or the corpse. "Where was she found?"

"Devil's Hole." Tick tapped the large map hanging on the wall. His voice remained angry and subdued, the line of his body still carrying the tension he'd taken away from the King residence. "Ten, eleven miles from here. Couple of miles down Jackson Dairy Road."

"Jackson Dairy isn't far from US 19, is it?" she asked, eyes narrowed as she studied the map. "Sharon Ingler's body was just a mile off from there."

"Right."

"And the area where you found the girl today is only a mile or so from the same highway."

Cookie nodded. "Yeah, but she could have gone into the river anywhere. What are you getting at?"

Tick frowned at the map. "Not anywhere," he corrected, tracing the snaky blue line of the Flint River with his finger. "She had to go in between the power dam and Plant Chandler."

"Ah, shit." Cookie pulled a tin of smokeless tobacco from his back pocket. He looked at it and laid it aside, his sigh regretful. Instead, he rummaged in his shirt pocket for a pack of gum. "That's still ten miles of river."

"Yes, but where are your access points?" Caitlin rose to stand by Tick, looking more closely at the map, her shoulder brushing his arm. His body heat radiated through her thin silk blouse, warming her. Awareness hummed inside her, ears attuned to his even breathing. "I mean, where would someone be able to put the body in without being noticed?"

"Here." He reached around her to point to an area just over the county line. Sheltered by his lean frame, her senses full of his male scent, she struggled to focus on his words. Memories of his tenderness with Lauree King wafted through her mind. What would it have been like, to have that strong, gentle support when she'd needed it most? She shrugged off the thought and straightened, tuning in to his voice more closely. "Probably anywhere along Veteran's Park. The woods off Highway 3. And the public boat ramp off Radium Springs Road. Maybe the crime lab can lift bacteria or chemicals from her body. If so, one of our Department of Natural Resources biologists might be able to tell us where she went into the river."

"And all this tells us what?" Schaefer joined them.

Caitlin glanced at him, his dark brown brows drawn together over earnest blue eyes. He was younger than Tick and Cookie, late twenties, thirty maybe, but his slow, methodical demeanor made him seem more mature than his age.

"He's most likely working the highway. He's dumping where he can get in and out without being noticed and where he thinks the bodies won't be found for days or even weeks. Obviously, he's not as good at picking dump sites as he thinks he is."

Schaefer's expression turned sharp and interested. "Why do you say that?"

"If he was that good, you wouldn't have two bodies in as many days."

"Unless he wanted us to find them that quickly," Schaefer said with an off-hand shrug.

"True." Caitlin held his gaze a moment. "He could merely be getting bolder."

"He?" Cookie brightened and straightened in his chair. He chewed harder, popping his gum. "So, we're looking for just one guy."

"Don't get excited," Caitlin said. "It might be one person. Or it might be four deaths that are coincidentally alike. If it is one person, he probably won't be easy to find."

"Coincidence, my ass, with those bruises." Cookie crossed his arms over his chest, his gray stare measuring. "You'll be able to help us find him, right?"

"I'll do my best." She turned back to the files on the table. "But, remember, my job is to help you narrow your field of possible suspects."

"Right." Tick stepped away, his jaw tense. "Given the opportunity, you'll take over."

"Hey, works for me." Cookie grinned. "Means less overtime on my part."

"Probably more overtime on everyone's part," Caitlin mused aloud, skimming the autopsy report on the first victim, the Jane Doe discovered nearly two weeks before. Strangulation, no sign of sexual assault, bruising to the arms and torso. She looked up. "We'll need to really work your command center—lay out the photos and reports, track your evidence—so we can get a feel for who this guy is."

She met Tick's hard eyes. "VICAP didn't register anything?"

Schaefer pulled a printout from a folder. "A list of cases with the same MO. Most of which were out of state or already solved. I've been checking them out anyway."

Sighing, she rubbed the tension knot developing at the base of her neck. "So tell me about Sharon Ingler and Amy Gillabeaux."

Tick leaned against the table, arms folded across his chest. "Sharon's daddy has a produce farm out on the highway. He's got three sons and they all went to work farming with him right out of high school. Sharon was his baby and the only girl. Smart, graduated at the top of her class, received a full scholarship to the University of Georgia. Had all A's her first semester."

"Her daddy was proud, too." Cookie drummed a pen against the table, his face pensive.

"I'll bet." Caitlin studied Sharon in the photo clipped to her file. The man with her had to be her father, his arm around her shoulder, the pride Cookie mentioned glimmering in his eyes. She tapped a fingernail against the photograph. Proud daddies were not part of her personal experience, but it was obvious Ingler had adored his daughter. "What happened?"

Jeff shrugged. "She came home for the summer. Her car was found along Highway 112. She'd broken down. Four days later, another farmer found her body in a culvert while he was clearing a ditch."

"Ashleigh Hardison." She frowned over the name on the witness report, a memory niggling at the edges of her mind. "Ash Hardison?"

"Yeah." Tick's terse voice had her looking up. He watched her, frowning. "Why?"

"Unusual name. I think he went to military school with my brother Vince."

"Probably." Cookie was folding his foil gum wrapper into an intricate swan. "He's ex-army, not from around here. Moved into the area last year."

"Small world." She shrugged off the coincidence. "Did Sharon know Amy Gillabeaux?"

"Around here, everyone knows everyone." Tick still watched her, his frown remaining. "They graduated together, had gone to the same schools since kindergarten, attended the same church. I'm sure they knew each other. Did they hang out in the same crowds? Probably not."

Something about his voice raised a flag in her mind. "Why not?"

"If Sharon was the local golden girl, Amy was the town wild child." Jeff's expression twisted with distaste.

Tick shook his head. "She was a little spoiled, had her daddy wrapped around her little finger. She was smart, too, wasn't far behind Sharon in class ranking, got into UGA as well. She just wasn't interested in studying. She flunked out her first semester and Tommy made her transfer to the local state university. She liked to flirt and she liked to party."

"She liked older men, too." A taunting leer lurked around Cookie's mouth. "Didn't she, Tick?"

"Shut up, Cookie."

Unease shivered along Caitlin's nerve endings. "Were you involved with her?"

"No."

Cookie rubbed a finger over his bottom lip. "Not for a lack of trying."

On whose part? She swallowed the question and dropped her gaze from Tick's. What he did, who he saw, was none of her business anymore. But he had to know he couldn't work a murder case where he'd been involved with the victim.

"You have to tell her the story." Wicked amusement laced Cookie's voice.

"Holy hell, Cookie, sometimes you talk too damn much." Tick's anger seemed to hover in the air. "It was no big deal. Yeah, Amy made a play for me. The last time I had to go by to see Tommy, she met me at the door."

"Wearing only the bottom to her itsy-bitsy bikini and a great big smile," Cookie added for him, earning an inarticulate growl of frustration from his colleague.

"Like Tick said, no big deal. Amy lived for being outrageous." Jeff's calm tone soothed the rising tension in the room. "She's hit on just about every guy in the county over twenty-five and under fifty. She wasn't into guys her age."

Which meant a huge field of possible suspects, and maybe the possibility that her death wasn't related to the others.

Caitlin flipped to the next page in the file, a missing

person's report, Tick's slashing signature at the bottom. "What were the circumstances of her death?"

"She didn't come home Tuesday night." Tick cleared his throat. "Her daddy had half the law enforcement agencies in this end of the state looking for her. We found her car that night in the parking lot of the local football stadium. Like Sharon, a farmer found her body Wednesday afternoon in thick underbrush. He was cutting a fire break."

She frowned over the folder. Having all of this would have been helpful before she'd come down here, if ADIC Frazier hadn't been in such a rush for her to head out, to soothe Tommy Gillabeaux's political screaming. "There's no autopsy report."

"Hasn't been done yet." Cookie shrugged. "Backlog at the crime lab. We don't have Sharon Ingler's, either."

She looked up. "How much of a backlog?"

"Williams is talking about a week on the short side before she even gets to the preliminary."

"A week?" She should have brought Ransome, the medical examiner and resident lab geek on her team, with her. "Any idea on the cause of death for both girls? Same as your Jane Doe?"

"Looks like strangulation." Tick turned to scatter crime scene photos across the table. He arranged close-up pictures of the girls' torsos side-by-side.

Caitlin examined the bruising on each victim. "But not garroted."

"No, and not manual strangulation either. No finger marks. He used his forearm against the windpipe." Tick laid his wrist lightly against her throat to demonstrate.

Caitlin jerked away. His eyes widened and she swallowed, sure the memories and horror lingered on her face. "Thanks but I don't need the visual."

She attempted a nonchalant smile and an ironic tone, but her voice quivered.

"Sorry." Tick frowned, his gaze thoughtful, piercing, assessing. "I didn't mean to startle you."

"No problem." She gave a scoffing laugh, aware they had

captured Cookie and Jeff's rapt attention. She ran a finger over the round mark on Sharon's throat, darker than the other contusions. "They all have the same bruise pattern."

"Probably his watch." Something indefinable, a soft questioning perhaps, remained in Tick's voice, but she refused to look at him.

She tilted her head, still eyeing the bruise. "Maybe he's left handed."

"They weren't quick deaths." Anger colored Cookie's quiet statement. "He toyed with them."

Caitlin nodded. Bruises scattered over the bodies. Small round burns on breasts and thighs, probably a lit cigarette pressed against the tender skin. Thin cuts on the arms and abdomen, enough to bleed, enough to cause pain and terror, but not death.

Except for Amy.

Caitlin picked up the photos depicting Amy's body. Her killing had been more violent, with bruising to her face absent from the other girls.

And the stab wounds.

She counted the jagged gashes. Seven in the abdominal area, three more on her upper torso.

A vicious, brutal death.

A personal murder.

She'd known her killer and he'd known her.

Why had he wanted her dead? To cut her out of his life? To keep her from belonging to someone else?

The ultimate control, maybe.

Darkness hovered at the edges of Caitlin's mind, trying to steal her breath. She forced it back, focusing on the process of getting oxygen in and out of her lungs. She couldn't fall prey to the panic, not here, not now.

Not in front of Tick.

She diverted her attention from the mutilation of Amy's body, studied the pictorial record as a whole again. The bodies were too clean, the scenes too clean. "You didn't find trace evidence on them, did you."

"No hairs, no fibers, no fluids. Bagged their hands, but I doubt Williams can pull anything." Tick nudged a picture with a long finger. "I think he washed them before dumping them."

"So no clues as to the whereabouts of his kill site. And no DNA."

"Right."

"He thinks he's smarter than us." Jeff's words held a note of annoyed offense.

"What else do you have?"

"Not much." Frustration darkened Tick's voice. "Witness statements from the night Sharon disappeared, preliminary interviews with the girls' friends and families. Some items pulled from Amy's apartment this morning—her address book, her laptop."

"Anything from those?"

"I'm still trying to access her files." Cookie slumped in his chair. "She password protected a lot of things. Checked out her MySpace page online, her little blog, that kind of stuff. Thousands of damn comments on her MySpace. I'm working through all of those."

"My partner might be able to help with that. She's a computer expert...she's amazing." Caitlin's concentration strayed to the photos once more and she traced a finger over the bruises at Amy's neck, down to the stab wounds. The girl had to have been terrified. Caitlin made herself shrug off the remembrances clamoring in her head. "I'll get you her number."

Jeff leaned forward, steepling his fingers together. "Where do you suggest we go from here?"

"Equivocal—"

"Forensic analysis," Tick finished for her in his deep drawl.

"Exactly."

"Mind repeating that in English?" Cookie chuckled.

"It means we're starting over," Tick said.

"Going through all the evidence." Caitlin avoided the urge to rub at her tired, burning eyes. The nightmares and periodic insomnia were bad enough; plunging back into the field with this case, working with Tick Calvert was even worse.

"Sharon didn't keep an address book." Cookie's musing

brought her attention around to him. "We should see if Vontressa did. We could set up a database and cross-reference the people they all knew. Since most murder victims know their killers, it makes sense that the three local girls may have known this guy."

Caitlin flicked a glance at him, admiration stirring to life in her. Brilliance lurked beneath the flippant façade. She smiled, the first real one all day, hell, probably the first one in weeks, maybe even months, if she was honest. "Good idea."

"I have lots of those." He grinned, a hint of salaciousness in the expression. "You and I should explore one or two."

Jeff groaned. "Oh, God, here we go."

"What we're going to explore is the rule of twenty-four." Tick's words held a steely warning. "We'll start with Amy, since she's our most recent victim, and Vontressa, since she's our most recent discovery."

"And delve into their lives." Distaste shivered down Caitlin's spine. Funny how her approach had changed once she'd walked on the other side. She'd hoped that once she was back in the field, she'd enjoy the chase again. She picked up one of the photos of Vontressa and looked at those staring, lifeless eyes.

No. She'd never find enjoyment in this again.

Chapter Two

She wasn't the same Caitlin Falconetti he'd known for years.

Tick eyed her bent head, unease slithering through him. He'd seen some of the changes back in March, when he'd come back from Mississippi and she'd summarily dumped his ass. He'd been too all-fired mad and hurt then to really think about how she'd changed, too busy afterward, with his grandmother's death, that mess with his brother Del's boy, and setting up the department from the ground up. He'd been grateful for the distractions, trying to use them to get her out of his mind.

His Caitlin, first his friend and later his lover, was bright and talented, intuitive and caring, with her emotions reflected in the deep green of her eyes. This woman was someone else. This woman, who rarely smiled and went through professional motions, couldn't be real.

Something about this Caitlin's eyes niggled at him, something he couldn't quite put his finger on yet.

His stomach, ignored since breakfast, chose that moment to gnaw at his spine with an audible growl.

Jeff snorted a laugh. Cookie snickered. Tick glared at both of them. God, he needed to get out of here.

What he *really* needed was a cigarette.

He ran a hand through his hair. A shower would be nice, too. "Why don't we take a dinner break, meet back here around eight thirty."

Cookie looked askance. "A dinner break? You're letting us out of the dungeon?"

Tick swallowed a biting reply. "Yeah. Get something to eat, take a walk, whatever. Just be ready to work when you get back."

Caitlin lifted her head, her expression unhappy. "We left my rental car—"

"At Ash's." Shit. Just what he needed—another little ride cooped up with her.

"I can take you." Cookie pushed up from his chair, the springs squeaking. Caitlin stiffened visibly, her gaze darting over the breadth of his shoulders. She shifted almost a full step backward, away from him.

What was that all about? Tick frowned and pulled his keys from his pocket. "I'll drive her."

"I'll do it." Cookie waved him away with a negligent gesture. "Go home. Take a shower."

"I said I'd take her." Tick stared him down, tired of the other man playing him. Jeff watched them and the surprised curiosity on his face sent a crawling itch down Tick's back.

With a deep chuckle, Cookie lifted both hands in surrender. "Sure thing, man."

Tick snatched his cap off the chair where he'd tossed it earlier. He didn't look at Caitlin. "Ready?"

Outside, Tick slid his sunglasses on against the onslaught of the evening sun. As he put the truck in gear and backed out of his parking space, he glanced sideways at Caitlin, her posture tense and tight.

He wanted to reach out, rub at her nape and shoulders, ease the visible tautness. Instead, he gripped the wheel harder. What in holy hell was wrong with him? "Hungry?"

"No." Her husky voice was quiet, stiff.

She had to be lying. He'd never known her not to be hungry. Her appetite had been legendary among their classmates at Quantico, but her high metabolism and penchant for exercise kept her body lean and toned. An image of her flat stomach quivering under his urgent touch flashed through his mind, and he pressed the brake down hard as he prepared to shift into drive. The truck jerked. Caitlin turned an odd look on him and he shook his head, face hot.

"Sorry."

He pulled out of the parking lot onto the two-lane highway and hooked a finger over the steering wheel. Eight miles. Ten minutes if he didn't get caught by both traffic lights or behind a slow-ass chicken truck.

Ten minutes. He could handle that.

His cell phone vibrated to life, offering a welcome distraction to the pulsing silence.

"Excuse me." He flipped it open. "Calvert."

"Where are you?" His younger brother Del greeted him.

"Headed north on Highway 3." He slowed for the first traffic light as it flared red. Damn it. Make that twelve minutes. "Why?"

"Thought I'd see if you'd had supper yet and wanted to meet me at Old Mexico."

"Sounds good." He knew Del was at loose ends with his wife and kids out of town, and maybe the company would keep his own mind off the woman occupying his passenger seat. "I have to run out to Ash's and I need a shower. Give me thirty minutes."

"Right. See you there."

Neither he nor Caitlin spoke until they reached Ash's and she asked for directions to her hotel. He rattled them off by rote, itching to get away. Once she'd pulled out on the highway and he headed in the opposite direction toward home, he released a slow, relieved breath.

A hot shower and quick shave did little to lessen the jumpy tension and make him feel more human. He pulled into the Old Mexico parking lot five minutes earlier than he'd told Del to expect him. He wasn't surprised that his ever-punctual brother stood outside, cell phone pressed to his ear, a wide grin on his face.

"I miss you, too, honey. Tick's here; I have to go. Love you." Del ended the call and clipped the phone on his belt as Tick approached. The brisk breeze toyed with his brother's tie, the pyramid pattern in green and brown echoing the apple green of his fine cotton shirt, tucked into a pair of khaki slacks. The bright lantern lights under the awning glimmered over his wedding ring. "Hey. You look like hell."

"Feel like it, too." Tick yanked the door open.

"Well, that's a new one." Del grabbed the knob and let Tick precede him. "Usually you're snarling at me to mind my own damn business."

"Yeah." Inside, cheerful mariachi music blended with the tinkle of a large fountain in the middle of the dining room. The noise crawled over him, making his jittery feeling worse. The scents of spices and cooked meat hovered in the air, but despite his physical hunger, the desire to eat just wasn't there. With a wave at the sole waitress, busy with another customer, Tick lifted two menus and headed for the corner booth he and his brother usually occupied.

Del waited until they'd ordered and their drinks had been delivered to speak again. He rested an arm along the back of the booth and twirled his beer bottle with his other hand. "Something you want to talk about?"

"No." Tick squeezed lemon into his iced tea. Maybe spilling his guts to someone he could trust would help take the edge off. "Yeah."

Del waited, silent.

"You lousy son of a bitch." Cookie shoved Tick's shoulder and dropped into the booth next to him. He grinned at the waitress. "Hey, Lola, honey, bring me an unsweet tea and a number twelve."

"Oh, Lord." Tick rested both elbows on the table and pressed the heels of his hands against his gritty eyes. Could it get any worse?

Cookie jabbed him, hard. "You've been holding out on me."

"Go away."

"Man, you are not going to tell me you didn't hit that." Cookie's very male laugh shredded Tick's already skinned nerves. His head jerked up and he gripped his knees hard instead of curling his hands into fists.

"Shut up, Mark. Don't talk about—" He swallowed the words, forcing them down with the urge to take a swing at his partner.

"Someone want to fill me in?" Del lifted his beer. "I'm completely lost over here."

Tick decided he'd just ignore Cookie's presence. It wasn't like it had worked before, but a guy's luck had to turn sometime. He exhaled.

"She's here."

"She?"

"Cait." Tick tried to relax into the booth, stretching out his legs. He relived the moment she'd stepped from that car, shivers traveling over him. "She's here and I have to freakin' work with her."

"Cait..." Del scratched his chin, frowning. "Should I know her?"

"Falconetti. The one who helped with Tori's—"

"Holy shit. The brunette with the legs? And the bedroom voice?"

"Bedroom voice?" Cookie snorted. He smiled as Lola set his tea before him and waited until she was out of earshot. "Fuck-me voice, you mean. Hot damn, she could just talk to me and I'd be happy."

Cold fury sizzled through Tick's brain. "I'm going to kill you if you don't shut the hell up."

"Wonder if I could get her to record me an MP3?"

Del muffled a laugh. "That's interesting. She's the one groveling didn't work with?"

"Move, Cookie." He was out of here. Even Del had turned on him.

"Now I'm lost." Cookie didn't budge. "*You* groveled? With a woman."

Hell, he'd done everything but get on his knees. And she hadn't given a damn. The memory of her cold voice and icy eyes flashed through his mind.

"So you have another chance to beg." Del pointed his beer in Tick's direction.

"Hardly." Holy hell, the idea appealed more than it should. He laughed, a raw, ugly sound. "Last time she threatened me with a sexual harassment suit."

Cookie sputtered over a mouthful of tea. "What?"

Shock slid over Del's face. "You're shittin' me. You?"

"Yeah, me." Not that she'd have done it. She'd just wanted to get rid of him and that was a surefire way to do it. At least he didn't think she would have. Hell, he wasn't certain of anything where she was concerned anymore. The woman he'd come home to after Mississippi was someone other than the one he'd left behind. He frowned. "She's changed."

"Changed?" Del leaned back to give Lola room to set down their plates. Steam drifted up from his platter of sizzling fajitas.

Tick pushed his number-two special aside, appetite gone. "She's cold, hard. Not that she wasn't cool before, but..."

How to explain the chilly professionalism Caitlin used like a shield against the bureau's old boy network? But she'd never turned it on him, at least not until he'd returned. He'd always gotten the real deal and during that week before he'd gone undercover, he'd thought she'd let him in, given him access to the woman who lived under the Betty Bureau façade.

"You know, people don't change without a reason," Del said.

"Yeah." Tick slumped, tracing a droplet of condensation down the side of his glass with a fingertip.

What did it matter why she changed? Knowing that wouldn't result in her taking him back.

"Wait a second." Cookie mixed his rice into his refried beans, a frown drawing his heavy brows together. Tick knew that expression well—he'd seen it often enough when they were working a case and Cookie was trying to fit all the pieces together. "We're talking about the same woman, right?"

"No, her evil twin."

"The way she watches you?"

"What are you—" Screw it. He was tired, and they were over. All he could hope for was to get through the next few days with his sanity intact.

"How does she watch him?" Del's quiet voice brought him back to reality. He looked up to meet his brother's dark eyes, the same chocolate brown as his own. Why the hell did Del have to go and ask that?

"Like a starving dog eyes a juicy T-bone steak." Cookie forked up a bite of chimichanga. "Man, you didn't make a move today that she didn't see, which doesn't make sense if she kicked your ass to the curb. Why'd she dump you?"

"I don't know." All he'd ever been able to get out of her was she didn't want him anymore.

Like a freakin' broken record. *Just go, Tick. It's over. Damn it, Tick, leave me alone. Please go. I don't want you anymore.* Hell, he'd heard those words in his dreams for weeks. No wonder he couldn't sleep. He didn't *want* to sleep.

What had turned Caitlin against him during those months he'd been away? He'd figured she'd simply changed her mind, as she claimed. He'd even wondered if she'd found someone else. But...today, being around her, getting a good close look...

The shuttered blankness of her gaze.

This Caitlin watched the world with the shadowed, expressionless eyes of a soul destroyed. What in holy hell had happened to her? To *them*?

ᘓ

Caitlin's running shoes hit the packed clay path in a steady, soothing rhythm. After checking into her room, she'd forgone the idea of food, her stomach twisted in tight knots. A park with a large pond and jogging path lay across the street from the hotel, and seeking to calm the adrenaline-inspired energy making her nerves tingle, she'd donned shorts and a T-shirt, clipped her holster and cell phone in place, slid her Bluetooth headpiece over her ear and set out.

The close-to-setting sun glared red and gold through the pine trees surrounding the pond, casting long shadows on the path, glimmering on the water in gilded wavelets. On the patch of grass to the north, a family gathered around a picnic table and a group of teenage boys played a game of pickup football. A twang of country music drifted from a truck parked in the gravel lot, a young couple leaning against the hood in a soft embrace.

The exercise and the peaceful setting weren't helping. Her entire body still jangled with tension. From the moment she'd learned she'd be working with Tick, she'd known this was going to be bad.

It had turned out to be worse than she ever expected.

Her control, the quality that had made her the Fed she was, had been shot all to hell for months now. She struggled with separating herself from the victims, and being with Tick didn't help.

The image of him in faded jeans and that damp, worn T-shirt rose in her mind. Even with him sweaty and smelly, she'd been hard put not to throw herself at him when she'd stepped out of the car. The intensity of that desire to be close to him, the bubbling of joy at being in his presence again, sent fear scrambling through her. He remained a dangerous distraction and she needed her focus. Only single-minded concentration would get her through this.

The headpiece pinged at her ear. "Falconetti."

"Well?" Concerned curiosity suffused Gina Bocaccio's voice and Caitlin sighed, surprised her partner hadn't called sooner, like five minutes after her estimated arrival time in Georgia.

"Well, what?" she asked, starting her second lap.

"Girl, don't even try that. Are you okay?"

"I'm fine." To her left, a duck gave a squawk and slid into the water, diving at June bugs skimming over the surface. "Why wouldn't I be?"

"God, you're such a bad liar. A bad liar with denial issues."

Silence hummed between them.

"Cait?"

"I'm here."

"You know what your problem is?"

"I'm sure you're going to tell me."

"You spend too much time trying to be perfect and too little time trying to be human. You are, you know. Things happen. Bad things, but it wasn't your fault and—"

"Gina. Stop." She skidded to a halt, bending over against the sudden sharp pain knifing through her chest and side. It wasn't all physical, she knew that, but she rested her elbows on her knees and tried to breathe through it. Black dots danced at the edges of her vision, the panic trying to get a hold on her mind. She dragged in a lungful of oxygen, staring at a lone pebble in the middle of the path. Focusing. "I can't do this. Not now."

"You need to tell him."

Caitlin recoiled from the bald statement. She straightened and swept a loose hank of hair from her face. Sweat trickled between her shoulder blades, sending an icy little frisson down her spine. "No."

"Cait—"

"I can't." She'd tried, didn't Gina get that? She'd always planned to tell him. God, she'd thought about it for *months*, waiting for him to come home from Mississippi. She'd practiced the damn words an infinite number of ways.

When he'd walked into her office that rainy morning, his dark gaze alight with joy and hunger, she hadn't been able to do it. Somehow, killing that joy by sending him away seemed more right than telling the truth, watching the hunger be replaced by duty.

If she'd told him, he'd have stayed and she'd never have known why. She wasn't doing that to either of them. At least this way, he didn't have to live with it every day. He could move on.

"This is going to blow up in your face, Cait. I know it and so do you."

"Look, Gina. He's the poster boy for the perfect family man. Loves his mom, loves kids, wants a house full of them one day." She choked over the words, over the lump of tears pushing up in her throat, and swallowed a curse. "I'm here to assist on a case. Do the job, get out, don't get involved. Just like always. Nothing's going to happen because I'm not going to let it."

She turned back toward the hotel, retracing her steps. A Chandler County sheriff's car pulled into the gravel lot, its tinted windows hiding the driver. It paused behind the pickup truck, brake lights flaring, before it purred onto the street again.

"Listen." Affectionate worry softened Gina's tone. "If you need anything—"

"I won't." She glanced at her watch. Long enough to shower, get herself together before she headed into the lion's den once more. "I have to go."

For long moments after she broke the connection, she

concentrated on steadying her breathing, fighting back another wave of stupid, hopeless tears.

CR

The squad room lay quiet and deserted. A subdued rumble of activity drifted up the stairs from the dispatch area, mixing with the scent of stale coffee lingering in the air.

The few bites of chile relleno Tick had forced himself to eat formed a lump in his stomach. He tucked his cigarettes in his pocket, the two he'd smoked back-to-back on the way over here not really settling him down.

He paused in the doorway to the conference room. Jeff and Cookie were nowhere in sight. Caitlin sat, reading the red leather-bound journal they'd taken from Amy's room, a cup from the local java joint at her elbow. He watched her, the thick black silk of her hair pulled into a loose knot, the Fibbie suit traded for jeans and a simple white T-shirt under a neat seersucker jacket. One loafer-clad foot tapped the floor, a frown of concentration wrinkling her brow.

Damn, she was beautiful.

Beautiful and scarred. Not visibly damaged, but *something* had stolen her away from him.

Damned if he wasn't going to find out what. If he was trapped into this working arrangement, so was she. This time, he'd make it a hell of a lot harder for her to dodge the issue.

"Find anything interesting?"

She startled like a scalded cat. The diary slid to the floor and one flailing hand collided with her coffee, sending the dark liquid across the table.

"Oh, hell!" She jumped to her feet and righted the cup. He grabbed a handful of napkins from the shelf by the door and began mopping up the mess. She glared, her eyes big and dark with fury in her pale face. "Don't sneak up on me like that, Calvert."

"Who's sneaking?" He dropped the sopping mass of napkins in the trash. "I just walked into my own department and asked a simple question."

She leaned down to retrieve the book, but he reached it first. They straightened and he proffered it, merely the length of the volume between them. She took it from him with ill grace. "A little advance warning would be nice."

"You're awful jumpy." He studied her as she sank into the chair again. The color didn't return to her face and tiny tremors shook her slender fingers. A warning flag waved in his mind.

"I was reading."

He pulled out the chair cater-cornered and closest to hers, an old interrogator's trick. She flicked a glance at him and shifted to the farthest edge of her seat.

"So how've you been?"

"Fine. Thank you."

"Busy?" He leaned back and folded his arms behind his head. He stretched his legs, crowding hers a little, forcing himself into a semblance of casual relaxation. "Probably had to drop a lot of things to come down here."

"Not really." She scratched a note on a legal pad, her knuckles white. "I've been out of the field."

That surprised him. She lived for the damn job. At one time, he'd been fully prepared to take a backseat to that drive of hers, as long as they could be together. "Why?"

Her Montblanc pen faltered, ink smearing on the paper. She dropped it and looked up, her eyes cool and shuttered. "Did I miss something, Calvert? When did we agree to play twenty questions?"

He smiled, the "aw-shucks-good-ol'-boy" one he used whenever he had to worm his way under the defenses of a local suspect. "You said it, Falconetti, we have to work together. I'm just playing nice, making conversation."

"Try selling that line of bull to someone who'll buy it." Her hands were in her lap now, but he'd bet his next pack of smokes her fingers were wound into fists. The whole line of her body screamed with tension and the need for escape. How many times had he seen that posture on a perp? "You're digging."

"That implies you're hiding something."

She pushed her chair back, obviously preparing to flee. "Hiding something? You're deluded—"

"What is it, Cait?" He grasped her wrist, holding her in the chair with a light touch. "What the hell happened while I was in Mississippi?"

"Let go."

"Tell me."

"Don't touch me." They stared at one another, the power struggle pulsing to life, growing and twisting between them. "I mean it, Tick, let go or—"

"Or what? You'll slap a sexual harassment suit on me? Ruin my career?" He leaned forward, ready to call her bluff. "Go for it, precious."

The endearment he'd only ever used with her slipped out and her eyes widened, darkened. She moistened her lips and tugged against his hold. "You're hurting me."

Not physically. He wasn't holding her tightly enough to do that, but he released her. She had a trapped, hunted air about her now and grim satisfaction curled through him. Oh, yeah, she was hiding something. If he could just find the weak point, break through that damn control of hers...

"I'd never hurt you and you know it."

"Stop." Her voice trembled and his chest tightened.

"Not until you—"

"Until nothing. We're colleagues, Tick," she said, cold dismissal not quite covering the lingering nervousness in her tone. "That's all."

"We used to be friends."

And lovers. The words hung in the air, unsaid.

"Well, this looks cozy."

Damn. Tick smothered a wave of frustrated anger. Cookie had the worst timing known to man. Tick straightened, making sure his expression was blank before he looked around at the other man. Cookie's face was a study in smooth guilelessness that didn't fool Tick for an instant. Jeff stood slightly behind him, a small frown creasing his brow.

Tick crossed his ankle over his knee. "Falconetti's been looking through Amy's diary."

Jeff pulled out a chair at the other end of the table. "Bet that's a hell of a read."

Rounding the table to the seat opposite Tick's, Cookie grinned. "Anything interesting?"

"A record of her sexual conquests." Caitlin held out the diary. "Look for yourself."

Cookie leaned forward to take it, his attention dropping to the scooped neckline of her T-shirt and the hint of cleavage exposed. An urge to smack him on the back of the head barreled through Tick. The guy was his friend, a crack investigator, but did he always have to be such a sleaze where women were concerned?

"Cookie, do me a favor, would you?" Tick jerked a thumb toward the door. "Go get my spare lighter out of my desk drawer."

His partner's eyebrows lifted, a knowing leer twisting his mouth. "I thought you quit."

"You thought wrong." He had quit, for the third time since January. This had been his longest stint so far, a whole three weeks without a smoke, but damn it, he needed another nicotine fix. Even worse, he needed Cookie away from Caitlin. "Are you going after it or not?"

"And contribute to your bad health choices? You're on your own, man."

"I'll get it." Jeff pushed up from his chair and disappeared through the door. Smiling, Cookie leaned back and opened the diary.

A pulsating silence so thick it was palpable descended, broken only by the soft tap of Caitlin's loafer on the tile. She folded her arms over her midriff, gaze trained on the book in Cookie's hands.

"Here you go." Jeff tossed him the lighter and Tick tugged the pack of menthols out of his pocket.

Caitlin eyed them. "What are you trying to do, commit suicide slowly?"

She didn't need to go there with him right now.

Cookie didn't look up from the diary. "You can't smoke in here anyway. State law."

Jeff gestured at the book. "So how many are there?"

"Several." Caitlin lifted a shoulder in that easy elegant

shrug of hers. "It spans a six-month period or so. She didn't write every day. And I like I said, a lot of it is a chronicle of her sexual activities. I think her father was aware of what was going on and it drove him crazy."

"Knowing Tommy, I imagine so." Tick creased the front of his jeans along his shin. "He'd be afraid it'd hurt his chances for reelection if it got out his daughter was the local nympho."

"Cynic." Cookie continued reading. "Not like the whole damn town didn't know anyway. Nobody can keep a secret around here."

Caitlin ignored him. "She doesn't really name names, although she does describe some men she's interested in."

Tick shifted. Ten bucks said Amy had recounted the whole bikini incident. Holy hell, he couldn't wait for that to be entered into evidence.

"A few weeks ago, the tone of the entries changes. She was involved with someone exclusively and that becomes her focus."

Jeff tapped his fingers on the scarred tabletop. "I don't suppose we're lucky enough to get a name."

Caitlin shook her head.

Tick pursed his lips. "Any clues as to who this mystery guy is?"

"She doesn't describe him, other than his prowess, but what she relates about his personality..." She shrugged again. "She should have run like hell."

"Why?" Genuine interest flared in Jeff's eyes. Tick hid a grin behind his hand. The kid was always reading psychology books, tomes on criminal profiling. He had to be eating this up.

"He reads like a narcissistic personality disorder. Throw in what sounds like some shadowy sociopathic tendencies, and I'd bet you my next paycheck the man she's describing is your killer."

Jeff frowned. "So why would she get involved with this guy in the first place?"

Ice flickered in Caitlin's eyes. "A narcissist is all about appearances and illusions. There is no real emotion or concern for others within them. All they see is their own desires and how to manipulate others to achieve those desires. They can make themselves into whatever you want them to be, but only as long as it suits their purposes. Amy probably didn't realize what she was dealing with until it was too late."

Cookie looked up, his gaze fixed on her face. "That sounds like the voice of experience."

Jeff groaned. "She's a criminal profiler, Cookie, for Pete's sake. Of course it's the voice of experience."

"My father," Caitlin said, her voice quiet. Tick watched the flash of understanding that flared between Caitlin and his partner, and jealousy tingled over him. He couldn't get her to open up, but Cookie could? "He was a textbook example and my mother couldn't extricate herself. It made for an interesting childhood."

Cookie tapped the book. "You see something else in here, don't you?"

She slanted a cautious glance at Tick. "I think he's a cop."

"What?" His stomach took a slow, sickening roll. "Hell, what makes you think that?"

"Probably the stuff like this." Cookie flipped back a page and began to read. "He'd just gotten off work. I had him leave his clothes on, including the holster and the gun. I love the idea of it, the power. It's the biggest turn-on ever."

"It's southwest Georgia." Jeff chuckled, a hint of derision in the sound. "Have you seen all the gun racks on pickups? Hell, just about every guy here has a gun and they wear them. All you need is a permit."

"It's more than that," Caitlin said softly. "She mentions the use of handcuffs—don't look at me like that, Calvert, I know anybody can buy them, but still—it's the way she talks about him. I simply...damn it, I think he's a cop."

Tick tugged a hand through his hair, frustrated. "Intuition?"

"Yes."

"Shit."

"Yes." She looked away. "I might be wrong."

He pushed up to pace. "And when, exactly, was the last time you were wrong about an offender profile?"

"Well..."

"Yeah, that's what I thought. Great. Just freakin' great." He didn't want to think about it. Now he'd be giving every guy he worked with, from every department in this end of the state, the once-over, wondering which one it could be.

"He could be an ex-cop. Or a wannabe who couldn't pass the psychological to get into the academy. God knows we see enough of those—"

"You realize this makes all three of us suspects." He stopped and faced her.

"Everyone's a suspect. That's the number one rule. You know that, Calvert. And I'm only theorizing. I don't know enough yet to say more. Besides, if we start trying to put any unsub offender into a neat little slot, we're bound to be disappointed."

"Hey, I'm in here." Cookie chuckled.

"Why am I not surprised?" Jeff cast a glance heavenward.

The weight of the day's events settled squarely in the middle of Tick's back. "Tell me you're kidding."

"Nah." Grinning, Cookie passed him the book. "May twenty-third."

Not wanting to read the account, but compelled to do so, Tick accepted the journal. He skimmed the entry, relief and disgust tangling in him. "Because you wrote her a flippin' speeding ticket. When are you going to grow up?"

"You're grown up enough for both of us. I've got to start on that database." He stood to rummage in the banker's box for the evidence bag holding Amy's address book. He tagged Jeff on the arm. "You can help me."

Rising, Jeff gestured between Tick and Caitlin. "What are you two going to do?"

Caitlin glanced at Tick and away. He cleared his throat. "What colleagues do in an investigation. Follow the rule of twenty-four and delve into Amy and Vontressa's lives."

 C3

During the minutes before the seven a.m. shift change,

quiet permeated the sheriff's office, and in the makeshift war room, Caitlin buried herself in the materials related to the case, free from the distraction of Tick's presence. The hours they'd spent after dinner the night before, interviewing Vontressa King's friends, had seemed a special kind of torture. After midnight and countless unsuccessful interviews, they'd parted with a polite distance between them.

That hadn't stopped her from dreaming of him.

She rubbed at her eyes, gritty and dry from lack of sleep. With Amy's diary and address book open before her, she jotted notes on a legal pad, adding to the twelve pages she'd already written since her arrival at the obscene hour of four a.m. She lifted her cup of coffee. The lukewarm liquid left an acidic aftertaste, much like the aftermath of her dreams, first the nightmares that left her smothering screams, later the dreams about Tick that always left her breathless and wanting.

Grimacing, she leaned back in the rickety chair and surveyed the photos on the bulletin board again. No matter what path she took, she returned to Amy Gillabeaux. Amy had to be the key to finding this killer—her death was different enough to provide a lead the others wouldn't. Before he'd gone home to catch a couple hours of sleep, Cookie had given her the folders organized for each victim, and she pulled Amy's forward, lifting her senior photo to study it. Amy stared at her with a cool smile and mischievous eyes.

Caitlin tilted her head, still studying the photo. She recognized that smile—she'd hidden behind one just like it most of her life. A persona to hide the fear and insecurity inside.

"What happened to you, Amy?" she whispered. "Who wanted you dead?"

The instinctive knowledge that Amy's killer had been someone she'd known well remained. The other three women seemed to be victims of opportunity, in the wrong place at the wrong time. Amy's death...this death had been one of purpose, of planning. She alone carried bruises on her face; she alone bore stab wounds. The others didn't. They still hadn't located Vontressa King's missing car. The doors had been unlocked on Sharon Ingler's car, the contents of her purse spread across the passenger seat. Amy's car had been discovered in a local parking lot, doors locked, her purse gone—as if she'd left to go with someone else.

Willingly.

"Agent Falconetti. You're up early." Jeff Schaefer's deep voice interrupted her reverie. He leaned in the doorway, alert and professional, two cups of coffee in hand. The fluorescent light glinted off his brown hair. "Brought you some fresh caffeine."

"Good morning, Investigator." She accepted the coffee and he dropped into the chair closest to her. A hint of sports deodorant wafted over her, and she shifted away. "Thanks."

"Call me Jeff." He glanced at the legal pad on the table. "Looks like you've been busy. What have you got?"

She shrugged and took a cautious sip of the hot, fresh brew. "Not much more than we talked about last night. I'm just organizing my thoughts. Tick's obviously right about his cleansing the bodies."

Schaefer nodded. "He doesn't want us to have any DNA or other trace evidence we can use to nail him."

"And he's dumping the bodies at a secondary location, so we can't analyze the actual kill site. He's an organized personality—thinks things through, is prepared for the kill, even if the women seem to be victims of opportunity."

"Like I said, he thinks he's smarter than us."

"Probably. We're going to prove him wrong. We'll start with our victimology, focusing on Amy Gillabeaux."

"Why Amy?"

"Rule of twenty-four. She's your most recent victim, even if she was found before Vontressa King. It'll be easier to backtrack the forty-eight hours before and after her death."

"So basically we're going to delve into Amy's secrets, huh? Figure her level of risk."

She studied him. Younger than Tick and Cookie, he nevertheless exuded quiet professionalism, from his appearance to his demeanor. He not only talked the talk, he seemed to walk the walk as well. "You have profiling experience?"

"Just watch a lot of that courtroom cable channel."

"Sure you do." Good training wasn't hard to see, and he had it. His earnest attitude reminded her of Tick as a young

Quantico recruit.

"Hey, I was a road cop for nine years before I got this job. I've picked some things up along the way. I read a lot, and I took a course on forensic profiling last summer." He chuckled, levering himself out of the chair. "Where do we start?"

He vibrated with eagerness. Caitlin hesitated; given a choice, she'd rather do this with Tick. She trusted him, despite everything, and they'd always worked well together. "Shouldn't we wait for Tick or Cook?"

Schaefer shook his head. "Tick called into dispatch a few minutes ago. Power outage at his place last night—his clock didn't go off and he overslept. He's running late. And Cook works a split shift today—he won't be in until twelve."

Well, she didn't have a choice, did she? "Then let's go talk to the parents."

CR

A discreet housekeeper ushered Caitlin and Schaefer into the Gillabeaux's elegant living room. Light bounced off gleaming hardwood floors, and tasteful accoutrements gave the room a magazine-photo quality. Caitlin glanced at the portraits hanging in a neat row above the couch. Amy looked down on the room with the same reserved smile and wicked eyes from her senior photo.

Eloise Gillabeaux rose from a tapestry wing chair to greet them, her face ravaged by grief, dark circles under her eyes, deep lines cut into the papery skin around her mouth. "Good morning, Investigator."

Schaefer nodded. "Mrs. Gillabeaux, this is Special Agent Falconetti, from the FBI."

Caitlin kept her smile soft, taking the woman's hand. "Mrs. Gillabeaux, I'm so sorry for your loss. Thank you for agreeing to see us this morning."

Eloise drew in a shaky breath. She sank into the chair, hands clenched in her lap. "I-I just want you to find the monster who did this to Amy. I'll do anything I can to help."

Caitlin took the wing chair nearest the couch. Schaefer

remained standing, resting his arm along the fireplace mantel. She balanced her notebook on her knee and smiled again. "Mrs. Gillabeaux, I need to know everything you can tell me about Amy. Her friends, her schedule, even if it doesn't seem important."

"She was our baby," Eloise said, tears glistening on sparse lashes. She swallowed and blinked rapidly. "We had four boys and then Amy. She was always Daddy's little girl...she was very much like Tommy, too. Strong willed, but she loved people. She was very popular."

Caitlin nodded. "Did she have close friends? Someone she would confide in?"

Eloise dabbed at her eyes with a crumpled, lace-trimmed handkerchief. "She'd just moved last semester into an apartment near the college. Her roommate was her best friend from high school, Laurie Gold. Laurie is the one who called us when Amy didn't come home Tuesday night."

Her voice broke over the words, and Caitlin leaned forward. How awful losing a child was. A cold pain settled around her heart, but she shut it off, tucked it away. Focus. She needed focus. "Take your time, Mrs. Gillabeaux. Whenever you're ready."

"This is just so hard to believe," Eloise sobbed, and Caitlin reached out to touch her clenched hands. "Why would anyone want to hurt her? Amy loved people...she was always wanting to help others. That's why she volunteered at the center—"

"The center?"

"The women's crisis center. Amy volunteered there two days a week, when she didn't have classes."

Caitlin nodded and jotted the information down. "Did Amy have a boyfriend?"

Eloise shook her head. "Oh, no. She wasn't ready to settle down yet. Her father used to tell her she had to date at least twenty-five men before she would be ready to make a decision regarding marriage. She would just laugh and tell him no one would compare to her daddy."

The revelation brought on fresh tears and Caitlin waited for the woman's composure to be restored before continuing. "Did you see Amy on Monday?"

"No. She went to church with us Sunday and spent the afternoon here. We usually talk on the phone every day, but I didn't...I didn't call her Monday."

Caitlin closed her notebook after removing a business card. "Mrs. Gillabeaux, this is my card. If you remember anything at all, even if it seems unimportant, please call me. My cellular number is there, or you can reach me at the sheriff's office. And thank you again for seeing us."

"Please don't thank me." Eloise struggled for composure. "Just find the person who killed my daughter."

The same maid appeared to show them out. "Where is the women's crisis center?" Caitlin asked as they walked to Schaefer's unmarked unit.

"It's in the old high school building," he said and unlocked the car by remote. He walked directly to the driver's side and, unlike Tick, he didn't bother to open the door for her. "Tori Calvert, Tick's sister, is the director."

"I know." She latched her seat belt. During their last phone conversation, when Tori had called with questions about a paper for her graduate courses in psychology, the younger woman had joked that she'd gotten the job because no one else wanted it. Caitlin smiled, aware that had to be as far from the truth as possible.

"That's right. You worked her case. Tick called in favors to get you to profile Reese." He adjusted the rearview mirror before backing out of the drive. "So let me guess—our next stop is the center?"

"Exactly."

She gazed out at the imposing façade of the Gillabeaux home. The house she'd grown up in possessed the same classic red brick, huge white columns and air of stately decorum. Homes like that, displaying the class and status of old money, pressed on their inhabitants, pushing them into socially appropriate roles. Here was one half of Amy's double life—the good daughter, the good girl, aching for freedom, seeking something this life didn't give her.

Something in her other life, the one where Amy hadn't had to be a good girl, had gotten her killed. Caitlin was sure of it.

CR

Caitlin's shoes clicked against the tile in the women's center lobby. Despite the institutional flooring, a sense of calm and comfort saturated the room thanks to soft pastels on the walls and even softer music coming from a CD player behind the reception desk.

The blonde working the desk glanced up, smiled at Schaefer and flicked a curious glance at Caitlin. "Hey, Jeff. How are you?"

He leaned against the waist-high desk and tapped his fingers against the white countertop. "I'm good. Is Tori in?"

"She's in her office, working on the budget, but she'll be glad to see you. You know the way."

"Come on." Schaefer motioned down a long, narrow hall. Caitlin shook her head and followed him. Professional he might be, but he lacked Tick's ingrained good manners. As much as she'd laughed over Tick's opening doors for her or rising when she entered a room, she missed the way it made her feel—special and very feminine. Or maybe he just made her feel that way.

And maybe she should simply focus on her job.

"Come here often?" Caitlin asked, and Schaefer chuckled.

"I handle most of our sexual assault cases since we don't have a female deputy yet," he explained. "Cookie doesn't always have the right, er, demeanor for them, and Tick...well, those cases set his teeth on edge, if you know what I mean."

"I do." She remembered Stanton having to drag Tick off rapist Billy Reese during the arrest. He'd been icily calm until Reese had started yelling taunts about Tori, then he had lost control. Caitlin had pulled him from the room, forcing him to look at her while she ordered him to calm down. His tortured expression had done her in—all she'd wanted was to make the rage and agony go away.

The whole tangled mess between them had probably started that night. It had simply taken three more years to come to fruition.

Schaefer's comment about Cookie surprised her, though.

Cook had layers and she'd already pegged the sleazy persona as a mask, maybe because she wore her own every day. After dinner, once they'd gotten down to business, the investigator had been quick, articulate and an utmost professional.

"Plus, Tick and I teach a women's self-defense course here a couple nights a week," Schaefer said. That comment brought Caitlin back to reality and a smile to her lips. She could imagine Tick doing so and doing a darned good job, too. She didn't understand why he had doubts about taking this position. He was the kind of guy who was always there when needed, and the community needed him.

He never shirked a responsibility.

Schaefer stopped at an open office door, rapping lightly on the frame. "Ms. Calvert, I'm with the sheriff's department and I need a word with you, please."

Her back to the door, Tori Calvert didn't turn from the computer screen. Long dark hair spilled over her shoulders in a shining fall. "Jeff, unless you're coming to tell me that you won the lottery and you're donating the money to the center, I don't have time."

"Would you have time for the FBI?" Caitlin asked.

"Oh my gosh, Cait!" Tori jumped from her chair and rushed to embrace her. Caitlin hugged back, affection surging through her. "What are you *doing* here?" She stopped, glancing from Caitlin to Schaefer and back, sobering quickly. "Oh. Of course. Amy and Sharon. And now Vontressa. When did you get here? Why didn't Tick tell me you were coming? Oh, gosh, it's good to see you!"

Caitlin smiled. Tori hadn't changed—happy or upset, she still bubbled over with questions. "I got in yesterday afternoon. I have no clue why Tick didn't tell you, so you'll have to ask him. And it's good to see you, too."

Tori stepped back. Her eyes, the same chocolate shade as Tick's, sparkled with excitement. "You look wonderful! But you always do." She wrapped her arm around Caitlin's waist and grinned up at Schaefer, who leaned in the doorway and watched them. "Jeff, did I ever tell you that when I was a teenager and first met Cait while she was at Quantico with Tick, I hoped they'd get married? He was so besotted with her it was pitiful. I just knew they'd make a great couple and have beautiful babies together. I even had names picked out."

Caitlin's breath stopped in her throat and she struggled to keep her composure. *Good God, Falconetti, she's only teasing. Pull it together.*

"Actually, no, you never shared that with me." Schaefer laughed. "Maybe we could have dinner Saturday night and you could tell me more."

Tori grinned. "Mikata's?"

He nodded, blue eyes glowing with male appreciation. "Sounds good. I'll pick you up around seven."

"How about I meet you there instead? We can walk over to the theater afterward."

Caitlin drew a sharp inhale. "Tori, I hate to interrupt, but I wanted to talk to you about Amy Gillabeaux. Her mother said she volunteered here."

"I'll tell you everything I can, but I need to get away from that awful budget for a while. Jeff, you're dismissed." She waved him away. "Cait, I can tell you about Amy over lunch."

Caitlin started to protest, but knew the gesture would be futile, like disagreeing with Tick when he had his mind set on something. Somehow, she'd keep Tori focused on Amy, not on catching up and all the places that could lead. Faking a smile, she gave the younger woman a teasing salute. "Yes, ma'am. Let's go."

Chapter Three

The lunch rush in Coney, Chandler's county seat, was in full force already. They ended up at the Hickory House, a long, squat concrete building on the highway. Pickup trucks and SUVs filled the parking lot, but Tori squeezed her silver sports car into a small space between a huge diesel Ford and a pecan tree.

The heat washed over Caitlin in waves when they stepped from the car.

Tori dropped her keys in her purse. "We may have to wait, but it'll be worth it. The food is great."

Her prediction proved true, as the line at the ordering counter stretched to the entrance. Caitlin glanced around at the country décor—hokey hand-painted signs, ceramic animals, lots of sunflowers. The spicy scent of smoked meat and barbeque sauce hung in the air, and her stomach grumbled.

Tori turned her back on the farmers in front of them and fixed Caitlin with a steady gaze. "I am so glad to see you. By the way, did I mention that my brother, the one I think you're perfect for, is still single?"

Perfect? Far from it. "So, tell me, are you and Schaefer serious?"

"Me, serious? Hardly ever. Jeff, always." She laughed at Caitlin's huff of exasperation. "No, we're not dating seriously. Not yet anyway. We've been to dinner a couple of times. He's a nice guy. I haven't had a chance to find out if there are any sparks." Tori's wicked grin, so like Tick's, lit her whole face. "Those sparks are a necessity, you know. Or so I've heard."

"Tick would have a fit if he heard you say that."

"Screw Tick." Affection tempered Tori's frustrated statement. "He plays big brother a little too heavily, and I've told him so on several occasions. Sooner or later, he's got to realize I'm not ten, and now is as good a time as any. And stop changing the subject. What did you think when you saw him again?"

"You really want to know?" Caitlin asked, and Tori nodded, leaning forward. Caitlin lowered her voice to a conspiratorial whisper. "That he needed a shower. He'd been involved in farm work."

"You have a serious case of denial." Tori turned around as the line moved forward.

"Don't try to analyze me," Caitlin warned, a note of real tension entering her voice. After the attack, she'd gone through the motions with a bureau counselor, and that had been painful enough. She didn't want Tori picking at her scars, too. "I have more training than you do, remember?"

"More classroom training," Tori conceded, her gaze fixed on the menu over the counter. "But I've had tons of experience with the real thing."

Darkness colored Tori's tone. Caitlin brushed her hair back, looking at the confident tilt of Tori's chin. The other woman was right. She was mature beyond her twenty-four years, a maturity brought on by the horror of her rape. Tori, with typical Calvert courage and Tick's unwavering support, had faced the aftermath dead on.

Caitlin shivered. Tori was right about the experience, too. Training and lectures had nothing on the real thing, the real horror. Caitlin had once thought she'd learned everything she needed to know between her doctoral degree in psychology and her FBI training.

Benjamin Fuller had taught her differently.

You know Tick would support you the same way, hold on to you, hold you up.

She tightened her arms over her stomach, the hollow ache there now having nothing to do with hunger. She was over it. She'd confronted the reality of what had happened to her, the way it affected her future, what it had taken from her. So she still had nightmares, the occasional panic attack. That was normal. It didn't mean she wasn't handling the aftermath, wasn't recovering.

And why even bring Tick into this? She'd made her choice about him. Best not to even go there.

"Cait?"

Startled from her reverie, Caitlin glanced up. "Sorry. I was thinking."

Tori continued to watch her carefully. "I didn't mean to bring up something that's hurting you."

Caitlin shrugged. Her weak smile hurt her face. "You didn't. I'm just trying to get my mind wrapped around this case."

"Sure." With seeming reluctance, Tori let the topic pass, and Caitlin's next breath became a relieved sigh. They ordered and made their way to a corner table. Within a few minutes, their food arrived, hot, fresh and delicious. Caitlin's usual hunger had fled, and she managed only a few bites, moving food around her plate with aimless movements.

Tori laid down her fork, her face brightening. "Hey, I've got a great idea. Why don't you come to church with me Sunday? And then you can come to Mama's for Sunday dinner. I'm telling you, that's an experience not to be missed."

Caitlin balked. She was here to work, not get further entangled in the Calvert family. "I don't—"

"You'll love it. Come on. Say yes. Besides, a little church never hurt anyone. Not that I know of, anyway."

Caitlin stared at her a moment. If she didn't give in, Tori wouldn't allow her a moment's peace. Besides, if she was lucky, she'd be back in Virginia by Sunday. "Okay, fine. I'll go. Now, tell me about Amy Gillabeaux."

Tori rested her chin on her hand, sadness invading her eyes. "The gossips like to paint her as a wild child, but she wasn't, not really. She liked to party and she liked attention, but she was a good person. She was doing well in school after the fiasco of her first semester, majoring in social work, and I think she genuinely enjoyed her volunteer duties at the center."

"What did she do there?"

"We have support groups for young women who've experienced domestic violence in dating situations, who've suffered date rape, any number of things. Amy organized and worked with several of those, and she helped coordinate our self-defense courses."

"Did she have a boyfriend?"

Tori sipped her tea. "Amy had lots of boyfriends. She liked uniforms, and she liked older men."

"You're the second person to tell me she liked older men. What kind of uniforms?"

"Cops. Marines—Albany has a major supply of those. Air Force boys from Valdosta."

"But you don't know of any guy in particular she was interested in? Someone who visited her at the center?"

"She was interested in lots of guys, Cait. Lord, she even made a play for Tick. She was very miffed that he wasn't interested."

Caitlin speared a cucumber slice with her fork. "So I've heard."

"I think Amy saw him as a challenge." Tori waved her fork toward the door. "Speak of the devil. I forgot it was the civic club's monthly lunch meeting."

Anticipation slid over Caitlin even before she cast a casual glance over her shoulder. Tick stood by the door to the meeting room, talking to a group of men, including Mark Cook, Stanton Reed and Jeff Schaefer. He grimaced and punctuated his words with his hands. Caitlin watched his mouth move and turned away before he caught her ogling him.

"Oh my Lord." Her voice gleeful, Tori stared at Caitlin. "I knew it! You've got the hots for him."

"I do not have the hots for your brother." Caitlin creased her napkin into a neat rectangle and laid it beside her plate. For telling that whopper, she would need to be in church Sunday.

"Sure. And Chandler County is a cultural Mecca. This is wonderful! I wish you could see the way you just looked at him."

"Tori. Stop." She wasn't letting this go further. "I'm not saying he's not an attractive man. We're old friends and we're working together. But that's all."

"Sure. Deny it all you want." Tori nodded, a knowing smile

curving her mouth. "You'd be perfect for each other. He needs someone who won't let him be in charge all the time, someone a little strong willed. And I think you need someone to take care of you, even if it's only every once in a while."

"You're deluded." Caitlin's laugh sounded shaky to her own ears. She picked up her notebook from the table and dropped a tip beside her nearly full plate. "Thank you for the information on Amy."

Tori's wave was dismissive. "Anything I can do to help. Just be forewarned—Tick's my mother's favorite, and she likes big weddings."

"Would you stop?" Caitlin pushed a hefty dose of irritation into her voice, and after a long searching look, Tori shrugged.

They walked out, squinting at the bright sunlight. Wishing for her sunglasses, Caitlin shielded her eyes from the glare. "Could you drop me by the sheriff's office? I need to interview Amy's roommate and my car is there—"

"Ready to go, Agent Falconetti?" Schaefer asked as he joined them. Even in the wilting heat, he maintained a crisp professional appearance. He pulled his sunglasses from his pocket and slid them on, smiling at Caitlin's quizzical look. "You wanted to talk to Laurie Gold, right?"

She nodded. "Tori, I guess I don't need that ride after all."

"That's Jeff for you. Always around when he's needed. Don't forget, Mr. Schaefer, Saturday night, I'm meeting you for outrageously expensive Japanese food."

"I won't." He brushed a quick kiss across her cheek.

"Cait?" Tori called after them as they walked to the car. "I'll pick you up at your hotel Sunday morning around ten."

Trapped at the restaurant entrance by Ray Lewis, the local newspaper editor who was all but demanding inside information on the murder investigation, Tick watched Caitlin walk away with Jeff. Envy twisted in his gut and he jerked a hand through his hair. The jealousy bothered him.

Her secrecy and the distance between them bothered him more.

Mentally, he cursed the rural power cooperative. Why today

of all days did his power have to go out? If the damn clock had gone off, he'd have spent the morning in Caitlin's company, using the opportunity to further the murder case and maybe getting answers out of her, rather than closeted in a meeting with Stanton and two testy county commissioners, explaining every freakin' line item on the proposed investigative budget.

His day had to get better. It just had to.

Yanking his cigarettes from his pocket, he glared at the insistent editor, now sputtering something about the first amendment and the public's right to information. "Ray, give it up. You'll get the prepared statement from the department this afternoon, just like everyone else."

Ray's thin hair, grown long to cover a spreading bald spot, lifted in the hot breeze. "Just tell me this—is it true that you have no evidence at all?"

"Of course we have evidence. You can't have a crime with no evidence. It's not possible." They just hadn't found it yet, but hell if he was letting Ray print that in the paper.

"Forensic evidence, Tick. I'm talking about DNA and carpet fibers and all that crap they're always talking about on television."

Tick blew out a long stream of smoke, letting the nicotine soothe his jangling nerves. Halfway to Jeff's unit, Caitlin stopped, smiling an apology as she pulled her cell phone from her jacket pocket. Lord, she was gorgeous when she smiled.

He turned to Ray. "I can't tell you that. If I told you what we have or don't have, you'd print it. And then I'd have Tom McMillian on my ass about screwing up his prosecution—"

"Well, you can't prosecute a suspect you don't have!" Ray snarled and stalked off, waving his hands in the air.

"What is Ray fussing about now?" Tori asked, joining him.

"You don't even want to know." He passed a hand over his nape. "Where are Cait and Jeff off to?"

"She wants to interview Amy's roommate." Tori poked him in the ribs affectionately and he winced, rubbing the spot. She had the sharpest nails known to man and knew right where to jab him. "Why didn't you tell me she was here?"

"You think I tell you everything?"

Mischief crinkled Tori's nose. "You don't have to. The local grapevine tells me sooner or later."

"We've found two bodies in as many days, Tor. I've been kind of busy." He dropped the cigarette to the gravel and ground it out with his heel.

"Are you happy to see her?"

"I'm glad to see her," Tick said, going for professional and noncommittal. Confiding in Del was one thing, Tori quite another. Del would listen, maybe offer advice, back off to let him figure things out. Tori would hound him to death. "She'll be a big help on this investigation."

"That is not what I meant." She blew out a long-suffering sigh. "Big brother, she is very into you."

"What are you, twelve? Into me? She is *not* into me," he protested, even though he knew the words to be false. Caitlin didn't want him near her right now, but they'd been as into one another as two people could be. That level of physical need didn't just go away.

He hated the knowing look that crossed his sister's face. Tori tossed back her hair. "Trust me. She's very attracted to you."

Attraction wasn't the issue. Trust was. He was finally figuring that out, now that the anger and hurt over her rejection was receding a little. The physical tug between them was too strong to ignore, but something kept her from letting it go deeper than that. The puzzle was driving him nuts.

Tori nudged his arm. "C'mon, Lamar Eugene, you're staring into space. What's going on? Tell little sister all about it."

"I'm not discussing this with you. Nothing's going on." He shook his head, walking away. Yeah, Caitlin was attracted to him. He'd have to be blind not to see that. During the myriad interviews they'd conducted last night, he'd looked up and caught her watching him more than once, a hunger in her eyes that made him burn.

Damn it all, none of this made sense.

He jerked the truck door open, gaze straying to Jeff's flaring brake lights as the unit pulled out of the parking lot. Footsteps crunched on the gravel behind him.

"You know what you need?" Tori leaned against his hood.

"Don't say it." He dropped his tone to the stern warning he'd used when she was a teenager. It hadn't worked then, so he didn't hold out a lot of hope that it would work now. She was like a runaway semi when she got on a tear, and she always felt she had to try to fix everyone's problems.

"Oh, get your mind out of the gutter, Lamar. I was going to say an afternoon fishing, but what you're thinking would do wonders for your mood."

"Tori, go away. Do your job. Help somebody."

"Good Lord, you're a grouch. And I'm trying to help somebody. I just...I want you to be happy, and I think you could find so much with her." Her expression turned sober. "What happened to her, Tick?"

His nerves jerked in response to the quiet, simple question. "What makes you ask that?"

She shrugged, brows drawn together in a puzzled frown. "She's...different. Tense, withdrawn. Doesn't look like she's had a decent night's sleep recently, either."

"She has a tough job, Tor."

She pinned him with a cynical look. "No one's job is that tough. She looks like she can't stand to be in her own skin."

She had to say that. Tick shuddered. He'd heard it before— Tori had screamed the same words at him in an agonized rage mere weeks after Reese had raped her. His stomach pitched and he lifted a hand to wipe beads of sweat from his upper lip. It was one thing for him to see changes in Caitlin, quite another for Tori to see the same. If Tori saw it, too, it might be real.

"Tick, what is going on?" Her worried voice penetrated the icy dread gripping him. "I haven't seen you look like that since—"

"I don't know." The raspy whisper hurt his throat, but the horrific possibilities rolling through his mind hurt worse. He pushed his hair away from his forehead, fingers pressing against his skull. Lord, what secret was Caitlin keeping locked up inside? "She hasn't said anything. Look, we're just speculating. Like I said, it could be nothing more than job stress."

Even he didn't believe his reassurances.

"If I were you, I'd keep an eye on her. I know that look."

He expelled the air from his lungs in a harsh breath. "Yeah?"

"Yeah. I used to see it in the mirror every day."

ℭ

From the nature CD, the soft strains of Mozart's "La Clemenza di Tito" blended with a pattering rain and croaking frogs. Eyes closed, Tick sat in his darkened office, glad the thick blinds and sheltering oak trees cut the insistent sunlight. Head tilted back, he pushed his shoulder blades into the chair and concentrated on breathing in and out in a slow rhythm. The five-minute relaxation technique was the only thing he'd gotten out of a three-date relationship with the yoga instructor at the local Y.

It wasn't working.

He still wanted a cigarette and couldn't clear his mind of budget figures, crime scene photos or Miss Lauree's sobs. Worse, the light rain on the CD made him think of Caitlin. Rain always brought her to mind, but the thoughts weren't pleasant this time. Memories of her pushing him away mingled with fear of what had caused the changes he saw in her.

She looks like she can't stand to be in her own skin.

With Tori's words echoing in his head, any relaxation he'd achieved evaporated. He rubbed at his eyes and pinched the bridge of his nose. Tori had nailed what he'd been seeing and been afraid to name. In his experience, the look Caitlin wore, the tension she carried, arose from some horrific event. What trauma caused the icy shadows in her eyes?

He had too much familiarity with every awful act that could be inflicted on a woman, and his mind insisted on conjuring terrible scenarios in realistic detail—screams, bruises, terror. His stomach turned, a slow, sick roll.

Not Caitlin. Not that.

With a curse, he rested his elbows on the desk and buried his head in his hands. Whatever had happened, she was dealing with it alone. Pride and stubbornness he understood, and she wouldn't want anyone to see her healing process as weakness.

Didn't she get that he wasn't just anyone?

Protectiveness stirred in him. He wanted to be there, to be the one person she could trust. He wanted to be her stability, a sanctuary she could hold on to when the memories and the horror became too much. A deep shudder traveled through him.

A rap at the door broke the quiet. He didn't raise his head. "It's open."

The hinges squeaked, and the cacophony of voices and a ringing phone flooded the room. Footsteps clicked on his office floor. He didn't need to look up to know who closed the door, shutting out the noise again. Lord, he could *feel* her. He rubbed slow circles over his aching temples.

"Tick?" Caitlin's husky voice sent soft shivers along his spine. "Are you all right?"

Sanctuary. He wanted to hold on to her as much as he wanted to stand strong for her. The real note of concern made him want to lie in the dark somewhere with her and spill all his worries and insecurities, her arms and that voice wrapped around him. Man, he was in bad shape.

Leather creaked, and the sound of rain swelled around them, thunder rumbling. "Not really, but I'll survive."

In the dimness, he could make out the outline of her form across from him, but not the expression on her face. "What's wrong?"

He laughed and leaned back to scrub his hands down his face. "It would be easier to tell you what's not. Four dead girls, no leads. You think it might be a cop. The county commission wants us to cut our budget further, and it's already so tight that..." He let the words trail away, irritated by his own self-pity. "Hell. I shouldn't have left the bureau."

She leaned forward and his ears picked up the whisper of silk against skin. "Why did you?"

"Because..." How to articulate that? How to put his stupid idealism into words she would understand? "Because it's home, and the people here deserve real service and protection. Because I owed it to Daddy to make sure that once the men who killed him were out of power, a decent department took their place."

"Are you doing that?"

"I'm trying."

"Then you did the right thing." Although he couldn't see her genuine smile, he knew it was there nonetheless, and the surge of warmth she sent through him with her approval had a frightening intensity.

Be careful, Lamar Eugene. Not like she hasn't kicked you in the balls before.

He pushed up from the chair and skirted the desk to hit the lights. A cold fluorescent glare flooded the room, and the air of intimacy disappeared. Caitlin blinked at him, her expression like someone waking from a wonderful dream to a bleak winter morning. He looked away and returned to his chair.

"What did you need?" He leaned over and cut off the CD player, stopping the rain and thunder and music. "How did your interviews go?"

She shrugged. "Just confirmation that Amy led a double life. According to her roommate, she was dating an older man, someone she didn't want her parents to know about. So much so that she wouldn't even divulge his name to her friends. Laurie, the roommate, said this seemed to be the first relationship where Amy wasn't the one in control. Whoever he was, she'd had to work to get him, and she was working to keep him."

He crossed his arms over his chest. "So if he's the killer, maybe she knew that, was using the knowledge to hold on to him."

Her mouth tightened a moment before her expression smoothed over. "Anything's possible. Could be a motive. So either she was dating your killer or she's not related to the other victims, and the similarities between her death and theirs are coincidental."

Frustration dug in with fierce claws. "So we're not any further along than we were. There are just more avenues to follow."

"I never figured you for a quitter, Calvert." A mocking light glinted in her eyes. "Throwing in the towel before we even get started?"

The frustration flashed into fury. She was calling him a

quitter? Like hell. Calverts didn't give up before the job was done. He bit his tongue to keep an angry retort from spilling forth. Like reminding her that she'd given up on them before they'd even started.

Kinda like you did, Lamar Eugene?

He inhaled sharply. He had quit. Hurt and confused, he'd let her push him away and he'd gotten on that plane back to Georgia, sought sanctuary in the familiarity of home.

Damn it, but he was a fool.

Releasing the breath slowly, he relaxed his frown. She still watched him, one eyebrow lifted in silent challenge.

"I'm not quitting, Falconetti." *Not on this case and not on you, either.*

"Good. So which of those avenues do you want to travel next?" Her smile faltered. "Or do you have another budget meeting?"

"No, thank God." He drummed his fingers on the desk, the nicotine urge winding its way around him again. He reached for a peppermint instead and offered her one. She shook her head. He tucked the mint into his cheek to speak. "Where would you go next?"

She pushed her hair back, feathering the strands between her fingers. "I'd like to see where Sharon and Amy's cars were discovered. Visiting Vontressa King's apartment could be helpful as well."

The idea of touring possible crime scenes with her wasn't supposed to give him a thrill, but it did. The more time spent in her presence meant more chances to convince her to let him back into her life, get to the bottom of what had gone wrong between them. He reached for his keys, lying atop his cigarettes on the desk.

"Let's do the apartment first."

"Great. I'll grab my things."

He followed her to the war room, enjoying the trim fit of her black pinstriped slacks over her taut rear end. Awareness hummed under his skin. Suppressing it, he looked at the neat stacks of files and papers on the table. "You've been busy."

Tucking her notebook into her small leather bag, she shook

her head. "I've been hanging out with Schaefer, doing interviews. Cook's been busy. He's compiling a database and doing a good job of it, too."

Tick lifted a paper from the closest pile, skimming the list of Vontressa King's friends. "Yeah. He can be really methodical when he's not being a major pain in my ass."

"According to a couple of Amy's friends, he's a really fun date, too. Are all of his girlfriends that young?"

"He doesn't date any of them long enough to call them girlfriends."

"Apparently, neither do you. Your name came up in a couple of those interviews. Amy's infatuation with you was common knowledge in her circle of friends."

"Amy wasn't infatuated with me, and she wasn't looking to date me, either. All she wanted was another notch on her bedpost. Are we going or not?"

The analytical way she studied him set his teeth on edge. "Whenever you're ready."

СЯ

An eerie silence hovered in Vontressa King's empty apartment. She'd never finished moving in—no furniture filled the rooms, boxes waited by the door, a television sat on a milk crate by the window. A half-empty Diet Pepsi stood open on the counter between the living area and kitchen.

In the middle of the large L-shaped living room, Caitlin looked at Tick over her shoulder. "It's like she's going to walk through the door any second, isn't it?"

He nodded. "Yeah."

"She was probably dead within three or four hours of her disappearance." She peered into the boxes. "I think the statistic is seventy-six percent of abductees are killed during that time frame. But why her? Why Sharon?"

"No 'why Amy'?"

"Amy's different. If it's the same guy, she's personal."

"It's the same guy." His voice hardened.

"You sound sure." She set one box to the side. "Intuition?"

"Yeah."

"I think he's an evolving killer." She flipped through the second carton's contents—spicy romance novels, R&B CDs, a collection of DVDs. "Fantasizes about the attacks, before and after, planning them, reliving them, figuring out how to make it better the next time." She frowned, nibbling her lower lip. "Maybe that's why VICAP didn't turn up anything. There's a distinct pattern to these deaths. Maybe he did it before somewhere else and changed his methods to elude detection."

"You don't think he's local?"

"Could be." She rolled one shoulder in a shrug. "Or he's local and he killed before elsewhere? A lot of times, we find these kinds of killers do a lot of trolling in different areas, driving around, looking for victims. They'll have high-mileage vehicles."

Tick nodded. "Maybe we need to have Schaefer expand the VICAP search, look for clusters of deaths that don't share this MO but are in the tri-state area."

"Good idea." She picked up a photo album from the next box and flipped it open. Vontressa's wide grin appeared in picture after picture chronicling her senior year of high school. The last few pages depicted the party atmosphere of a cruise ship. Another familiar smile caught Caitlin's eye. "Tick, look at this."

"What?" He moved to stand behind her and the warm scent of his soap enveloped her.

She passed a fingertip over Vontressa's face to the pretty blonde standing next to her, an arm around Vontressa's waist. "It's Amy."

"Their senior trip." He tapped a long finger against the photo above, a beach scene with several people in a group. With the movement, his arm brushed hers. "And there's Sharon."

Caitlin studied the pictures. In both, a long-haired teenage boy loitered at the edge of the action. In the bottom photo, he stared at Amy Gillabeaux with a hungry gaze. "Who is he?"

"Keith Lawson. His daddy runs a local garage." He paused. "And he applied to the police academy. They turned him down. He didn't have the grades."

She glanced up at Tick, intensely aware of his closeness. "We should talk to him."

"Tomorrow." His deep voice caressed her ears. "He's probably gone to the car auction in Thomasville with his daddy."

She nodded and looked away. This close to him, she wanted his mouth on hers, his hands on her skin. The silence enclosed them, much as the darkness had in his office earlier. She'd wanted to touch him then, too, to comfort him. A good thing he'd shifted to consummate professional and turned on the lights before she'd embarrassed both of them.

"Cait." If anything, his voice deepened, his drawl like sweet, smooth molasses. She looked at him again, desire sharpening the angles of his face, and her lungs slowed down, tried to stop. He cupped her shoulder, his fingers sliding over her thin silk blouse, leaving fire behind.

This was not good. She wanted him to go on touching her, to glide his hands down her body, to assuage the ache building low in her stomach, to fill in some way the yawning emptiness Fuller had left behind.

That wasn't possible.

Shaking back her hair, she stepped away and laid the photo album on the nearest box. "You said Vontressa's car hadn't been found, right?"

"Right." A muscle flicked in his cheek above his jaw.

"The car could have been a motive in her murder—"

The shrill beep of his cell phone cut her off. He tugged it from his belt and glanced at the screen. "Excuse me."

She stepped to the window, studying the parking lot below. Across the street, a strip mall squatted under a thundercloud. People hurried to and from the grocery store. Cars filled the spots in front of a Chinese restaurant and drugstore. A Chandler County patrol car sat in the corner of the lot, facing the street at an angle. A shiver traveled over her skin, and she turned away, letting the curtain fall back into place.

"Thanks, Williams. We'll see you in a while."

He flipped the phone closed and returned it to his belt. Her skin still crawling, Caitlin forced a polite smile. "Case related?"

"Yeah. Williams is ready to start on our autopsies. I thought you'd want to ride over for that."

"Definitely, I—"

His phone rang again and he grimaced at the repeat interruption.

"Holy hell." When he glanced at the caller ID, both his expression and stance softened. "Hello? Hey, Mama. What? I'm a little busy...work. I'll try, but I can't promise." Phone pressed to his ear, Tick glanced heavenward. "Yeah, I know I work too hard. I love you too. Bye."

"Do you mind if we make a quick run by the hospital on our way to Moultrie?" He tugged a hand through his hair in a tight, frustrated movement. "It won't take long and it'll make my mama happy."

"Not at all." She pointed at the window. "Tell me something first. Whose patrol car is in the lot across the street?"

Frowning, he moved to the window. "What patrol car?"

She joined him. The car had vanished. "It was one of yours, but it's gone."

The sense of unease the car invoked stayed with her during the drive to the hospital. Tick stopped at the front desk, picked up guest passes for them and ushered her to the elevator. "I can check the dispatch records and find out which car it was."

She nodded. A vision of that car, its occupant watching Vontressa leave her apartment, following her, invaded Caitlin's mind and brought with it remembered fear. She knew firsthand what it was like to be hunted.

ᥴᷧ

With a hushed ding, the elevator doors slid open, and they stepped into the corridor. Directly in front of them lay the maternity ward nursery and a different unease slid over Caitlin, trailing icy fear in its wake.

Oh, no. Not this. Not now.

With her shaking hands clenched behind her back, she looked up at Tick. "Tell me again why we're here?"

"To make my mama happy and see my new nephew. He's all of an hour old."

Pain twisted through her stomach. "Why don't I wait downstairs? A new baby in a family is a private thing and I wouldn't want to intrude."

"Cait, come on. It's not an intrusion. Mama would have my hide if I left you downstairs to wait. We won't stay long."

She didn't have a choice. If she protested, he'd want to know why. Suppressing the sickening hurt, she faked a smile. "Okay. Just don't forget we still have a lot to do this afternoon."

"Yes, ma'am." He knocked on the door to room 535 before pushing it open.

The pretty brunette lying in the bed opened her eyes. "Hey! You came."

"Like I'd miss this. How do you feel?" Tick leaned over to hug her. Caitlin stood close to the door, her attention locked on the clear plastic bassinet by the bed and the blanket-wrapped bundle it contained. The urge to run consumed her.

"I'm fine," the brunette answered, her curious gaze resting on Caitlin.

Tick waved her closer. "Cait? This is my sister-in-law Deanne. Dee, this is Caitlin Falconetti."

Ingrained politeness forced Caitlin to move forward. "It's nice to meet you." She darted a quick look at the bassinet, a wild mixture of agony and hunger twisting in her. "Congratulations."

"Thank you." Deanne eyed Tick with affectionate resignation. "Go ahead. I know you're dying to pick him up."

With a deep chuckle, Tick slid his hands under the baby and lifted him. A small fist escaped the blanket, waving, and Caitlin glimpsed a few wisps of dark hair on the tiny head. Tick settled into the vinyl chair, his nephew in his arms, and Caitlin swallowed hard. What had she been thinking when she agreed to this?

"He's, er, adorable, Dee." Tick's laugh emerged muffled and choked.

"Liar." Deanne's proud glow dispelled the exhaustion dragging at her features. "He's red and wrinkled, and he looks like a space alien. But he's mine, and yes, he's beautiful."

"Does he have a name yet?" Tick shifted the baby in his arms, holding the infant with familiar ease. He stroked a finger over the baby's cheek and Caitlin's throat tightened. He'd make a wonderful father.

This was what Benjamin Fuller had stolen from her. She hoped he rotted in hell.

Deanne's voice broke into her tortured thoughts. "We're still arguing about it. I want to name him Carter, but Chuck thinks he needs a more manly name."

"You don't have one named for Daddy yet." Tick's mouth quirked, and he shifted the baby to lie in the crook of his knee. He folded the blanket back and placed his fingertip in one tiny palm before lifting a small foot. Counting fingers and toes, Caitlin realized. "He kind of looks like a Lamar Eugene."

"We're leaving that name for you to use. And I know your mama's hoping you'll hurry up and use it."

"Give me time." Tucking the blanket about the baby again, Tick glanced at Caitlin and she swallowed hard at the emotions reflected in his dark gaze, joy and pride mingled with anticipation.

She had to get out. Her own feelings threatened to suffocate her. Caitlin smiled thinly, clutching her hands behind her back, fingernails biting into her palms. "Excuse me a minute."

With extreme care, she closed the door behind her. She walked to the restroom at the end of the hall, her vision blurred by tears demanding release. Blinking hard, Caitlin ran cold water over her wrists, splashing a few drops on her face. God, how was she supposed to deal with this?

"All right, Falconetti," she whispered, pressing her fingertips to her burning eyes. "You've been over all this before. Whining and crying doesn't change anything. Just suck it up and get on with it."

The door behind her creaked open, followed by Tori's cheerful voice. "Go *on*, Mama. I'll be right there."

Caitlin grabbed a couple of rough paper towels to dry her hands. Tori paused just inside, letting the door swing shut. "Cait? Are you okay?"

She closed her eyes against the concern in the other

woman's voice. She nodded and drew in a deep, fortifying breath before turning around. "Fine. Why?"

"I don't know. You seemed...sad or something."

"I'm fine," she repeated with a mocking little laugh. Tucking a strand of hair behind her ear, she straightened her blouse.

Tori nodded, remnants of suspicion on her face. "Sure."

Caitlin pulled up her best bureau smile, a brittle expression that made her cheeks ache. Pride and self-preservation demanded she convince Tick's sister nothing was wrong. "I'm going to make a couple of phone calls. Would you let Tick know I'll wait for him downstairs?"

She left the restroom and took the elevator to the ground floor. She turned in her guest pass and walked out into the hot afternoon sun. Despite all her efforts, the tears fell. Damn it, she hated crying, and she hated having a runny nose. She rummaged in her bag for tissues, trying to smother the sobs that rattled her chest.

God, what had she been thinking? She should have run as soon as they stepped out on the maternity floor. Or as soon as she'd seen him at that damned chicken farm, filthy and sweaty and still attractive as hell.

She wanted him. But the wanting went deeper than the physical desire. She wanted him, the man, all of him. She wanted him to love her, and she wanted him to be the father of her children. It was too late for all of that and the futility made her want to scream.

Instead, she began the slow process of pulling herself back together.

"Hey, lady, you all right?" An orderly pushing an empty wheelchair back to the main door paused, concern etching deeper lines around his eyes. "Somebody die or something?"

His bedside manner was atrocious. Laughter bubbled in her throat and she covered her mouth, stifling the sound. "Yes, I guess you could say somebody died."

Benjamin Fuller needed her dead so she couldn't want another man. She still wanted, but Fuller had succeeded in killing the woman inside, the one who planned for a hazy future. She was left with the shell and clear, cold reality.

Fuller had killed more than her spirit.

"I'm sorry to hear that."

"So am I." Caitlin dragged in a deep breath of humid air, redolent with the scent of camellia blossoms and coming rain.

"Anything I can do for you?"

"No." She dried her eyes again. "There's nothing anyone can do. But thank you."

In the confusion of having most of his family, including his aunts Ella and Maureen, in Deanne's room at once, Tick failed to notice immediately that Caitlin didn't return. Once Chuck's four older children arrived with their maternal grandmother to see their new brother, three-year-old Charlie burst into tears because the baby was in Uncle Tick's arms.

Returning the baby to Chuck, Tick swung Charlie up into his embrace, blowing raspberries on her neck and making her giggle through her tears. He laughed, too, affection thrumming through him. "Come on, Charlie, don't you want to see your baby?"

"No." Her bottom lip jutted again and he grinned. Her pout was a miniature version of the one Tori sported when irritated. He held her close, catching a glimpse of glimmering emotion in Chuck's eyes as he settled the baby in Deanne's arms and brushed a soft kiss over her mouth.

Tick shifted Charlie higher on his arm. Hell, it was too damn easy picturing himself in the same situation, with Caitlin. A holdover from too many nights dreaming of her while he'd been undercover.

Holding Chuck's son earlier, he'd watched Caitlin, heat slamming into him as he wondered what it would be like to make love to her again, knowing he might give her a child.

She hadn't returned. Frowning, he glanced around at the crowd and passed Charlie off to Tori. "Where's Cait?"

She pressed a kiss to Charlie's chubby cheek, her expression serene. "She went to make a couple of calls. Said she'd wait for you downstairs."

Apprehension tickled through him. "When?"

"I don't know...five or ten minutes ago. What's the problem?"

"No problem. None at all." He swallowed hard, forcing a cheerfulness he didn't feel. "Mama? I'm gone."

He caught an elevator, worry over Caitlin's absence churning in his stomach. She was making calls, so why was he getting edgy? It didn't make sense, but his instincts were screaming.

Outside, he glanced up at the thunderclouds gathering in the western sky, backlit by the afternoon sun. He couldn't shake the gut intuition that said Caitlin's disappearance had more to do with him than with something case related.

She waited under the porte-cochere, leaning against a column, staring across the parking lot, tapping her cell phone against her lips.

"Cait?"

Not looking at him, she straightened. "Ready?"

Her voice sounded raw, strangled, the aftereffects of tears plain on her face. His chest tightened and he reached for her. "What's wrong?"

She pulled free of his light hold, her movements jerky. "Can we go, please?"

"Not yet." A couple entering the lobby cast them a curious look and he lowered his voice. "You were fine earlier and you've been crying. Tell me what's going on."

"It's none of your business and I wish you'd simply leave me alone." She turned on him, eyes narrowed to green slits, sparking with bad temper. "Which part of 'we're colleagues' did you not get, Calvert? I don't go around sharing my personal life with Cook or Schaefer. What makes you different?"

Her anger set him back for all of two seconds before his own rose to match it. "Maybe the fact we had a personal relationship? Remember that, Cait? That's what sets me apart from Cookie or Jeff, the fact you all but told me you loved me, the fact I've had you wrapped around me and screaming my name."

"So the sex was good." She strode toward the parking lot. "Get over it. I did."

"No." He caught up to her halfway to his truck, grabbed her arm, spun her to him. He leaned down, his face close to hers. "It was more than that and you know it. Something got in the way and hell if I know what it is—"

"God, you're stubborn." She fairly growled the words at him, pushing away, continuing toward his dusty Z71. "Did it ever occur to you that maybe I met someone else while you were gone? Or maybe I decided I wanted something different? Or even that *maybe* I just didn't want you anymore! How many times do I have to say it before it sinks through that thick skull of yours?"

Holy hell, but he was tired of this. "So that's it?"

"That's it." She tugged at the door handle. "Unlock it."

"You don't want me."

Ire flushed her face. "Didn't I—"

He smothered her protest with his mouth. For a half second, she stiffened in his embrace and lifted her hands, probably to shove him away, before she clutched the front of his shirt and pulled him to her, kissing him with a hunger close to desperation. Desire barreled through him, blending with the frustrated anger, making the kiss rougher than any they'd shared before. He flattened her back against the truck, opening his mouth over hers, stroking his tongue between her lips.

She wound her arms around his waist, arching into him, and he pulled her closer, as near to him as he could get her. She stroked the bunched muscles at his lower back and he groaned into her mouth. Lord, he loved the way she touched him and it had been too damn long since he'd had her hands on him. He'd needed this since she stepped out of that car at Ash's, since he'd come home from Missisippi. Hell, he'd needed this, needed her, the whole damn time he'd been gone, pretending to be everything he wasn't.

He splayed his fingers at the curve of her hips. She tasted of mint and passion, the essence of her rocking him to the core. He was growing hard and heavy, an uncomfortable snugness at his groin. Heat trailed through him.

She nipped at his bottom lip, then soothed it with the tip of her tongue, pushing his need higher.

An engine rumbled on the side street and brakes whined. A horn blared, followed by a piercing male wolf whistle. Caitlin went rigid in his arms. Tick pulled away and stared into green eyes almost black with desire. His chest heaved as he struggled to catch his breath and get his body under control.

"Now tell me you don't want me."

"Damn you, Calvert," she whispered, her face pale. "Let it go. Please."

"I can't, Cait. Don't ask me to."

A tear slipped from beneath her lashes and he caught it with his thumb. She shoved his hand aside.

"We need to go to Moultrie." Her voice quivered.

He might be stubborn, but he knew when to back off. If he pushed any more right now, she'd close herself completely off from him and he'd be right back where he started. He unlocked the door, wrenched it open for her. She climbed in and he stood in the opening while she latched her seat belt with hands that trembled.

She didn't look at him.

"The conversation is simply postponed, Falconetti." He rested a hand along the top of the doorframe and studied the averted curve of her face. "This isn't over, precious, not by a long shot."

Chapter Four

No matter where it was in the country, the distinctive smell of an autopsy room never changed—a strong, sharp disinfectant that couldn't quite cover the lingering odor of decomposition. With Tick holding the door, Caitlin took a quick, shallow breath through her lips as she stepped into the examination room. She knew it wouldn't help. The overwhelming scent would linger with her the rest of the day, infiltrating her clothes, hair, everything.

A nude body rested on the stainless steel table, a tall, slender blonde Caitlin recognized from the crime scene photos as Amy Gillabeaux. Tick let the door close behind them with a quiet click and the woman clad in scrubs and a face mask peered up from arranging her tools. Her hazel eyes crinkled at the edges. "Hey, Tick."

"Hey, Jolie." His voice was quiet, tense, and Caitlin didn't look at him. They'd driven the entire thirty miles to Moultrie in silence. "Cait, Agent Jolie Williams, GBI. Jolie, this is Agent Caitlin Falconetti, FBI."

"Talk about alphabet soup." Williams pulled on a pair of thin latex gloves. Picking up a scalpel with ruler markings along the edge, she glanced at Caitlin. "So you're the profiler Tommy Gillabeaux wanted down here so bad."

Caitlin nodded. "I'd like to talk to you about the victims and the autopsy results."

"Can you talk while I cut? It's the only way you're going to get results soon." The other woman gestured toward the refrigerated room behind her. "We have a backlog."

"Sure."

Williams scrutinized Tick, who had turned his back on the bodies to stare at a chart on the wall, one hand covering his nose and mouth. "Calvert, don't you have some calls you need to make or something?"

He spun, his face pale. "Yeah. I'm going to check in with Palmer and Price, see if they have anything on that forgery case we've been working. Let me know when you're ready."

Caitlin held her breath until he left, releasing the pent-up tension with a slow exhale. She faced Williams, whose eyes creased in an unseen grin as she lifted the scalpel. "He's okay until I get out the saw or crack the skull. I thought he'd throw up the one time he was in here when I started pulling the lungs."

He'd been teased without mercy at Quantico about his sporadically queasy stomach. A gory crime scene he could handle—an autopsy was another thing all together. He wasn't alone, either. Caitlin had seen many seasoned detectives undone by the sights, sounds and smells of an autopsy room.

Williams tilted her head toward a shelf over a long sink. "Gloves and face masks are over there if you want them."

While Williams talked into the overhead microphone, describing Amy's age, height and weight, along with the external condition of her body, Caitlin listened. She eyed the bruising along the girl's throat, noting the circular bruising Tick had pointed out in the crime scene photos.

Over the next hour and a half, Williams removed organs, weighed and examined them, including an analysis of the stomach contents. Watching closely, Caitlin took notes and asked questions, wincing a little at the squishing sound the lungs made as they were pulled free. When Williams reached the lower abdomen, she paused, an odd look flashing over her face.

Caitlin leaned forward. "What?"

"She was pregnant."

Caitlin's intuition tingled to life again. They'd already established in the preliminary examination that Amy had had intercourse in the hours before her death, although there was no seminal fluid present. "How far along?"

"Ten, maybe twelve weeks. I can take some measurements

to determine the exact gestational age."

"You'll run a DNA profile on the fetus, right?" Caitlin snapped her notebook shut and tugged off her face mask. She pulled a card from the book and laid it on the table next to Williams's tools. "My cell number's on the card. Would you call me when that's done?"

Thanking her again, Caitlin went searching for Tick. She found him in the reception area, leaning against the empty front desk, talking to a trim redhead holding a stack of file folders.

"I swear, Tick, she said you were the worst blind date she'd ever had," the redhead was saying. "What is wrong with you lately? Did you really call her by the wrong name?"

At the click of Caitlin's shoes against the tile floor, he looked around. "Ready?"

She managed a nod and wrapped her arms around her midriff. She ached deep inside and it had nothing to do with how much or how little she'd eaten at lunch.

"Think about what I said about asking her out again, making things up to her, Tick. She's good-looking and really smart, unlike your recent string of dates," the redhead said, walking down the hall. "You could do worse."

"Later, Kath." Tick turned an inquiring look on Caitlin. "Jolie come up with anything interesting?"

She leaned on the counter next to him. "Amy had sex before she died."

His brows lowered in a deep frown, and she knew he was thinking about Tori. "Rape?"

Caitlin shook her head. "No bruising in the vaginal area consistent with a sexual assault. Williams thinks it was consensual." She paused, her throat tightening. "And she was pregnant."

"Good Lord." Tick gave a low whistle. "Wonder if Tommy knew about that? Hey, are you okay?"

"Of course." Adopting a scoffing tone, she turned and blinked away yet another wave of the weak tears. This was ridiculous. She'd dealt with pregnant victims before. Amy Gillabeaux's pregnancy shouldn't affect her this way.

You're just tired. It was unexpected and you weren't

prepared. The method of strangulation, the stab wounds, the pregnancy...it was just too close to her experiences for comfort. She rubbed a hand over her eyes.

"Caitlin? Are you sure you're okay?"

She dredged up her professional mask. "I'm sure. Just thinking."

"About?"

"That her pregnancy could be a motive for her murder. It could help explain the increased violence of her death, why it seems so personal." Her throat threatened to close. She could not deal with this, not with him here, not after his pushing for answers and that damn kiss earlier. Once they returned to Coney, maybe she'd find a way to get away from him for a while. Right now, with the memories crawling under her skin, digging in, she couldn't handle him. "We should head back. I want to start on my preliminary profile."

"Sure thing. Then we can run out and look at the stadium lot and Highway 112, where we found Amy and Sharon's cars."

"I can do that alone." She settled for honesty. Maybe it would work, since nothing else seemed to. "I'd rather not be with you right now, Calvert."

He blinked, obviously taken aback. For several long seconds, he studied her, frowning, before he nodded. "Okay. I've got payroll and some other paperwork to catch up on. And I'll check in with you later."

◌ଃ

She tried working on the preliminary profile, but her heart and concentration weren't in it. A quick shower washed the smell of the autopsy lab away but not the edgy tension dogging her. The walls of the generic hotel room pressed in on her, and in desperation she picked up her keys and notebook and went in search of Stadium Drive.

Set off from the street, Centennial Stadium loomed over the empty parking lot. The falling sun backlit the structure, casting deep shadows on the gravel parking area, offering pockets of coolness.

Caitlin stepped from her rental car and leaned against the hood. Hands tucked in her pockets, she surveyed the surroundings. To the north lay a set of recreation baseball fields. The administrative offices were to the south, blocking the view of the parking lot from the road.

If Amy had left her car here, meeting someone, leaving willingly with him, as Caitlin suspected, maybe the relative seclusion had been the reason. Maybe that someone didn't want to be seen with her, or was someone her father would disapprove of.

Opposite the stadium, several pecan warehouses lined the street. They sat deserted in the off-season. Caitlin shivered. This might as well be the middle of nowhere, even in the midst of town.

A pickup rumbled down the street, followed seconds later by a sheriff's patrol car with dark tinted windows. It slowed, turned into the long, tight drive before the warehouses. Caitlin watched, eyes narrowed, as it eased onto the street and headed in the opposite direction. She caught a glimpse of the tag on the front end: *C-7.*

With tiny frissons moving down her spine, she returned to the car and pulled out in the direction of the sheriff's department. She stopped at the front desk.

"May I help you?" If the eager young man working the desk had had a tail, it would have been wagging.

She held her credentials aloft. "Agent Falconetti, FBI. I'm assisting with—"

He pointed down the hall. "Straight down—"

"I know where it is. Thank you."

A young male voice drifted into the hallway. "I swear to God, she steps out of the car, buck naked, and starts putting her clothes on, right there by the highway—"

The moment Caitlin stepped into the squad room, silence descended. Cookie was tipped back in his chair. To the right, Tick's office door was closed. Two other officers leaned against the counter. Discomfort twisted the two deputies' faces. She'd interrupted a bull session.

Cookie grinned, a lascivious expression, his gray gaze sweeping over her in a calculating glance.

"Falconetti. What a pleasant surprise." He shot a pointed look at the other officers. "Don't you guys have anything to do?"

The deputies trooped out of the room, albeit reluctantly, mumbling about reports that had to be filed.

"What can I do for you?" His tone implied he hoped it was something out of the line of duty.

She regarded him with a cool stare. She was not in the mood for his flirtation, but she didn't relish sitting in her hotel room with her memories, either. "I just went out and looked at the stadium lot where Amy Gillabeaux's car was discovered. I'd like to drive through the route Sharon Ingler would have taken on her way home from school. I wondered if you'd go with me. Show me where the car was actually found."

Cookie rose so quickly his chair toppled over. "Sure."

"One thing."

"Yeah?"

"You even think of hitting on me and I'll shoot you with your own gun."

"Yes, ma'am."

Even with that assurance, she didn't have complete trust in him. He wasn't Tick. Why did *he* have to be her benchmark for everything, anyway? If she were with him, she wouldn't be gauging the distance from town as the countryside deepened around them or surreptitiously checking her holstered weapon.

The sun slid below the heavy tree line that made up the western horizon as they left Coney behind. At night, the memories were always closer, stronger, and she concentrated on keeping them at bay, watching pecan groves and houses and the occasional chicken barn flash by.

Cookie pulled over just beyond a green mile-marker sign, its reflective number glowing in the headlights. "Here it is."

They left the Blazer, their footsteps loud in the silence. A whip-o-will called in the woods surrounding the road, and Caitlin grew uneasy standing in the dark by the side of the isolated two-lane highway. No one knew they were out here. She glanced back at Cookie. Completely relaxed, he leaned against the hood of his Blazer and unwrapped a piece of gum.

"Both the deputies on duty the night Sharon disappeared

placed the car here?"

He nodded, pushing off the hood and adjusting his holster. "Yeah."

She scuffed the bottom of her loafer in the loose gravel at the edge of the road. Tiny pieces of a broken beer bottle glittered up at her in the light from the truck's headlights. "You said the three wrecker drivers in the area swap out nights. Each one takes calls on different nights?"

"Most of the time. Bobby Gene Butler is a vulture, though."

"A vulture?"

"He goes out and rides the roads, looking for breakdowns. He'll steal them out from under the others if he can." He popped his gum, sweeping a foot at the knee-high weeds in the ditch.

"Bet everyone loves him."

"Yeah, well, he ain't too popular in the county, anyway. He's an ex-con and he'll steal you blind."

"An ex-con? He served time? For what?"

"Manslaughter."

"He killed someone?" A glimmer of excitement sprang to life. Maybe, just maybe, this was a lead. And she'd much prefer to have a suspect who was *not* a cop.

"Yeah. Caught some guy in bed with his wife and shot him."

The anticipation flickered and died. She heaved an inward sigh. A crime of passion just wasn't the same as a well-planned murder. But, maybe...if he wasn't a suspect, he might be an important witness.

"So, who was on the road that night?" She walked out a circle in the thick grass. It whispered against her jeans and she resisted a shudder. Maybe all the snakes were in bed for the night.

"Mike Lawson was scheduled." A slow grin spread over Cookie's face. "But Bobby Gene Butler caught the tow."

"How convenient. Where did he say the car was?"

"He says the first time he saw it, it was about two miles back, at the twenty-third mile mark."

"The first time?"

"Well, that was about ten p.m. Then Chris Parker called him out to tow the car from here at just after one a.m."

She lifted an eyebrow, intrigued. "So either he was wrong about where he saw the car the first time, or the car was moved. Or..."

"Or he lied," he finished for her and shook his head. "Only thing is, Schaefer and Chris saw the car at the twenty-three, too. Jeff was doing a fill-in shift that night."

She nodded. "So the car was moved."

"Looks that way." Cookie glanced at his watch. "Hey, it's after nine and I'm off duty. Let's go get a beer."

She sent him a warning look, and he held up his hands.

"And work!" he protested. "I've got my copies of the files and we can go over them. I want to hear about your profile ideas. I'll even buy you a Big Cheesy."

"A Big Cheesy."

"An experience not to be missed." He chuckled. "Kind of like the Big Cookie."

"You know, Cook, you're really pushing your luck." She followed him to the truck. In the morning, she was going to look for Bobby Gene Butler. She wanted to hear his story of the magical moving car firsthand.

The Big Cheesy turned out to be the house specialty of the Cue Club, a little bar and grill on the outskirts of Coney. The huge chili dog dripped with melted cheddar and she watched in awe as Cookie polished off three of them. "It would take Drano to clear your arteries."

He wiped a dribble of greasy chili from his chin. "Probably. But, damn, it's good. Just like the—"

"Don't say it." She pushed away the uneaten half of her own Big Cheesy.

"You got it." From the chair beside him, he lifted a small handful of file folders and dropped them on the table. He slanted a wicked smile at her. "But it is really, really good. You don't know what you're missing."

She didn't get guys naming their anatomies. Did she and Gina go around calling their breasts by nicknames? Well, actually, she could see Gina doing so, but Gina went in for a lot of things Caitlin didn't.

"I guess you're *not* on intimate terms with Little Lamar?"

Reaching for the folders, she froze and raised her gaze to his expectant face. "He doesn't call it that."

Cookie leaned back in his chair, rubbing his stomach. "Damn sure does. Or he did, back when we were partnered the first time."

Her attempt at impassivity failed, and she laughed, the sound a little shaky, and covered her face with her hands. "God, I can't believe I'm having this conversation with you. When were you partnered with him?"

"When we were both at the Dougherty County PD and he was a skinny, piss-ant rookie."

"Oh, I can't imagine..."

"The stories I could tell, huh?"

"Seriously." She picked up the top folder. She pushed away the desire to learn more about Tick, to find out what she didn't know. She had to get her equilibrium back where he was concerned. Like she'd ever had any to begin with. "Quick question. How are your cars assigned here?"

"For road officers? By dispatch number, except for Tick."

"What do you mean?"

"He drives his personal vehicle and submits the mileage. He has an unnatural attachment to that damn truck of his. The cars are given dispatch numbers to match up with the deputies, starting with me, C-3."

"So who's C-7?"

"Chris Parker. He's our K-9 officer. Why?"

She shrugged. "I saw the car earlier and was curious. He was the one who found Sharon Ingler's car?"

"That would be Chris-boy."

"So her car breaks down. We know it wasn't operable, right?"

He nodded, taking a long swig of his beer. "Yeah. Slung a rod through the oil pan."

She tapped her fingers on the paper in front of her, thinking out loud. "The car breaks down. No cell phone?"

"We didn't find it. Not in the car, not in her parents' home. Never got any pings off of it. It wouldn't have been useful anyway if she did have it with her. That whole area is a cellular black hole. Can't get a signal."

"Okay. So does she get out and walk, or does she wait?"

"Nearest house is a quarter mile away."

"She drives that route every week when she comes home from college. She knows where the houses are. But it's dark, and that's a long way to walk alone. Maybe someone stopped."

He frowned, unconvinced. "And she got out of the car?"

"Maybe. A vehicle she recognizes or someone who represents safety, security. A cop, a tow truck driver, a volunteer fireman. A lot of women would get out of the car."

Cookie scratched the back of his neck. "You're a woman. If you were stranded, who would you get out of the car for?"

She regarded him with a level stare. "No one."

After almost three hours spent putting the department's weekly paperwork in order, Tick emerged from his office. The mind-numbing tedium always left him feeling shell-shocked and a little brain dead.

The odor of scorched coffee hung in the deserted squad room. The conference area held only Jeff surrounded by file folders and Caitlin's notes. Tick eyed her neat handwriting, regret pulsing in him.

He'd tried calling her cell, twice, and both times had gotten her voice mail.

She hadn't returned his calls.

I'd rather not be with you right now, Calvert. Yeah, he'd definitely pushed the issues between them too hard today.

Tick paused in the doorway, watching the young investigator scribble in his notebook. "Jeff, have you seen Agent Falconetti?"

Jeff didn't look up. "She's with Cookie."

That didn't make him feel better. "Got any idea where?"

"He's off duty. He went ten-six right after nine o'clock when I signed on."

He glanced at his watch. Almost ten thirty now. Tension curdled in his stomach. No way. She wouldn't. Not Cookie, not after kissing him the way she had. And Cookie wouldn't, not knowing his past with Caitlin.

Damn it, Cookie wasn't her type, and she definitely wasn't Cookie's. He couldn't deny Cookie had a way with women, but the other man's taste ran to loud, blatantly sexual women who wore too much makeup and too little clothing, women turned on because he had a badge, women who didn't care that he wouldn't call again.

Except Tick had pushed every button she had earlier and hell if he could predict how she'd react.

Hell, Cookie would, too, if Caitlin showed the least amount of interest. Who was Tick kidding?

He was jealous. And he hated it.

"He's probably at the Cue Club," Jeff offered, and Tick snapped out of his reverie to find the younger man watching him with a quizzical expression. "You know it's his usual Friday night hangout."

"No, he didn't." Caitlin covered her mouth, muffling her amusement. The simple act of laughing felt so *good*. Giving in to the temptation to learn more about Tick felt even better.

Cookie chuckled, wiping tears of mirth from his eyes. "Damn sure did. Ol' Tick calmly stops the cruiser, shoos the chicken out of the car and heads on to the call. We left chicken feathers in his locker for weeks."

She relaxed into the seat, holding her stomach. "Oh, that's funny. I'd love to have seen his face."

"Then there was the freak ice storm we had. Roads slick as owl snot, wrecks everywhere. We pull up at the 41 and 336 crossroads and Lamar Eugene is gonna run from the car to the latest fender bender. Only he's wearing shiny new duty shoes. One good stride and he was on his ass."

"And of course, you just stood and laughed at him."

"Hell, no. I went to help him up and fell on my ass. We had to freakin' crawl back and use the car to get on our feet. Everybody at the little curb store was standing outside, hooting and hollering at us. Of course, by then, we were laughing so hard neither of us could stand up."

She could picture it, could almost hear the rich sound of Tick's deep laugh. She ran a fingertip down her longneck. Okay, she'd indulged enough. Time to change the subject. "Too bad Gina and I are so normal, or I could—"

"You should give Calvert a chance." He leaned back and steepled his fingers together. "You two would be good together."

"I don't know what you're talking about." She took a nonchalant sip of the beer she'd been nursing all night, the bottle still half-full. Good together? If Cookie only knew. They'd been better than good, in bed and out. At one time, she'd had hopes for the two of them, based on how absolutely incredible it had felt between them.

"Right. You never noticed the guy tripping all over himself when you're around."

She pinned him with a withering look. He was on a fishing expedition, but if he thought she'd fall for the oldest interrogation trick in the book, she had news for him. "I don't know what you're talking about."

"Sure you don't."

"If you don't shut up about it, Cook, I'm going to kick your ass. Right here, right now."

"Stop." He picked up a toothpick and began cleaning under his thumbnail. "You're turning me on."

"Get this straight. There is nothing between Tick Calvert and me." Not anymore.

"Sure, there's not. And that's why he's headed this way, ready to knock my dick in the dirt."

Startled, she glanced up, straight into Tick's infuriated gaze. Her stomach fluttered, but she dredged up a smile and a little false courage. "Tick. I didn't know you were here."

"Yeah," Tick snapped, brows drawn together in a dark frown. "What's going on?"

Cookie slid an arm along the back of his seat. "We've just been going over the particulars of the Ingler case."

"Over beers in a bar?"

She didn't like the note of accusation in his tone. "We're both off duty."

"It doesn't look right, Cait."

She analyzed his attitude with ridiculous ease. He was, amazingly, jealous of Cookie. She wasn't above using the emotion to her advantage, either.

With an effort, she relaxed and smiled at him, injecting just the right amount of ice into the expression. "You and I did the same thing over the Reese case a few years ago, and several times while you were prepping for that undercover assignment in Mississippi. Was that different?"

He stiffened, his gaze freezing over, and he stared at her, the moments stretching out in slow motion. Hands shoved in his pockets, he rocked back on his heels. "No, I guess it's not. Cookie, give us a minute, would you?"

"Yeah. Be right back." He levered himself up from the booth and ambled toward the bar.

Tick slid into the vacated seat. He looked at her for a long moment, confusion darkening his eyes to black. "You want to tell me what the hell is going on?"

She pointed at the files scattered over the table. "We're working."

"That's not what I meant. Why not let me know where you'd be?" His voice vibrated with pained anger and that jealousy that made her stomach turn. Damn it, she was hurting him, but it didn't have to be this way, if he'd just let things *go*. Maybe if she pushed as hard as he did?

She poured on the frost. "The last time I checked, I was an adult. I haven't checked in with anyone since I was sixteen."

Frustration tightened his face. "Is this because I kissed you?"

She straightened the folders into a neat stack and glanced up at him, making a dismissing gesture with one hand. "What happened earlier today doesn't matter."

"So you can turn it on and off like a switch. When did you get so damned cold? I feel like I don't even know you anymore."

She lifted one shoulder in a shrug. "A lot happens in a year. People change."

"Obviously." His voice dropped. "What did I do, Cait? What turned you against me while I was gone?"

"Nothing. I'm just not interested—"

"Get real. We already covered that this afternoon."

"No, you get real." She leaned forward. "When are you going to realize it doesn't matter how hard you push or how long you try to hold on to me, Tick? It's over and there's nothing you can do about it. You can't make me want you, you can't *make* me take you back."

"You know, from where I'm sitting it doesn't feel over."

"What if it was Tori we were talking about and some guy who just wouldn't back off? How would you feel then?"

His face paled, and he jerked as if she'd slapped him. "You know, Falconetti, sometimes I just don't like you."

She couldn't look as stricken as he did. Her mask was too practiced. "Like I haven't heard that one before, Calvert. Why don't you go ahead and get it over with—call me a bitch. You'll feel better."

He stood, contempt tightening his mouth. "Because my mother taught me to treat a woman with more respect than that, whether she deserved it or not."

Refusing to flinch from the insult, she simply regarded him with a tiny smile. "Funny. You must have missed a couple of lessons. You respect me too much to call me a bitch, but not enough to honor my wishes."

She wouldn't have thought his face could lose more color, but it did, his eyes burning black with fury.

"You wanted us to be just colleagues," he snapped, the words harsh and clipped. "Well, you got your damn wish, Falconetti. Believe me, beyond finding this son of a bitch, I want nothing more to do with you." He leaned in, holding her gaze with his. "I'm done."

He threaded his way through the crowd, but never looked back. She swallowed the rising lump in her throat and left enough money on the table to cover her bill and a generous tip. However, she didn't have his strength, because as she approached Cookie at the bar, she couldn't resist the urge to cast a surreptitious glance over her shoulder.

He'd stopped at the side entrance, talking to the small group of people who'd just entered, including the redhead from the GBI lab earlier. She touched Tick's arm, drawing his attention to the curvy brunette with her. He smiled at both women, his stance taut with tension.

Caitlin turned away, her throat tight and hurting, and met Cookie's knowing gaze. When she was able to speak, her voice came out a painful rasp. "Not one word, Cook. Not one."

His sharp gray eyes held something a lot like sympathy. "I wasn't going to say a damn thing, Falconetti. You ready to get out of here?"

"Sure. Let's go take a look at Devil's Hole, where the first body was found."

"Don't you want to wait until morning? That's the middle of nowhere and it's going to be hard to see anything in the dark, even with a spotlight."

"Then drop me back at the sheriff's office. I can work on the victimologies."

He pushed the door open, humid air rolling over them as they walked into the parking lot. Distant sheet lightning brightened the purple sky in a burst of flashes. "Geez, Falconetti, you were in the office at four this morning, and it's after eleven now. Don't you ever sleep?"

"I don't need—"

"Of course you don't sleep. Not unless you're exhausted." He answered his own question. "And you have nightmares when you do, right? I doubt you have the flares of anger. You're too controlled for that. But I bet you're hiding some major mood swings."

Horrified by his insight, she stared at him. She shook her head, a slow, disjointed movement. "You—"

"I get it, now." Comprehension spread over his face, and he snapped his fingers. "Calvert's too close, and you're pushing him away while you tell yourself you're protecting him. But you're the one who needs protection, aren't you? You don't want to hurt him, but you're more afraid of being hurt yourself."

She stepped back, still shaking her head. Those keen gray eyes saw too much. "You've been watching too many talk shows, Cook."

"No, I lived it. Let me tell you something, Falconetti. Alone is an awful place to be."

Hell, she knew that. She didn't need him to tell her anything. Icy anger curled through her. "Thanks for sharing, but I really would like to get back to work. Can we go now?"

"Sure thing." The lascivious mask fell into place again. "You know, if you wanted to indulge in a meaningless, purely sexual fling, I'm available."

"I thought I warned you about hitting on me."

"You did. Sorry, I'm just not scared of you. Right now, I'm more afraid of Calvert shooting me."

She wanted to laugh, wanted to pretend she didn't care. She settled for a nonchalant shrug. Tick would find someone else. That's what she wanted him to do, wasn't it? "I don't think you have to worry about that anymore."

"Then you don't know him as well as you think you do." He pulled his keys from his pocket. "Know why his father called him Tick?"

She waited for him to unlock the door. "Because when he was little, he was as stubborn as a tick on a hound dog—once he got a grip, he wouldn't let go."

"Think about that." Cookie swung the door open, his arm resting along the top. "Right now, he wants you. You might have just kicked him in the teeth, but he's not going to give up as easily as you want him to."

She shuddered at the thought. She really couldn't take much more of this.

Well, she'd simply have to find a way to tell him the truth. Then they'd see how long he wanted her.

Hours later, Caitlin kicked the sheets away with a frustrated sigh. Even with the air conditioner running, she was hot, her skin flushed and damp. She left the bed and went to stand in front of the unit. Scooping her hair up from her neck, she let the cool air wash over her.

The glowing red numerals of the clock mocked her inability to fall asleep. Tick's hurt expression and Cookie's direct questions jumbled together in her mind. Why did she keep pushing him away? Who did she really want to protect? Him? Or herself? What really frightened her?

That one was easy. Her susceptibility to him terrified her. Tick Calvert didn't even have to touch her—one easy grin, the sound of his deep drawl—and her defenses were breached. When he did touch her, she forgot everything but him, and that was dangerous.

The way he'd looked at her today had gone beyond sexual. There'd been something else in that expression, a tenderness and affection deeper than friendship. In that hospital room, he looked like a man in love, and she couldn't allow that to happen.

Who was she kidding? Last year, before he'd left for that undercover job in Mississippi, he'd done everything but say the words. So had she. The proof of those feelings had lain in how eagerly, at first, she'd waited for him to come home, how eagerly he'd sought her out once he did.

But he was right. By the time he walked back into her life, everything had changed.

She had changed.

He wanted children. That fact was indisputable. Even ten years ago, at Quantico, when they'd talked about what their futures held, fatherhood colored his goals. So if she held him off, she protected him from the loss.

Yeah, right. Face facts, Falconetti. You know if he finds out about the truth and walks, and you know he will, it'll destroy you. You're protecting yourself.

She pushed away from the air conditioner, frustration burning along her nerves. Damn him anyway for being everything she wanted. Damn him for making her feel again.

She had to get out.

If she stayed in this room one more minute, the questions and what-ifs swirling in her mind would drive her crazy. The front desk clerk had assured her earlier that the fitness center was available at all hours for guests. A little exhaustion should push him straight out of her mind.

Because of the late hour, the fitness center was quiet and deserted. Out of habit, she clipped her holster to her shorts and chose a treadmill that faced the door. She set it for a brisk run. Determined to forget all about Tick Calvert, she let her mind wander through the information in Amy's diary. In one of the last entries, with the sexual relationship with her mystery man deepening, Amy had poured out her impressions of him.

He's not what he appears to be.

The words rang in her mind. "He's not what he appears to be," she whispered, her gaze riveted on the open door, her senses hyperaware. "Who *is* he, Amy?"

The facts tumbled around in her mind. A sketchy profile was forming, and she didn't like the picture at all. A narcissist—self-centered, controlling, outwardly charming. A man who hid behind a mask, who smiled and made polite conversation while he put his victim at ease. Women would love him.

A shiver trailed down her spine as she remembered another man who hid behind the friendly mask while he created a delusional fantasy with her as the center. When that fantasy shattered, he'd wanted to destroy her.

He'd succeeded.

What was going to happen if the killer was a cop, was in Tick's department, and he realized his façade was in danger?

She pushed the thought away. They would find him, stop him before that happened. Eyes closed, she took a deep breath, clearing her mind.

In the adjacent lobby, a phone rang, and she jumped, eyes jerking open. Laughing at her own nerves, she picked up her pace a little.

The memories nudged their way into her unwilling consciousness—his arm crushing her throat, the knife tearing—*carving*—into her abdomen, her mind not accepting the reality.

The glass slammed the reality home—the awful, grinding pain of broken glass slicing the skin of her lower back in a dozen places through her thin silk robe, her grandmother's crystal vase shattered on the floor, and Fuller's weight on her as he shoved harder against her throat. And the fury in his eyes, the absolute need to destroy her, made stronger by the fact that she carried a child that wasn't his. She was *everything* to him, he'd repeated over and over. She was his everything, and she'd dared to want, to give herself to another man.

She shuddered. When had Amy realized what was happening to her? When he grabbed her? When the gravel ground into her skin? When the knife pierced her womb, seeking to destroy the life within? When he smashed his arm against her larynx, cutting off all hope?

She stumbled, grabbing the rails for support while she shut off the treadmill motor. Sudden, stabbing sobs tore at her chest, and she sank onto the nearby weight bench, burying her face in her hands. She identified too easily with Amy Gillabeaux, and if she had any sense at all, she'd tell ADIC Frazer and Tommy Gillabeaux to go to hell and excuse herself from this case. She couldn't, though. She couldn't walk away and chance it happening to another unsuspecting woman.

Arms wrapped around her stomach, she cried, hating the weakness of the tears but needing the release. She cried for Amy and for herself, for everything lost. In her mind, she saw again the baby cradled in Tick's strong hands and wept with renewed bitterness, wishing Fuller had succeeded in his murderous intent. She shied from the thought, shoving it away, and at last, the tears abated.

Eyes burning, she dragged herself back to her room, exchanging her workout clothes for her discarded sleepwear with listless movements. Cold now, she slipped beneath the covers and wrapped her arms around the extra pillow, resting her cheek on it. Exhaustion pulled at her, and the last image in her mind before sleep came was of the raw pain invading Tick's dark gaze as she let him believe he meant nothing.

Two jailers and a dispatcher fell victim to undercooked takeout from the local grocery's deli, tanking Tick's plan to kick back with a beer and Jimmy Buffet and wallow in self-pity before going to bed early. When he returned to the department, Jeff was gone and thankfully neither Cookie nor Caitlin was anywhere to be found. Tonight, that was a good thing. He prided himself on being a patient man, but even he had limits.

The desire to shake the truth from her, to take a punch at his partner, curled through him again, but after lights out, he settled for slipping into the tiny weight room on the jail level and hitting the heavy bag until his knuckles hurt.

She was right. He couldn't *make* her do anything, couldn't make her want him in her life, make her take him back. He'd lost her, it seemed like for good this time, and there wasn't a damn thing he could do about it.

The knowledge stuck in his craw, eating at him.

Damn it. He drove his fist into the bag. She'd sat there and put him on the same level as Cookie, reduced those few precious nights he'd had with her before Mississippi to nothing. He'd lived on those memories, taking them out at night after he'd said and done things that turned his stomach, holding on to her, to them.

Yeah, they'd sat and talked over beers in a bar several nights in a row, and part of it had been work. She'd delved into his head, into the heart of who he was, helping him figure out how to be what he wasn't, teaching him to hold tight to what he was. By the third night, he hadn't been able to help himself and when he'd walked her to her car, he rested a hand atop the Volvo and leaned down, taking her mouth in an easy kiss of discovery and exploration, a kiss nine years in the making. He hadn't misread the emotion glittering in those green eyes as she looked up at him afterward, either. More than wanting, more than desire.

He slugged the bag harder. The fourth night, she'd taken him back to her apartment, to her bed. And the fifth night? He'd been trying to distance himself, getting ready to get on that damn plane, and she'd pushed beneath his barriers, until they'd ended up back at his hotel and the way she loved him blew his mind. God, sometimes he woke up, still able to feel her.

Sweat trickled down his neck and another punch slammed into the bag.

Oh, yes. There. Tick, please...

The sultry whisper of her voice filtered through him with the memory of being wrapped around her, the lush heat of her body closing on him.

"Shit." The raw, hoarse voice couldn't be his. He threw a hit so hard it jarred his elbow. What if she...what if Cookie...?

Damn it, she could do what she wanted. He wouldn't let it matter any longer, any more than those words she'd whispered that last night in Virginia. He'd leaned over her, an "I love you" on his tongue, and she'd pressed her fingers to his lips, her green eyes gleaming in the soft light.

No, not yet. When you come home...

He'd come home to nothing.

His wild swing missed the bag completely and he lost his rhythm. The sturdy sack smacked into his chest and abdomen. He stumbled, steadying it with shaking arms.

Trying to catch his breath, he rested his forehead against the rough canvas. He was done, they were over, she was out of his life.

Holy hell, let her do whatever she wanted. He was too damned tired to care anymore.

Later, after the relief jailer finally made an appearance, Tick tried stretching out on the cot in the guards' break room, but sleep wouldn't come. He folded his arms behind his head and forced himself to focus on the case, running through everything they knew so far. Wriggling his shoulder blades against the thin mattress and its unforgiving springs, he closed his eyes. The connections were there, but damned if he could see them yet.

God only knew how that young Jane Doe had ended up in Chandler County. A runaway, maybe, like Jeff theorized, although none of the missing persons reports he'd looked at so far matched her description. He'd almost think she wasn't related to the others, if not for that round little bruise on her neck.

Sharon. Vontressa. Amy.

Same high school. Same graduating class. Other than that, not a lot to connect them, either. But Keith Lawson had known each of them. That might be the link. He could see Sharon getting out of her disabled car for Keith, especially if he'd been driving his daddy's wrecker.

Was Keith smart enough to do this?

Tick muffled a yawn with his fist. Maybe he'd talk to his nephew Blake, who knew Keith, see if that helped build a preliminary sketch of the boy's personality.

Gut instinct told him he was looking for an older suspect, one with some experience on him. Caitlin didn't think this was a first kill. She painted a picture of a predator, maybe someone who'd killed elsewhere then turned his attention on Chandler County.

His eyes snapped open and he studied the water stains on the ceiling with its peeling paint. Lord, he just couldn't get away from her, could he? He needed her to finish the damn profile and go back to Virginia. He needed that, so he could start putting his life back together again.

The massive back door to the jail slammed with a metallic clang and he jumped. His body felt heavy, reactions slurred by exhaustion. He rubbed a hand over his eyes and twisted his wrist to look at his watch.

Nearly five.

He rolled to sit on the cot's edge, staring at his feet and shaking his head to clear the fuzz and cobwebs. Shower. Coffee. Cigarette. Then he'd get moving again. Jeff would be on duty until nine and they could toss around ideas, maybe ride out and talk to Keith Lawson, get a read on the kid, find out if he could send them in any new directions.

Cookie was off today, thank God.

A quick tepid shower in the bathroom off the employee locker room and a round with his electric razor had him looking more human. He rubbed a thin towel over his hair, frowning at his reflection. Damn, he had to find ten minutes to go get a haircut. Maybe Becky could fit him in during his lunch break. She'd chatter him to death the whole time, but that would work. If he was listening to her, he wouldn't have to think.

He brushed his teeth, avoiding his troubled eyes. He was avoiding a lot of things this morning, making sure his thoughts stayed on the straight and narrow path of what he needed to do during the day.

Dressed and feeling more awake, he plodded upstairs, the low buzz of radio traffic following him from the dispatch office. A hum of terse male conversation drifted from the squad room.

"All I'm saying is, maybe you should think about the fact you have to work with him after this." Contempt laced Jeff's steady voice. "Thought y'all were friends. Is a piece of ass worth losing that?"

"Maybe you should think about the fact that working here a couple of months doesn't make you one of us yet," Cookie retorted as Tick walked through the door. "Or even better, maybe that you're not as damn smart as you think you are."

Tick ignored them in favor of the coffee station. His nape prickled under Jeff's watchful stare. A wet wool blanket of silence smothered the room. Warm mug in hand, Tick turned and rested against the counter. He gestured with the cup in Cookie's direction.

"Your day off. What are you doing here?"

"Couldn't sleep." Cookie shrugged and unwrapped a fresh pack of gum. His brown hair was damp at the edges, a Florida State T-shirt untucked over his clean jeans and the boat-and-deck shoes he wore without socks.

"Yeah." Tick scowled at the oily swirls atop his coffee. The muscles in his neck and shoulders seized up.

"Guilty conscience," Jeff muttered, tapping his pen on his blotter. Tick tensed further. The kid wasn't helping matters.

"Kept thinking about Sharon Ingler and her car." Cookie folded the foil over and over until it resembled a lopsided swan. "Been riding the roads, trying to get my mind around it."

Tick nodded.

"You look like shit," Cookie said. "Go home and get some sleep. Let me take your shift."

"Like that, would you?" Tick set the mug aside with deadly precision, the chilly fury burning him again.

"Hell, that's it. I'm done bothering with you." Cookie pushed up, his chair squawking with the movement. He shook his head, face twisted with disdain. "Let me know when you get your brain out of your ass."

"What is that supposed to mean?"

Heading for the door and the hallway beyond, Cookie lifted a hand in dismissal. "It means you're wrung out and not firing on all cylinders."

Tick followed, the overworked muscles in his arms throbbing with renewed tension. "You got a problem with me, Cook?"

"Tick, let him go." Jeff rose with an uneasy movement. "This isn't worth it."

Waving him off, Tick caught up with Cookie in the hall. "Spit it out."

"Ain't talking to you, Tick. I'm going home to enjoy my day off."

"Like you enjoyed last night."

"You're an idiot." Cookie halted and blew out a harsh, long-suffering breath. "Would you stop and think for two seconds before one of us ends up doing something both of us will regret later?"

"Like one of already didn't, right?"

Cookie threw his hands heavenward. "Yeah, fine, whatever. I did her, the whole night long. That's why I'm up at five in the damn morning. The sex was so freakin' fantastic that's all I can think about. Happy now?"

Anger flushing his entire body, Tick stepped forward. "You son of a bitch."

"Try it, Calvert, and I'll whip your ass, seniority or not."

"Like to see you try." Even feeling like the walking dead, he was two years younger, three inches taller and a hell of a lot madder than Cookie.

"Think." Cookie thumped him on the forehead. "Did you see how shook up she was last night? Do you really believe she'd be interested in sleeping with me? And like I'd go to bed with a woman who'd be thinking about you the whole time. I have standards, you know."

Tick blinked. "I—"

"She plays you so easy it isn't even funny."

"Plays me?"

"And hell, you let her. She pushes your buttons and you lose all God-given common sense."

"I do not—"

"She got rid of your ass again, didn't she? You let her. Now, you're pissed at me. Probably spent the whole damn night picturing what you thought was going on between us." Cookie shook his head. "Damn, but I wish you'd wise up and use that legendary intelligence of yours where she's concerned. This is getting old."

Shit. He hated when Cookie was right. She had done it again; he'd *let* her do it again. And hell, he was no closer to figuring out why she kept pushing him away.

He slanted a look at Cookie's patient expression. "Yeah, yeah, you're right."

"Oh, no, Lamar Eugene, you have to say it."

"Fine, I'm an idiot and I let her do it to me again."

"You're whipped already, man, and—"

The newly installed department door slammed open, the glass rattling in the frame. His and Cookie's heads jerked toward the tiny lobby. A pair of teenagers stood inside, their faces pale and frightened. Tick's stomach dropped. This wasn't going to be good.

"Mr. Calvert! I'm so glad you're here." The blonde, one of his nephew's friends he was sure, stepped forward, her blue eyes big and shocked. "You're not going to believe what we just found."

Rain fell, sheets of water blowing in a wild wind, rattling the windows on the long corridor. She'd been here before and it never ceased to terrify her. Horrible things sought her in the shadows, breathing, pulsing, lurking.

You cold-hearted bitch.

God, he was here, hiding, waiting for her.

You think I'm letting you have this baby, letting you have his baby? Do you?

I'll kill you first.

The pain tore through her and she ran, the dark surrounding her, unseen hands pulling at her ankles, making her stumble. Somewhere, beyond the inky black, a baby cried.

Her baby. Tick's son.

No matter how many times the dark invaded her dreams, how many times she'd searched for him here, she'd never been able to find him.

He was lost to her.

A noise shrilled, drowning out the baby's cries, and she frowned, the sound louder and louder, filling her consciousness, pulling her from the fear, the pain, the loss.

Her phone. Without opening her eyes, she grabbed the vibrating square from the nightstand.

"Falconetti." Her voice came out even huskier than usual, her throat aching from last night's tears.

"It's Tick." Tension dripped from the words.

She opened her eyes. The lights blazed around her. Thirty-three years old and she slept with the lights on away from home. That would kill her reputation in a heartbeat if her colleagues ever found out.

"It's barely six. What do you want?"

A pause hummed over the line. "We just found number five."

Not again. "Oh, God. Give me directions, and I'll meet you there."

"You'd never find it. I'll pick you up. Be ready in fifteen minutes."

Chapter Five

So much for interviewing Bobby Gene Butler or pulling work schedules for the night Sharon Ingler disappeared. Caitlin rubbed at her burning eyes. Another body, another crime scene. Another day trapped with the man who surely, *finally*, didn't want her now. That was supposed to make her feel better.

It didn't.

Tick's truck bounced over a rut in the red clay dirt road and Caitlin clung to the armrest. He slowed to navigate around a large gully, the remnant of a long-ago torrential rain. Erosion had taken its toll on the area and clay walls rose on either side of them, three or four feet above the wide ditches, with exposed tree roots snaking down through the dirt.

The sun lay just above the horizon, throwing golden and crimson light over everything. Caitlin stared out at fields and trees, trying to resist the urge to study him. He wouldn't even look at her, and guilt coiled in her chest like an angry rattlesnake. He looked awful, his face pale, jaw tight, red-rimmed eyes heavy with lack of sleep.

Braking, he swung the truck into an overgrown driveway, almost hidden by low-hanging branches. Evidence of tire tracks showed that the trail was not as abandoned as it first appeared. Within a few yards, the trees opened up, revealing a wide path that circled a chasm almost a half-mile in diameter. Tick stopped the truck behind a county unit and killed the engine. Caitlin stared at the miniature canyon, marveling at the colors revealed in the layers of rock.

"This is it." The words came from between clenched teeth, and he shoved the door open and stalked over to speak to the deputy leaning against the patrol car. The sudden absence of his habitual courtesy stung, but she pushed the emotion away. She stepped from the truck and trailed behind him across the pocked, gravel drive.

Tick tugged his department cap lower over his eyes as she approached. "Ready?"

"When you are." She followed him down into the pit. He moved on the narrow path with easy familiarity, but she picked her way with caution, every loose rock skidding over the edge making her nervous. The steep sides cut off the budding sunlight and brought an eerie, unnatural dimness to the morning. Despite the muggy humidity, she shivered, glad she'd donned her black duty jacket with her T-shirt, jeans and sturdy hiking boots.

At the bottom of the rocky trail, a young deputy stood at the edge of the taped-off scene. This was the true middle of nowhere—a hell of a place to hide a corpse. "Who found her?"

"Couple of teenage kids camping out up on the ridge. They were planning to go for a sunrise swim in the pond." Tick ducked under the tape after a brief word with the deputy.

"Hell of a walk for a swim."

"Privacy. It's a local make-out hot spot. I doubt swimming was all they had in mind."

The putrid smell of decayed flesh swamped her first, and she covered her nose and mouth, choking back the gag reflex. She never got used to the peculiar stench of death, no matter how many times she smelled it.

A nondescript brown blanket lay near a small cove of scraggly long-leaf pines. Remnants of clothing scattered the area and pieces of stained, yellowish bones peeked from among the cloth and pine straw.

Caitlin stepped closer. The remains weren't intact and drag marks marred the damp earth. She cringed, her gaze tracing over the tracks leading away from the blanket. Whoever she was, the animals had been at her. "God."

Tick glanced sideways at her, his mouth taut. "Yeah. I know."

He passed her two pairs of latex gloves and she snapped them on, one over the other, although they wouldn't touch anything until the scene was catalogued and photographed. A thin T-shirt lay next to the blanket, a wide tear along the shoulder seam. What looked like an arm bone rested beneath the fabric, and a silver bracelet gleamed dully in the early morning sunlight. The jeans, a few feet away, were new, fashionable and bore a designer label.

The torso remained, the skull still attached, a few strands of long blonde hair intact. Not all of the flesh had decayed, and Caitlin eyed the level of decomposition and the insects crawling on the corpse. The maggots present could help determine how long she'd been out here. Weeks. Maybe as long as a month.

Tick hunkered down by the head and pointed to a smudgy area almost indiscernible against the decomposing layers of skin. "Looks like she might have had a tattoo on her shoulder."

Straightening, she glanced around the canyon. "Doesn't appear to be any sign of a struggle, either."

"We had those heavy rains last weekend." He indicated dried rivulet marks in the dirt. "From the rate of decomposition, she's been out here at least a couple of weeks, if not longer. Any footprints would have washed away."

"How is this different from the others?" She knew, but she wanted to hear it from him.

"The blanket for one thing, and her clothes are here. The others were nude."

"I think she's the first one he killed here. Maybe not his first ever, but still an early kill. He evolved after her, which is why the others are different. And he's escalating." She tilted her head, studying the scene from a different angle. He'd obviously learned since this one—taking the clothes and washing the bodies of trace evidence.

Even the amount of time between her death and the discovery of her body seemed important, weeks instead of the days between the other murders and the discovery of the bodies. He'd gotten away with this murder, and the confidence he'd gained had induced him to leave the later bodies in more obvious places. He'd wanted the other girls to be found. She'd seen it before. The recognition, the notoriety, the heady sense of winning a game against the local police became an addiction.

Tick stood motionless, staring down at the remains. Caitlin

watched him, gauging the play of expression over his face. "What is it?"

He glanced away. "The damn blanket. It's identical to the ones we carry in our patrol cars. Holy hell, I didn't need this."

She squashed the sympathy that leapt to life in her. Turning back to the body, she lifted one shoulder in a nonchalant shrug. "We'll match the dye, match the lot, find the distributor. It may be a coincidence, and we'll find it didn't come out of a Chandler unit at all."

"Sure." Resignation colored his voice. He rubbed a wrist over his face and turned toward the deputy standing by the crime scene tape. "Troy Lee, go get the camera and crime scene markers out of your unit."

Caitlin crouched by the body and looked up at the towering walls. "I don't think he killed her here. It would be too hard to get her down that path in the dark, especially if she struggled. Too much of a chance that she'd go over the edge and take him with her."

With a curt nod, he walked a few feet away, staring at the ground. Caitlin remained where she was, watching him. Minutes passed, the silence between them growing deeper with tension. "I think your deputy got lost."

He didn't smile. "I wouldn't be surprised. I told Stan he was too young. Cookie says—"

She winced at the way he bit the sentence off, the line of his back rigid. "Tick, I'm sorry about—"

"Not now, Cait." Without looking at her, he held up a hand before he sighed, tugging at the bill of his cap. "I'm going to walk up and wait for Stanton and the coroner."

Shaken, she watched him go, a sense of loss nagging at her. She wouldn't even come away from this with his friendship, and the thought sent the hated tears pricking at her eyelids again. With a deep breath, she forced them down. So she'd lost something irreplaceable. It certainly wasn't the first time.

ʒ

While the glaring heat of a Georgia summer day set in, the

tension grew. A throbbing headache hovered at Caitlin's temples and radiated through her skull. For once, she sought ironic refuge in an autopsy lab, assuming Tick wouldn't hang around the cool, quiet room where Jolie Williams worked.

They'd pulled in every favor they had between them to get the latest victim moved to the front of the autopsy schedule. Tick surprised her by returning to the lab after disappearing briefly to run their victim's statistics through the missing-person database. Arms folded over his chest, he lounged against the long table that ran along one wall. His face closed and expressionless, he watched Williams.

Caitlin ignored his presence as much as possible, forcing her mind to focus on the medical examiner's comments.

"See these fractures here?" Williams asked, pointing at the throat with her scalpel. "Tick, care to have a look?"

"I'll pass."

"Her larynx is crushed." Caitlin twisted her back to relieve the dull pain sitting at the base of her spine.

"What's left of it anyway. He probably put his forearm across her throat to restrain her."

The memories deluged her without warning. Caitlin sucked in a sharp breath, tiny dots of ink dancing at the edge of her vision, the room going out of focus. She clutched the edge of the table and concentrated on breathing through her mouth, a slow in-and-out rhythm.

William's eyes widened. "Okay?"

"I'm fine. The smell got me for a second."

Tick pushed away from the table. "Do you see anything remotely helpful, Williams?"

She tilted her scalpel toward the lower abdomen, the remaining skin and layers of muscle beneath open along a neat incision. "She had a hysterectomy. In a woman her age, that's pretty rare."

Tick peered closer. "Are you sure it wasn't the animals?"

"I'm sure. Animals don't cauterize the surrounding tissue when they rip out your organs."

Caitlin continued to focus on the simple act of getting air in and out of her lungs. Damn it, was there any aspect of this case that wasn't going to throw the past in her face? She resisted the urge to lay a hand on her own flat stomach, dizziness attacking her head.

With a sharp tug, she pulled the surgical mask from her face. "I'm going out for a second."

Outside, the damp, heavy air made it hard to breathe, but she dragged in gulps, trying to fill her lungs and settle the nausea churning below her heart. She leaned her forehead against the metal support post beneath the aluminum awning and closed her eyes. It was just stress. Simply stress and exhaustion and lack of food...the last thing she'd eaten had been half of that godawful chili dog with Cookie the night before.

"Hey, I'm supposed to be the one who gets sick in the autopsy room. Are you all right?" Genuine concern colored Tick's words.

She didn't open her eyes. He was the last person she wanted to deal with right now. She was too damned weary and heartsick. "Go away, Tick. You're done, remember?"

"Damn it, would you just talk to me?" His low, rough voice shook with frustration. "Tell me what's going on."

"Nothing."

"Don't lie to me." Anger vibrated the deep timbre of his drawl, and she felt him move closer. "I'm not taking that bullshit this time. You tell me now, or I'll have you pulled from this case."

She opened her eyes, glaring at him. "If I recall correctly, I was ordered down here by an ADIC at the request of your state senator. And you're going to pull rank, how?"

"Trust me, between me and Stan, we could do it. Spill it, Falconetti."

"I don't do ultimatums, Calvert." She stepped away, moving toward the door.

With a muttered curse, he grabbed her arm, pulling her back to face him, an odd gentleness in the action. Bare inches between them, she stared up at him. His hair stood out in spikes at weird angles, from the cap he'd worn earlier and his habit of running his hands through it. Shadowy stubble darkened his jaw, but the emotion in his eyes claimed her attention. She'd seen that haunted concern before, four years ago when he'd looked at Tori.

"Tell me," he said, his voice a raw, painful sound.

She shook her head, aware of the strength in the hand still holding her arm, a strength that ran throughout his long, lean frame. A desire to fold herself into him trembled through her, but instead she stiffened.

"I can't."

His lashes lowered briefly, and when they lifted, his chocolate gaze burned. "Yes, you can. You mean you won't."

"I can't." The words, with all of their double meaning, broke on a muffled sob. She couldn't tell him. Not here. Not now. Not like this. "I just can't."

The frustration remained in his eyes, but he nodded. "Tori, then. Let me call her. She'll meet you—"

"I don't *want* to talk about it." The words came in a fierce whisper, and she brushed her hair back, avoiding his gaze. "Talking about it doesn't change anything. Talking about it doesn't make it go away."

He cupped her face, thumbs sliding along her cheekbones in a gentle caress. With subtle pressure, he tilted her head up, forcing her to look at him. "And keeping it locked inside is killing you."

With a harsh laugh, she pulled away, struggling to regain her equilibrium. She dredged up an icy sarcasm. "Killing me? How dramatic. I'm under a little stress, that's all. I'm doing my job. You can't complain there."

Hands jammed in his pockets, he stared at her. "It's not your job I'm worried about."

Smile. Pretend nothing's wrong. The commands rang in her mind. "Your concern is touching, Calvert, especially after everything we had to say last night. But I'm fine."

"Damn it, Cait, why won't you let me help you?"

He spun. After the door closed behind him, she sagged against the pole and covered her eyes with a shaky hand. Resisting the overwhelming temptation to tell him everything left her wrung out. She took a few moments to gather her flagging inner strength before she followed him inside.

CR

Tick slumped in one of the leather chairs facing Stanton's desk and watched the other man pace. Caitlin stood in the doorway, leaning against the doorjamb. Exhaustion dulled her eyes and dust smudged one high cheekbone. He tried to remember if he'd seen her eat anything during the day. Worry nagged at his gut again. She looked like hell.

Earlier, she'd all but admitted to suffering some horrific act.

Talking about it doesn't make it go away.

It had been in her eyes then, the pain and terror, still holding her prisoner. He wanted to make it go away for her, knew from experience he couldn't. All he could do was stand by her, be there when the memories were too much. Except she wouldn't let him.

And he didn't know what to do to reach her.

Stanton dropped into his chair. "So what did we end up with?"

Caitlin lifted a shoulder in her familiar, elegant shrug. "Not much. The blanket. A couple of hairs that probably aren't human. A very smudgy partial print, which doesn't even look usable, from her bracelet. It may be hers. Fibers from her clothes."

"What do we have to do? Catch this guy in the act?"

Tick sighed at Stanton's frustrated outburst, but if Caitlin was disturbed, she didn't show it. "That would be helpful, but it's unlikely."

"I was being facetious, Falconetti. You don't have to take everything so damned literally."

"Gee, I'm sorry, Reed. I didn't realize you actually possessed a sense of humor."

Tick muffled a weary laugh at Stanton's outraged expression, but resisted the urge to play peacemaker. One thing Caitlin had made perfectly clear—she didn't want his help.

Jeff Schaefer appeared in the doorway, and Caitlin glanced

at him before moving farther into the office. "Hey, Tick, there's a call on line two for you."

He unfolded himself from the chair. "I'll be right back. Y'all try not to kill each other while I'm gone. I'd rather not process another crime scene today."

CR

Caitlin leaned against the counter running along the wall in the squad room. Trying to ignore the headache four acetaminophen tablets hadn't dulled, she paged through the work schedules Cookie had printed for her. He poured the last of the coffee into a dark green mug bearing the department's insignia and she eyed the thick, scorched liquid. "You're not going to drink that, are you?"

"You planning on running a fresh pot?" He set the empty carafe on the counter and reached for the cream and sugar.

"Do you really want me to answer that?"

He laughed. When he turned toward his desk, his elbow brushed the glass carafe and it tumbled to the floor, shattering on the dingy gray floor.

The sound singed Caitlin's senses, and the printouts slid from her nerveless fingers. *Her grandmother's crystal vase exploding against the Mexican tile, Fuller's weight hitting her from behind, searing pain ripping into her consciousness. The wild fluttering of her unborn child, the knife piercing her body, those whispery movements dying away.* Her vision blurred, darkness rising in a dull red tide. The fear wrapped tentacles around her throat and lungs, cutting off her breath. She struggled to breathe, the panic intensifying.

Oh, God, not now. She pressed against the counter. Pulse thudding in her ears, she fought the tremors attacking her body. Eyes closed, she heard Cookie's uneasy voice from a distance, but she remained trapped in the overwhelming terror she couldn't control. She counted, the rhythm of numbers doing little to stop the fear.

"Cait?" Tick's voice, rough with concern, broke through the darkness, his arms supporting her. "Cookie, what happened?"

"I broke the carafe, and she just went white as a damn sheet."

Icy perspiration dampened her skin. Caitlin grasped his arms, riding out the receding horror. She sagged into him, Tick brushing her hair from her face. The sensations weakened, leaving her shaking in the aftermath. Her ability to breathe returning in ragged gasps, she buried her face against his throat. His scent surrounded her and she rested her palms against his back, wanting the solid connection. Relief trembled in her. He was here; she wasn't alone.

The episodes only lasted a few minutes—her body could only sustain the fight-or-flight rush that long. What frightened her more than the attacks themselves was that she never knew one was coming until it was slamming into her full force. And there was absolutely nothing she could do to stop it once it began, other than counting and trying to breathe through the panic.

Tick rubbed her spine in a long, soothing motion. "Cait?"

"Anxiety attack," she whispered, her mind clearing enough for her to realize they were alone in the squad room. "It's over."

"You're shaking." He pulled back but didn't release her. "Does this happen often?"

She shook her head, blowing out a long, uneven exhale. "Not as often now. I haven't had one in weeks. At first, it was several times a day."

"Sit down." He tugged the chair out from Cookie's desk and eased her onto it. Caitlin leaned her head back, eyes closed. He moved away, but her perception still felt fuzzy, unreal. "Here."

She opened her eyes and took the paper cup he pressed into her hands. Grateful, she sipped the cool water. Tick crouched in front of her, cradling her knees, thumbs kneading her lower thighs in a gentle, circular motion. Worry darkened his eyes and she forced a smile. "Thank you."

A frown drew his brows together. "This was happening several times a day?"

"Yes." She attempted a laugh, the shaky sound without humor. "Gina took my car keys. I had to talk Vince out of assigning me a keeper."

The warmth of his caressing hands began to seep into the

chill gripping her body. "You're taking meds for this, right?"

"Yes, I'm taking something. It helps, but—"

"Now will you talk to me?" A pleading note hoarsened his voice.

"Tick, please." Exhausted, she passed a hand over her eyes. "It's been a hellish day, and I could use several hours of uninterrupted sleep."

Not that she'd probably get it. Most often the panic attacks increased the frequency and intensity of her nightmares.

"Precious, please talk to me." His long fingers pressed against the outside of her thighs. "Let me help you."

Help her? Didn't he get it yet? The tension and exhaustion overwhelmed her, flashing into anger. "God, what do you want to know? How I can tell you what was in Amy Gillabeaux's mind as he killed her, because I've been there? How it all happens so fast and so slow at the same time?"

She stumbled over the words as they rushed out. "She was terrified...he caught her off guard and she couldn't figure out what was happening...why he was hurting her..."

Oh, dear Lord in heaven. The squad room blurred in front of him. Her words painted a picture, not of what had happened to Amy Gillabeaux, but of her own experience. He tightened his grip on her legs and closed his eyes briefly, opening them to find her watching him with a haunted gaze that glittered, bright and unnatural, against the pallor of her skin.

He swallowed hard. "Cait, you—"

"He worked for my grandfather." The anger drained from her voice, leaving only the desolation. "I was home for Troupe's birthday. Troupe...we call him by his name, my grandfather."

The words tumbled out of her in a wild disconnected stream. "He...Fuller thought I was in love with him. I...I smiled at him once too often, I guess, and he created this whole life for us in his head. I came home from the party early, I wasn't feeling well and he was waiting for me in the kitchen..."

His throat tight, he leaned forward, pulling her from the chair and into his arms. He smoothed his palms over her back, wanting to absorb her anguish.

"He kept talking to me, saying all these crazy things that made no sense. I-I started upstairs, my gun was in my room and I just wanted to get away. He came after me. He put his arm over my throat, I couldn't breathe, and then h-he was stabbing me. And there was nothing I could do..."

Her voice broke and she wept, her face pressed into his neck. Tick held her even closer, trying to take away the pain wracking her body. A familiar rage smoldered under his skin, a rage he thought he'd locked away with Billy Reese. Someone had hurt her, and he hadn't been around to stop it happening.

Someone had hurt her and she'd kept it from him, bottled all the pain inside.

Hating the bastard who'd attacked her, he rubbed his face against her hair and pressed a kiss to her temple. She stilled, huddled into him, her hands splayed against his back, her breath coming in shuddery sighs. "I'm so tired."

"Come on. I'm getting you out of here." He rose, pulling her up with him, still enveloped in his embrace. She swayed on her feet, the top of her head brushing his chin.

In the parking lot, he ushered her into the truck from the driver's side, and she slid as far as the middle of the bench seat. He fired the ignition and tugged her closer, her head against his shoulder. She shifted nearer, her hand resting above his knee, and his chest tightened. When he reached the road, he deliberated for only a second before turning in the direction of his home.

"Tick?" Her voice was a drowsy whisper.

"What, Cait?"

"It's not you. I didn't want you hurt, and I can't...I wanted..."

"Hush." He rubbed his fingers over her knee in a firm caress. "Not right now."

She subsided into silence, the only sound in the cab the hum of the engine and her occasional shaky breath.

Minutes later, he turned into his driveway, headlights sweeping the pine trees. She straightened. "Where are we?"

"Home." He slid from the truck and helped her out. A muggy breeze washed over them, carrying the scent and whisper of the river with it.

With a glance at his house, she stiffened. "Tick, I can't—"

"It's not up for discussion." He traced a fingertip along her jaw. "I'm not leaving you alone tonight."

Inside, he rummaged in his bureau and came up with his favorite Jimmy Buffet T-shirt, soft and faded from repeated washings. He pushed it into her hands and then gently bullied her into the bathroom to change.

"Are you hungry? I can fix you something—"

"No." She passed a hand over her flat stomach, her expression twisting. "Thank you. I don't want anything."

Food was the last thing on his mind, too. All he wanted was that awful look off her face. He brushed back a strand of her hair. "I think there's an extra toothbrush in the medicine cabinet. Towels are on the shelf by the shower."

She twisted the shirt around her hand, looking everywhere but at him. "Thanks. I'll just be a minute."

Seconds later, the sound of rushing water filtered through the closed door. Tick squashed the image of her in his shower, water sluicing over her slender frame, of him joining her under the spray. That was not what either of them needed tonight. After flipping the bedcovers back, he went to the closet and pulled down another of his grandmother's handpieced quilts and an extra pillow.

In the living room, he tossed them on the couch and picked up the remote, tuning to the late news. The pretty blonde anchor prattled on about a wreck on the Albany bypass and the latest efforts to clean up abandoned properties in Dougherty County. Tick leaned back, rubbing his hands over his face. His body ached with exhaustion, but his mind was running ninety-to-nothing, thoughts tumbling over each other in a wild scramble. He'd never get to sleep tonight.

The shower stopped, and he tried to focus on the weather report rather than what was going on in his bathroom. A sunny Sunday coming up, high of ninety-eight, late afternoon thundershowers. Not a towel easing water from a flat stomach, an elegant back and long, runner's legs. Not haunted green eyes and a full mouth trembling with remembered fear.

"Damn it," he muttered, staring at the ceiling.

The bathroom door creaked, and bare feet whispered on his

hardwood floor. He glanced up. Caitlin appeared in the doorway to his bedroom, hair damp at the edges, his T-shirt covering her to upper thigh, arms wrapped around her midriff. "I feel badly about taking your bed."

Letting his head fall back again, Tick closed his eyes. "Don't worry about it."

"I...I should warn you that I have nightmares." Her voice held an uncertain attempt at humor. "I haven't roused the neighbors yet, but I wake up screaming. Gina bought earplugs when I moved in with her."

Rage chased everything from his mind. He'd kill the bastard. One way or another, he'd kill him. "Nearest neighbors are two miles away. I don't think you'll bother them."

"Well, good night, then."

"Good night." He waited for her to leave, but heard nothing.

"Tick?" A tentative note colored her voice.

He sighed and straightened. "Yeah?"

She glanced away. "I don't know how...damn it, Tick, I don't want to sleep alone tonight."

The words shivered through him. Lord, Cookie was right. He was already whipped. He'd crawl into bed with her and hold her like the honorable man his father had raised him to be. Even if it killed him, he wouldn't do any of the other things his body clamored for—pull her close, kiss her until he couldn't remember his own name, slide his hands beneath that T-shirt, bury himself within her.

He stood, cut off the television and the lamps, aware of her gaze on him the whole time. He crossed the room to her, massaging her shoulders. "Then I won't leave you alone."

In the bedroom, he turned off the lights. The sheets rustled as she climbed into his bed. He tugged his shirt over his head, kicked off his shoes and stepped out of his jeans, pulling his socks off at the same time. Clad only in his boxer briefs, he slid in beside her.

Caitlin lay on her side, and Tick rolled so his chest was against her back, her bottom tucked against his groin, and the back of her legs lay along his thighs. Lord, she fit him to perfection. The tension eased from her body, muscles relaxing against him. His arm draped over her waist, he dropped a kiss on her neck. "Comfortable?"

Her palm rested on his arm, and she turned her head, her cheek brushing his biceps. "Better than comfortable."

"Yeah?" He yawned. Sleep tugged at him, surprising him.

"Yes. I'm safe."

Good. He meant to keep her that way. He spread his hand across her abdomen and her pulse beat against his palm. He pulled her closer and she covered his wrist, tracing a random design on the back. His skin tingled under her easy touch. Heavy contentment settled in him. Damn, but he never wanted to move again. His eyes slid closed.

"I should have been able to stop him." The darkness of her memories trembled in her voice. "I tried, Tick, I swear I did..."

He snapped to full alertness, staring into the blackness over her head. "Baby, don't."

Her hair swept across his chin. "I'm an FBI agent, with over a decade of training. Hell, I've taught other people how to—"

"It wasn't your fault." He tightened his hold. "You can't think that, Cait."

Her finger continued drawing circles and squares on his hand. "I relive it in my head, trying to figure out what I could have done differently. If I'd waited for my brother or my grandfather to drive me home, if I'd taken my gun that night. Even if I'd stayed in Virginia instead of going home in the first place. Or if the training had kicked in sooner, before he had the upper hand. But he had me down and I couldn't breathe, couldn't get free...if Vince hadn't come home when he did..."

The pictures took over his brain with horrifying intensity. He buried his face in her hair, wanting to absorb the pain making her voice hoarse and tremulous.

The way Tori sounded when she talked about the rape. His stomach roiled, more images tumbling through his mind. He rubbed his thumb across her stomach and pressed his mouth to her cheek.

"I know what you're thinking." Her tone steadied and her finger stilled on his hand. "It wasn't about rape. He wanted more power than that. He needed to make sure I never wanted another man, and the only way he could do that was to leave me dead, to kill my—"

Her voice halted.

"It was the only way he could *control* me." She shuddered against him. "God, I hate that word. Your guy, he's all about control. He needed to control Amy. He wanted to prove his ultimate control with the others—"

"Enough." He smoothed her hair, tucked her head beneath his chin. "Get some rest. We'll talk about it tomorrow."

She burrowed closer. "This is my first case back in the field since it happened, Calvert. I can't screw this up."

"You won't, Falconetti. You won't."

And neither would he.

Chapter Six

The phone shrilled, jerking Tick from a deep, dreamless sleep. Eyes closed against the bright sunlight spilling into the room, he snatched the phone from the nightstand after the first ring. "Hello?"

"Good morning, big brother." Tori's cheerful voice vibrated along the line. "Did I wake you?"

"Do you care?" He kept his tone low, aware of Caitlin sleeping beside him. Sometime during the night, he'd rolled to his back, and she'd followed, her head now pillowed on his chest, her hand splayed over his stomach, each and every finger imprinted on his bare skin.

"Not really."

"What time is it?"

"Nine thirty. Do you know where Caitlin is? I'm supposed to pick her up at ten to go to church with me, but she's not answering at the hotel."

"She's here with me." It was a state of affairs he could definitely get used to. He opened his eyes. Lord, she was beautiful. Black lashes fanned over her cheekbones, the dark circles of fatigue under her eyes faded almost to nothing. He resisted the urge to run a finger over her parted lips.

"Really. How interesting." Absolute glee flowed through his sister's words. "Maybe you want to go church with us, too. I think the sermon is on the sins of the flesh. You can repent."

"Tori." He ground his teeth. "I haven't done anything to repent for. Nothing happened."

"You know, you keep saying that. I'm disappointed."

"Did you want anything else or just to torture me?"

"Caitlin as a sister-in-law would be nice. I'd like to see you married off with a couple of kids. You'd be too busy to interfere in my life."

"Victoria." He tried to make her name a stern warning, but her response was a light laugh. Her teasing built a picture in his mind, of the way things could be, and he liked the scenario way too much. "Do me a favor. Pick Mama up and take her to church."

"Sure thing. What do you want me to tell her if she asks where you are?"

"Tell her something came up." He sighed at her giggle. "Do not comment on that. I'll talk to you later."

He replaced the receiver, watching the light play off Caitlin's dark hair. She slept on, undisturbed. Her body must have finally given in to months of exhaustion. Careful not to wake her, he extracted his arm from under her neck and slid from the bed. If he didn't get up now, he never would.

Intending to cover her, he reached for the quilt and stilled. His faded blue T-shirt bunched around her waist, inches above the tiniest pair of lilac silk panties he'd ever seen. But her flat stomach drew his attention, his gaze riveted on the scars marring her smooth skin, two jagged stab wounds and lower, a precise, surgical incision. Above her abdomen, just visible at her rib cage, beneath the shadow of the cotton shirt, lay two more ragged scars.

His nerves clenched, a chill sweeping his body at the evidence of the horror she'd endured. Smothering the urge to touch her, he pulled the quilt over her shoulders and slipped from the room.

Sleep faded away, and Caitlin surfaced to an incredible sense of peace. Eyes squeezed shut against the bright sunlight, she stretched, pointing her toes toward the end of the bed. Tick's clean, subtle scent clung to the quilt, enveloping her, and she drew in a deep breath, remembering the solid strength of him next to her.

She'd gotten through the night without a single nightmare.

"Someone's been sleeping in my bed, and here she is," his

lazy voice said. "Rise and shine, Sleeping Beauty."

"I think you've got your fairy tales mixed up." She rolled over. Dressed in jeans and a dark red polo shirt, he leaned against the doorframe, holding a coffee mug sporting a tractor slogan.

"Probably." His smile was the sexiest thing Caitlin had ever seen. She fought down an urge to open her arms and invite him back to bed. "Sleep well?"

She nodded, watching him saunter toward the bed, loving the easy way he moved. The sheet pooled about her waist when she sat up against the headboard, and she twisted her hands in it to keep from reaching for him. He held out the mug, and she accepted it, inhaling the brisk aroma of fresh coffee. "You?"

"Very." He sat on the edge of the bed, fiddling with the hem of the quilt. "I have a confession to make."

She sipped the strong brew. "Really."

"I committed a breaking and entering this morning. Actually, more entering than breaking."

"What are you talking about?"

"I thought maybe we'd work from here today." He took the mug from her and drank slowly. "I didn't think you'd want to put on the same clothes this morning. I filched your card key and picked up some of your things—a change of clothes, your laptop and your files. Oh, and Amy's diary."

"You didn't have to do that." She shook her disheveled hair from her face. This close to him, heat curled in her stomach. To start every day this way, to have this much consideration and affection wrapped around her.

"You were sleeping and I didn't want to disturb you. You needed the rest." He looked away for a moment, his jaw tightening. "I have the department schedules Cookie ran off for you, too."

"Tick, we have to check." She touched his hand, his skin warm under her fingertips.

"I know." He ducked his head, but when he looked up at her, his eyes were clear, his smile rueful. "But I don't have to like it."

She stole the mug from him, relishing for just a moment

the intimacy of their interaction. They would be so good together, if only...she brushed the thought away. "What time is it, anyway?"

"Twelve fifteen."

"What? I've slept half the day—"

"Cait, calm down. It's Sunday. You've worked nonstop for the last three days."

A hand over her eyes, she groaned. "I was supposed to meet Tori at ten."

"I've already talked to her. Stop worrying. Take a shower and get dressed. You can satisfy your workaholic tendencies by working on your profile all afternoon. You know, it's just a job. You're allowed to take a break every now and then."

"I let you look after me for one night, and you think you can just take over, don't you, Lamar Eugene?"

He leaned in, brushing his mouth over hers in a quick, casual caress that set her nerves on fire. "Pretty much."

"Don't get used to it."

"I wouldn't dare." He rose from the bed. "Your things are on the chair. Shower's all yours."

He closed the door behind him. She pushed the covers away and climbed out of the bed, taking a few moments to straighten the sheets and quilt and set the pillows against the black iron headboard. Retrieving her clothes from the armchair in the corner, she laid them out, smiling at his thoughtfulness. He'd brought not only her clothing, but the small bag containing her jewelry and cosmetics.

She picked up her underwear and let the lacy bra dangle from a finger. He'd managed to find the sheerest set of lingerie she owned.

In the bathroom, she brushed her teeth and turned on the tiled shower in the corner, casting a wistful glance at the large antique clawfoot tub dominating the center of the room. It would easily hold two people. Her body tingled with the images her mind conjured—water sliding over his tanned skin, their bodies intertwined, caressed by warm suds.

Casting aside her panties and his T-shirt, she stepped into the shower, the hot water flowing over her skin like one long lover's caress. The soap lather filled the small enclosure with the scent she associated with him and she leaned against the wall, last night's terror forgotten. Eyes closed, she pressed trembling fingers to the sweet ache pooling in her lower stomach. Right now, she wanted nothing more than to be back in his bed, in his arms, with sleep the last thing on their minds.

The night before, she'd given into the temptation to lose the darkness in his arms. This morning, she simply wanted to lose herself there. Straightening, she turned the water to cold and gasped at the icy jets pummeling her skin. She'd told him about the attack and she'd survived. Surely she could tell him the rest.

She *should* tell him the rest.

Her fingertips brushed the surgical scar, cold reality dissipating the lazy well-being and piercing desire. How on earth to begin? How would he react?

A shiver completely unrelated to the cold water traveled over her. Telling him would change everything and she wasn't even sure where they were now.

She needed time, enough time to discern where they were headed, what really lay between them.

Pushing back her wet hair, she turned off the shower. She didn't have to tell him yet. A little more time to figure out how, to make sure she was doing the right thing, wasn't too much to ask.

When she came out of the bedroom, Tick sat at the kitchen island, a file folder spread open in front of him. A slow smile crossed his face as he took in her jeans and white buttondown. His slow survey of her felt like a touch and her breasts tightened inside the sheer bra he'd chosen.

"You look nice."

"Thank you," she said. He flicked a look up at her hair, restrained in a loose knot, and an odd expression flashed through his dark eyes. "What?"

"It's your hair...I'm going to spend the entire day wanting to take it down. We need to find this guy soon because my objectivity is already shot to hell."

Feeling a desperate need to change the subject, she peeked over his shoulder at the folder. "What are you doing?"

He held up a missing person flier with a grainy photo. "We might have a possible ID on yesterday's victim. Kimberly Johnson, twenty-eight. She's a cop, Cait. Atlanta PD. She disappeared three weeks ago on her way to Florida. Williams's trying to get her dental records since she couldn't get prints from the body."

She lifted the report lying on top of the thin stack of papers and skimmed. "You've been busy this morning."

"I want this son of a bitch locked up." His low voice vibrated with intensity. Dropping the report on the stack, she stepped away, brushing his arm with her movement. His eyes darkened to black and the breath he sucked in was audible.

She backed up, putting space between them. "Did Williams say anything about our labs?"

"Yeah. They're not done, and with the backlog, they probably won't be for at least a week."

"A week?" The prospect horrified her.

"If not longer. We've waited almost three months for results to come through."

"We're not waiting that long. We can have the evidence transferred to the FBI lab."

A slow smile curved his mouth. "You really can't resist taking charge, can you?"

The teasing note in his voice warmed her. "You're not going to freak out like Reed, are you?"

"Unlike Stan, I don't have a problem relinquishing control. Sometimes, it can be pretty darn interesting."

Her lungs not working, she stared at him, knowing full well he wasn't talking about their case any longer. With an effort, she pulled her gaze away from his. She wasn't ready for this. "You know what I need? Food."

He gestured toward the counter. "Help yourself. I think there are some bakery rolls in the breadbox. Mama called and fussed at me for not going to church, but I can redeem myself by showing up for Sunday dinner. We're supposed to be over there before one thirty and she always cooks for an army, so save room for—"

"I'm not going to your mother's for dinner." Keeping her

back to him, she peered at the cellophane-wrapped sweet rolls, her stomach telling her if she ate one of those stale things, she'd be sorry. Sleeping in his bed had been bad enough, even if all they had done was sleep. Sunday dinner with his family? She didn't think so.

She *really* wasn't ready for that.

"Yes, you are. She specifically asked me to bring you, and I told her I would. I'm in charge right now, remember? You can have your turn later."

She laughed. "You are—"

"Planning to take care of you today," he finished, near her ear. She startled, aware now of the warmth of his body behind her. He rested his hands at her waist. When he spoke again, his voice was serious, all playfulness gone. "You need a break. I don't ever again want to see you like you were last night."

She closed her eyes. He wanted to take care of her, take her to his mother's. Oh, God, that had to mean something.

Probably the same thing it would mean if she took him home to her grandfather.

Fine. She would find a way to handle whatever that meant and maybe by the end of the day, she'd know how she was going to tell him what really stood between them.

She sidestepped, turning to face him, pasting on a smile that hurt. "I give in. When do we leave?"

"I should warn you that the entire mob will be at Mama's." Tick glanced at Caitlin as he turned onto Boll Weevil Road. "She's been keeping Chuck's crew. He's bringing Deanne home from the hospital today, and I imagine they'll be at the house. And my brother Del's family was due home from the beach last night. They should be here as well."

"Sounds crowded." Her gaze lingered on the cornfields lining the road. She was quiet, a little reserved today, but less tense.

And she wasn't fighting him on every little thing, on every step of the way.

He was closer to having his Caitlin back.

The scars. He gnawed at the inside of his bottom lip.

Everything—all the changes in her, the distance she kept placing between them—it had to be because of the attack she'd suffered. Slowing for a small yet crowded residential area, he studied her sideways. She didn't trust him. What did she think, that he'd turn away once he knew? Where the *hell* did she get that idea? If she believed that, she didn't know him at all.

Maybe he didn't really know her either. At one time, he'd thought he knew everything about her. Now, he wasn't so sure. Where did the necessity for all those walls of hers come from?

He slung an arm along the back of the seat, brushing her shoulder, the fine cotton of her blouse smooth under his fingertips. "You come from a big family, too, don't you?"

Her posture tightened. "My father was one of seven children. I have Falconetti cousins scattered all over. My mother was an only child, so no Cavanaugh cousins. Just me and Vince."

"Was?" His forefinger stroked down her arm.

She shrugged, dislodging the easy contact. "She died when I was six. Father when I was sixteen."

Concern tempered his slight hurt that she didn't seem to want him touching her. Even sixteen years after his father's murder, grief still knifed through him at the most unexpected times. "I'm sorry."

"Don't be. I barely remember Mother because she was not well when I was small, and Father and I weren't exactly close." She sounded disconnected, as if speaking of someone else's life. Something indefinable, beyond ice, tainted the word *Father* when she said it and sent unease skittering down his back.

"Why not?" Had she meant it when she told Cookie her father was a narcissist? And what kind of unseen scars did that leave on a child? Still looking out the window, she appeared unaffected by the conversation.

"He didn't want a relationship with me beyond paternal responsibility and daughterly obedience. He didn't want me, period." One shoulder lifted in another elegant shrug. "I never could please him. First, I had the audacity to be born. Second, I had the nerve to be a girl. From what I've been told, I wasn't the easiest child to live with, especially after Mother died, so that probably didn't help. He liked an orderly household."

So did his mother, but she also understood children. An image of Caitlin as a small, motherless child in a magazine-perfect home flickered through his mind, and he swallowed hard. "You had your brother, right?"

She shook her head. "Military school for him, boarding school for me. That's where he knows your buddy Hardison from." A bittersweet smile tempered by true affection tilted the corners of her mouth. "He was at West Point when Father died and I went to live with Troupe and Grandmother. When he was around, he was always trying to make sure I was protected and virginal. A lot like you and Tori."

"There's nothing wrong with a guy looking out for his sister."

"There is when he tries to change her to do it." An edge entered her voice.

"I don't try to change Tori."

She laughed. "I didn't say you did. I love Vince, I do. Lots of hero worship there on my part, but I never got to really be myself with him. Like my father, it was all about meeting expectations."

Not sure what to say to that, he turned into his mother's neat gravel drive. An assortment of vehicles fanned out along the front of the sprawling red brick two-story. The sensible white sedan caught his attention and he groaned.

Caitlin glanced up from studying her nails. "What's wrong?"

Easing the truck into the spot next to Tori's little silver car, he killed the engine. He clenched the steering wheel, relaxed his fingers, flexed them once more. "Jeff's here."

"That's a problem?"

"It could be."

"He's dating Tori, right? Maybe he's with her."

"That's what I'm afraid of. She's never brought a guy home for Sunday dinner before." He pushed the door open and walked to the passenger side to help Caitlin down. He made an effort to unwind, wishing his mother would let him smoke in her presence. "Come on."

The excited laughter and squeals of his nieces and nephews drifted from the backyard. He led Caitlin around to the side door, remembering at the last moment not to let the screen door slam behind him. The interior of the house was cool, spotless and filled with the enticing aromas of his mother's traditional Sunday dinner—fried chicken, garden-fresh vegetables and hot, homemade biscuits.

The familiarity calmed his jangling nerves somewhat. The dining-room table was already set with his mother's good china, another Sunday tradition. He knew the kitchen table would be arranged for the children. With his hand at the small of Caitlin's back, they crossed the hall and the family room, entering the huge kitchen, which overflowed with activity.

"Lamar! You're early." His mother's pleasure settled his emotions further. It was damned hard to be upset in her calm presence.

"Hey, Mama." He wrapped her in a swift, hard hug. The sharp scent of VO5 hairdressing clung to her, mixing with the rose lotion she'd used for years, and awakening sensory memories from his childhood. He inhaled and held on a moment longer. "You remember Caitlin?"

"Of course!" Caitlin received a quick embrace as well. "I'm so glad you could come."

"Thank you." Caitlin smiled, a pretty, genuine curve of her lips, and Tick was glad to see her customary reserve didn't extend to his mother. "Is there anything I can do to help?"

"Maybe in a minute." His mother waved the offer away. "Everything's almost ready. Tori will get you some tea and we can get to know each other better. Lamar, Jeff and your brothers are in the backyard with the children."

That was a definite dismissal from his mother's female domain. Any other time, he'd have taken Caitlin with him, but he knew what "getting to know each other better" meant—his mother was going to subject Caitlin to an interrogation unlike anything the Federal Bureau of Investigation could produce. He grinned on his way out the door. Caitlin thought he was pushy?

He almost felt sorry for her.

Besides a master interrogator, Lenora Calvert was also ninety-percent drill sergeant. After fifteen minutes in which she ended up divulging details of her early life, her college years and her career at the FBI, Caitlin watched, amused, as the petite woman organized the women in her kitchen, getting a meal large enough to feed a small army to the long, cherry-wood dining table. Even Deanne, looking more rested than she had Friday night, pitched in while her newborn dozed in a padded infant carrier.

"How about buttering these for me?" Lenora pressed a butter container into Caitlin's hands.

"Of course." She smiled, warmed at being included. Standing at the long counter near the back door, she brushed butter on the hot, flaky biscuits. Happy chatter and affectionate teasing wrapped around the room, and a lump settled in her throat. Being a part of this family would be such a sweet blessing.

The baby, named Charles Carter after all, stirred, and Tori swooped down, lifting him into her arms. She nuzzled his cheek. "I still wish you had named him Lamar, Dee. I'm sorry, but he looks more like Tick than he does Chuck."

"Don't let Chuck hear you say that. He's convinced this is his spitting image. But you're right. I was looking through your mom's baby photos earlier, and he does look a lot like Tick as a baby. But Tick is the junior, he should get to have Lamar Eugene III."

Tori sighed. "He'd probably call him Trey or something. And if he doesn't hurry up and do something, there won't be a Lamar Eugene III."

Intensely uncomfortable, Caitlin stuck her hands in the back pockets of her jeans and wondered how she could make a graceful exit.

"What do you think, Cait?" Tori asked, settling the baby into Caitlin's startled hold. "Does he look like grumpy old Tick?"

The last words were emphasized with loving baby talk. Carter yawned, his eyes drifting shut.

Caitlin stood, frozen by the sweet barely-there weight of the infant in her arms. Hardly breathing, she dared to glance down. His tiny mouth pursed as he turned his head toward her with little snuffling sounds. Minuscule fingers curled and uncurled against the curve of his face. Long, dark lashes brushed his cheeks, matching the soft wisps of dark hair that covered his head. He showed the beginnings of what would be a strong jaw and stubborn chin.

Oh, dear God, he did look like Tick.

Is this what their son would have looked like, if he'd been born?

The crushing agony pounded at her, a sob pushing at her throat. She swallowed it with difficulty, holding the baby close and hurting.

Pretending would come so easily—fooling herself for only a moment that this was her baby and Tick's, and any minute he would come strolling through that door with his long, lazy stride and call her precious. Letting herself believe for a moment that Fuller had never existed, that she'd been allowed a chance to hold her baby.

This should have been real, could have been real. She should be here under different circumstances, holding a dark-haired boy only months older than the one in her arms. Tick should have had the opportunity to cradle that baby with joy and pride, to count those little fingers and toes. So many should-haves and what-ifs that she wanted to scream until the pain and loss was spent.

"You look sick," Tori said with characteristic bluntness.

"I think I'm just not used to the heat." She handed Carter back to his mother and fanned herself with a hand, small beads of icy perspiration breaking on her upper lip. Nausea churned in her stomach. "I'm fine."

Tori scrutinized her face. "Maybe you need some air."

Lenora waved them toward the door. "Tori, take her out and show her the rose garden. We've got a few minutes before dinner."

Relief coursed through Caitlin as she followed Tori to the front door. The rose garden took up most of the front yard, with wrought iron benches scattered among the fragrant shrubs. Oak trees curved overhead, providing pockets of cooling shade. The shouts and giggles of children flowed from the backyard, interspersed with the low hum of a male conversation. A deep voice murmured and Tick's rich laugh carried to her.

She wrapped her arms around her midriff, trying to staunch the tide of loss sweeping her.

"What happened in there?"

"Nothing." Caitlin sank onto a bench. "I just felt ill for a moment."

"I know ill, Cait. That wasn't ill. That was a nervous reaction."

"I'm fine."

"You have a serious case of denial if you think that."

Caitlin tossed her an infuriated look. "You don't quit, do you? Just like—"

She bit the sentence off.

But Tori picked up as though Caitlin had finished the thought. "Just like Tick? He cares about you. He spends a lot of time worrying about the people he loves and—"

"Loves?" A low, dull throbbing started at her temples. No, she didn't want to think about that, not right now. "You are so deluded."

"What?" Tori demanded, a hint of anger nudging at her voice. "So I said it out loud. My brother loves you, is so in love with you that everyone but the two of you can see it. And you know what I think? I think you could love him, too, if you'd just let yourself."

"You're wrong." The words emerged deadly quiet, devoid of emotion. Even as she uttered them, she knew them for the obvious lie they were. Yes, he was in love with her, but he didn't have all the facts, either. How long would he love her if she told him the whole truth?

If she told him he had been a father, that Fuller's attack had stolen that from them both? That more than not being able to protect herself, she'd failed to keep their baby safe?

Tori folded her arms over her chest, chin tilted at a defiant angle. "So, say it. Say, 'I am not interested in Tick Calvert'."

"Damn it, I am not interested in *anyone*!" The ache became a grim pounding. "I'm not interested in love, or in marriage and babies, or any of the other fairy tales you're cooking up. Got that?"

Tori stared at her for a several long moments, sympathy and concern glowing in her eyes. "Sure. I got it."

"So the conversation is closed."

"Whatever you want."

Yeah, right. Whatever she wanted. She wished that were so, because she could still feel the baby in her embrace and Tick's arms around her from the night before.

She deserved an Oscar for her performance at dinner. Caitlin smiled and made polite conversation, answering questions and complimenting Lenora on food she never tasted. Tick sat at the head of the table, Caitlin to his right. His three-year-old niece Charlie insisted on sitting on his knee, and he ate with his right hand, steadying Charlie's still-shaky fork with his left.

Caitlin avoided looking at him and instead studied her barely touched plate. Surely this meal couldn't drag out all day.

"Tori, what did you do last night?" Deanne passed Tick an extra napkin for her daughter.

"Jeff and I went to Mikata's." Tori grinned up at Schaefer, nudging his arm with hers. "And we saw that new romantic comedy everyone's raving about. Save your money and rent the video."

Deanne laughed. "Honey, we always rent the video."

A cell phone jingled, and Schaefer slid his chair back from the table. "I'm sorry." He pulled the phone from his belt and checked the display. "I need to take this. Would you excuse me a minute?"

Lenora smiled. "Of course."

He left the room, and seconds later the kitchen door shut with a click. Tori leaned back in her chair and glared at Tick. "There's that look again."

He set his fork down, his face impassive. "What look?"

"The same one you get whenever I say anything about going out with Jeff."

He attempted to wipe sweet potatoes from Charlie's face. "He's too old for you."

"Six years! How is that too old? Mason Jordan was too irresponsible. Donny Thurston was too serious too soon. It doesn't matter who I date—you're not going to approve of anyone. Besides, how can you say he's too old for me? Your last girlfriend was twenty-one."

"Twenty-three. And two dates don't qualify her as my girlfriend." He lifted his tea glass and took a long swallow.

"Whatever. Maybe I'll just go out with Cookie."

He choked. "That'll never happen."

"And why not?"

"Because he knows I'd kill him."

"Victoria. Lamar. We have guests." Lenora's voice was a gentle, steely reminder.

Tori subsided with a pout. Tick shifted a drowsy Charlie on his lap, and she rested her head under his chin, eyes drifting shut. Deanne laid her fork beside her plate. "Let me go put her down."

Tick waved her back to a seated position, rising with the little girl cradled to his chest. "I'll put her on Mama's bed."

"I wish she'd go down that easily at night." Chuck placed another helping of butterbeans on his plate.

Deanne laughed. "Well, if someone didn't get her all riled up by playing airplane right before bedtime, she probably would."

Tick eased out of the room. Caitlin pushed the food around her plate one more time. Having her fingernails pulled out one by one couldn't be worse than this.

When was this day going to end?

After settling Charlie on his mother's bed, Tick spread the light blanket over her. A smudge of sweet potato still colored her chin, and he grinned. She hated having her face washed and she'd give Chuck a fit later when he tried.

His cell phone emitted the opening notes of his favorite Gary Allan tune, and he stepped into the hallway, pulling the slim device from his belt. "Calvert."

"We've got a positive ID on your lime-mine victim from the dental records. It is Kimberly Johnson." Williams's voice was brisk. "Her partner from Atlanta PD drove down. He wants to talk to you."

"Is he still there?"

"Yeah. He wanted a minute with her."

He took a quick glance at his watch. "Give him directions to the sheriff's office. Tell him I'll meet him there in a half hour."

"You got it." With a click, she was gone.

He walked back to the dining room. Jeff had returned to the table. Tick's gaze settled on Caitlin's bent head. Her food seemed untouched. "Cait, we've got to go."

Jeff watched him with a troubled expression. "It's not another one, is it?"

"No, thank God."

"Do you need me to come with you?"

He waved away the question. "No. Finish your meal. Cait and I can handle this."

Caitlin met his gaze, and he saw that her relaxed smile was nothing more than a polite mask. She stood, thanking his mother before following him into the hall. "What is it?"

"Our vic from yesterday is Kimberly Johnson. Her partner made the identification and he's on his way over from Moultrie to talk to us."

"That was fast." Excitement flickered through her eyes. "Maybe we'll get a lead from this."

"Yeah." He fought the impulse to tuck a stray lock of her hair behind her ear. As much as he wanted this case solved, he didn't want her to go and he needed more time to convince her, to get through those layers of hers. "I hope so, too."

Chapter Seven

Caitlin leaned against the railing on the steps outside the sheriff's office. Her shoulder brushed Tick's arm and warmth rushed along her skin. He cupped his hands around his lighter as he lifted it to a cigarette.

"You know those things will kill you," she said.

"Yeah, but someone has to support the tobacco farmers."

"When did you start that, anyway?" Pique twisted through her. She resisted the desire to snatch the glowing white cylinder out of his hold.

"Mississippi." He tucked his lighter in his pocket, his gaze flickering toward the street. "Helped take the edge off."

"Do you realize what you're doing to your lungs? Could you even pass a physical training run right now?"

He laughed. "I'll have you know I conduct our training runs every week."

"Standing on the track with a stop watch does not count." Unimpressed, she crossed her arms over her chest. She shouldn't even make a big deal of this, but it irked her. Besides, it was definitely easier to talk about this than another topic she could think of. "And kissing you after you've had one of those things is less than pleasant."

"Does that mean you'll kiss me more often if I quit?" Devilment glowed in his dark gaze, and her breath stopped in her throat, the urge to kiss him right now strong, cigarette or not. He tilted his head toward her; she raised her mouth.

"Are you Investigator Calvert?"

Regret flared in his eyes, sparking an answering twinge in her chest. They turned to face the man climbing the steps, a thick manila folder in hand. He had closely cropped hair and the professional bearing of a young cop.

Tick crushed the cigarette out in the adjacent ash can and extended a hand. "Yes, and this is Agent Falconetti, FBI."

The man took his hand in a quick handshake and nodded at Caitlin. He didn't smile. "Tripp Payton, Atlanta PD. Kimberly Johnson was my partner. Agent Williams said I could find you here."

"I'm sorry about your partner, Officer Payton," Caitlin said, eyeing his tense movements. The anger lurking in his eyes was too personal. Losing a partner was the worst thing in the world for a cop, but his expression hinted that Kimberly Johnson had been more than his partner.

"Thanks." He ran a hand over his short brown hair. "Is there somewhere we can talk?"

"We can use my office," Tick said. "Or there's a diner down the street if you're hungry."

"I could use some caffeine." He jammed his free hand in his pocket. "I haven't had anything all day."

The Sunday dinner rush was over and the small storefront diner held only a couple of older men lingering over gossip and slices of pecan pie. Tick chose a corner table at the back of the restaurant and let Payton order first, a cheeseburger and cola, before ordering sweet tea for Caitlin and himself.

Payton rubbed his hands over his face. "Seeing her was harder than I thought it would be."

"How long were you partners?" Caitlin asked.

He dropped his hands to the table. "Three years. Since she graduated from the academy. Kim loves...loved the job. She wanted to change the world. She never lost that idealism most rookies have."

"She was more than your partner, wasn't she?" Tick kept the question soft, even.

Payton nodded, staring at the green Formica tabletop. "We started dating last year, after she got sick. We kept it a secret because we didn't want them to split us up as partners. I wanted to marry her."

"Sick?" Tick leaned back to allow the waitress greater access to the table. Ice tinkled in tall glasses with wedges of lemon clinging to the rims.

"Cervical cancer." Payton wrapped both hands around his tumbler, ignoring the hamburger. "It's supposed to be really rare in women her age, but it was vicious. She went through the whole bit—surgery, chemo, radiation. But she beat it. I used to tell her she was my superhero—strong, brave—nothing could touch her."

"She sounds like a great person," Tick said, his voice quiet.

"She is...was. I wanted to spend my life with her, but she...she wanted some time before she answered me. The surgery, well, that meant we couldn't have kids. I told her it didn't matter, that I only wanted her. She thought I'd change my mind later, maybe start to resent her."

Unable to give the conversation the concentration it demanded, Caitlin stared at a distant point over Payton's shoulder. As much as she hungered to hear the same words from the man sitting beside her, she understood Kimberly's reluctance to accept them at face value. Who wanted to live life waiting for the man she loved to decide she wasn't enough after all?

"That must have been hard for her." Empathy colored Tick's words, dragging Caitlin from her thoughts.

Payton nodded. "That's why she was going to Florida. She wanted to walk on the beach, get her thoughts together. She was supposed to give me an answer when she got back. Only she never made it. When she didn't call and let me know she'd gotten to Panama City, I got worried. Then the hotel said she'd never checked in."

"That was three weeks ago, right?"

"Three weeks and four days. I knew she'd been here, but I didn't expect to...I didn't expect her to be found here." Payton flipped open the file, pulling a record of credit card transactions. "She bought gas locally, but the next transaction was in Tallahassee a couple of hours later—a fast-food joint. Then Lake City, Gainesville. I thought if anything happened to her, it was there. I went down, but didn't find anything. Then when someone tried to use the card again, in Orlando, the credit card company called the police. The woman they arrested said she'd found it in a bus-station parking lot in Thomasville. That's why I focused my attention there."

Caitlin picked up the record. "May we keep this?"

He pushed the entire folder across the table. "That's why I brought it. That's everything I have—cell phone details, witness interviews, everything. I just want you to find the bastard."

Three weeks' worth of legwork in one convenient package. Caitlin knew what Tick was thinking—it was better than Christmas. Tick flipped through the interview notes on top. "Did you talk to anyone here?"

"I stopped at the convenience store where she bought gas. No one remembered her." Payton's voice betrayed disbelief that anyone could not remember.

"It's the Tank and Tummy." Tick underlined the name with his finger on the credit card record. "They just installed security cameras a couple of months ago after their third armed robbery. We can get the tape."

Payton drained his soda. "I've got to head back. I...I need to talk to her mama tonight. I want her to hear it from me, that it really is Kim."

He reached for his wallet, and Tick waved him back to a seated position. "I've got it. Cait, let me have one of your cards." Tick scrawled his name and number on the back of her card. "You need to know anything, you call me or Agent Falconetti. And I promise you, as soon as we know something, you'll be the first call I make."

Rising to his feet, Payton pocketed the card and took Tick's proffered hand. "Thanks."

Payton walked to the door, the line of his shoulders screaming dejection. Caitlin rested her chin on her hand. "God, that poor guy. Can you imagine what he's going through?"

"Yeah, I can." Tick stood and tossed a bill on the table. He grabbed her hand, his gaze intent on her face. "And I don't want to. Come on, let's get out of here."

She picked up the folder, thankful for the excuse to avert her eyes. Resisting him was so damn hard when he looked at her like that. He made her want to let go of the fear and just believe in him, but the old habit of self-preservation dug in with tenacious claws.

He tugged her toward the door, and she pulled her hand from his. "Tick, slow down. Where are we going?"

"I want to get that tape."

Caitlin matched his stride on the way to the truck, glad to have the force of his attention concentrated on something other than her for the moment. She needed to get her equilibrium back after that conversation and focused on latching her seat belt as he fired the engine.

"You know what I don't get?" He braked for the first traffic light, a slight frown wrinkling his brow. "Why did she think her not being able to have children would matter to him?"

She swallowed, choosing her words with care. "Because to some men, I guess it would make a difference."

His laugh resembled a derisive snort. "Sure, shallow ones."

"With your recent dating record, you're not allowed to call anyone shallow." The desire to change the subject was strong, but the need to probe his feelings was stronger. She forced herself to use a casual tone. "How would you react in his situation?"

"The murder?"

"The infertility."

"I don't know. I never thought about it." He shrugged, steering into the left turning lane. A semi loaded with crates of live chickens rumbled through the intersection. "I guess I'd be disappointed, but would it change my feelings? No. And, hell, people adopt every day."

"Yes, they do," she murmured. People underwent fertility treatments every day, too. Intellectually, she accepted both as an option. The bureau counselor persisted in pointing that out during their rare meetings, but right now the grief and loss were too strong, overpowering acceptance and hope. She didn't have the necessary strength to consider the merry-go-round. A five percent chance at successfully bearing a child meant a ninety-five percent chance of failure. How did anyone deal with odds like that?

She'd already lost one very loved, very wanted baby. She wasn't ready to travel that road again yet. And if she was, would Tick want to?

They left the city limits behind, and he pressed down on

the gas. "How would you react?"

Startled from her thoughts, she twisted in the seat to look at him. "What do you mean?"

Squinting, he pulled his sunglasses from the visor and slid them on. "If the situation were reversed and you found out the guy you were interested in was sterile, would it matter?"

"No."

"There you go, then. I don't get it. Why did she think it would change anything?" He slowed to pull into the dusty parking lot of a squat metal convenience store with a faded, hand-painted sign advertising gas, hot cooked food and boiled peanuts.

"Maybe she didn't want to cheat him."

He parked behind an ancient blue El Camino to the rear of the building. With a quizzical expression, he killed the engine. "Cheat him?"

"The infertility was probably a blow to her identity, especially if she'd wanted children. If she leaves, he can find someone else, someone capable of bearing his child."

"That's the most illogical thing I've ever heard." His chuckle infuriated her and she pushed the door open, her feet kicking up little puffs of dust when she stepped down.

"People's emotions aren't always logical, Calvert."

He met her at the back of the truck. "It's a moot point, anyway. She's dead. I wonder what her answer would have been if she'd known that she'd never see him again."

"What-ifs are a waste of time."

"Yeah, but sometimes you can't help thinking about them, and I have a lot where you're concerned, Falconetti. Hell, Carter is a breathing what-if. I look at him and see what was in the back of my mind during that whole undercover detail. I was damned irresponsible with you."

"We were both careless." Being with him, coupled with the conversation, suffused her with a wanting that went beyond physical desire. Beneath the wanting, hope whispered of possibilities long abandoned. She wouldn't be able to resist him long, not when he looked at her like this, with tenderness and desire burning in his dark eyes.

"Yeah." He rubbed a hand over his nape and glanced across the parking lot. He laughed, a low, rueful sound. "But you're the only woman I've ever lost my head like that with."

She wanted to be that only woman in his life, more than she would admit to herself. Pushing the craving away, she pulled up a cool smile. "I'm flattered, Calvert, really, but I thought you were in a hurry to get this tape?"

He quirked one eyebrow at her tone. "Yeah. Come on."

The aroma of stale grease and cigarette smoke permeated the store's dim interior. A woman in her late forties sat on a stool behind the counter, reading the Sunday paper. Her bleached blonde hair rose in a teased bubble over her forehead. A half-burnt cigarette dangled from her cracked, heavily rouged lips.

When the cheap wind chimes over the door announced their arrival, she huffed a sigh and slowly raised her eyes, speaking around the cigarette. "Well, look what the cat done drug in."

"Hey, Jeanette," Tick drawled, his posture relaxing. He transformed into his slow country farm-boy role and Caitlin smiled at the ease with which he put it on. He leaned on the counter. "I need a favor."

Jeanette stubbed her cigarette out in an ashtray shaped like a tractor wheel. "Why is it every time I hear those words come out of your mouth, there's trouble?"

"Now, that is not true—"

"Who's your friend?" Eyes narrowed in suspicion, Jeanette waved a hand at Caitlin, the fluorescent light bouncing off garish red nails.

He slid a slow grin in Caitlin's direction and an insidious thrill of desire pinched low in her stomach. Oh, God, he had the sexiest mouth ever.

"That's Caitlin. We've just come from Mama's."

Jeanette's sharp blue gaze flickered over Caitlin. "Well, that explains it then."

"Explains what?"

"Why you haven't been in here lately."

"What do you mean? I filled up the truck yesterday."

"Shanna tells me you just quit hanging around, all of a sudden like. Your taste change? Skinny brunettes your thing now?"

A flush touched his cheekbones. "I've been busy. You know, cop stuff."

Jeanette made an elaborate show of folding the newspaper. "She said if you showed up to tell you she misses seeing you."

His flush deepened, and despite the jealousy biting at her, Caitlin enjoyed watching him squirm.

Tick rubbed a hand across his jaw. "Tell her I said hey."

"Tell her yourself." Tearing off a piece of register tape, Jeanette scrawled a number and slid it across the counter. "She wants you to call her."

He tucked the paper scrap in his back pocket. "Thanks."

"Now what do you want, sweet thing?"

Caitlin choked on a laugh and he shot a warning look her way. "I need your security tape from the nineteenth of May."

"No."

"What?"

"No. I ain't giving you the tape. I don't have to, and I'm not gonna."

Color rose up his nape. "Jeanette, just give me the tape."

She arched pencil-thin plucked brows at him. "You got a warrant?"

"I don't *need* a warrant, but believe me, I could get one. Course, I'd have to drive all the way out to Virgil Holton's and disturb him on Sunday afternoon, then drive all the way back here, which is going to put me in a really bad mood."

Jeanette leaned back on the stool and regarded him with deep suspicion. "How do I know this ain't some kind of undercover sting?"

He waved an arm at the cluttered store. "A sting? Do I look like I'm undercover? What would I be looking for?"

"Oh, I don't know...you might be looking to see if we was carding people for our alcohol sales. Or you might have some mistaken ideas about Wilford's friendly little card games." She tilted her head toward the two long folding tables set up by the

147

front windows.

He exhaled hard, dropping his head. "If I was looking for that and I wanted the tape, then I'd need a warrant. But I'm not looking for that. I'm not interested in your poker games either."

She narrowed her eyes. "Then what are you looking for?"

He pulled the snapshot of Kimberly Johnson from his pocket. "I think she was in here that night. I need to see who else was in the store."

Jeanette studied the photo. "This that girl y'all found out at the lime mine?"

"Yeah. That's her. Probably murdered by the same guy who killed Sharon Ingler and Amy Gillabeaux. You do want me to catch him, right?"

"Of course I do! I mean, a single woman's not safe in this county anymore. I figure next I'll be murdered in my own bed."

From Tick's exasperated expression, Caitlin figured there was a distinct possibility of her being murdered, right here, right now. He leaned forward. "Then give me the damn tape."

She slapped down her folded newspaper with a huff. "What date did you say again?"

"The nineteenth." He followed her to the doorway of the back room and watched as she eyed the tapes lining a rough, wooden bookshelf. He grinned at Caitlin over his shoulder, his hair falling onto his forehead.

Jeanette pulled a box from the shelf and held it to her chest. Head high, she walked back to the counter and set the tape down. She laid her hand on the videotape as he reached for it. "You buying anything?"

He pointed a finger at her. "That's extortion, Jeanette."

He walked to the drink box and grabbed two glass-bottled Cokes, picking up a pack of salted peanuts on the way back to the counter.

"That'll be two-seventy-nine."

He pulled three ones from his wallet and tossed them on the counter. "Drop the change in the penny cup."

With a wide smile, she slid the tape across the scarred surface before she reached over her head to pull down a pack of his cigarettes. "On the house."

"I can't." He pushed the pack back to her. "I'm trying to quit again."

"So am I." She laughed, a hoarse, rattling guffaw. "Been trying for ten years."

With a muttered curse, he grabbed the pack and shoved it in his pocket. Juggling the tape, the sodas and peanuts, he pushed the door with his hip, keeping it propped open. He glanced at Caitlin, his jaw tight. "You ready?"

Caitlin waited to laugh until they were outside. "Sweet thing? Oh my God, you should have seen your face."

He cast her a dark look, setting the tape and sodas on the hood of his truck before tugging the scrap of register tape from his pocket and shredding it.

Caitlin watched him drop it in a nearby trash barrel. "Who is Shanna anyway? Another of your blondes?"

"Shanna is...Shanna. I've been trying to get that phone number for two weeks."

Jealousy pricked at her again, making her voice waspish. "Well, don't trash it on my account. You never know, sweet thing, you might need it."

Two of his long strides and she was trapped between the truck and the solid line of his chest, his hands braced against the hood on either side of her. Heat flushed her body, pooling in her stomach, flowing between her thighs.

"I don't need Shanna's number." He stared down at her, a grin quirking at his mouth. "Call me sweet thing again, precious. I kind of like it when you do. Course, I like just about everything you do."

"Do you call Shanna precious?"

"No. Just you." He leaned in. "You're damned cute when you're jealous, Falconetti."

"I am not jealous." She struggled for a lofty tone, wanting nothing more than to pull him closer and wrap herself around him. How did he make her want him so easily?

His gaze dropped to her mouth. "Sure you are. The same way I was when you took off with Cookie Friday night."

"That is not the same thing."

"Like hell it's not."

He took her hand and pressed it along the fly of his jeans. Against the denim, her fingers curved around his semi-aroused length. Reawakened desire licked at her stomach with a fiery tongue, intensified by the roughening of his voice.

"Feel that? I've been living with that, only in a more intense state since, you showed up at Ash's. Your voice alone makes me so hard my teeth hurt. Throw in the way you kiss me and having to sleep with you last night without touching you, and it's a wonder I can think at all. But I can assure you...I'm not thinking about any woman other than you."

Unable to resist, she flexed her fingers against him, wringing a guttural groan from his throat. He lowered his head, mouth covering hers. She opened to him, kissing him back, continuing to caress him through the faded denim.

With a harsh gasp, he pulled his mouth from hers and cupped her face. "I want you. I want you back in my bed tonight—"

"I hate to interrupt." Cookie's voice had the same effect as a blaring car horn, and Tick jerked against her. She glanced over his shoulder. Cookie's Blazer waited at the gas pump, and he stood just feet away. A blush swept her face, and he grinned. "And I really mean that, because I'd love to watch."

Tick muttered a curse. "If I shoot him..."

"I'll swear it was justified." Caitlin tried to smile. It could be worse. Reed could have walked up on them in a public parking lot while she was groping him. At least Tick had parked to the rear of the building, and on Sunday afternoon, the highway near the store was deserted. She closed her eyes on a hopeless sigh. He made her lose her head way too easily.

"Boy, don't you know Georgia has laws about lewd and lascivious behavior in public?" Fiendish amusement rumbled in Cookie's voice. "I ought to run both of you in."

"Cookie." Tick spoke between gritted teeth. He didn't turn to face the other man, and she realized he was trying to get his body's reaction to her under control. "How would you like to work midnights for a solid year? I can arrange it."

"Indecent public behavior and abuse of power. You're corrupting him, Falconetti. Want to corrupt me?"

"Want to make that midnights and doubles for a year?"

Tick reached over her and picked up the sodas, handing one to her. He popped the top from his bottle and ripped open the packet of roasted, salted peanuts with his teeth, pouring them into his Coke.

Cookie hooked his thumbs in his belt. "Schaefer says we got a positive ID on yesterday's vic."

"Yeah." Tick pointed at the tape lying on the hood. "She was in here the night she disappeared. I want to see who else was."

A wicked grin curved Cookie's full bottom lip. "If shapely Shanna was working, it's a sure bet you're on there."

"Shut up, Cookie. Don't you have somewhere to be?"

With elaborate casualness, Cookie consulted his watch. "Nope. Not for a couple of hours. Can't I hang out with y'all?"

Tick gave Caitlin a nudge toward the passenger side. "No."

"Oh, come on." Cookie leaned over the truck bed, hands clasped loosely. "You two are together, Jeff's off with your sister. I'm all alone here."

"Go find Angel."

"Can't. She and Jimbo are back together. I have morals, remember?"

Tick made a disparaging sound in his throat and tugged the passenger door open. "Like a tomcat."

"I'm offended." Cookie slanted a calculating glance in Caitlin's direction. "Hey, Falconetti, we had an awful damn interesting phone call come into the station earlier."

She halted, sheltered between Tick's lean body and the truck cab. "What do you mean?"

"I had the opportunity to talk with the CEO of Falcon Security Enterprises."

"Oh, holy Mother of God." She rolled her eyes. She'd kill him, if he was up to his old tricks. "What did he want?"

"Seems someone important is sending his phone calls straight to voice mail and he's trying to track her down. Wanted to use me as his personal messenger boy. The guy's a real prick."

"You have no idea." She let the soda's icy bite trickle down her throat. Damn it, didn't Vince have anything better to do than keep tabs on her?

"Would y'all like to fill me in here?" Tick rested his forearm on the doorframe.

"My brother. He can't stand it when I'm off the leash and he can't find me."

"What do you want me to say if he calls back?" Cookie grimaced. "Something tells me he will."

She couldn't very well ask him to pass on what she normally said to Vince when he shifted into his imperious overprotective mode. "Tell him to cool his jets and I'll call him when I'm ready."

After retrieving Caitlin's rental car, they spent the next few hours in Tick's living room, going through Tripp Payton's file, making notes, tossing theories about, arguing over the importance of different details. They worked well together and the easy camaraderie relaxed Caitlin further.

"I inventoried the blankets, both in our cars and in the supply closet. Each one is accounted for." Tick spoke around a pencil clenched in his teeth. Even with his voice muffled, his relief was obvious.

Caitlin looked up from the department schedules. She'd read over them so often that afternoon, she almost had them memorized. If there was something off in them, she didn't see it. "Isn't tomorrow Amy Gillabeaux's funeral?"

"Yeah. Vontressa's, too."

She returned her attention to the spreadsheet. "We should go. Actually, you might want to videotape the crowd."

"I'd already made arrangements to do that." Tick stretched, a long, lazy movement, and rolled to his feet. "I'm thirsty. You want anything?"

You. The word trembled on her lips, and she swallowed with difficulty, imagining his reaction. "Water's fine."

He ambled into the kitchen, rummaging in the refrigerator. She couldn't pull her gaze from him. Low-slung jeans clung to his hips below the polo shirt and there was no sign of the heaviness many cops developed around the waistline, despite the amount of time he spent behind a desk or in a vehicle. She knew agents who lived in the gym trying to bring that same muscle tone to their bodies.

I want you back in my bed tonight. She wanted to be there, too. Needed to be there, to touch him and have his hands and mouth on her.

Not wanting him to catch her staring, she lowered her gaze as he closed the refrigerator door. She took the bottled water he proffered, drinking deeply to quench the sudden dryness invading her mouth.

He twisted the cap off his beer and reached for Payton's folder again. "I cannot believe what this guy has accomplished in three weeks."

"He was trying to bring her home."

"Yeah." He tapped a finger against the photo of Kimberly Johnson clipped to the inside of the folder. "She still looks familiar, like I know her from somewhere."

"Her missing poster was hanging on the bulletin board right outside your office door. You were looking at it every day."

"I guess." He tipped the bottle up and she found herself watching the muscles in his throat move as he swallowed. She wanted to shove the paperwork out of the way and jump on him, take him right there on the floor.

With difficulty, she looked away, forcing herself to focus on the artifacts he'd arranged on the table. He thumped the credit card record. "Bet that fast-food place had a security camera, too. We should check on that tomorrow. We could go down Tuesday morning to view their tapes. I'd like to see who used her credit card in Tallahassee."

"Speaking of tapes, for someone who was so eager to get the one from the Tank and Tummy..."

A sheepish expression flashed over his face. "I got distracted."

He pushed the videotape into the VCR and sank down behind her on the floor, close enough to warm her with his body heat. Her lungs decided to stop working, her entire body flushed with an awareness of him. He fast-forwarded through the afternoon hours, utilizing the numbers in the corner as a guide. As they neared seven o'clock, he returned to normal play.

Caitlin listened to his quiet breathing, reveled in his warmth at her back. She could hold on to these few precious moments, these memories to dwell on later.

On the screen, two familiar figures walked into the store. "That's you and Schaefer."

He coughed. "Yeah. I'm coming off duty; he's coming on."

Another pair of men walked through the doors. Cookie slapped Tick on the back. "Who's the other guy?"

"Chris Parker. Our K-9 officer. They were coming back from a training exercise over in Lowndes County."

On the television Schaefer paid for his purchases and left. Tick leaned a hip against the counter, smiling at the busty blonde working the register. Cookie and Parker ambled out.

Caitlin elbowed Tick in the ribs. "You're flirting with her."

He winced. "I'm having a conversation with her."

"With her chest. I'll give her this, she had a great plastic surgeon. I guess that's Shanna."

"Yeah. That's Shanna."

"God, Tick, you've been in there nearly ten minutes. You must really like this girl."

"You're going to give me a fit, aren't you?"

"At every opportunity. I hate to tell you this, Calvert, but either she's not interested or she's really good at playing hard to get."

"Cait, cut it out, would you?"

She grabbed for the remote. "Run it back. Were you flexing a muscle at her?"

He held it out of reach. "No, I wasn't. Would you let this go?"

Twisting, she leaned across his chest, fingernails digging lightly into his side. He rotated sideways, chuckling, and dropped the remote on the table. With an agile movement, he pushed her back on the floor, pinning her hands by her head.

"Shanna's a nice girl, a pretty girl, but she isn't *you*." He shook his head, all playfulness gone. "I've been dating, a lot, but that's all. Dating. I was looking for a way to forget you. It didn't work. Now, will you quit?"

His weight pressing into her aroused old memories and intensified the desire throbbing to life low in her stomach. She stared up at him, wanting his mouth on hers. The knowledge she could get away if she really wanted hung between them and mingled with the blatant craving in his gaze. She swallowed and held still, absorbing the feel of him against her.

"Hey, wait—that's her." He jerked to a sitting position, grabbed the remote and rewound the film. "My God."

Caitlin straightened to sit beside him. On the screen, Kimberly Johnson held out a map for his inspection. He traced a route with his finger, grinning at her. A couple of minutes later, the young woman signed her credit card receipt and left.

He stared, his jaw slack. "I talked to her. That's why she seemed so familiar. Damn it, Cait, I talked to her."

"Rewind it again." She stared at the images, noting Kimberly's clothing, her purse, her purchases. She watched Tick punctuating his directions with his hands. Kimberly smiled, thanking him. Picked up her receipt. Walked out the door.

And within hours, minutes maybe, became the victim of a brutal murder.

Caitlin shivered. Seconds. It only took seconds for the presence of a stranger to forever change a life. Or take one.

Tick hunched over, elbows on his knees, head in his hands. "I talked to her. I was one of the last people to see her alive. And I don't remember."

The desire to comfort him was strong. She smoothed her hand over his back. "Don't—"

He lifted his head, staring at the screen with haunted eyes. "I don't remember what I said to her. Hell, that poster was hanging outside my office, and I didn't even recognize her."

"Stop. You didn't know, and there's nothing you could have done. The only thing you can do now is—"

"Find the son of a bitch so the state can put a needle in his arm." Suppressed rage trembled in his voice.

"Tick, don't. It's not your fault."

A shudder ran through him and he caught her hand in his, keeping her fingers pressed to his face. "I want this guy, Cait. I want him bad."

He gestured at the television with his free hand, Kimberly Johnson frozen there in the moments before she disappeared.

"Look at her. She has no idea what's waiting for her. Neither did Sharon when she got out of her car. Then Vontressa and Amy. The son of a bitch has destroyed Miss Lauree's life. Eloise Gillabeaux has taken to her bed because the grief is too much. I want him locked away."

His light stubble abraded her fingers. The heat of his skin traveled along her nerves, sending delicious shivers through her. "I know. We'll get him."

Their gazes met, clung, the anger in his shifting to a different type of heat. He smiled, a wry twist of his lips, and he turned his mouth into her palm. "I want you worse. Don't go back to the hotel tonight."

You can have this. Live for the moment, take this opportunity. You may not get another. "Are you sure?"

A slow nod moved his skin against hers again. "But I want it to be about us, not about comfort. I need it to mean something."

"I can't make you any promises, Tick." Her heart swelled with all the promises she yearned to make, the promises she craved from him.

"I'm not asking for any." He leaned closer. "Just tell me you want me."

Rising to kneel before him, she cupped his face in both hands and met his fiery dark gaze without hesitation.

"I want this. I want *you*." Her long, slow smile matched the burn between her thighs. She'd take these moments while she could, figure out how to deal with the rest later. "Take me to bed, sweet thing, and I promise you won't be sorry."

Chapter Eight

Sorry? How could he be sorry, with Caitlin's lips against his, her urgent hands on his skin? Tick cradled her head, dipping his tongue into the dark heat of her mouth. She moaned, the sound sending a heavy rush of need to his groin, before she pulled away, grasped the hem of his shirt and tugged it over his head.

Her desire-shadowed gaze lay on him like a touch and stoked his need higher. Eyes locked on his, she settled her hands on his shoulders and eased forward, her thighs straddling his. "What do you want?"

He smiled at the naughty whisper and gripped her waist, the cotton of her blouse soft against his palms. "I've got everything I want right here."

From beneath her lashes, she flicked a glance at him. She trailed a slender finger down his chest, leaving unbearable excitement in its path. Her fingernail traced a circle around his navel, the muscles in his gut jumping under the soft touch, his erection growing to press against his fly with excruciating intensity. The maddening finger slid down to skim along his waistband.

She lifted her other hand to release her hair. She shook the sleek mass back and he reached up, itching to bury his hands in it. She caught his wrists, her thighs pressing harder into his.

"You must have some fantasies, Calvert." She leaned toward him, her blouse gapping to offer him a glimpse of the sheer bra he'd dreamed of all day. She nuzzled his throat, almost purring. "Something that pushes your buttons." Her husky voice, a dark whisper, shivered over his ear. Thumbs caressed his wrists, but continued to hold his hands at his sides. "Whatever turns you on."

Everything she did turned him on. She'd been every one of his fantasies since he'd taken her to his bed. Or hell, if he was really honest, since that first week at Quantico, during a course on takedown methods, when she'd knocked him on his ass.

"Cait—"

"Or maybe you want me to figure it out."

Lean thigh muscles flexed against his legs and she pushed at his chest, a light shove, until he lay flat, reclining on his elbows. He laughed, the sound emerging rusty and strangled. "We've been here before, Falconetti."

"No." She curled her fingers into his waistband, and his stomach contracted. "Definitely not here, Calvert."

Knuckles brushing his abdomen, she popped free the metal button, and his breath stopped. The slow trace of her lowering his zipper felt like a caress. Desperate to touch her, he reached for her, intending to drag her down for a kiss.

She caught his hands. "No. You're not touching yet."

"Cait." The frustrated sound was close to a strangled plea and he swallowed hard. He caught her teasing smile before her hair fell forward to shield her face. How the hell did she think he'd keep his hands from her? He was hard, straining and ready now, and she'd barely touched him.

She pushed his arms above his head again. Stretching forward, she nipped his shoulder, her breasts rubbing against his chest.

"Damn it, Cait, you're killing me." The words were wrung from him on a gasp when she ran her nails down his torso in a light rake, stopping just short of his open fly.

He grasped her waist and found his wrists captured in a firm grip. She held him down this time, leaning over him, her body cupping him intimately. She moved in a slow, sinuous circle against his straining erection, her low laugh doing incredible things to his nerves. "I don't have to get out the cuffs, do I, Calvert?"

The scary thing was he'd let her. He'd let her do anything she wanted to him and enjoy every minute of it. He was hers.

Great. He was already a goner.

"Whatever you want, Falconetti."

"Giving me control can be a dangerous thing," she murmured against his ear. Easing his hands above his head once more, she rotated her hips into his, and he ground his teeth, aching to be inside her.

"And I told you, I don't have a problem relinquishing control. Sometimes it can be damned interesting."

Releasing him, she kissed him, a slow, teasing caress. "Let's find out how interesting."

Metal clinked before the cold circle closed around his right wrist. He jerked, and the other cuff rasped shut on his left wrist. His fingers brushed the heavy wood post on his coffee table, and surprised, he stared into green eyes near black with passion and mischief. She rested her hands on the floor, either side of his torso, a smile quirking at her mouth, and excitement burned in his gut.

Interesting wasn't the word.

She didn't speak, but blazed a trail of kisses down his abdomen. Her fingers curled in his waistband again and she tugged downward, jeans and boxer briefs sliding over his hips. At the rush of cool air, his dick twitched, and he caught another glimpse of her wayward smile. She pulled the garments free of his body and tossed them aside.

Tracing a design on the inside of his thigh, she tilted her head. "You said something about giving me control?"

Considering he was the one naked, incredibly aroused and handcuffed, he figured she already had it. "It's...interesting."

Her fingertip moved up his leg, eased over his scrotum in a featherweight caress. Uncontrollably, his back arched, his eyes slid closed. "God, precious."

She skimmed the finger along the length of his erection, the light touch shivering through him, sending sparks to every nerve.

The lush wetness of her mouth closed around him. He bowed again, his stomach clenching, the cuff chain rattling against the table leg.

"Holy hell," he gasped, his breathing coming in uneven

bursts. More than anything, he wanted to touch her, the smoothness of her skin under his hands, and he could do nothing but give himself over to the pure sin of her mouth.

She had him completely at her mercy.

The smooth motion of her tongue flicking against him, the massaging warmth of her fingers at his balls—all coalesced into sheer sensation, swirling and flooding from his groin, into his belly, out through his blood stream. Nothing existed but the pull of her lips, the brush of her hair against his stomach. Pressure built, a fiery tingle that burst into a full-fledged inferno, threatening to burn him alive.

"Cait," he groaned, while he could still speak, still think. "It's...been a long time. I'm not...gonna last."

That was her intent, he gathered with the last part of his brain capable of coherence. She didn't slow, and if anything, tightened the incredible paradise around him, taking him deeper. The inferno burned higher, melting away everything, until nothing remained but the sensation, until he came with a ferocity that left him shattered and winded.

Heart thudding against his ribs with a painful rhythm, he struggled to catch his breath. His arms ached, and aftershocks ran through his body, along his nerve endings. He opened his eyes to find her sitting against the coffee table, fully clothed, hair tousled, a satisfied smirk on her beautiful, talented mouth. She lifted his beer bottle and swallowed.

The edge was off his desire, but the need to touch her, to bury himself inside her burned as strong as ever. He shifted his elbows, rattling the cuff chain. "Take 'em off."

She lifted one elegant eyebrow. "No."

Damn, she had layers he'd never suspected existed, and oh, hell, he liked them. "You know, sooner or later you have to let me go."

And payback's a bitch.

The unspoken promise of sweet retaliation lay between them and her smile widened. "I can handle it."

She lifted the beer again and he shifted under her steady gaze. Head tilted, she set the beer aside. "Are you sorry?"

"Hell, no."

She smiled again, fingers moving to the buttons on her blouse. In slow motion, she popped each one free and shrugged out of the fine fabric. Clearly outlined, hardened nipples pressed against the sheer lace of her bra. She wriggled out of her jeans, leaving only the tiny thong he'd chosen that morning.

His gaze fell on the scars, and he frowned, a little of the playfulness fading. "Precious—"

She kissed him, swallowing the endearment, and he tasted the sharp mix of beer and his own come, blended with the dark sweetness of her mouth. Her tongue danced against his, withdrew, and she pulled away, licking and nipping her way down his throat with open-mouthed kisses. Unbelievably, desire rushed through him again, as strong and sure as before. She nuzzled his pecs, hands stroking down his ribcage to his waist, legs tangling with his.

His renewing erection pressed into her, the lacy fabric of her thong an exquisite torture to his sensitized skin. Velvety and damp, she rocked into him, and the reality shook him to the core. She was as wet for him as he was hard for her. He wanted to make her wetter, drive her as crazy as she did him, until she was writhing and moaning his name.

She traced the line of his ribs with her mouth and he shifted under her, tugging against the handcuffs again. "Cait, come on. I want to touch you."

With a feline stretch, she aligned herself along him, eyes locked with his. She fingered the line of his jaw. "You relinquished control, Calvert. That means we play by my rules."

"Uncuff me and I'll make it worth your while." He lifted his head the inch or so necessary to bring their lips together, but she pulled back, an impish light in her eyes. Frustration curled through him, but didn't temper the desire.

She shifted to slide a hand between them and swept a caress down the length of his hard-on, fisting him in a slow up-and-down motion. "Oh, it'll be worth my while regardless."

He struggled to catch his breath. "Turn me loose and we can take this in the bedroom."

Her fingers fanned over his balls. "I keep you locked up, and I can take you right here."

"Protection." Holy hell, she made it hard to think. "Kitchen, top drawer by the door."

"Be right back." She brushed a kiss against his stomach and eased away. Moments later she returned with the multicolored package, which she dropped on his abdomen. At the tiny impact, he jerked, every nerve ending sensitized beyond belief. "Calvert, do I want to know why you keep a box of condoms in your kitchen?"

"Bought 'em this morning when I went for your stuff. Thought we might need them."

With a twist of her bra's front clasp, the garment fell away, the sight of her taking his breath again. He curled his hands into fists, fingertips tingling with need. She eased the thong down and tossed it aside.

A wicked smile played around her mouth as she reached for the small box. "Let's see what's in here."

A shower of cellophane packets rained down, and she laughed, the dark husky sound shivering over him.

She shook her head, hair shifting against her shoulders, and ripped the package open, withdrawing a scrap of bright pink latex. With exquisite slowness, she unrolled the condom on his length, and Tick gritted his teeth, hips bucking. She straddled his thighs and leaned forward, her mouth a whisper away from his.

"I'm going to take you," she murmured and flicked her tongue against his lips. He groaned. She lifted away, poising over him, and anticipation dried his mouth. He ached to be inside her, to have her take him, right here, as she'd promised, fast, slow, however she wanted, as long as it was soon.

God, he was whipped.

Her gaze tangled with his. "Are you sorry, Calvert?"

"Cait..."

"I wouldn't want you to have any doubts." She leaned forward, breasts pressed to his chest. "I want you to be very, very sure."

If he was any more sure, he'd die. "No doubts, Falconetti."

"Positive?" She lowered her hips, hot wetness just taking the tip of him. Fire erupted in his gut.

He thrust upward, sheathing himself in her. She gasped,

the passion-filled noise vibrating through him. He laughed, the guttural sound torn from his throat. "Absolutely."

"Good." She settled more firmly against him, her body a blazing, tight glove around him. She lifted and fell, posting slowly. "Because if you give me some choir-boy apology later, I'll kick your ass."

"You're kicking it now." He pushed the words through clenched teeth. The smooth movement of her body on his was reminiscent of what her mouth had done to him earlier, and the unbearable tension coiled in his gut again.

She pushed harder against him, and he grimaced at the pleasure bordering on pain. Her unbound breasts, nipples hard, swayed above him, and he wrapped his hands around the table leg, dying to touch her. The enforced denial added an edge to the desire. She shook her hair back, eyes sliding closed. Her lips pursed, parted, and he tightened his fists again.

He needed to touch her, needed more than simply being able to thrust inside her.

He needed her eyes open, so he could watch the pleasure darken them when she came.

He needed more.

A slight bend of his knees allowed him to drive further into her as she ground down on him, and a moan slipped past her lips.

He chuckled deep in his throat. "Are you sorry, Falconetti?"

Shaking her head, she bit her lip.

His fingers slipped on the slick, varnished wood, the metal bracelets clinking. He drank in every nuance of her expression, seeking some way to forge the connection he wanted. She liked his voice, liked having him whisper to her while he made love to her. He remembered that from those nights before Mississippi.

Maybe he'd given her physical control, maybe he couldn't touch her, but he could damn well talk to her.

"I've missed you, Cait," he murmured and she faltered slightly in her easy rhythm. He shifted his hips under hers, altering the angle of his thrusts. "I dreamed about you, about this, the whole time I was gone."

Her lashes fluttered, desperate hunger sharpening her face.

"Don't."

"Why?" The seductive drag and lift tried to steal his breath once more and his voice came out a hoarse rasp. "You don't want to hear that I'd wake up hard and shaking, like I could feel you around me? That I wanted your breasts in my hands, my mouth—"

"Calvert, stop." She moved faster, their bodies sliding together in a maelstrom of soft wet sounds and softer moans. "Please."

"No. Tell me you didn't think about it, that every time it rained, I wasn't in your head." He lunged harder against her, a broken whimper that dripped with arousal escaping her parted lips. "Because you were in mine, constantly. Hell, even when I took a shower and all I could think about was taking you against the wall in that hotel room, how damn tight you were, how hot and wet you were for me—"

"Stop."

"Do you remember, baby? We were both soaked from the rain and I followed the drops on your skin with my tongue. I couldn't get enough of you, your feel, your taste."

"You tore my blouse." The accusation emerged on another of those sexy, shaken moans. "Ruined it and all I wanted was you, hard and inside me..."

Hell yeah, she remembered. Her body tightened on his, a flush spreading up her belly, over breasts and tightly budded nipples, suffusing her neck and face. Fighting back a climax, he watched the orgasm wash over her, a slight frown drawing elegant brows together, his name slipping from her lips.

The wet clench of her muscles around him sent desire punching into his gut. Fingernails digging into the wood table leg, he exploded, pushing deeper, higher. Lights and shadows danced at the edges of his vision, his heart thudding as it tried to escape his chest.

She collapsed, slumping against his chest, face pressed to his throat. "Oh, God, Calvert."

He wanted to hold on to her, to wrap his arms around her. Growling, he tugged at the cuffs. "Take 'em off *now*, Falconetti."

Pushing her hair back, she lifted her head and pulled her bag close, rummaging without looking and coming up with a small key ring. She stretched forward, and the first cuff gave. Arm burning as circulation returned, he wrapped it around her waist. The second cuff sprang free, and he tangled his hand in her hair. The metal bracelets clattered to the floor, and Caitlin rested against his chest again.

Tick stretched protesting muscles. She'd been right—no way would he regret this night when morning came. He nuzzled her shoulder, inhaling the unique perfume of her bare skin. Pure Caitlin, but bearing the imprint of his scent.

This was what his life could be. She'd refused to make him any promises, but surely she had to see what they could have. And surely her being with him like this meant something. One step closer to regaining the Caitlin he'd lost.

He trailed a finger down her spine. Already, she was under his skin. One little push and he'd be over his head in love with her. The kind of love where he'd do anything for her, even if that meant leaving his department and the idealism of what he was doing to return to the bureau so they could be together.

He kissed the curve of her neck and she shifted with a murmuring sigh. The sound shot through him, sending a hot flood of emotion along his body. He tightened his hand on her waist and slid it up her side, fingers cupping the side of her breast.

"Down, boy." She moved, patting her palm against his chest. "Time for a nap."

Laughing, he brushed her ear with his nose and kissed behind it, finding the spot he knew made her moan in pleasure. "Boy? How big do they grow the men where you come from, Falconetti?"

"I'm from Texas, remember?" She dragged out her drawl. "Everything's bigger there. It takes a lot to impress a Texas girl."

"Yeah?" He nibbled at her throat, his body still joined to hers in an intimate embrace. The hot, wet feel of her wrung a groan from him. Damn, he could stay like this with her forever, even with his back protesting the unyielding hardwood floor. He'd be sore as all get-out tomorrow, but hell if he cared right now.

"Yes." Her hands tangled in his hair, she pushed against him. "But I'm most impressed, sweet thing."

He chuckled, holding her close, and she wrapped her arms around him, giggling into his throat. With a satisfied grunt, he rubbed both hands down her back. "A nap, huh?"

"Mmm." She kissed his collarbone. "And an encore later."

℣

Caitlin jerked into awareness, senses on full alert. A delicious ache pulsed between her thighs. Darkness surrounded her; weight and warmth lay next to her. A distinct male scent sank into her consciousness and she relaxed. Tick. She was in Tick's bed and he slept beside her, a soft intermittent snore tickling her ears. She could stay here forever.

But somewhere, beyond the dimness of the bedroom, her phone beeped. She disentangled from Tick's easy hold and slid from the bed. He turned his face into the pillow, murmuring in his sleep.

She picked up his polo and tugged it over her head before padding into the living room. A light from the kitchen illuminated the area and she retrieved her cell phone. The display indicated voice mail waiting, despite a weak signal. She listened to Gina's single message and Vince's six.

Letting the phone redial, she slipped out the back door. Frogs croaked above humming crickets in the moist night air, and she settled into the rocker near the door.

"Geez, Cait, do you know what time it is?" Gina said after the fourth ring. The cellular connection hissed, Gina's voice fading in and out.

Caitlin tucked her feet beneath her. "Actually, I don't."

"It's almost three in the morning. Where have you been?" A suspicion-filled pause hung on the line. "Is Calvert's nose bleeding?"

If it weren't, it wasn't for a lack of trying. Her body quivered with remembered sensations of having him inside her. "Something like that."

"Good for you." Gina's words ended on a yawn. "It's about time you loosened up a little. You need something more than the job in your life."

"It's just sex, Bocaccio." She'd made sure of that. This time, she hadn't let the emotional connection take place. She'd held complete control.

Or rather, she'd tried to, until he'd started talking and had wrapped that gorgeous voice and the decadently sensual memories around her.

Silence hovered on the hissing line. "Did you tell him?"

A tiny green frog hopped across the floor, tapped her toe and turned the other way. Moonlight washed the pine trees lining the river with silver. She swallowed. "No."

"And you're putting up the don't-touch-me walls, aren't you?"

Caitlin laughed, the small, brittle sound hurting her already tight throat. "I have no clue what you mean."

"Come on, Cait, this is me. You can be honest now. You're scared to death someone's going to get close enough to see the real you because you think once they see the reality, they won't want you anymore. I could lay odds that's what you're doing with Calvert, too. The sex is a diversion to keep him from getting too close."

Tears burned her eyes. "I'm the one with a psych degree, remember? You're the computer expert. Stick to analyzing cache records and virus codes, would you?"

Another silence fell between them. "You're falling for him all over again, aren't you?"

Damn Gina for never taking a hint, never beating around the bush. "Yes."

"You're playing a dangerous game." Hesitancy hovered in Gina's voice. "You said yourself he's all about truth, justice and the American way. Those kinds of men don't like secrets."

"I know." She pressed her fingers against her closed eyelids. "Believe me, I know."

Caitlin couldn't be sure if Gina sighed or if the sound was merely another hiss on the line. "Cait, tell him. He obviously wants you, too. Waiting is only going to make things worse."

She shuddered. "I can't. Not yet."

"Think about it, okay?"

She didn't need to. Eyes closed, she pushed her tangled

167

hair away from her face. The smell of him lingered on her skin and invaded her nostrils with the movement. He'd permeated every pore on her body. "I need a favor."

"Anything."

"I'm going to email you a department roster. I need background checks on each officer, and I also want you to see if there are open homicides or missing person cases anywhere they've lived or worked before."

"You don't ask for much, do you? Is Calvert on this roster?"

"He is."

"Want me to run him, too?"

Guilt pricked at her, but she smothered it. They wouldn't want any questions later. If the killer turned out to be one of Tick's colleagues, a good defense attorney would have a field day with her not having his background rechecked. "Yes. Run him, too."

"Whatever you say. And Cait? Take care."

"You, too."

Killing the connection, she tapped the phone against her lips, staring into the darkness beyond the bluish mercury light. What she should do, right now, was dress and go back to her hotel before this insanity went any farther.

What she was going to do was crawl back into Tick's bed and get as close to him as possible.

The phone buzzed in her hand and emitted a loud chirping, and she startled. With a soft curse, she checked the screen. She flipped it open once more, lifted it to her ear and waited.

"Where in hell are you?" Annoyance bordering on anger simmered in Vince's voice.

She pushed a foot against the floor and set the chair rocking. "Wouldn't you like to know?"

"I asked you a question."

"I'm in Georgia, working a case."

"Caitlin." He was obviously grinding his teeth and she smiled. He made getting under his skin too easy. "I know that. I also know you're not in your hotel room because I've called you more times than I care to count. I know you're not at that piss-ant one-pony sheriff's department because I've talked to the most insubordinate fucker I've ever encountered there twice already. Now, where the fuck are you?"

"Does Troupe know you talk like that?"

"Is there a reason you're making this difficult?"

"Is there a reason you're checking up on me?"

"Yes. It involves still having nightmares about finding you in a pool of blood, fighting off a psychopathic son of a bitch." A raw hint of pain invaded his tone. "Not to mention the fact I know who the hell you're working with and as smart as you are, you make the most asinine personal decisions I've ever seen."

Any sisterly affection engendered by his concern evaporated. "Go screw yourself, Vince."

"Does Troupe know you talk like that?"

Silence hummed over the line and she stared at the dark silhouettes of the pine trees flanking the river.

He sighed. "Cait."

She pushed her foot a little harder against the floor. A couple of fireflies flickered through the yard.

"Come on." Honest apology lurked in the plea. "I worry. I don't want to see you hurt. I can't find anything negative on this Calvert guy except a letter in his file for being mildly insubordinate to a training officer when he was a rookie cop but—"

"What did you do?" God, he was unbelievable.

"I had Tony work up a dossier on him when I found out where you were." He seemed unaware of her seething. "What do you want to know?"

And she made the stupidest personal decisions? Holy...

It wasn't like he was going to change. "You can't go investigating everyone I meet. And I'm offended that you'd check Tick out. He would be, too."

"I'm the one who let Fuller into our lives," he said, residual fury and frustration in his words. "I did that. If I'd looked further, convinced Troupe to have new staff undergo psych evaluations, maybe we wouldn't have hired him and *maybe*—"

"Things would be different. I know." Melancholy drifted through her. Beyond the porch, a dove called and a twig snapped sharply in the distance. She rubbed a hand over her eyes. "Stop worrying."

"Why don't I just stop breathing? Same thing, Angel Face."

"It's not your fault, Vinnie. It's Fuller's." She swallowed, blinking back tears. "There wasn't anything you could do."

Hadn't Tick said the same thing to her the night before? He didn't place the blame with her, anymore than she did with Vince.

No, the responsibility lay solely with Fuller. A weight of darkness lifted from her.

"Right." Her brother sounded less than convinced. "Just do me a favor, would you, Cait?"

"What?" Visions of convents and vows of chastity danced in her head.

"Be careful." His voice roughened. "And keep in touch."

"I will." She blew him a kiss into the phone. "Goodnight, Vinnie."

"Night, Angel Face."

She flipped the phone closed and laid it on the small table beside the chair. An unaccustomed peace wrapped around her, highlighted by the soft chorus of frogs and crickets.

Floorboards creaked under quiet footsteps. Tick's silhouette appeared at the kitchen door. "What are you doing out here?"

"I had to return a call and didn't want to bother you." Warmth and hope pulsed through her. Pushing out of the chair, she walked to stand before him. He settled his hands on her hips, sliding beneath the cotton polo shirt.

"Something wrong?" His mouth caressed her temple and she blinked away a wash of tears.

"Just checking in with Gina." She wrapped her arms around his waist and leaned into him. "And Vince."

"Is he looking for me with a shotgun?"

"No." Inhaling deeply, she turned her face into his throat. In his embrace, everything had to be all right. "He's just worried."

And guilt-ridden over something that wasn't his fault.

"I can understand that." Tick nuzzled below her ear, his hold tightening. "A guy has to look out for his sister."

"Hmmm." His mouth was doing wicked things to her senses, and there was something rich and sweet about being here in his arms in the dark. This was her moment. "Tick, I need to—"

"You feel so good, precious. I love what you do to me." He pulled her into him, his arousal a hard ridge against her stomach, even through his jeans. "I want you again."

"Um, me too, but..." The words trailed away under the playful temptation of his marauding hands. With a soft laugh, she tilted her head back and tried to read the expression in his glittering eyes. "You're insatiable."

"Only for you." He tangled his fingers in her hair, holding her head at an angle, and lowered his own. The kiss was wild, a mingling of passion and desperation. She opened her mouth, tongue stroking his, possessing him. Moving her arms to his neck, she held him tighter. She burned, her skin hot wherever he touched. Desire pooled in her stomach, and between her legs, she pulsed with each caress. He was hard, hot, heavy, and she pushed against him, aching, wanting, needing.

He lifted his head and brushed his nose against the curve of her ear, his breath a warm rush against her neck. "This time I get to be in charge." Excitement shivered through her. Nipping at her throat, he chuckled and backed her deeper onto the porch. "Maybe I'd better make sure you're not carrying those cuffs."

She stroked down to his waist, loving the warmth and texture of his skin. "Now just where would I hide them, Calvert?"

The porch railing bumped against her back and legs. Enough light from the mercury lamp and the sliver of moon illuminated his face, revealing the devilish glint in his dark eyes. His hands slid down her arms to her wrists, fingers a strong, sure grasp there. "You know as well as I do that a thorough search is key to any arrest, Agent Falconetti."

Tick Calvert searching her. Oh, God. Images flashed in her head, and heavy yearning shot through her, a low, harsh rhythm. She laughed, the sound shaky and too husky. "An arrest? What charge?"

"You held me prisoner in my own living room." He tugged at her wrists, spreading her arms wider on the railing. "Sounds

171

like kidnapping to me."

His teeth rasped against her neck again and she let her head fall back, offering him greater access. "It's not kidnapping if you were a willing participant."

"Details. We'll work 'em out later." He gazed down, fingers tightening on her. "Assume the position, Falconetti."

Her breath strangled in her throat, lungs ceasing to work. Beneath the soft fabric of his shirt, her nipples beaded, and burning excitement leapt higher in her abdomen. He stepped backward, pulling her forward just enough to turn her and wrap her fingers around the porch railing once more.

He nudged his knee between her thighs, denim rough on her skin. With his foot, he widened her stance. She swallowed, her mouth unbearably dry.

"This isn't textbook technique," she said, injecting sophisticated mockery into her tone. Her voice shook, completely ruining the effect. "Two moves and I'd have you down and incapacitated."

He brushed her hair aside, mouth against her nape. His hips pressed into hers. "You really want me incapacitated?"

Shifting away, he ran his hands along her waist, under the shirt. "This is in the way." Grasping the hem, he tugged the garment upward, over her head, and tossed it aside. Cool night air kissed her skin and he slid his hands to her wrists once more, fastening her hold on the railing.

He moved over her in a slow facsimile of the classic search—from her waist to her head, fingers sifting through her hair, caressing her neck and shoulders, sliding over her arms. Traveling down her chest, they cupped her breasts, hefting, molding, teasing until she moaned. His rough laugh tickled her ears again, and he dropped his hands, spanning her waist, stroking along her hips and thighs, sweeping to her calves and ankles and up the inside of her trembling legs.

Fire danced in the wake of his touch, and his mouth dampened the back of her knee, the small of her back, her nape once more. One hand covered her stomach, the other slid between her thighs, a long finger dipping inside her, tantalizing, driving her crazy.

"Tick, please." She pushed into him. A second finger joined

the first, but it wasn't enough—she needed more, all of him, the connection of having him within her. Heat flushed her stomach, suffusing her body.

"God, you're wet. And so damn hot." He bit her shoulder, a light graze of teeth against skin. "I guess you're clean," he mumbled, erection pressed to her. "Still gonna knock my technique?"

"No." With his fingers pushing her toward the edge? She shook her head, hair brushing his throat. The steamy line of his chest pressed to her spine, the rough cradle of his denim clad legs cupping her—he was all over her and still she wanted more, wanted them so close she didn't know where she ended and he began. "I need you inside me, Calvert."

A breeze tinged with earth and river swept over them, the cool air tightening her breasts further. He nuzzled the sensitive skin beneath her ear, increasing the wet pulsing between her thighs, sliding his thumb over her clitoris. "Like I needed to touch you earlier?"

The pressure intensified, and she gasped, wanting the end to come with him hard inside her, as deep and hard inside her as he could get. "Just...hurry."

His maddening fingers left her and she shivered, trembling, every nerve ending sensitized, every sensation heightened. A zipper rasped, cellophane crinkled, denim rustled. A harsh intake of breath behind her, and he grasped her waist, widening her stance once more. She held her own breath, anticipation intensifying, and he entered her on a slow, driving thrust that filled the aching within.

She closed her eyes at the hard perfection of him. Her body throbbed and trembled around him, ready to tumble over the edge just from one stroke. "Oh, God, Calvert."

He withdrew and plunged deeper, a hand slipping from her waist to plunder and tease between her legs. She tossed her head in a restless side-to-side motion, the exquisite sensation of him driving into her too much, his fingers vibrating over too-sensitive areas, until she thought she'd scream with the need for release.

"Tell me, Cait," he murmured near her ear. "Tell me what you want."

"You." The torn whisper didn't sound like her and she caught her bottom lip between her teeth. "I want you, all of you."

"Like that?" He adjusted his stance, tilting her so his next thrust was impossibly intense. Shivers coursed through her.

"*Tick*, yes." She let her head fall back and he dragged his open lips across her neck to her shoulder, biting gently. "Please..."

When she came, the painful pleasure firing through her, she clamped the cry down, much as she could feel her own muscles clamping on his hardened length. He gasped a chuckle and tightened his hold on her, wrapping her close, maintaining the rhythm of his thrusts until her orgasm faded. She sagged into him, legs quivering like jelly and refusing to support her.

He laughed, winded and hoarse, against her shoulder. "Holy hell, you're going to kill me."

Unable to speak, she struggled for air, clutching his denim-clad thighs. The zipper at his open fly scratched against tender skin, but was nothing compared to the aftershock rocking her. Finally, she blew out a slow breath, eyes closed, sliding her palms over his legs. He kissed the side of her neck and shifted his hips, still hard within her.

A sweet emotion curled in her, and she turned her head to brush her mouth over his cheek.

"Come back to bed," he whispered, a dark, deep drawl.

"Yes." She curved a hand along his jaw, entire being infused with his warmth, with him. "Whatever you want, Lamar Eugene."

Disengaging from her body, he took her hand and drew her inside.

In the bedroom, he stripped off his jeans and reached to turn on the lamp. Caitlin, standing by his bed, blinked at the muted light, a new unease running over her. One hand drifted down to conceal the physical proof of the damage Fuller had inflicted. "Tick—"

"Sshh." Under his kiss, her nervousness faded, disappearing completely as he pushed her gently onto the mattress and followed her down, as he parted her thighs and entered her again, setting a deep, steady rhythm that made her forget everything but him.

When it was over, with thrums of pleasure still running through her body, Caitlin tried to regain her ability to breathe. Lying where he'd collapsed against her, Tick gasped, his face pressed into her throat. Filled by a surge of happiness so strong she wanted to laugh aloud, she caressed the strong line of his back. Oh, she'd missed this, missed *him.*

He traced the curve of her jaw with a fingertip. "You're beautiful."

She swallowed hard at the reverence in his rough whisper. The same finger traveled over her lips and across her cheek, stopping to stroke the skin below her ear. He kissed her neck, temple, cheekbone and finally her lips. "So, so beautiful."

Caitlin closed her eyes, letting his drawl wash over her, soaking in the pure emotion in his words. She let her hands wander up his arms, pressing into his shoulders, his muscles bunching and trembling under her touch.

He kissed her, mouth finding hers again in a caress containing more affection than desire. He slid his palms along her skin, skimming her waist and easing up her rib cage before he pulled away.

"I want to see you," he whispered, voice raw as he stared at her, his eyes glittering. He smoothed his lips against her shoulder. "You're perfect."

Digging into his hair, she closed her eyes and held him. Tears burned behind her lids. She wasn't perfect, not in the way that counted, the way that would really matter to him.

He whispered kisses over the line of her ribs with long, lazy movements, moving lower.

The scars.

For all she knew, he'd already seen them. Hell, she knew he had in the living room earlier. Somehow, knowing he would see them now was worse. She reached for him, to pull him up to her before he saw the disfigurements, but the harsh hiss of his indrawn breath stopped her. She cringed. He cradled the jut of her hip bones, and the warmth of his cheek rested against the damaged flesh.

"God, precious, I'm so sorry this happened to you, so sorry I wasn't there."

She couldn't bear the concern in his voice. Dread settled into an icy lump in her stomach, dissipating the warmth left by their lovemaking. She pushed away, up against the pillows, completely separated from him now.

"Don't."

A confused frown drew his brows together over worried brown eyes. "Cait, they don't matter."

How could he say that? Sitting, she pulled up her knees and reached for the sheet, the mingled scent of their bodies embracing her. He could say it because he didn't realize what they represented. Didn't realize exactly how those scars stood between them.

"Oh, hell." Frustration shook his voice.

Fighting the chill invading her limbs, she pulled the sheet higher. "What?"

Sitting at the edge of the mattress, he didn't look at her, his face set in grim lines. "The damned condom broke. I'll be right back."

After he left the bed, she rolled to her side. Water ran in the bathroom. Black night hovered beyond the window, the rumpled bed reflected in the glass. Her pleasure disappeared, like water evaporating under a hot summer sun. She'd assured him he wouldn't be sorry in the morning, but could she really do that? She swallowed the tightness gripping her throat and willed the tears away.

His form appeared in the reflection, distorted by the old wavy glass. She closed her eyes, and the bed dipped behind her. He covered her stomach with one hand, kissed her shoulder. "Cait? I'm sorry about that—"

"It's all right." She fought against the compulsion to turn into his touch. "It happens."

He shifted to lie down, his arm across her chest as he pulled her down with him. "You don't have to worry about an STD."

Like he had to tell her that. If that had been a worry, he wouldn't have taken her to bed. Surely he realized she knew that much about him. "You either."

With gentle pressure, he turned her in his easy embrace, his expression intense as he stared down. "If you get pregnant—"

"No worries there, either." She pushed away from him. "I'm not going to get pregnant."

He stared at her a long moment. "You're sure?"

"I'm sure." She clenched her fists until her knuckles burned and her nails bit into her skin. "It's not in my future, Calvert."

Just saying the words hurt. She'd surprised him, the sudden tension in his body betraying him. "Not ever?"

"Not ever."

"And that's not negotiable?"

Throat too tight to form words, she shook her head. Arguing with the facts—the removal of an ovary and Fallopian tube, a uterus so damaged by Fuller's attack her doctor doubted it would support a pregnancy past the second trimester, if she made it that far—was pointless.

She sucked in a deep breath and swallowed. "The attack...he damaged me."

"Don't say that." He cradled her nape, his eyes fierce. "Not like that."

"The chances that I could conceive are small and I probably wouldn't be able to carry a baby to term if I did."

He caressed her chin with long, gentle fingers. "I guess you think that changes things."

She tugged free of his easy hold. "There's more—"

"It doesn't matter."

"Of course it does," she scoffed. "It has to and we both know it does matter. It's already changed things. You're different. I can feel it."

"I don't want to rush things. I'm learning not to push with you, precious." A wry smile curved his mouth. "Why don't we do this one step at a time? I'll promise not to push; you promise not to pull away all the time."

"I haven't gone anywhere."

"Yeah, you have. Somewhere I can't follow." He stroked her face. "Come back to me, Cait, and hold on to me, just for tonight."

She let him pull her closer, tucked into his side, and she wrapped an arm around his waist, wanting to believe. He reached over to flick off the lamp, darkness surrounding them. She traced her thumb over his ribcage, he smoothed his hand over her hair.

Two sleepless hours later, she slipped away from his easy hold and gathered her clothes, dressing in the dim light filtering from the kitchen.

"Tick?" Tying her blouse into a loose knot at the waist, Caitlin perched on the edge of the bed. He'd slept, finally, although she'd felt the tension in him for at least an hour after his plea that she come back to him. He didn't stir now.

She traced his features, relaxed in sleep, tousled hair falling over his forehead in dark strands. Her heart ached, a hard, clenching pain in her chest. She wouldn't trade this time with him for anything.

And she wanted more. She wanted everything. Only there was so much still in the way.

One step at a time, he'd said.

She leaned down, pressing a kiss to his stubbled jaw, letting his clean scent fill her nose. He shifted, mumbled, lashes lifting for a moment. "What?"

Sleepy and rumpled, he was incredibly appealing, and she smiled. She feathered his hair away from his forehead.

"I have to go," she whispered. "I'll see you later."

He nodded, eyes slipping closed again. "Careful, okay?"

She kissed him and made herself pull away. "Always."

CR

Someone had been outside his house.

Anger simmering under his skin, Tick eyed the footprints at the edge of the clay path. He'd discovered them when he'd set out to check the timed fish feeder on the dock.

He looked around at Cookie and Jeff. He'd called Cookie upon finding the prints and been surprised when the two showed up together. "What do you think?"

Cookie rubbed a hand over his mouth. "A poacher, maybe?"

"Could be." Tick frowned. The woods surrounding the place were rich in deer and other wildlife but something about those impressions bothered him. It didn't *feel* like a wayward hunter. He glanced toward the river and his dock, hidden by a bend in the trail. Whoever it was had stopped here, paced a while, leaned against a tree.

Cookie came to stand beside him. He lifted his head, sharp gray eyes trained on the woods stretching away along the riverbed. "Heck of a place to be stumbling about in the dark. One wrong step and you're in a mess of trouble. Wicked currents."

"How about I photo and cast 'em?" Jeff's leather gunbelt creaked as he shifted his weight. "I need the practice and if it is a poacher, you'll have the evidence for the forestry ranger."

Tick turned back toward the house. "Y'all want some breakfast—"

The offer strangled in his throat.

Jeff looked at him. "What?"

Facing the house, Tick was looking straight at his driveway, the sun deck...

And the back porch.

Holy hell.

Nausea rose in his belly and for a second he thought he'd actually vomit. Images tumbled through his mind, the sweet surrender of Caitlin's body to his, her subdued cry when she came. The idea of someone watching that, watching them in those moments of ultimate intimacy...hell, he felt worse than invaded.

He felt violated.

"Tick?" Cookie nudged his shoulder. "You all right?"

"Yeah." He blinked, surveyed the area where they stood, glanced at the house. Shit. "Come on. We'll let Jeff play."

On the porch, he stopped at the railing. In the morning light, he could just barely make out Jeff's form crouched over the task of casting the footprints. At night, one wouldn't able to see anything there.

But the mercury light would make everything on the porch

visible from the woods.

"Freakin' hell." He restrained himself from kicking something and shoved the back door open.

"Yeah, you look like freakin' hell," Cookie said. He pulled mugs from the cabinet while Tick started the coffee maker with stiff movements. "Did you sleep last night?"

"Not really." He'd slept, in short bursts between making love to Caitlin. And after that conversation about her probable inability to have children, he'd lain awake, staring into the dark until exhaustion took him around five thirty. He dimly remembered her leaving him shortly after.

A cold blend of fear and distaste slithered down his spine. Had whoever'd been in the woods been there when she left?

Arms crossed over his chest, Cookie shook his head. "Me, either. Trying to get my mind around this case."

Tick pulled the carafe out and stuck his mug under the stream of coffee, then repeated the act with Cookie's. Taking a cautious sip of the steaming brew, he watched Cookie add an inordinate amount of sugar and cream. "Lord, Cookie, would you like a little coffee with your sugar rush?"

Cookie chuckled, stirring. "So Falconetti's okay, huh?"

Better than okay. Spectacular. Incredible. Mind blowing. And more capable of pissing him off than any woman he'd ever met. More capable of hurting him without trying, too. "What do you mean?"

"She was in bad shape Saturday night, but she didn't look any the worse for wear yesterday when y'all were liplocked in the Tank and Tummy parking lot."

"I swear, if I hear one word about that in the county, I'll—"

"I ain't going to say anything. I might want to embarrass you, but not her."

Tick stared at him, struck by the real respect in Cookie's voice. "You like her, don't you?"

"She's all right for a Fibbie. What she sees in you I'll never understand." Cookie sucked the end of his coffee spoon and laid it aside. "She did you, didn't she?"

Tick choked. Coughing, he grabbed a napkin and wiped his mouth. "What?"

"You have 'just got laid' all over you." Cookie surveyed him. "And what looks like a good case of mad, too."

With a glance at the door and the porch behind, Tick sighed. "From where those prints are? You can see everything on my porch."

"Yeah? And...oh. Shit. So some of the action happened out there."

"Yeah." Tick dragged a hand down his face. "I don't think it was a damn poacher in my woods."

"Well, that explains why you're wound so tight. I was wondering, if you'd gotten laid by a woman whose voice is a wet dream, what was up to make you so pissy."

"Would you stop referring to it that way? I wasn't looking to get laid. I was looking for—"

"Oh, shit. If you say love and forever, or anything else along those lines, I'll puke, Lamar. Seriously."

"Why do I bother trying to talk to you?" Tick said with an irritated grunt. "You'd never get it."

"Man, I don't want to get it." Cookie snorted but sobered quickly. "Having someone watching your house is not good, Tick. It could be our guy, and I doubt he's got his eyes on you."

Tick's head jerked up. He didn't want to know what Cookie was getting at, although his mind had already gone there, too. "What do you mean?"

Cradling his mug, Cookie settled onto an island stool. "He's been laughing at us for days, probably, if not weeks. I'm not completely sold on Falconetti's theory that he's a cop, but somehow, I think the son of a bitch knows everything we're doing. Like he's watching and laughing. In his head, he's calling us country bumpkin county mounties, probably. Not intimidated by us in the least. Your girl? Now she could be a challenge."

"She's not—" Oh, hell, why deny it? He grabbed the cordless phone. And right now, he didn't actually know where his girl was. Before he could punch in Caitlin's number, the device shrilled to life. "Calvert."

"Do you by any chance have my cell?" Her husky voice washed over him, bringing with it a surge of relief. She was annoyed but safe, obviously.

"No, why?"

"When I packed up this morning, I couldn't find it." In the background, he heard a rustling—paper, clothing, maybe. Her voice dropped away for a moment and came back. "I thought I'd left it on your porch table, but it wasn't there. I wondered if maybe you'd picked it up."

Sheer dread skittered over his nerves. He pinched the bridge of his nose. "No, I haven't seen it. Where are you?"

"Um..." Again, her voice faded. "My hotel, trying to get dressed. I went for a run. Am I late?"

"No, actually, I'm not at the office yet." He met Cookie's steady gaze. "Listen, Cait, I want you to be careful. More careful than you normally would."

A pause hummed over the line. "Why?"

Lord, he didn't want to tell her this. "Someone was outside the house last night. In the woods."

"Outside." Horrified realization slipped into her tone. "Oh, God."

"Yeah." His stomach knotted. "It could just be a poacher, a local kid maybe, but I want you to be...alert."

"You don't think it's a poacher or a kid."

Lying wasn't an option. "No. Just be careful, precious."

"I will. I'll see you at the station."

He dropped the phone in the charging cradle and frowned.

"What?"

He looked up and met Cookie's incisive gaze. "She can't find her cell. She thought she'd left it on the porch last night. It could be somewhere else but—"

"But we didn't find Amy or Sharon or Vontressa's cell phones. Anywhere."

"Yeah. Exactly."

"She can take care of herself, Tick. You know that."

He did, only...he hadn't been there once before to stop her being hurt. A shudder worked its way over him.

"So what about the tape?" Cookie jerked his chin toward the television. "Was Johnson on it?"

Regret stirred in Tick's stomach again. "Yeah. Would you

believe I talked to her? Gave her directions."

"And knowing you, you're wracked with guilt."

Voices outside heralded Jeff's return. Tick glanced through the glass of his kitchen door to see Stanton standing on the brick walk, with Jeff showing him the completed casts.

Eyeing his former partner's grim expression, Tick frowned. "What is he doing here?"

"He doesn't look happy," Cookie said, smirking. "What did you do?"

"Who knows?" He had a good idea, though.

"Probably knows where you've been dipping your wick. Can't stand her, can he?"

"No." With a sigh, Tick grabbed his mug and crossed to open the door. "Want some coffee, Stanny-boy?"

"Not really." Stanton strode up the steps.

"I'm going to take a look at those casts." Cookie shot a less-than-sympathetic look at Tick and rose. "They look like crap from here."

"They are crap," Stanton said. "Too smudgy to do anything with."

Tick settled onto one of the two stools facing the island and waited.

Stanton crossed his arms over his chest and rested a hip against the counter. "Tell me Falconetti's coming up with something."

Oh, here they went again. "She's working on it. She wants to send our evidence to the FBI lab, and she's right. We'll get the results back a heck of a lot quicker. Kimberly Johnson's partner brought us a ton of information last night, and we've been wading through—"

"Is she profiling or investigating?"

Tick knew that snide tone and he didn't like it. "A victimology involves investigating. You know that as well as I do. Back off."

"You're sleeping with her again, aren't you?"

"Stan, that's really not—"

"Her rental car was here last night and y'all didn't even

bother to move it from the station lot the night before. It doesn't take a rocket scientist to figure out what's going on. And believe me, Troy Lee is all over this one."

Irritation licked at Tick's gut. He didn't have to explain his actions to anyone. "I'm allowed to have a personal life. You know what that is, right? It's what I do on my own time."

Stanton leaned forward. "It's not what you're doing, it's *who* you're doing. You're a commanding officer in this department. These guys, not to mention the community, watch every move you make. She's a visiting agent who hasn't been here a week yet, and y'all are already in the sack."

"You're the sheriff, and you're doing the public defender."

A flush darkened Stanton's face, and his jaw tightened. "That's not the same thing."

Tick tried to appear relaxed, not like he wanted to go for his best friend's throat. "Isn't it? Where was Autry Holton's car parked last night? Her drive or yours?"

Stanton slapped a hand on the counter. "Damn it, Tick, we're not talking about Autry."

"Why? Because she's more deserving of respect than Cait is?" The words emerged with cold, deadly precision.

"I did not say that."

"No, but you sure as hell implied it. Go ahead and say it, Stan. What's really on your mind?"

"I'm worried about you."

"You have a weird way of showing it."

"Would you shut up and listen a minute? You're getting in over your head, and I'd rather not watch you get kicked in the gut."

"What are you talking about?"

"What are you going to do when she leaves?"

The question hit him like the kick to the gut Stanton alluded to. What would he do? "I—"

"Think about it, Tick. She's a bureau profiler, one of ten. It's a career that's taken her a decade to build. What does this place have to offer her?" Stanton's voice was intense, concerned.

Him. It offered her him, but would that be enough? Damn, he needed a cigarette. "I don't know."

"Then what the hell are you doing?"

He was doing the only thing he could—falling for her again and making the most of the time he had. His feelings weren't going to go away, and he couldn't let her leave without at least trying to convince her they had a future. "You don't understand."

"No, I don't. I really don't want to, either. It's like watching you put yourself in the line of fire, knowing you're going to get your ass blown away and not being able to do anything about it." Stanton glowered. "Damn it, Tick, this is the same woman who jeopardized your safety when you were down in Mississippi."

Tick stiffened. "What? She wouldn't—"

"She called me to try to contact you while you were gone. And she knew the risks involved in getting a message to you. It was hell trying to get her to back off." Stanton shook his head, disparagement heavy in his voice. "Know what that tells me? That what she wants is more important than protocol, than your life."

A tap on the door forestalled Tick's reply and Jeff stuck his head in the room. "Just thought you two would like to know we can hear every word out here. Cookie's laying odds on who's going to throw the first punch."

"Great." Tick rubbed a hand over his face.

"And dispatch is calling, Sheriff. Bubba Bostick wants to see you before you go in this morning."

"Thanks, Jeff." Stanton waited until the younger man was gone. He fixed Tick with a steady look. "Just be careful."

Once he had all of them gone, he shut off the coffee maker, rinsed the carafe and mugs and started gathering together the investigative material Caitlin hadn't taken with her.

Her presence hovered around him in the quiet room, her voice echoing in his head, snatches of conversation.

How would you react in the same situation?

Yesterday, she'd tossed the casual question at him while they talked about Kimberly Johnson's inability to have children.

That conversation had been anything but hypothetical. Cold certainty nailed him like an unexpected fist to the jaw. She'd been gauging his reaction, even then, worried that her possible infertility would change the way he saw her.

The odds are against it.

His muscles tightened like someone had kicked him, hard. When he'd seen that broken condom, he'd worried. In the back of his mind, he'd been laying out a future with her, but he hadn't wanted to start with the stress of an unplanned pregnancy. But if Caitlin couldn't have children, there would be no pregnancy, planned or unplanned, in their future.

The reality still didn't want to sink in. He stared at the shelf by his television, which held a small collection of snapshots featuring his nieces and nephews, among them one of him holding Charlie when she was just hours old, another of his sister Ruthie's youngest at six months, the newest a Polaroid of Carter in the hospital. Everyone kept commenting on how much Carter looked like him, but the truth was all Calvert babies looked alike.

The sense of loss took another punch at him. Caitlin couldn't have children. For them, there wouldn't be a Calvert baby who looked like all the others. He would never know what it felt like to make love to her, knowing he might make her pregnant. Her body wouldn't swell with his unborn child.

He speared his fingers through his hair, struggling with the confused jumble of emotions rushing through him. This was why she kept pulling away from him.

Maybe she didn't want to cheat him.

The scary thing was it made a weird kind of sense. In her position, he'd be tempted to do the same, to attempt to protect her from loss and disappointment by giving her up. Her sense of self-preservation had to be at work as well. She was afraid his feelings for her would change.

He didn't want that to happen. He didn't want it to matter this much. He wanted to say, "I'm falling in love with you, and nothing can change that." But he wasn't sure it didn't and he couldn't hurt her with his doubts. What he needed was time and distance to put his confused feelings into perspective.

What he had was a job to do and two funerals to attend.

So much for perspective.

Chapter Nine

"Cookie, you know what bothers me the most?" Caitlin sat on the edge of the conference table, staring at their notes on the large dry-erase board. The process of breaking down leads and evidence had kept them busy all morning, and she was glad for the diversion. She needed something to think about other than Tick Calvert, who sat in his office with Jeff Schaefer, comparing Amy Gillabeaux's phone records to her address book. Something to think about other than the possibility that someone had watched them the night before. The idea made every millimeter of her skin crawl.

She could only think of one person who might do that on purpose. Having his interest left her feeling sickly nervous.

"Not having a clue who this guy is?" Cookie lounged in a chair, eyes closed.

"That, too." She drummed her fingers on the table's edge. "Sharon Ingler's car."

With a rough sigh, he sat up. "You know, that gets me. Always has."

"How far can you drive a vehicle once it slings a rod? Is it immediately out of operation?"

"It could go a couple of miles, but once you'd shut it off, you wouldn't get it started again."

"So when, how and why was that car moved?" She swiveled, sorting through the stack of reports beside her. "Did we get any prints off the car?"

"Yeah. Tick's and Jeff's. Oh, and Bobby Gene Butler, which is to be expected, since he towed it."

She blew out an exasperated breath. Tick, at least, should know better. "Don't they know what gloves are? What about Amy's car?"

He unwrapped a piece of gum and popped it in his mouth. "Remembered the gloves that time. Only prints belonged to Amy's family."

"All right, tell me this. There had to be other traffic on the highway the night Sharon disappeared. Did you check in any way to see who would have been out there?"

"We set up a roadblock, talked to all the locals who use the road regularly." He folded the foil wrapper into an intricate pyramid and flicked it into the trashcan.

"Did you keep a list?"

"What do you think?" He flipped through the file in front of him and pulled out a single sheet of paper. "There you go."

"This is great." She ran a finger down the page of typed names and addresses. A few had notes beside them, written in Tick's slashing handwriting. "Want to go out and knock on some doors?"

"I'm game." With a teasing leer, he slumped in the chair, his gaze roving over her. "But I'm up for just about anything."

She glowered at him, suppressing a grin. He was hopeless. "Everything boils down to sex with you, doesn't it?"

"Hate to break it to you, Falconetti, but everything between a woman and a man boils down to sex."

"Really?" She lifted an eyebrow at him. Sure, sex was an important component, but it wasn't everything. "Somehow I get the feeling you're going to try to enlighten me."

"I don't care how smart or 'enlightened' a guy might be— sooner or later, he's going to do his thinking with his dick."

"That's an old cliché, Cook."

"Sure it is. But it's true—why do you think it's a cliché? Look at Calvert. He's got a brain quicker than a greyhound, but that's not what he's thinking with lately."

"We're not going there."

"Oh, face it, Falconetti. The poor guy's so hot for you his brain is fried. His focus is not on this case—it's on you. If working this case gets him close to you, he'll do it."

"You—"

"Now, one of two things can happen—either you give him a little and that'll break the tension, or you don't, you leave, and the tension goes away. He'll get back those lightning-quick thought processes we all love so much because either way that dog's been collared, if you know what I mean."

"Unfortunately, I do." Ice dripped from each word. And Calvert's brain should be in perfect working order this morning, but damned if she wanted Cookie to know that. "No self-respecting woman would ever get involved with you."

"Who said I wanted a self-respecting woman? They're no fun."

"Neanderthal."

He chuckled. "Yeah. But I'm also a damn good cop."

Another smile tugged at her mouth, but she firmed her lips. She hated to admit it, but he was right. She tapped a fingernail on the list of interviewees. "Who would you start with?"

"Nate Holton. Get him out of the way while he's still sober."

"Did you get much out of him when you interviewed him before?"

"Yeah, Tick almost got shot. Jeff ended up doing the interview, but he didn't get a lot of information."

"Dislikes cops, does he?"

Contempt twisted Cookie's mouth. "Nate dislikes pretty much everybody, but he's jealous of Tick."

"Why?"

"Tick's daddy and Virgil Holton were big buddies. Virgil tends to treat Tick like the son he never had, if you get my meaning."

"I do."

Cookie shifted in his chair, hands folded behind his head. "And then there was Helen."

She darted a look at him. "Helen?"

"Nate's wife. She took off a few weeks ago, took the kids with her. She was a good mother, too." He tilted the chair back. "Tried to be a good wife. Nate can be a mean drunk, and we answered a lot of domestic calls at their place."

"That's not the entire story."

"Nate swears Tick helped Helen get away—gave her money, moved her stuff. I don't know for sure if he did or not, but yeah, he probably helped her. He has a soft spot for kids. And pretty young blondes, which Helen definitely was."

"Oh, please, Cookie. He's not the type to date another man's wife, and you know it."

"Yeah, I know, but it's fun to push your buttons. You're awful cute when you're jealous, Falconetti. Makes those Irish-green eyes of yours glitter like crazy. I'll bet you can turn on the mean real quick."

"Keep it up and I'll give you an example of turning on the mean."

"Just for me?"

"Yes, and you won't like it."

"Wanna bet? You don't know me that well. I *like* mean women."

"Shut up, Cookie." He was irrepressible, a lot like General Beauregard, her grandfather's favorite beagle—always nipping at her ankles. "Do you want to drive, or shall I?"

"Hmmm. Putting you in the driver's seat could be fun, but I thought you were going to Amy Gillabeaux's funeral."

"I am." She checked her watch, frowning. Ten twenty already. Scheduled for eleven, the funeral was sure to draw a massive crowd.

"If we're going, we need to leave." Tick spoke from the doorway and she glanced over her shoulder at him. He couldn't have heard much of the conversation. At least she hoped not. Heat flushed her face, but his impassive expression revealed nothing.

Exactly as it had all morning. He'd been quiet and reserved, seemed uncomfortable in her presence. Everything between them had shifted, changed, and she didn't think it was because of the lovemaking. She'd told him she might be incapable of having his child, and already he was pulling away. Hold on to him, he'd said. Sure. And what was she supposed to do when he decided to let her go?

"You have a phone call at the front desk." Tick pointed at

the multiline phone sitting in the middle of the table. "I told Lydia to transfer it in here. You need to make it quick, though."

"Thanks." The phone buzzed and she lifted the receiver as Tick and Cookie made themselves scarce. "Falconetti."

"Hey, it's me," Gina said. "God, where are you? I've been calling your cell all morning. It's going directly to voice mail."

"I can't find it. What's up?"

"I've started on your background checks. Began with Reed and Calvert. They're both clean. Running the ones with Georgia law enforcement records now. I can't believe I let you talk me into running this many checks. Cook, Schaefer, Monroe and two of the others...can't remember the names...may take a little longer. They worked in Florida, and some virus has taken down their entire database."

"Thanks. I owe you. You're the best, Gina."

"Yeah, yeah, I know. I want to borrow your Blahniks tonight."

"They're not even your size."

"Who cares? I'm just wearing them to dinner and maybe a little dancing, and it's not like I plan to keep 'em on all night. My roommate is in Georgia chasing a serial killer. I can bring Sergeant Spence home and be as loud as I want."

"You're crazy." Caitlin laughed. "And it's not you being loud that bothers me. It's hearing Spence wheezing in the throes of passion through those thin damn walls of ours. Fine, wear the shoes. And let me know when you have anything else."

"Sure thing, partner."

She dropped the receiver in the cradle and reached for her portfolio. With Tick already tense, she didn't want to keep him waiting.

The latch on the leather binder wasn't secure and the contents spilled across the floor.

"Damn it," she muttered and bent to retrieve the reports and notes scattered over the dingy tile.

"Jesus H. Christ, what's up with Calvert this morning? Shit, he just bit my head off." A young male voice carried through from the hallway beyond the squad room. "You'd think if he was finally getting laid that he'd be in a better mood—"

"Shut up, Troy Lee." Cookie's tone brooked no argument. "Clock out and go home."

Damn, damn, damn. She finished gathering her papers. So their involvement was all over the department. She shouldn't be surprised; they'd been less than discreet. Was that the reason for Tick's terse distraction?

Or was it the possible infertility after all? God, she hated not knowing where she stood with him. And if it was the infertility that had him pulling back, what would happen when she told him about their baby?

With everything shoved haphazardly in her portfolio, she hurried from the building. Her attention trained on trying to straighten out the painstaking notes she'd taken on Amy's diary, she collided with a deputy jogging up the steps.

"Excuse me."

"I'm sorry."

Firm hands steadied her and she looked up. Dark hair, a chiseled face, the iciest blue eyes she'd ever seen. She dropped her gaze to his nametag.

C. Parker.

"Agent Falconetti, right? The FBI profiler?" He let his hands fall and tilted his chin, expression not softening. "I've heard a lot about you."

She bet he had. She stepped away. "Excuse me, Deputy. I have somewhere to be."

"Cait, come on. This traffic is going to be a bitch." Annoyance sharpened Tick's drawl. At the bottom of the steps, he jingled his keys.

Not sparing Parker a glance, she moved down the steps to Tick's side. He lifted a finger in acknowledgement to Parker's "Later, Tick". Her nape prickled with awareness as they walked to Tick's truck, her intuition whispering that if she turned, she would find Parker still standing on the steps, watching them.

He could be the one. Hell, any of them could. She hated this, too, not knowing where the threat lay.

"How well do you know him?" At the truck, she shifted as Tick opened the passenger door, placing his tall body between her and Parker.

"Parker? He's a good cop."

"That's not what I asked." She latched her seat belt. "I asked how well you knew him."

"Not very. He's new to us and he's a private guy. I like what I have seen though, which is more than I can say for Troy Lee." He moved to shut the door. "We've got to get going or we'll be late."

Tick remained withdrawn during the drive to the church, silence and tension coating the air in his truck. Cars spilled out of the parking lot, lining both sides of the country road. A few trucks and SUVs were parked in an adjacent field. Tick swung into a space between a Camaro and an Expedition.

Caitlin held him back, watching the last few straggling mourners enter the church. His jaw tightening, he glanced down at her hand on his arm, but didn't move. They were among the last to slip inside. Mourners packed every pew, and several people stood along the outer aisles. No one looked their way.

She tilted her head, peering at him from beneath her lashes. "Is the whole town here?"

"Looks that way." The words were short and clipped, his breath stirring the hair at her temple. A middle-aged woman squeezed by them on her way to a pew, forcing Caitlin into closer contact with him.

She turned toward the front where the immediate family sat and then let her gaze travel back along the rows, pausing if she saw a familiar face or something that nudged at her intuition. When the congregation stood for the opening prayer, she didn't lower her head, but continued tracking the crowd, aware Tick was doing the same behind her.

Near the middle of the church, Stanton Reed stood beside a woman, her sun-streaked chestnut head barely reaching his shoulder. An older woman was next to her, a distinguished gray-haired man at her side. One pew behind them stood Tori, dark head bent in reverence, with her mother to her left and Jeff Schaefer to her right.

A young man hovering inside the door caught Caitlin's attention. Unlike the other mourners wearing their Sunday best, he wore jeans and a pullover shirt and kept running his hands down his legs. Long hair that didn't appear to have seen shampoo in weeks brushed his collar, kicking up in greasy wisps. Keith Lawson, the boy from Vontressa's picture album.

The prayer ended, the mourners sitting with a soft wave of rustling. Caitlin touched Tick's arm and lowered her voice to a breath of a whisper. "Tick. Look."

"I saw."

The minister launched a glowing description of Amy and the joy she found in everyday life. A sob rose from the first row, where Eloise Gillabeaux sat huddled into her husband's side.

Caitlin closed her eyes briefly, sympathy stabbing through her. If losing her unborn baby was devastating, how much worse to lose a child loved and nurtured to young adulthood.

When she opened her eyes again, Keith Lawson had disappeared.

Caitlin tilted her head toward Tick. "I'll be right back."

Outside, Keith paced the neatly trimmed grass in front of the church, hands shaking as he tried to light a cigarette. He turned at the soft click of her heels on the brick steps. Caitlin smiled, straightening her navy suit jacket. "Some crowd, huh?"

His eyes betrayed a bitterness lurking below the surface. "Yeah. Bunch of damned hypocrites. All they could do was talk about her while she was alive, but now they're crying like—"

He bit the words off, and Caitlin nodded. Sometimes silence was the best interview question.

Eyeing her with distrust, he jerked his head toward the church. "You one of her fancy Atlanta cousins?"

She produced her credentials for his inspection. "No. I'm with the FBI. I'm assisting the sheriff's department with their investigation—"

"Yeah." His short laugh was a derisive snort. "Don't expect a lot of help from them."

"Why is that?"

"Because it was probably one of them." He tossed the cigarette away and glared, his gaze hot with resentment. "But you wouldn't believe that, would you? All you cops stick together."

"I'm not one of them." She lowered her voice to a

conspiratorial tone. "Ever watch detective shows? The local cops hate when the FBI shows up."

"Yeah, I seen that."

"You and Amy were close." Caitlin made sure it came out a statement of fact. Right now, she wanted him firmly on her side.

"Yeah."

"I want to find the person who did this to her. I think you can help me."

He glowered at the imposing brick façade behind them. "Not here."

"Then let's go for a walk."

They strolled into the adjacent cemetery with its softly rolling hills, where Chandler County's dead reposed under ancient moss-laden oaks interspersed with the occasional pine tree.

"You said you and Amy were close?"

"We were, at least until this summer. She...changed."

"Changed? How?"

He shook his hair out of his eyes. "She used to want to hang out, do stuff, you know? Even though her daddy didn't like me, she used to invite me over to swim or whatever. Then she just stopped. Didn't want to talk to me or see me unless she needed something."

Stopping in front of a large family plot enclosed by rusted wrought iron, he pulled out his cigarettes and offered her one.

She shook her head. "Keith, why did you say someone with the sheriff's department killed her?"

"She was screwing one of them." He blew out a long stream of smoke and a couple of obscenities. "And if that son of a bitch killed her, they'll protect him."

Caitlin had to ask, although she already knew the answer. If Amy didn't name her lover in her diary, she surely wouldn't have told this boy. "I don't suppose you know who in the department she was seeing?"

"No, she wouldn't tell me. She just liked to rub it in my face because I didn't get in at the police academy. She had a thing for that Calvert guy, though. Probably because messing around with him would make her daddy crazy." He pushed his hair

196

back, the oily strands clinging together.

With a slight nod, Caitlin wrapped her fingers around a finial on the fence corner. "Anything else? Any other secrets she was keeping that you know of?"

"She banged up the side of her car and didn't want her daddy to know it—I just finished a paint-and-body course out at the tech school. I fixed it up for her. She'd hang around talking to me while I worked on it."

"How did she mess up her car?"

He shrugged. "She said she backed into another car in a parking lot. She didn't report it or nothing. She'd had some speeding tickets and her daddy told her if one more thing happened with that car, he'd take the keys."

She pulled one of her cards, scribbled her hotel extension on it and handed it to him. "If you remember anything—even if it doesn't seem important, I want you to call me."

"Yeah." He shoved the vellum rectangle in his back pocket. He waved a hand toward the church, where people gathered out front. "Just find the son of a bitch who hurt her."

He stalked back to the church and to his turquoise low-rider pickup, skirting the other mourners. From a distance, she eyed the group. Stanton and Tick walked away, deep in conversation. Within moments, Schaefer and Cookie joined them, along with a couple of other deputies. A shiver tickled her spine, raising gooseflesh on her arms, despite the hot summer sun. This was going to be ugly before it was over.

Dozens of law enforcement officers, including jailers and dispatchers. One of them could be a cold-blooded killer. And one of them was the man she was falling for.

Tick walked toward the cemetery gate, hands in his pockets, his charcoal suit jacket falling open. Sunlight glittered off the badge clipped to his belt. She'd give almost anything to know what thoughts lay behind his unsmiling expression.

He inclined his head. "Cookie says you want to reinterview witnesses. We have time for a couple before Vontressa's funeral."

Once they were on their way, he drove with one hand, often with just his wrist hooked over the wheel. His handheld radio emitted the crackling dialogue of a rural, although busy, department. Unease tugged at her stomach. She glanced at him. He stared at the road, his face set in tense lines. Where was the man who'd loved her so well last night?

"So what did Keith Lawson have to say?" Tick turned onto Old Lonely Road.

Grateful, she seized the distraction. "He was infatuated with Amy. Fixed some body damage to her car for free."

He snorted. "For free? More likely he fixed it, and she gave him a little to do it. Did he say anything else?"

Keith's insistence that Amy's killer had been a Chandler County deputy whispered through her mind. All suspects, including, if she was completely honest, the man sitting in the driver's seat. "He swears Amy was seeing someone in the sheriff's department."

"Oh, crap." He smacked a hand against the steering wheel. "I didn't need to hear that."

"I'm sure. About like I didn't need to hear him mention your name as the person she was interested in 'messing around with'."

He looked her way, his jaw tight. "I was not—"

"I know. I didn't say you were." She straightened her skirt. "But I think you have to be prepared to deal with the way your name keeps coming up during this investigation."

The truck bottomed out on a couple of deep ruts before he pulled to a stop in front of a dingy white-and-green singlewide trailer. A small deck had been tacked on the front, but looked as lopsided as the mailbox. The grass was more than ankle-high, except for the circular bare track worn down by a sad-looking mutt tied to a small tree at the end of the trailer.

Caitlin glanced at the list. "Which one is this?"

"Nathaniel Holton. His daddy's a local judge and his sister's the county public defender."

"I take it he didn't go to law school." She climbed out of the truck and followed him to the steps, looking for snakes as she walked. The mangy dog woofed at them a couple of times, half-heartedly.

"Barely made it through high school. He tries to farm, does a little truck-driving on the side, but he's got so many DUIs it's a wonder anyone will hire him."

As they started up the steps, he unsnapped his holster. Caitlin felt under her jacket and did the same. At the top of the steps, Tick put his shoulder against the wall and reached over, banging on the door with his fist.

No sound came from the trailer, but the blinds in the door's small window moved slightly. Tick hammered on the door again. "Nate! Open up. It's Tick. I'm not serving a warrant. We just need to talk to you."

The door opened a crack and a young man, his chiseled face marred by a scraggly beard, peeked out. "We?"

Tick jerked a thumb in Caitlin's direction. "This is Agent Falconetti, FBI. She's looking into Sharon Ingler's death. We want to talk to you, that's all."

He regarded them with equal suspicion and belligerence. "I'm busy."

Caitlin smiled. "We'll only take a few minutes of your time."

With a huff, he swung the door open and waved his arm in an elaborate flourish. "Come on in."

The dark interior smelled of stale garbage, sour alcohol and unwashed clothing. Nate pushed a pile of clothes in an indeterminate state of cleanliness off the couch. "Have a seat. I'm gonna get a beer."

Caitlin glanced at the stained upholstery and forced herself to sit. She'd have her suit dry cleaned before she wore it again. Tick sat next to her, distaste curling his lip. The smooth fabric of his slacks brushed the bare skin above her knee.

Nate returned, popped opened a fresh beer and dropped into the vinyl recliner. He scratched his bare chest. "So what do you want to know?"

Tick leaned back, stretching his arm along the back of the couch, propping his ankle on his knee. "You told Jeff you saw Sharon's car on the road that night."

Nate's chin jutted with hostility. "Yeah? So?"

Caitlin crossed one leg over the other, resting her hands in her lap. "Were you working?"

"I was driving a load of chickens."

"I've heard that's difficult—with the load shifting and all."

He relaxed in the chair, warming to the subject. "It can be. I've seen guys dump a whole load before."

"You sound very experienced. So it's second nature to you, handling that truck."

He took a swig of his beer, nodding. "Yeah, I guess it is."

"I would really appreciate it if you'd tell me what you saw that night." Another perfect bureau smile. "It's just so much better than trying to read someone else's report."

Nate threw an arm over his head, exposing an inordinate amount of underarm hair. "Well, I'd just picked up a load of chickens from Ash Hardison's place."

She pulled out her notepad and Montblanc. "Do you mind if I take a few notes?"

He waved permission. Another swig from the can and he wiped his wrist across his mouth. "Anyway, I was headed out to the chicken plant. On my way back I saw the car sitting off on the side of the road. It was empty and I didn't think nothing about it. People break down out here all the time."

She looked up. "About what time was that?"

"Quarter to ten or so."

"And do you remember where you saw the car? Any landmarks or anything?"

"It was right at the twenty-third mile marker."

She jotted a note and met his bleary gaze. "Did you notice anyone else on the road? Pass any cars coming or going?"

He grimaced as though he had an appointment with the Queen of England and her questions were delaying it. "Hell, I don't know...I passed a sheriff's car going the other way. An empty chicken truck going out to pick up another load at Hardison's." He waved a hand in Tick's direction, active dislike flaring in his eyes. "Oh, yeah, and him going the same way I was. He had his boat hooked up and I went around him."

She wrote down the information, casting a quick glance at Tick's stony face. "We won't take up any more of your time. Thank you for talking with us."

Nate took the card she proffered and flicked it into the array of beer cans and empty potato chip bags on the coffee table. "You can find your way out, right?"

Outside, she dragged in deep breaths of fresh air and laughed. "I've been at crime scenes that smelled better."

"Yeah." Scowling, Tick waited for her to fasten her seat belt before starting the truck. "What the hell was that, anyway?"

"What?"

"That smile you kept giving him. And the flattery—"

"Did you see Ingler's car?"

"What?" He shot an irritated look in her direction. "No. I was on my way back from the lake and passed through at about eight thirty. It wasn't there. Dispatch called me back out at around quarter to one when Chris checked the car."

"How long does it take to unload one of those chicken trucks?"

"Why don't you ask Nate? He's the expert."

"Why don't you stop being an ass and answer the question?"

"An hour, maybe two, depending on the number of workers. Why?"

"Just wondering if his time frame checks out."

"It does. And so does his story. I talked to Ash and the plant foreman after Schaefer interviewed Nate. Besides, he's not smart enough to pull off something like these murders. He'd screw it up like he does everything else."

"You can't stand him either, can you?"

He glanced her way, his expression dark and sullen. "Cookie has a big mouth. What, you don't want to ask me if I helped Helen leave him?"

"It doesn't matter if you did or not. It's irrelevant to this case." She struggled to keep her tone noncommittal. What she really wanted to know was whether or not he'd been interested in the cute little blonde who was already a great mother.

What she *really* wanted to know was what he thought about the fact she might never be a mother at all.

CR

Hands in his pockets, Tick leaned a shoulder against a column at the far edge of the church's porch. In the hot, still air, no leaves moved on the pecan trees surrounding the small clapboard building. A trickle of sweat ran between his shoulder blades to pool at the small of his back. Pockets of mourners gathered under the trees, waving funeral home fans in a vain attempt to alleviate the heat.

Beneath one of those trees, Caitlin stood with two of Vontressa's cousins. Sympathy softened her face, a genuine smile flitting across the curve of her lips. Damn, but he loved that smile, the way it shaped her mouth and lit her eyes.

She was the one.

He'd wondered if the infertility, knowing he might never make her pregnant, would affect his feelings for her. Hell, anybody who knew him knew he looked forward to being a father, raising a family in his grandmother's house. The goal held importance for him, and he'd always assumed he'd be raising Calvert kids who looked like all the rest. Now? Now looking at Caitlin, he had his answer.

He couldn't imagine any other woman in his life.

If that meant he lived without becoming a father, so be it. Because one thing was for sure—he didn't see himself fathering another woman's child. So maybe that meant he'd redefine having a family. Maybe all he needed was the woman in front of him, filling every day of the rest of their lives with that incredible smile of hers.

Now, the problem lay in convincing Caitlin that the infertility didn't matter, that she could gamble on him and he'd never hurt her. That he could deal with the darkness she danced in, as long as she let him be her light.

"Man, she has you whipped already." Thumbs hitched in his belt, Cookie stopped beside him. "You should see the look on your face."

"Cut it out, Cookie." He shrugged, a tight, irritable movement. His suit sat too heavily on his shoulders, but maybe it was his own unease, his dissatisfaction, weighing him down.

Cookie jerked his head in Caitlin's direction. "Read her initial profile, that little list do-hickey she did."

Tick grunted. He hadn't read it yet. He'd been too busy

getting his mind blown and then his gut tied in knots. Oh, and watching her smile at Nate Holton as she flattered him. That had been a fun little way to kill some time. "Yeah?"

Cookie nodded, his expression serious for once. "Yeah. She thinks the guy is all about control. Can't connect with women except on a superficial level, has issues with his mother, probably too close to her with some underlying anger or hatred. For a second, I thought she was profiling you."

"Funny." Tick shot him a look. "Or you."

"Superficial." Cookie grinned, unrepentant. "Yep, that's me."

"...control issues." Jeff's voice, even pitched low, carried from the church's tiny foyer to Tick's right. "I could have come up with that."

Troy Lee murmured in reply, his words indistinct.

Brows lifted, Tick glanced at Cookie, who shrugged. "He's dissing your girl. I think Stanton's rubbing off on him. Sheriff's been bitching about her for two days."

"Stan's a control freak."

"No." Cookie feigned a shocked expression and ruined it by smirking. "And so is she."

"She took over one of his cases not long after we were out of Quantico. He's never forgotten it. And you know Jeff wants those lieutenant's bars. He's just kissing up."

"Seems like he'd be remembering who puts the department schedule together." He nudged Tick's ribs. "Or who will do his performance review before he gets those bars. I'd be kissing *your* ass."

Tick winced. "Really didn't need that mental picture, Cookie."

With a soft laugh, Cookie rubbed a finger over his mouth. "Yeah, it's pretty plain who you do want kissing your ass."

That particular mental picture sent a pleasurable shiver through him. "Shut up, would you? Remember where we are."

"Of course, Schaefer may not be worried about you. Probably figures if he makes Tori happy, you'll be happy, y'know?"

A frown tugged at Tick's brows. "She brought him to

Mama's Sunday."

"Whoa. Big commitment there." A couple of kids chased each other around one of the pecan trees. Cookie prodded his shoulder. "And who did you take to your mama's house Sunday?"

"You getting anywhere with that database? Any patterns?"

Cookie pulled his gum from his pocket. He popped a piece in his mouth, the scent of wintergreen exploding around them. "Just the people Sharon, Amy and Vontressa knew from high school. Keith Lawson, a couple others. They're easy to connect. It's that Jane Doe and Kimberly Johnson who throw the patterns off."

"Cait thinks they're all random. Victims of opportunity. Except for Amy." Tick watched as Caitlin spoke to Vontressa's Auntee Frances. She nodded, listening, and tucked her hair behind her ear.

Cookie regarded him, a knowing smirk on his face. "She's probably right. Could be mere coincidence that the three girls graduated together."

"Wish we knew where Vontressa actually disappeared. No signs of a struggle in the apartment, so I don't think she was taken from there."

"The cars could be the key. Money might be part of the motivation. Take the cars for parts or the black market, and the girls are just gravy."

"Wish you wouldn't put it that way." As a motive, it made sense, except...car thieves weren't usually people who knew to cleanse a body before dumping it. "Besides, that only explains Johnson and Vontressa. Their cars are the only ones missing. Doesn't hold true for Sharon and Amy."

A wave of mourners exited the church, including Miss Lauree, supported by two of her sons. Tick closed his eyes, trying to block out the grief on her face. Fury pulsed in him, a stinging heat that burned under his skin. Damn it, they would find this guy.

Standing around talking to Cookie wasn't getting the job done, though. Opening his eyes, he tagged Cookie's arm. People drifted to cars, along the way stopping to hug necks and share their grief. "Come on. Cait and I have interviews to finish up."

Cookie rolled his eyes. "And I have pages of names and numbers to finish going through. Why is it you get to hang out with Ms. Sex on a Stick and I'm banished to the war room?"

"Benefits of rank. And you're not her type."

"And you are? She's got old money written all over her. Hell, boy, her shoes cost more than your last set of tires."

Squinting, Tick examined the shoes in question. Navy slingbacks, an incredibly pointy toe, thin heels. And the most fantastic legs he'd even seen. "How do you know that?"

"Hey, I'm fashionably aware."

"You been reading *Cosmo* again?" Shaking his head, Tick jogged down the steps.

"Something like that." Cookie shrugged. "I googled her."

"You what?"

"Hell, I google everybody. Her family's loaded. Her father held fifty-one percent of Falcon Oil Refining when he died. Brother runs one of the most lucrative private security firms in the country. Their grandfather is real big in politics in Texas. Like I said, makes me wonder what she sees in you."

"Thanks a lot, *partner*."

Holding on to her daughter's arm, Vontressa's Auntee Frances moved to her car and left Caitlin standing alone under the spreading shade of the pecan tree. Joining her with Cookie on his heels, Tick resisted the urge to lay his hand along the small of her back.

She glanced over her shoulder at him. "Ready?"

More than she knew. Now all he had to do was convince her. "Whenever you are."

Cookie heaved an exaggerated sigh. "I guess I'm just going to head back to my dark little dungeon."

Caitlin laughed, the husky sound sending shivers over Tick. In the next second, her laugh faded into a startled exhale and she stumbled into Tick's side.

"Oh!" A hand on his chest, the other at his waist, she steadied herself, and he stared, all of his sensations shrinking to the space around them. A giggle rose between them, and he shook himself free of her magnetic pull and glanced down. One of Vontressa's nieces, her brother David's youngest daughter, grinned up at him, her smile missing a couple of pearly teeth.

"Hey, Mr. Tick." Neat braids swung around her face, the tiny beads holding the ends clicking together.

He grinned back. "Hey, Cartavia."

She tugged at his suit jacket. "Is Luke with you?"

He shook his head, knowing she'd sat in front of Chuck's oldest all through first grade. "Not today."

"Tell him I said hey." She bounded away, braids flying behind her.

He laughed and glanced at Caitlin. She stood, her expression carefully blank. His stomach performed a slow flip and he gestured after Cartavia, his chest tight. "Vontressa's niece. I know her daddy."

She nodded, but neither her face nor her posture relaxed. "She's adorable."

Cookie bumped Tick's shoulder. "Keep hanging out with him, Falconetti, and he can probably arrange for you to have a couple of adorable rugrats. You know, barefoot, pregnant, six kids and a singlewide."

Tick froze as a cold smile lifted her lips.

"Not likely, Cook. Tick? We have things to do." She turned and strode toward his truck.

Tick groaned. "Thanks a lot, Cookie."

"What did I say?"

He followed her, having trouble catching up despite the length of his stride. "Cait, wait up."

She didn't slow. He closed the distance and grasped her arm, pulling her around to face him. She stared up at him, her eyes narrowed. "Which witness are we interviewing next?"

He jerked a hand through his hair. They couldn't have this conversation here and he didn't relish trying to have it between interviews either. And she didn't look particularly receptive to anything he might say right now.

"Calvert?" She arched an elegant eyebrow. "Are we going or are we standing around here all day? I think we've given your deputies enough to talk about already."

"Yeah." He wanted to pull her close, whisper in her ear that she was everything that mattered. But she was right—sometimes the job had to come first. And judging from her expression, she'd knock him flat on his ass if he tried to touch her any time soon. "Let's go."

Chapter Ten

Several hours and twice as many interviews later, Caitlin surveyed the dry-erase board in the war room. She'd devoted an entire section to the information they'd gleaned from those interviews and spent another hour refining the outline, moving items, adding question marks, making connections. The second largest section was Amy's information, but the other victims' sections were almost as full.

Hunger clawed at her stomach and she recapped her marker, dropping it in the tray. A few leads looked promising, but there was nothing earthshaking before her.

"You think your partner can help us track down the car Amy backed into?" Intent on the charts, she startled at Tick's quiet voice. He made a neat stack of their files in the middle of the table.

"If the other person filed an insurance claim—and who wouldn't—and if it's in a computer somewhere, Bocaccio will find it." She'd tried to call Gina again earlier, but kept getting her voice mail. Caitlin stretched. Waiting wasn't always her strong suit.

He rubbed a hand over his neck, his face weary. "I'm starving. You want to get out of here for a little while?"

Relief cascaded through her. She'd missed his good-natured teasing throughout the day, missed *him*. Their gazes met, clung, and she smiled. "I'd like that."

"Why are Cookie and Chris listed under Amy's section?"

"The two speeding tickets she got in May, the ones her father was so upset about? They wrote them."

"Why is my name up there?"

"We talked about this, remember? Keith Lawson's statement?" She looked up at him. His suit jacket and tie had disappeared, the top two buttons on his shirt open. He appeared as tired and as covered with the invisible grime of a day's investigation as she felt. "And because two of the interviewees mentioned seeing you on the highway the night Sharon Ingler disappeared."

"Great. So I'm a possible suspect. I can't wait for the newspaper to get a hold of that." He grimaced and stared at the board a moment longer. "We can pick up our warrant for the fast-food place's security tape in Tallahassee tomorrow morning."

Brushing her hair back, she nodded. "Sounds good. And I want to talk to Bobby Gene Butler before we go."

He jerked his head toward the door. "Let's go get a bite. You have your choice of barbeque, Mexican or—"

"Investigator Calvert." The young man who sometimes worked the front desk burst through the door, out of breath, his eyes wide. "We have a problem downstairs."

As he related the situation before scurrying out again, Caitlin realized Tick wouldn't be going anywhere anytime soon. With a harried expression, Tick blew out a long, frustrated breath. "I'm sorry about this."

"It happens. Don't worry about it." She half-shrugged. He seriously worked too hard. Chief deputy-slash-investigator with an understaffed department or not, he couldn't keep running himself ragged like this. "I'm just going to work with this a little more, see if anything jumps out at me, then I may go back to the hotel."

"Don't work too late. Be careful when you leave." He cast a glance at the door and leaned in to brush a quick, sweet kiss over her lips. "See you later."

"Good night." A curious emptiness descended on the room with his departure, and she tried to concentrate on the patterns, her focus gone. At last, she gave up, gathered her things and headed to her hotel. She'd try again later.

A long, hot shower washed away the grime and some of the exhaustion, and a delivery of Chinese takeout took care of the hunger. But nothing—reading Amy's diary, reviewing autopsy reports, adding to her profile—dispelled the loneliness. In desperation, she changed into shorts and a T-shirt, slipped on her running shoes, and struck out for the small lake across the street from the hotel.

The run didn't help. An hour later, sweaty and frustrated, Caitlin tugged off her clothes and stepped into another hot shower. Her mind remained a confused jumble—case facts and Tick's voice bouncing around in her head.

Toweling off, she tried reaching Gina once more, with no success. Ten to one, her partner was boogieing down with the handsome Marine sergeant who was way too young for her.

A sharp knock on the door echoed through the hotel room, and she froze, instincts going on alert.

She discarded the towel and slid her arms into her short robe. With shaking hands, she tied the belt and went to the door, collecting her SIG along the way.

Another knock, more impatient this time. She peeked through the peephole and relaxed. Tick stood on the sidewalk and she swung the door open. He'd showered and changed, looking refreshed if still tired, and she wanted to snatch him inside the room.

"Hey," he drawled. The intensity in his dark eyes made her mouth go dry.

"Hey, yourself."

"I covered the jail." He rested an arm against the doorframe. "Figured I'd see if you were still hungry."

"Are you?"

"What do you think?"

"I think you look tired."

That slow, sexy grin of his bloomed on his face. "Maybe I should go to bed for a while."

Curling the fingers of her free hand around the open collar of his shirt, she smiled and tugged him forward. "Come inside with me, Lamar Eugene."

He jerked her into his embrace, and his lips came down on hers. Banked desire flared and she opened to him, slipping her arms around his neck.

A ragged sigh shaking his lean frame, he broke the kiss, nuzzling close to her ear. With one hand, he pushed the door shut behind them and fumbled the lock into place. She managed to make sure her gun hit the table and not the floor. His other hand tangled in her damp hair and he angled her face beneath his.

While he kissed her, his easy hold crept to her shoulders, the silky material of her robe sliding against her skin. His hands roamed over her arms and back in long, sweeping touches. "You're so beautiful."

The rough whisper shivered over her. She smiled, stroking inside the collar of his shirt. "You're not so bad—"

"No." He caressed the small of her back. "Not like that. Not tonight."

He lowered his mouth again, tasting and teasing. The hot, dragging ache in her stomach radiated out to become a moist heat between her thighs and a heaviness in her breasts. His clean scent enveloped her. She kneaded the tight, shifting muscles at his shoulders. What did he mean, not like that? The night before, he'd been playful, enthusiastic, creative. He'd made her feel like no other man ever had.

His tongue plundered her mouth, the erotic rhythm a reminder of having his body thrusting into hers. He cradled her hips and urged her closer. She burned hotter and held on. An urge to rub against him, take him fully inside her, filled her.

He was right; this was different. Every touch, each caress, held a single-minded intent—stealing her control, making her need him.

She fisted his shirt and pulled her head back, breaking the kiss. He stared at her, fiery desire lighting his dark eyes. Tilting her head, she tugged him toward the bed.

She expected him to tumble her down, the laughter and playfulness to take over and lead them into a sweet coming together. Instead, he eased her back and leaned over her, his gaze still burning. He didn't smile, but traced the line of her face with a finger. The simple caress shimmered over her, that fingertip traveling down the line of her throat, following the lapel of her robe to rest between her breasts, over her heart. Blood pulsed in her ears; he had to feel the thud under his hand.

He lowered his head, mouth teasing beneath her ear. One of his thighs slid between hers, the starched fabric of his khakis rough against her sensitized skin. She arched into him, needing more than his weight and the feel of his mouth on her skin. She needed everything, all of him.

His teeth rasped across the tender spot between her shoulder and neck, and he eased the robe open. She caught her breath, wanting his touch on her breasts, aching and heavy with anticipation. Desperate for the heat of skin on skin, she ran her hands down his chest and around his lean waist to tug his shirt free. At the first brush of her fingers on the sloping muscles of his back, he groaned.

He rose to his knees, long enough to strip the shirt over his head and toss it behind him, and she reached for him, wanting to learn the line of each tight tendon and muscle again. Instead, he caught her hands and placed her wrists above her head, his gaze hungry as it swept her body. She shifted under that look, feeling its weight as surely as if he'd run his hands along her form.

She moved a knee up the inside of his thigh and laughed lightly when his whole body jumped. "You're wearing too many clothes."

He stared down, thumbs caressing her wrists. "This isn't about me."

"Tick, I—"

He dipped his head to kiss her. "Let me, Cait," he murmured. "Let me love you tonight."

Her eyes stung, and she turned away. She wanted it and the depth of that wanting frightened her. With long fingers, he captured her chin and tilted her face back to his. Emotion glimmered deep in his eyes.

"Stop thinking," he said, still whispering. "No more analyzing. Just feel."

She closed her eyes. Yes, she could do that. For a little while, she could give herself over to the way he made her feel. Cherished. Desired. Precious.

"Open your eyes, Cait. No hiding. I want to see your eyes while I love you."

Her lashes fluttered, lifted. He kissed her again, a slow

devouring that went on and on, until she was suffused with need, pushing into him to assuage the craving he'd created. He lavished attention on her, hands shaping the sides of her breasts while his lips and tongue worshipped tight nipples. He trailed a caress over her stomach to the heat pulsing between her thighs. The teasing fingers lingered, sending a torturous delight through her, until she was writhing and moaning beneath him.

He left her long enough to shuck the remainder of his clothing, and then he returned to her arms, spreading her thighs to cradle his body. He entered her with a long, smooth movement, and she arched into him, biting back a cry.

"No," he whispered against her ear. "Don't hold back. Let me hear it. Let me have it all."

He withdrew and thrust again, her body stretching to accommodate his. Gripping her hips, he angled her body up to his, so she felt all of him. "Look at me, Cait."

Their gazes locked, his body moved into hers with a deep, binding rhythm, and inside, she shattered, a confused jumble of emotions flooding her.

Pressure built low in her body, a desperate desire only he could satisfy. She fluttered her hands over his waist and settled at the small of his back, pulling him deeper.

"Feel that?" He murmured the words against her temple. "We could have this, precious. Forever."

Her eyes slid closed. Yes, she could have this. The pleasure swirled in her body. She met his thrusts, reveling in the rough sound of his breathing next to her ear. She could have this. She could have *him*. The pressure increased, a restless yearning making her cling tighter to him.

His movements were hard now, hurried, exactly what she needed. Pulling his mouth from hers, he buried his face against her throat. His voice rasped over her ear. "Tell me what you want."

"You." The same question, the same answer. Her hands clutched at his shoulder blades, the words he wanted torn from her on a gasp. "I want you. Always you, Tick."

The ache expanded, the pressure radiating out. He pulled her hips harder into his. The orgasm washed over her, the exquisite heaviness bursting into an intense, painful pleasure. He plunged deeper, the sensations unbearably sweet, and she sobbed his name against his neck.

He tightened, pushing higher as his own climax took him, and she pressed closer, pulling him deeper still, feeling him pulse inside her. Gasping, he collapsed, one arm bearing his weight. She slid her palms from his shoulders to his chest, his heart thundering under her light touch.

He brushed his palm along her hip and thigh, their bodies still entwined, and he rubbed his cheek against hers. His satisfied sigh hummed through her.

Pleasure still thrummed in her body, but her vision blurred and shimmered. Sudden tears trickled from the corners of her eyes. She squeezed them tighter, trying to stem the flow, but more followed, seeping beneath her lashes, wetting her temples, dampening her hair. Breathy sobs shook her.

Tick pulled back, smoothing her hair away from her face. "Cait?"

She sat up, knees to her chest, the sobs getting stronger. "God, what a cliché," she said, her voice coming out harsh and strained. "Crying after sex."

Gently, he pulled her against him. "That wasn't just sex."

She rubbed at the tears on her cheeks. "I know."

He pressed a tender kiss to her temple, massaged her shoulder with his thumb. "I've been thinking about us."

"Wait." She tried to spin in his arms, but he held her still.

"Listen to me, Cait—"

"There's something I have to tell you first—"

"Chandler to C-2." The small radio buzzed from the floor, slightly muffled by his crumpled slacks.

"Oh, hell." He released her and leaned down to retrieve the offending square. "Go ahead, Chandler."

"C-13 requests your 10-78 at the old school."

Tick dropped his head, sighed and lifted the radio to his mouth. "10-4, Chandler. 10-76."

God, not now. Not when she finally had her courage in place.

"Damn Troy Lee's hide. Give him a badge, give him a gun and I still have to go hold his freakin' hand." He rolled from the bed and pulled on his clothes. "Told them I was out of service when I left. I'm not even supposed to be on call tonight."

Caitlin pulled the sheet around her and watched him, frustration a wicked sting. "We..." She swallowed. "I need to talk to you as soon as you're done."

"Who knows when that will be, the way the night's going?" He slanted a harried smile at her, tucking his shirt in. "This is what your life will be like if we're together."

Together. A wonderful sound wrapped up in a simple word. She rested her chin on her knees. "I can handle your job if you can handle mine."

"It's a deal." He dropped to the edge of the bed to put on his socks and shoes. A long breath shook his lean frame and he lifted his head to look at her. "I'll give it up, Cait, go back to the bureau, to Virginia, if that's what it takes. You're more important."

For a second, she couldn't breathe. She couldn't let him say these things, not until he knew everything. "Tick—"

"I've got to go." Fully dressed, he leaned to graze his mouth over hers. "You could meet me back at the department, if you're planning on working anymore tonight. Feel free to commandeer my office."

She bit her lip. This was it. She would tell him, tonight, before things went any further. He deserved to know and she *needed* to tell him. "And we'll talk later."

"Sounds good." He was already moving toward the door, his mind on the call. "Be careful, precious."

Tick ended up trying to teach Troy Lee one more time how to write an incident report. If they managed to turn the kid into a real cop, he'd give up smoking for good.

Fat chance that was going to happen. Across his desk, he eyed the unhappy slump of the younger man's shoulders as Troy Lee balanced his notebook on one knee, the clipboard with his report on the other.

Tick's ancient desk chair creaked as he leaned back, dragging his hands down his face. He was so wiped out his skin felt numb.

"I didn't say you had to agree with me, Schaefer. I just said I think it's important." Beyond the closed door of his office, Caitlin's husky tones carried to him.

"Yeah, but you can't explain *why*." Frustration twisted Jeff's voice as it faded down the hall.

Tick frowned. He needed to talk to Tori about him, find out exactly where that little relationship was going.

"Damn it." Troy Lee ripped the report free, crumpled it and tossed it toward the trashcan. He missed and the paper ball joined the two others on the floor.

Tick swallowed a long-suffering groan. They'd be here all night, but damn if he was going to do it for the kid.

Surely he hadn't given Cookie this much grief when he'd been wet-behind-the-ears.

Troy Lee settled in to write again. Tick turned sideways and nudged his mouse, bringing his computer screen to life, intending to play a couple of hands of solitaire while he waited.

Feeling a little like a teenage boy with a crush, he clicked on the Internet browser icon instead. The aging CPU whirred and the search page opened. With a grin, feeling a lot like a teenage boy with a crush, he typed Caitlin's name in the search box and hit enter.

Couldn't let Cookie know more than he did.

The first couple of hits were recent society columns in her hometown newspaper. The third mentioned her as the granddaughter of Judge Troupe Cavanaugh in a report on some political shindig back in February. There was a photo there, of Caitlin in a sleek, simple black gown that blew his mind, on the arm of a distinguished gray-haired man in his seventies or eighties. Everything below that turned his stomach.

News articles on the attack.

He moved the mouse, intending to shut the browser. He didn't need to read this stuff. His imagination had done a fine job of conjuring images of what had happened to her without his reading about it.

He paused, moved the arrow back, clicked on the first story.

It was a transcript of a news video, the written form awkward. Beside the brief column was a mug shot of one Benjamin James Fuller.

The rage stirred to life in Tick's chest, curling tenacious tentacles along his nerve endings.

So this was the guy. Besides being disheveled and sporting long scratches on one cheek, the bastard looked damned normal—neat professional haircut, clean shaven, intelligent blue eyes.

Tick's gaze tracked to the article. Fuller had been her grandfather's personal administrative assistant, with access to the home on a regular basis. He possessed no prior criminal record, not even a traffic offense.

"Tick?" Caitlin's husky voice shivered over his ears and he jerked like a guilty teenage boy caught...well, doing what teenage boys did.

"Hey." He closed the browser window, sure she wouldn't be too happy with his reading about her. He rose.

"I thought I'd see if you were able to take a break."

At the sound of her voice, Troy Lee studied her also, his attention seemingly riveted to the length of her legs as well as the curve of her other assets in a pair of jeans. Tick restrained himself from smacking the kid on the back of the head.

"Troy Lee, finish that damn report." He clipped his cell phone and handheld radio on his belt and picked up an unopened pack of cigarettes. "Let's go."

Outside the air was redolent with the smells of summer: camellias, jasmine, a hint of rain. He gestured toward the coffeehouse on the corner, its neon light still glowing. "Want a drink or something?"

"Actually..." Her gaze darted toward the small park on the other side of the sheriff's department, where two huge oak trees curved over a brick patio scattered with benches. "Why don't we take a walk?"

"Sure." He scrutinized her as they strolled down the block. Fiddling with the light necklace at her throat, she carried an edgy nervous excitement with her he wasn't used to. Unconfident, insecure almost. Apprehension prickled to life in him.

The dark shadows beneath the trees offered a sense of privacy and he slipped an arm about her waist as they stepped into the dimness. She surprised him by turning into his embrace in front of one of the benches. She smoothed his collar. "I need to talk to you. I need you to listen to me."

Her voice shook and his apprehension morphed into anxiety. He'd almost swear she was trembling. He curved a hand over her shoulder, rubbing his thumb across the soft skin revealed by the neckline of her thin T-shirt. "What's wrong?"

"I have to tell you..." She tugged free of his easy hold and dropped onto the stone bench. Leaning forward, she buried her face in her hands. "Oh, God, this is so *hard.*"

His stomach fell. Holy hell, she knew who their murderer was. It was probably someone in his damn department.

Lord, please don't let it be Cookie.

He discarded the thought as soon as it popped into his head. Cookie couldn't kill someone in cold blood.

He lowered himself to sit beside her. "Just tell me, Cait."

"While you were in Mississippi...when you came home and I told you I didn't want you anymore..."

There'd been someone else. His chest tightened as if he'd been delivered a heart punch.

Not Ransome. He could handle a lot, but not hearing she'd been sleeping with that lab jerk while he'd been in Mississippi dreaming of her every night.

"You're killing me here, precious." He laughed roughly and rubbed a hand over his mouth. "Just get to the point."

She pulled in a shaky, audible breath. The soft moonlight filtering through the shadows highlighted silver traces of tears on her cheeks.

"Cait, baby." He grasped her right hand in his left. "Don't."

With her free fingers, she covered her mouth and he felt the shuddery sigh that traveled through her. "Remember saying Carter was a breathing what-if?"

His brain shut down. It had to because everything just stopped. His heart froze, his lungs ceased, his thoughts ground to a halt.

"What are you telling me?"

Her grasp on his hand tightened to a painful level, his knuckles grinding under the pressure. "The month after you left, I learned I was pregnant."

"Oh, God." The raw groan couldn't be his.

"That's what put Fuller over the edge." She swiped at the tears, sniffling. "I'd told...I'd finally told Troupe because I couldn't very well keep it from him and heaven knows Troupe Cavanaugh can't keep a secret. I didn't want everyone knowing yet because you didn't but I was starting to show and..."

He rocked forward, his burning eyes squeezed shut, their clenched hands pressed to his forehead. This wasn't happening, he wasn't hearing this, she wasn't *saying* this.

She was not telling him she'd been pregnant with his child, that the son of a bitch had killed his baby.

Their baby.

She'd never told him. After he'd come home, she'd had every opportunity and she'd never said a word—not when he turned up in her office, not when she sent him away with that sexual-harassment bluff of hers, not when she'd arrived to assist on this case, not when she'd gone to bed with him again.

Not when he'd cajoled, pleaded, *begged* for the truth.

The agony of that silence settled deep inside, twisting his heart into a painful knot.

Why hadn't she said anything?

He lifted his head, pressed his mouth against her trembling fingers linked with his. "And you couldn't tell me this? God, Cait, why?"

"I wanted to. I tried...I know that's hard to believe, but I practiced how and...then when you walked in, I c-couldn't get the words out. I looked at you and I just *couldn't*." Her gasping sob tore at him. She leaned into him, her face against his, her tears wetting his skin. "I'm sorry...I'm so sorry. Please don't hate me, Tick, I can't bear that, I don't think—"

"Hate you?" His voice cracked. She thought he'd hate her? He pulled her closer, wrapped her as tightly as he could in his embrace. "Precious, I'd never hate you."

She cried harder, shaking. He buried his face in the curve of her shoulder and held on. She clung to him, her fingers digging in to his back, a need in her touch he'd never felt before. "I'd lost him and I knew...thought I'd lose you, too, especially once the doctors...once they said I c-couldn't..."

Him. A son. His throat closed.

She tightened her hold on him, huddling into him, still trembling.

Months of this. His heart, hell, his entire chest hurt for the suffering that poured out of her. He cupped the back of her head, shifted on the bench so he could draw her nearer. The ragged dampness of her weeping puffed against his throat. She'd carried this loss and desperation, this fear and pain, around for months, alone.

She hadn't trusted him enough to let him shoulder it with her and that slashed deep in his soul, at the core of who he was.

But she trusted him enough to bring it to him now. He had to hang on to that as the most important thing.

He turned his head, pressed his mouth to her temple. "You're not going to lose me."

Her weeping showed no signs of abating. He rocked them, stroking the length of her spine in long, slow sweeps, murmuring the comforting nonsense he used with Charlie.

His radio squawked, a garbled transmission between Jeff and Chris, and he squelched it to a low buzz. Above them, a whip-o-will called its lonesome song. Across the street at the take-out fried chicken stand, a group of teenagers laughed and cut the fool around a picnic table. He closed his eyes, cradling, loving, letting the dark soothe the anguish.

Finally, he felt a certain sense of calm claim her. She released a slow, shuddery breath against his neck and he knew she was pulling herself together. He swept his mouth against her temple once more, smoothed her hair. "Better?"

She nodded, brushing at her cheeks. He tipped her face up, the filtered mingling of moonlight and streetlights giving him just enough illumination to see her eyes glittering. Free of shadows for once, a little wary still, but holding an emotion that stole his breath and curled through him, binding him to her.

He was already bound. He rubbed a thumb over her lips, traced the back of one finger along her jaw and let himself simply look at her, drinking in the barely visible details of her tearstained face.

This was the mother of his child and that tied him to her on a level he'd never really understood before.

Words danced on his lips, wanting to be said, but he held them back. There'd be time for those words, he was sure of it now, and the wound of her silence still beat in his soul. This was enough for now, having her in his arms, having her trust in him.

The rest would come.

The radio crackled low at his side. "C-4 to C-2."

Jeff. Damn it. What now?

With a frustrated growl, he released Caitlin and lifted the mike to his mouth. She didn't move away, her leg still pressed along his. "Go ahead, C-4."

"What's your 10-20?"

It was starting again, he was certain of it. A full-moon night for sure. "I'm outside the station. Why?"

"Got a 10-10 out at the Rite Aid parking lot. Chris is busy and I'd rather not deal with Jed Stinson without backup."

Yeah, Jed had probably been drinking and more than likely it would turn out to be a domestic disturbance instead of a reported fight. "10-4, 10-76."

He slapped both hands against his thighs and stood. "I've got to go."

A ghost of a smile curved her mouth as she rose to stand beside him. "I figured as much."

Her hair was ruffled, more disheveled than he'd ever seen her, and he reached out, tucked a stray lock behind her ear. "Go get some sleep and I'll see you in the morning."

Her startled gaze jerked to his, fear and questions in the green depths. "You're not...I thought..."

"Not tonight." He caressed her damp cheek, trying to pick his words. He didn't want to hurt her but at the same time he wanted to crawl into a deep, dark hole, alone. "I need..."

"Time to deal."

"Yeah." His relief and gratitude blended into the single

syllable.

She leaned up, let her lips linger over his and folded him in an intense embrace, as if she wanted to never let go. "Be careful."

"You, too. Now let me go cover Jeff's sorry self."

CR

"I'm gonna sue your ass, Tick!"

"Go ahead." Tick threw the lock on the holding cell with an audible clang. A monster headache pounded at his temples, along his forehead and over the top of his head and Jed's incensed screaming wasn't helping. "I have liability insurance."

"I got rights." Jed slumped on the bottom bunk and glared with bleary eyes. "The law's on my side."

"Yeah?" Tick hitched a hip on the stool at the intake counter and started filling out his arrest report. "What law's that?"

"Georgia law says I can beat my wife."

He closed his eyes, spots dancing across his lids. Sweet Jesus save him. He really wished the legislature would take that archaic little legal loophole off the books.

"That's on Friday night with a twelve-inch stick, Jed-boy. Not midnight on Monday with your fists in the Rite-Aid parking lot." He rubbed a hand over his sore jaw. Jed had good aim for a drunk. Why did the idiot always have to put up a fight? "And the law don't say anything about letting you pop me one."

Jed hiccupped. "'s Tuesday."

"Yep, it is." He scrawled his signature at the bottom of the form and dropped it in the basket. "Night, Jed."

"Screw you."

"Whatever." He trudged upstairs to the squad room. From up the hall, he could hear Maggie Stinson at the front desk, already trying to bail Jed out. Some things never changed. At least he'd finished the paperwork this time before she showed up.

"You headed home?" In the squad room, Jeff tilted back in

his desk chair; Chris Parker leaned against the coffee counter, drinking a canned soda.

"Yeah." As soon as he found the bottle of sipping whiskey he'd carried around with him for the last ten years or so. The couple of long necks in his fridge weren't going to take the edge off tonight.

He pushed open his office door and frowned. Where'd he put it, anyway?

"You look rough," Chris called after him.

"Thanks." He dragged the dust-coated banker's box from beneath the credenza and lifted the lid. He grabbed the bottle of Ol' Ezra Del had given him upon his graduation from the police academy and shoved the box back in its spot.

An anger bordering on fury simmered under his skin and he had nowhere to direct it.

The Texas Department of Corrections had Benjamin Fuller locked up for two to twenty and Tick doubted they'd give him face-to-face alone time with the guy.

He needed to punch someone, to destroy something.

He'd settle for getting good and drunk.

Leaving his handheld in the charger, he settled his cap on his head, tucked the bottle under his arm and returned to the squad room. "I don't care what else goes on tonight. If you need anything, call Stanton."

Chris chuckled. Jeff's gaze locked on the bottle of whiskey. "What are you doing?"

"Going home to get wasted. And I don't want to be disturbed. Got that?"

Jeff jumped to his feet. "I'll walk out with you."

Tick headed for the side door. "This is not a good time."

The younger man followed him into the muggy night, his shoes clattering on the worn concrete steps. "It might help to talk about it."

Pulling his keys from his pocket, Tick slanted him a disbelieving look. Since when did Jeff think he was Tick's confidant? "Thanks for the offer."

"This has to do with Agent Falconetti, doesn't it?"

Tick paused in the act of unlocking his truck. The anger he was trying so hard to bank flared hotter, sending tendrils along his veins, heating his neck and ears. "Jeff. I'm serious. Not a good time."

"You haven't been yourself since she's been here."

That sounded like Stanton. Tick jerked the door open and tossed the bottle across the cab onto the passenger seat. "Don't kid yourself. You might be dating my sister and working in my department, but you don't know me that well."

"You'd be surprised." Confidence strengthened Jeff's voice. "I know it's not normal for you to be tied in knots like this all the time, to have to rein in your temper like you did with Jed earlier."

Jeff had better be glad he was reining it in now. His jaw ached from being clenched so hard. Hell, his whole head hurt from how hard he was grinding his teeth together. "I appreciate the effort, Schaefer. I realize at this point I'll be looking at you across Mama's table on a regular basis. But I'm not discussing this with you. Not tonight. Not ever. It's none of your goddamn business."

"Don't you think we'd all be better off if she'd finish her damn profile and go back to Virginia?"

"No." He spun to thrust a trembling finger in Jeff's face. "But I think we'd both be better off if you get the hell away from me tonight."

An arrogant smirk bloomed over Jeff's features. "See what I'm talking about?"

He would not take a swing at him. If he took one, he'd want another, would take all the aggression screaming in him out on the other guy and Tori would never forgive him. He turned, climbed behind the wheel and fired the engine. "Goodnight, Jeff."

The fury shadowed him all the way home.

He didn't even bother to go inside but stalked down to the dock. Once there, with the river whispering around him, he slouched in one of the Adirondack chairs and broke the seal on the whiskey.

The sipping alcohol sizzled into his gut, doing little to kill the smoldering rage, to drown the keening anguish.

He would've had a son. Probably a dark-haired, dark-eyed little boy who looked like all the rest of his mother's grandchildren.

But different, special, because it was *his* child.

His and Caitlin's.

She'd carried his child, growing and moving under her heart. She'd wanted that baby, he'd heard it in her voice earlier. If things had been different, if Fuller hadn't...hell, the pain and confusion of the last few months would have been filled with joy and love instead.

He tossed off another long swallow.

Fuller had stolen that from them and there wasn't a damn thing Tick could do about it.

And he most likely wouldn't be able to give her another child to ease the sorrow, either.

Dealing with the loss of the baby he'd never had a chance to hold was hard enough. Dealing with the loss of those future possible children made it worse.

Was this what losing his brother had been like for his parents?

He still remembered those desolate days after Will's death in a hunting accident. His father had been torn between comforting his devastated mother and trying to reach Del, who'd been mired in grief and misguided guilt.

One night Tick had found his father—his strong, invincible father—on his knees in the living room, Bible open on the couch before him, sobs shaking his sturdy frame.

Tick wished he could cry. Instead, the grief sat like a frozen knot in his chest.

He tilted the bottle up again. His eyes watered with the burn this time.

Another trickling swallow of Ol' Ezra scorched his raw throat. His fingers were going all tingly-numb. That had to be a good sign. Maybe if he drank enough, the rest of him would go numb, too. He slouched further in the chair and took one more pull.

His eyelids dropped closed and he relaxed, the bottle slipping in his grip. He startled, catching it before it slid to the dock and shattered. His head spun and he rubbed a thumb over the raised relief on the bottle. Drinking on a near-empty stomach probably wasn't the best idea he'd had in a while.

He set the bottle by the chair. Beneath the wood slats, water rushed and murmured. He scuffed the toe of his shoe over a bent nail. Probably he or Del had driven that crooked nail, during the summer his father had repaired the dock for his grandparents. A smile pulled at his mouth. He'd been ten, Del nine, and they'd probably been more hindrance to Daddy than anything else.

Leaning forward, he rested his elbows on his knees and his face in his hands. He wasn't going to show that baby how to place a nail between the teeth of a comb to hold it for the hammer. He wasn't going to teach him to fish or fuss at him to be still in the pew on Sunday morning. He wouldn't set him down in Lloyd Beall's barbershop chair for a first haircut or take him down the red clay stretch of Old Bainbridge Road for his first time behind a steering wheel.

"Lord, help me," he whispered. The rustling water caught the anguished plea and carried it away. How was he supposed to deal with fathering a child, but never being that boy's daddy?

CR

Tick jerked awake and recoiled from the light bouncing off his ceiling. His eyes stung and his mouth tasted fuzzy and dead. With a groan, he rolled over and buried his face in the other pillow.

A soft, unique smell tickled his nose. Caitlin...the spicy shampoo she used blended with the scent of her skin.

Loss swept through him again, and he closed his eyes, teeth clenched. The action worsened the pounding in his head. He had to get up, get dressed, get going.

He stumbled from the bed, his brain protesting the too-quick movement. Trying to focus his thoughts on the case, he showered and donned a black suit, the somber color matching his disposition. In the kitchen, he ate a bowl of microwaved grits and drank a glass of milk while standing up, his mind circling despite his best efforts to concentrate. He kept coming back to the same place, exactly where he didn't want to be.

Why did he feel like he'd lost everything? He hadn't. He had his family, his job, his friends.

He had Caitlin. He was fairly sure of that.

But he still felt like a dog who'd been kicked one too many times.

Depression plaguing him, he placed his dishes in the dishwasher and left, locking the house behind him. He had an hour before he actually had to be in the office and nothing was going to fall apart if he showed up on time rather than early.

At the crossroads, he turned left rather than continuing straight. Minutes later, he pulled into his mother's drive and parked by her car.

Humidity saturated the still morning, trapping the muggy heat that promised to be suffocating before noon. His mother's morning newspaper under his arm, Tick plodded up the side steps and let himself in. Blessed cool air washed over him as he opened the door.

"Mama?" He dropped the newspaper in her mail basket in the hall. The mingled scent of fresh-brewed coffee and cinnamon wafted from the kitchen.

"On the back porch."

He poured a cup of coffee, filched a cinnamon roll from the pan on the counter and followed her voice to the screened room just outside. Her fat marmalade cat twitched an annoyed tail at him as he stepped over her. His mother sat on the glider, shelling peas into a large bowl.

"Lamar." Affection suffused her face and he leaned over to hug her. She kissed his cheek, her embrace a sweet weight around his neck. "I'm very glad to see you."

"You, too." His eyes burned and he blinked, holding his cheek against hers before letting go. A rough breath rattled his body.

She patted the cushion beside her and shifted the bag of purple-hull beans closer to her thigh. He settled and let the smooth rhythm of her pulling strings and snapping ends soothe him. A soft rain of peas tinkled into the enamelware bowl on her lap. She didn't speak, didn't ask him any questions, and after he had finished the coffee and sweet roll, he picked up a handful of beans from the bag.

A fine mist cascaded over his fingertips when he snapped the first one, the clean acidic scent hitting his nostrils, bringing back a dozen memories of moments like this.

"Your father and I used to sit out here and talk over this very task. He said it let him think, having something to do with his hands." She patted his leg above his knee. "You remind me so much of him."

He smiled, a half-hearted gesture at best.

"I enjoyed having your Caitlin here Sunday."

"Yeah. Me, too."

"So maybe I'll finally get to plan a big wedding for one of you?"

He winced. Since Del had eloped, Chuck had opted for a courthouse wedding, and Ruthie had married overseas, his mama had missed out on all the excitement of marrying off her children in style. "Mama, please don't say that. Not today. We're...nothing's settled between us."

She gave him a wry look. The paper bag rustled between them as she lifted another handful of beans. "Lamar, who do you think you're talking to? You couldn't fib to me when you were eight and broke your Aunt Maureen's heirloom cake plate and it's not working now. You look at that young lady the same way your father used to look at me."

Another pat on his leg, this time with an affectionate squeeze. The silence descended around them again. Outside, birds fluttered around her feeders and down at the pond a duck plopped into the water, her ducklings following. A rope swing dangled from an oak tree, its edges a little threadbare. That swing had been Del's idea and how many times had the four of them—Tick, Del, Will and Chuck—competed to see who could swing the farthest out into the water on a hot summer day?

The whole house had to hold memories he didn't know about, memories of Will. Did they haunt his mother? Why did he feel like he'd be having those what-ifs about this baby forever?

"Mama, did it get any easier? Losing Will, I mean."

Her hands never paused in the smooth strip, snap, zip of hulling peas. "Well, I don't know if easier is the right word.

Losing a child changes what normal is. Things never go back to the way they were. But time soothes, a little."

He pushed another line of tiny peas into the bowl.

"After a while, you're able to remember all the good times, the sweet times, again." She tilted her head, gaze trained on the long thin beans in her hand. "But you know, somehow losing the baby was almost as bad as losing Will?"

He looked up sharply. "The baby?"

"Um-hmm. The one we lost." She lifted her eyes, staring out across the rolling green lawn. "About a year after Ruthie was born, while your daddy was in training with the Marshall service. It was such a shock, because I'd had easy pregnancies with all of you and everything had been going well. I'd even felt her moving...when I miscarried, it was far enough along for them to tell me it would have been a girl."

"I never knew that."

She laughed, a bittersweet sound. "You were six, honey. I don't expect you to remember."

"That was the summer we spent all that time at Grandma's. She said you weren't feeling well."

"You could say that." Her voice was wistful. "It was like a big dark weight, losing that child. Now they'd call it a depression but pure old-fashioned grief is what it was. And it didn't matter how many times people told me I had all of you still and that there could be other babies...oh, my, I grieved for that baby girl."

He bent his head, eyes closed. "You said it was nearly as bad as losing Will."

"I'd had the chance to love Will, to hold him, to raise him, when he died. I didn't have any of that to cling to with that baby." He felt her small shrug and heard the change in her tone when she spoke again. "But a few years later, along came Tori, completely unexpected and what a blessing and a joy the Lord sent us in her."

An unwilling smile tugged at his mouth. "A joy, Mama?"

"Sometimes you have to look for your joy, Lamar Eugene." She gave his leg one final pat. "And sometimes our greatest joys come out of our greatest pain."

By the time he left his mother's, he felt calmer and his headache had dissipated somewhat. He detoured by the courthouse to pick up warrants, and once he extricated himself from the clerk of court, it was after nine when he arrived at the office.

"Morning, Lydia." He rapped a hand lightly on the front desk. "Stanton in his office?"

She nodded, passing him a thin stack of pink message slips. "He's looking for you. And he's on the warpath."

"What else is new?" He leaned against the counter, flipping through his messages. He liked the fact that she held them and didn't tape them to his door like the other dispatchers did, where God and everyone could see them. "What did I do this time?"

"I don't think it's you. The Thomas case was dismissed this morning because the evidence never made it out of the GBI lab."

He shook his head. Underfunded, the GBI crime lab suffered under a massive backlog of cases, and Chandler County wasn't the only one losing cases before they ever made it to trial because of it. "I guess that means our lab results from the Kimberly Johnson case haven't come in, either."

Lydia pursed her thin, heavily colored lips. "I think Agent Falconetti is working on that this morning. I believe she and Cookie have been communicating back and forth with Moultrie and Quantico. She's taken over your office."

"Thanks." On his way through the squad room, he stopped at the soda machine. His body was screaming for nicotine, and he hoped a caffeine overload would appease the craving. So far, the nicotine jones was winning.

Cookie sat at his desk, laptop open, a legal pad before him, a pen between his teeth. "Yo, Lamar Eugene."

"Hey." He grimaced over the icy bite of cola as it hit his throat.

Cookie glanced at his computer screen, tapped a few keys and hit enter. "You look like shit."

"Probably because I feel like it." Tick drained the soda in a couple of gulps. "Let me go see what bug is up Stan's ass this morning."

"Good luck. He's loaded for bear. Jeff told him you went off last night."

Great. Just freakin' great.

Stanton's door stood halfway open and Tick entered without knocking. "Heard about the Thomas case."

"There's got to be a better way. Like we build our own crime lab and hire the people to staff it."

"While you're dreaming there, Stanny-boy, let's replace all of our units with brand new Chargers."

Stanton didn't smile. "What's this I hear about you going off the deep end with Jeff last night?"

"I didn't go off the deep end. I was in a lousy mood and he wanted to push a point. Quit worrying. I'm not going to kill your golden boy."

"He's a good cop. And tension between y'all will do more than damage morale, it'll come between you and Tori if you're not careful."

"He needs to understand a line is a line if we're going to work together, Stan."

Stanton's attention returned to the budget spreadsheet on his desk. "Still planning to go to Tallahassee today?"

"Yeah, right after we talk to Bobby Gene Butler. Cait wants to check out his story on Sharon Ingler's car."

Without looking up, Stanton nodded. "Good deal. And Tick?"

"What?"

"Try to hold it together."

He wandered back out to the squad room and filled a mug with Cookie's too-strong brew. Ill-temper settled over him, bringing his headache back full force. Damn it, he didn't like Jeff running his mouth to Stanton. What had happened between them had been guy-to-guy, not cop-to-cop.

He dropped into Jeff's chair opposite Cookie. Lord, the guy's desk was too neat. If he lived like this, and he and Tori got serious, she'd drive him nuts with all her stuff. He sipped at the godawful coffee. He'd better face facts—his sister had brought the guy to Sunday dinner at Mama's. She was already serious, despite anything she said to the contrary.

Shit, he didn't like her dating Jeff. It stuck in his craw, bad.

He should have wiped that goddamn smirk off the son of a bitch's face when he had the chance.

A quiet chime emanated from Cookie's laptop. He glanced at it, sighed, punched some keys, hit enter and returned to studying his notes.

Tick shook his head. "What are you doing?"

"Talking to Falconetti. She's harassing Botine over at the Moultrie GBI office by email. I suspect our labs will get moved to the top of the priority list if she doesn't end up transferring them to the FBI. She's harassing some guy up there about it, too. And we're tossing ideas around about this database."

"You're instant messaging her?"

"Well, yeah. I couldn't very well call her cell, could I? She still can't find her phone. And wherever it is, it ain't turned on. We tried to trace it by pings earlier. No luck."

The tension knot in Tick's neck tightened. "I thought she was in my office."

"She is." Cookie made a face. "But you don't want me yelling this stuff across the room, do you? We're multitasking."

"You're a nut is what you are." Tick rose and returned Jeff's chair to its customary just-so position. He picked up his mug.

Cookie rolled his gaze toward the ceiling. "She's got the brother from Texas and the FBI guy from Virginia on voice chat, probably dealing with one of the two."

"Do you know how ridiculous this is? You're in the same building. She could just work out here and then y'all wouldn't need the whole messaging thing. Hell, why don't you use the conference room?"

"You mean the dungeon? Sitting in there gives me the creeps and I like technology. So shoot me." Cookie shrugged. "And for some unfathomable reason, she likes you. Maybe that's why she wanted to use your office, to soak in your aura or some crap like that. Now go away and let me think."

Hard to argue with that. Tick gave him a light smack on the head and headed for his office. He tapped once and opened the door.

Eyes closed, legs crossed, Caitlin sat in his desk chair. Her laptop was open and an earpiece ran from the side to her ear. She made a moue of aggravation. "Vince. Stop. Being. An. Ass."

At Tick's entrance, she opened her eyes. After shutting the door, he set his coffee on the edge of the desk and reached for the files in his inbox, some of his tension falling away. He liked having her in his space.

"No. Because I said so." She caught Tick's gaze and rolled her eyes. She sighed and leaned her forehead on her hand. "You're impossible."

A pause. Frustration twisted her mouth. "No, it's not the same thing. Not even in the same ballpark."

Tick dropped into the chair in front of his desk, crossed one ankle over his knee and opened the topmost folder, skimming the dispatcher's report from the night before.

"Vinnie, I have to go. Because I have a job. Because...goodbye, Vince."

She slapped the laptop closed and jerked the earpiece free. With her elbows on his desk, she covered her face and blew out an audible breath.

An unwilling smile tugged at Tick's mouth. "Problems?"

"He's an ass. An overprotective ass who makes you look like an uninvolved bystander in Tori's life. I should talk to Troupe and get him cut out of the will."

Surprised, he stopped with his mug halfway to his lips. "What?"

"It's a regular thing. I've been disinherited more times than I can count."

His spurt of rusty laughter felt good, even if it did make his chest hurt. "For what?"

"Most recently?" She stretched and slipped from the chair. "A girls' night at Lingerlongs that went horribly wrong. It was all my cousin Lanie's fault. She's always been the rowdiest of us, although maybe I shouldn't have worn the hooker dress."

Tick sputtered on a mouthful of coffee. "The hooker dress?"

"That's Vince's name for it. I wear it when I really want to piss him off." She skirted his desk and leaned on the top. A pretty smile of reminiscence lit her face. "We were all right as long as it was just the Marines involved, but then the SEALs showed up and things just went downhill from there."

"The SEALS. I really don't want to know, do I?"

"Probably not." She lifted the mug from his easy hold and sipped. "That was before Lanie settled down to be a wife and mom. And before you."

Her voice softened with the words. She extended the cup in his direction, and when he shook his head, set it aside. Leaning down, she touched his jaw, her eyes warm and gentle. "I didn't sleep very much last night. I was worried about you."

"I didn't get a lot of sleep either." He'd spent a lot of time staring at the ceiling and when he did doze off, weird dreams had invaded his head. He stood, resting his hands at her waist. "I'm glad to see you this morning."

"Me, too." Her gaze clung to his. She'd never looked at him this way before, without the shuttered mistrust she turned on the world. Warmth suffused his chest, melting some of the cold grief still knotted there.

Sometimes you have to look for your joy, Lamar Eugene.

He lowered his head and slanted his mouth over hers. She lifted her arms to embrace him, her lips moving under his in a soft kiss of renewal. The promise in that exchange washed over him like a steady rain on a parched cornfield.

He pulled back with a shaky exhale. "We've got work to do."

With great caution, Caitlin picked her way across Bobby Gene Butler's overgrown yard, her gaze peeled for the first sign of a slithering reptile. "Did I mention I'm deathly afraid of snakes?"

"Snake's more scared of you than you are of it." Tick loosened his tie, having left his suit jacket in the truck.

"Thank you, Lamar Eugene, for that kernel of farm-boy wisdom. I feel so comforted." She watched him move, concern lingering in her. He seemed to be his normal easy-going self, yet she sensed a brewing tension in him that matched the low storm clouds gathering in the eastern sky.

He laughed softly, hands tucked in his pockets as they walked to the metal shed that housed Butler's wrecker. Vehicles in varying states of repair lined the rusted chain-link fence.

Tick slapped the side of the shed. "Bobby Gene!"

Butler waddled from the tiny office in the back of the shed, wiping his grease-stained hands on an even greasier rag. He offered Tick his hand. "What you know good, Tick?"

"It's hot. Bobby Gene, this is Agent Falconetti. We need to talk to you about Sharon's car."

His face closed. "I already told Schaefer everything I saw. I told you that."

Tick turned his shirt cuffs back a couple of times. "Yeah, but Jeff doesn't take the best notes, and I just want to make sure he didn't forget to write anything down."

Butler huffed a heavy sigh. "What do you want to know?"

"Just run through what you told Jeff."

He turned away, lifting a wrench from the workbench and rubbing it with the rag. "I'd been to the auction, and I was bringing the parts car I'd bought back. I came down Long Lonesome Road about ten, turned off on 112 and there's the car, sitting off on the shoulder. The hazards weren't on or anything."

Tick rocked back slightly on his heels. "Where was that again?"

"Twenty-third-mile marker. I made a note of it so I could circle around, in case they needed help or something."

"So you could beat Lawson out of a tow, you mean."

"Aw, hell, Tick, a man's got to make a living."

"I know. You didn't see Sharon? Not walking on the road or anything?"

Butler replaced the wrench and picked up a screwdriver, giving it the same treatment. "I didn't see nobody. And I didn't see the car again until Chris Parker called me out to tow it in. That was about one in the morning. But you know that. You was there."

"And the car had been moved?"

"Yeah. It was almost to the twenty-five then."

Tick nodded, rubbing his chin with a finger. "Listen, what have you got out back? My brother's looking for something he can fix up for my nephew."

Butler's eyes lit with the prospect of a sale. "Come on back. We'll take a look."

Tick tossed Caitlin a quick smile. "I won't be long."

No way he was car-shopping in the middle of an investigation. Caitlin watched him walk away with Butler. He wanted a look at the junk lot, and Butler had just fallen for the slow country boy act, swallowing not just the hook, line and sinker, but the whole damn rod. From the front of the shed, she eyed the vehicles lining the fence. Curiosity rising, she walked to the closest one, a beige late-model sedan missing the hood and front quarter panel.

She leaned over, checking the lower corner of the windshield on the driver's side. No small metal plate with the required vehicle identification number.

A quick survey of the other vehicles found three more with the VIN removed. She shot a speculative glance at the lot behind the shed, packed with vehicles. Butler ran more than a wrecker service. Looked like he also traded in stolen cars. Sharon's car didn't move on its own, and Vontressa's car had yet to be located. Kimberly Johnson's vehicle remained missing as well. Maybe Butler was involved.

Only the girls' deaths didn't fit the whole stolen-cars-as-motive scenario.

"You ready?" Tick strode out of the shed. He waved at Butler and pulled his sunglasses from his pocket, sliding them on against the sun.

Caitlin didn't glance back at the shed as they walked to his truck. "He's lying."

"Hell, yeah, he's lying." He opened the passenger door for her.

"I don't think he killed her, though. But he knows something."

"Yeah." He slid behind the wheel. "What kind of car did Johnson drive again?"

"White Nissan Altima. Early nineties model."

"That's what I thought. Guess what's sitting way at the back of his junk lot?"

"A white Altima. I bet the VIN plate is missing."

"I couldn't get close enough to see without spooking him. He thinks I'm a dumb ol' country boy, and right now, I want to keep it that way."

"We need a warrant for that car. Add Vontressa's to it."

Steering with one hand, he fished his cell phone from his pocket. "I'll call Lydia. She can handle the warrant, and we'll have Cookie and Schaefer bring in the car. They can toss Bobby Gene in holding for possessing stolen property—there's got to be a stolen car somewhere in that mess. He sits there a couple of hours while we run to Tallahassee, and believe me, he'll be ready to talk when we get back."

Chapter Eleven

Tallahassee's capital building gleamed in the midday sun. Caitlin leaned her head against the seat and watched Tick navigate the lunch-hour traffic surrounding the city's business district.

She reached over and shut off the radio, stopping Kenny Chesney midnote. "If you were going to Panama City, would you come this way?"

He didn't take his gaze from the white SUV in front of them. "No. And I wouldn't have sent Kimberly Johnson through here, either. I'd have sent her through Chattahoochee. He killed her, panicked and thought using the credit card here would cover his tracks. Or at least keep the focus off Chandler County."

"And it worked, temporarily at least. He'd killed, and he'd gotten away with it. He comes across Sharon on the road and can't resist the challenge of trying again. Same thing with Vontressa and your Jane Doe. Victims of opportunity. But he'd had time to think after Kim. To regroup, to plan for the next opportunity."

"Explaining the lack of physical evidence. But you left out Amy."

"I didn't leave Amy out. Amy's different, Tick, she always has been. She's a victim of purpose. He planned to kill her. She was prey, and he went after her."

He slammed on the brakes, muttering curses at the SUV's driver. "Because of the pregnancy."

"I don't know. It could be. He's a narcissist—he cares about his public persona, and he'll protect that persona at all costs. But he could have just married her and become a state senator's son-in-law. Amy was pushing for that; it's in the last couple of entries in her diary. Except that being forced into a shotgun marriage would have taken away his sense of control, and he's not going to let that happen."

He turned into the crowded parking lot of a colorful fast-food restaurant. "She never knew what hit her."

Caitlin shivered, pushing aside the mental images his words invoked. "No, she knew. He made sure of it."

Eyeing the bank of clouds building over the cityscape, she walked with him into the restaurant and let him take the lead in talking with the cooperative manager, who produced the tape and offered his office for immediate viewing.

In the tiny office, Caitlin pushed the tape into the VCR. Tick leaned against the metal desk and waited while the television flickered to life. A split screen appeared, showing the views from four separate security cameras.

They watched the flow of customers on the tape—families with kids in soccer or baseball uniforms, teenagers, young couples. White numbers at the bottom corner ticked off the time. Caitlin frowned. None of the customers remotely resembled Kimberly Johnson.

Tick blew out a long breath. "What time was the card used?"

"Eleven thirteen."

"We should be getting close—"

"Oh, my God." The shocked whisper slid past Caitlin's lips. She stared at the blonde who'd entered the restaurant, disbelief shivering in her mind. Her gaze jerked to Tick's stunned face. "That's—"

"Yeah. Oh, holy hell."

On the screen, Amy Gillabeaux brushed back her long blonde hair and swiped a credit card through the point-of-sale terminal. She slid the card into the pocket of her tight hip-hugger jeans, gathered her purchases and sashayed out.

Tick leaned forward, eyeing the portions of the screen that showed the parking lot views. "She didn't go to a car. She walked in the direction of the street."

"To a hotel maybe?" Caitlin frowned. "Do you think she

knew what she was doing?"

"I don't think so. She's too relaxed, too natural."

"Didn't she even look at that credit card?"

"I doubt it. If he gave it to her...she trusted him. Why should she question him?"

"Let's go see if there's a hotel nearby."

The first two hotels, both well-known, moderately priced chains, offered nothing. As they approached the third, Caitlin eyed the cracked asphalt and peeling paint. A pool, the water thick and green, sat in the middle of the horseshoe created by the low, squatty buildings.

She sidestepped a puddle of indeterminate origin on the sidewalk. "It's a dump. They probably rent by the hour."

"So he has lousy taste. You can add that to your profile." He pulled open the office door, jingling the cheap wind chimes attached.

Over the desk, Elvis stared down at them from a black velvet painting. An oscillating fan stirred air saturated with cigarette smoke.

Tick leaned down. "Does it count against me if I inhale deeply?"

A college-aged boy emerged from the small room behind the office. Curly dark hair surrounded a bored face sporting a scraggly goatee. "Y'all need a room?"

Nice to know customer courtesy was still alive and well. Caitlin produced her FBI credentials and held out Amy's snapshot. "Actually, we're looking for information on this young lady. She may have stayed here a few weeks ago."

He studied the photo and looked up, suspicion replacing the boredom. "Don't remember her."

"She was murdered," Tick said. "Do you remember her now?"

He nodded. "Yeah, she was here. Changed rooms three times—kept finding things wrong."

Tick glanced around the office. "Imagine that."

Caitlin glared at him before turning another polite bureau smile on the clerk. "Do you remember if anyone was with her?"

"Yeah. There was a guy with her. I thought maybe he was her brother or her dad—he looked old enough. You know, in his thirties. She registered for the room, though, instead of him, which I thought was kinda weird."

Tick scratched his jaw. "What did he look like?"

He shrugged. "Tall, dark hair. I don't remember too well—I was looking at her, you know?"

Caitlin leaned forward. "We need to see her registration."

He crossed his arms over his chest. "I'm not supposed to. Privacy and all that. I guess you could get a warrant."

She glanced at Tick and he sighed, reaching for his wallet. He pulled a twenty and laid it on the counter. The kid pocketed the bill and produced a cardboard box from under the counter, flipping through the cards. "Here it is."

Tick lifted the card. "Amy Smith. Original, wasn't she? You don't ask for ID?"

The young man laughed. "Yeah, right."

Caitlin tapped a fingernail on the highlighted asterisk at the top of the card. "What does this mean?"

"They left something in the room." He picked up a red ledger, turning back several pages. "A bag."

"Do you still have it?" Caitlin asked.

"Just a minute." The clerk disappeared into the back room.

"I could have called Helen over at the PD and saved twenty bucks," Tick muttered.

She rapped her fingers on the desk, anticipation flaring. What kind of bag? What was in it? "Don't worry. I'll make it up to you."

"Really? I have suggestions."

The clerk reappeared, small black fanny pack in hand. "Here you go."

He set it on the desk. Caitlin took the handkerchief Tick proffered and used it to cover her fingers as she unzipped the bag. She spread the sides to peer inside. A twenty-dollar bill, a small pad, an ink pen. "Well, it wasn't Amy's."

Tick leaned closer. "Why not?"

"Other than it's hideously ugly and completely

unfashionable? No lipstick, no mirror, no tampons. Any questions?"

"I guess not."

"Look." She separated a strip of hook-and-loop fastening to reveal a compartment at the back of the bag. "To conceal a gun."

A triangle of white cardstock peeked out from the edge of the opening. Grasping it with the handkerchief, Caitlin pulled it free. Her stomach clenched, even as excitement bubbled in her throat. A lead. An honest-to-God lead.

Tick swore.

She smiled at the clerk, who stared at Tick. "Thank you. For everything."

"Yeah."

Back at the truck, Tick pointed at the card in her hand. "I did not need to see that."

Caitlin glanced down at the business card, bearing the logo and phone number of the Chandler County Sheriff's Department, but no name. "It doesn't necessarily mean he's one of you. He could have gotten it at any time. It could be a coincidence."

He tugged a hand through his hair, swearing again. "Do you believe that?"

"Well, no, but anything to get that look off your face. Get me an evidence bag, would you? Maybe we'll luck out and get prints, hair or fibers from it." She tucked the fanny pack and its contents in the bag he held out. "Hmm...tall, dark hair, thirties...sounds like Reed to me. Let's question him. I want to be the bad cop."

"That is not funny."

"Look on the bright side—the kid didn't finger you."

"Does that mean my name is coming off the damn board?"

"No. It stays there until we make an arrest. So how many deputies fit that description?"

He grimaced. "About half the department. Cookie, Jeff, Chris, Monroe...want me to keep going?"

"Not Cookie. He's not socially competent enough." A memory of icy blue eyes filtered through her mind, bringing a shiver with it. "Chris is Parker, right?"

"Yeah, the K-9 officer. We stole him from Tifton's PD."

She stretched against the seat. "We could put together a photo lineup and bring it back down for the kid to look at."

"A lineup full of cops. Lord, Ray over at the paper will have a field day when this gets out. His circulation will triple."

"Cheer up. Maybe Bobby Gene Butler will tell us something earthshaking, and we'll make a quick arrest."

"Sure. Only one problem with that."

"What?"

"This ain't television."

Back in traffic, he lapsed into silence, thumping a hand against the steering wheel as he drove.

"Tick, stop it." She reached over, rubbing at his shoulder, the muscles tense under her touch. "Stop blaming yourself."

"Stan and I handpicked these guys. We went through applications with the proverbial fine-tooth comb. We interviewed and I ran the damn background checks myself." He slammed the flat of his hand against the steering column. "Son of a bitch! How did he get by us?"

"It happens, even to the bureau. Remember the agent prosecuted last year for spying?"

"It's not the same thing." He spit the words out, grinding his teeth. "It's just not the same."

"He wouldn't be that easy to spot. He's of above-average intelligence, very socially competent—"

"You don't get it, Cait." His mood matched the thunderclouds gathering ahead of them. "We cleaned that department out and started all over again. We were supposed to be wiping out years of corruption. We promised the people in that county they'd be safe—we were there to serve and protect. And instead we turned a killer loose on them. *I* turned a killer loose on them."

The storm broke when they were forty-five minutes south of Chandler County. Rain slammed into the windshield in sheets, and wind pushed at the truck like a child's toy. Even on high, the windshield wipers were useless and Tick struggled to keep the truck between the yellow lines.

Caitlin tightened her seat belt. "Tick, the guy behind us almost slid into the guard rail."

"I know. I'm trying to find a place to stop."

With a white-knuckled grip on the wheel, he pulled to the shoulder, flipping on the emergency flashers and leaving the engine running. He turned the wipers off and stared at the windshield, jaw set in a tight line.

Wind battered the vehicle, whistling around it. Caitlin watched the water stream down the window.

With a sudden movement, he twisted in his seat, grasping her headrest. "Last night, you said you'd lost *him*."

The haunting pain in his dark eyes took her breath and the remembered loss swept her. She'd expected more of his tension about their case, but not this. She studied him for a long, silent moment, taking in the weariness and stress straining his features. "Oh, Tick, let's not...are you sure you want to hear this now?"

"I have to." The raw words seemed ripped from somewhere deep inside him. "I need to know, need you to share him with me, Cait."

She understood, simply because she needed to share her memories with him, had always needed to share this child with this man. "I'd had a sonogram at eighteen weeks, a few days before Fuller...it was a boy." A wash of tears clogged her throat. "Things were going well; he was growing, thriving. I tried to get in touch with you then. I wanted you to know. I knew...I knew you'd be thrilled."

"I would have been." The low whisper emerged rough and grating.

She brushed a stray tear from her cheek. "I have those photos, from the sonogram, and the video, back home at Troupe's with some other things. I put them away...after... Because it hurt too much to look at them."

He took her hand, rubbing his thumb over her knuckles. He didn't speak and rain drummed down around them, creating an intimate curtain of sound. She flexed her fingers, curved them around his.

"Did you see him?" He lifted his head, his eyes glittering and damp. "After, I mean...what did he look like?"

"No, I didn't..." Pain fluttered in her chest. "I was in ICU for more than a week, so hysterical the first time I came to and Vince told me about him, that they sedated me. I was out of it almost completely for several of those days."

His lashes fell, shadowing his cheekbones.

She held on tight to his hand. "Vince claimed him for me. He's buried with my mother and grandmother, between them. I didn't name him...I couldn't without..." She swallowed against the ache in her throat. "Not without you."

He nodded, his head bent once more, his nape exposed and vulnerable. Fine tremors moved through his shoulders.

"I thought about names, before." She lifted her other hand to stroke over his hair, the thick dark strands soft under her fingertips. "I'd feel him moving around, at night, and I was missing you so badly, wanting to share him with you, wanting you with me—"

A strangled moan rose between them and her voice died in her throat. He was shaking, harsh choking sobs attacking his lean form. She caught the glimmer of tears on his face.

"Oh, Tick." She moved, kneeling on the seat to enfold him in a tight embrace. Her shoes slid to the floorboard. He buried his face in her hair, arms coming around her with bruising intensity. With the rain falling around them, she closed her eyes and ran soothing hands down his back, holding on as he cried.

ভ

Tick stopped at the top of the steps and stared at the stenciled star on the recently installed department door. He still felt raw and exposed, and the last thing he wanted was to go in there and tell Stanton the killer was one of theirs. Sitting down and talking to his mother about his sex life held more appeal. He wouldn't even have Caitlin for moral support—she'd insisted on going back to her hotel to check for messages.

His hand tightening on the evidence bag, he pulled the door open and stepped into the familiar controlled chaos. Voices drifted into the hall from the squad room and he bypassed his own office, heading in that direction.

Might as well get it over with.

The rich smell of Big Dawg hamburgers hung in the squad-room air. Cookie and Jeff sat at their desks, eating. Stanton had pulled up a chair. He grinned at Tick. "Hey, looks like we caught a break."

He couldn't return the smile. "Yeah?"

Jeff wiped his mouth. "The white Nissan? Belongs to Kimberly Johnson. Got a match on the VIN."

That surprised him. "It still had the plate on it?"

Cookie sucked mayonnaise off his thumb. "The one on the dash was gone. But Nissans have one on the firewall. Bobby Gene forgot that one. Chris and I brought him in. He's in holding."

Stanton's grin widened. "Won't say a word. Asked for a lawyer. Looks like we might have our man."

Tick shook his head. "It's not him."

Jeff dropped his burger on the wrapper. "What do you mean, it's not him? His prints are on Ingler's car, he has possession of Johnson's car, what else do you want? A signed confession?"

"It's not him."

"If it's not him, why'd you have us bring him in?" Cookie leaned back in his chair, a frown drawing his heavy brows together.

"Because we think he knows something. He—"

Jeff exchanged a disparaging look with Stanton. "We."

Anger tightened his chest. "What the hell is that supposed to mean?"

"It means you're not exactly objective," Stanton said.

Tick stared at the man who'd been his partner, who was still his close friend. "I don't believe this."

Jeff rested an elbow on the arm of his chair. "Okay, so if it's not Bobby Gene Butler, who is it?"

"A cop. One of ours."

"What the hell?"

"Bullshit!"

With the simultaneous outbursts, Stanton and Jeff

exchanged another look. Cookie, remaining silent, glanced between the three men. Stanton ran a hand over his eyes. "Son of a bitch. Lord, she's done it again—you've lost your everlovin' mind."

Blood pounded in Tick's ears. "Why do you keep bringing her into this? This has nothing to do with her—"

Jeff's humorless laugh rang in the room. "This whole cop thing was her idea, wasn't it? Your name's on the damn board in there as a possible suspect. Cookie's, too. And Chris. Hell, guess I'm next."

"Tick." Stanton's voice was calm, firm. "Look, we've got a viable suspect."

He refused to be soothed. "What we have is a possible witness who we damned well know is going to be uncooperative."

Jeff pointed across the desk. "Cookie, don't you have anything to say?"

Cookie shrugged, his face impassive. "What do you want me to say? It could be possible."

Groaning, Jeff rolled his eyes. "What did I expect? She's female, and you're...you."

Stanton's rough exhale bordered on a sigh. "Look, Tick, Tommy Gillabeaux wanted her here. She came down. She looked at everything—she's been a big help organizing what we had. We'll take her profile, and we'll use it. But a cop? One of our cops? Come on."

Tick blew out a long breath, staring at the ceiling. "Is this because Cait's involved or because you don't want to face the truth?"

"We don't have a truth yet."

Jeff snorted. "The truth is you're screwing her, and you'd do anything to draw this investigation out just to keep her here."

Anger washed the room in a red haze. "Shut up, Schaefer."

"Damn it, Tick, he's right. You're never yourself around her and—"

"So the general consensus is that I'd let a killer run loose so I can get laid? Is that it?"

Cookie ran a finger over his chin. "I think that's what they're saying, yeah."

"Then explain that." Tick flung the evidence bag on the desk, the card with its department logo face up on top of the bag inside. A neat stack of incident reports exploded, fluttering to the floor.

Silence descended. Stanton lifted the bag, his face white. "Where did this come from?"

"Someone left it in a motel room Amy Gillabeaux rented in Tallahassee the night Kimberly Johnson was killed, the same night Amy used Johnson's credit card. Looks to me like one of our guys killed Johnson and tried to use Amy to cover his tracks, then killed Amy, either because she was pregnant or she was figuring things out. The same guy probably offed Sharon, Vontressa and our Jane Doe." He threw his hands up in the air. "But what do I know? I'm only interested in getting my brains fu—"

"Does that mean you're not charging my client?" Autry Holton, the county's public defender, dropped her briefcase on the empty desk nearest the door.

"We may charge him with possessing stolen property," Tick growled. "But we might be able to work out a deal if he talks to us."

Stanton pinched the bridge of his nose, shoulders slumped with absolute defeat. "Cookie, go get Butler out of holding. Maybe he'll talk to us now."

Tick turned away, not able to look at Stanton, not wanting to feel sorry for him. He rubbed a hand over his nape, hurt anger clutching at his chest. Damn it, he wished Stanton could see past the wall of his stubborn dislike for Caitlin. Scratch that—he wished Stanton had seen past it months ago, when she'd wanted to tell Tick about their son. Shit, another "if only" to live with. Just what he needed.

Autry grabbed the nearest chair. "Do you guys always get along this well? Y'all sound about as friendly as the DA and I do when we're arguing motions."

"Autry, please," Stanton said, his voice weary. "Not now."

Awareness prickled along Tick's neck, down his spine. He looked sideways, his gaze clashing with Jeff's steady one. The younger man regarded him with a weighing, assessing expression that set Tick's teeth on edge.

Lord help him if Tori ended up wanting to marry the guy.

Cookie appeared at the doorway, out of breath. "Somebody might want to call the GBI."

Stanton looked up, a sick expression tightening his face. "Why?"

"Because Bobby Gene is dead."

Chapter Twelve

Ignoring the *No Smoking* sign above his head, Tick used the butt of his third cigarette to light his fourth. He leaned against the wall opposite the holding cell. GBI agents came and went, talking to Stanton, taking pictures, and conferring amongst themselves.

After a deep drag, he offered the pack to Cookie next to him. "Want one?"

"I thought you were quitting."

"Yeah, so did I." He stared at Bobby Gene Butler's body, now lying on the floor, still able to see him as he'd been when they'd run down the stairs to the cell area. Butler, face a deep purple, had twisted in a slow rotation, his body suspended from the top of the iron cage by his pants, knotted around his neck.

Supposedly he'd jumped from the top bunk. Tick figured he'd had a little help.

"Don't you know it's against the law to smoke in a municipal building in Georgia?" Will Botine, agent in charge of the Moultrie GBI office, slapped Tick on the arm.

Without a word, Tick extended the pack of cigarettes. Botine grinned and shook one out, pulling his lighter from his pocket. "Thanks. You boys didn't have enough excitement over here with that nut running around strangling women?"

Tick glanced at the holding cell, where two agents were lifting Butler's corpse into a body bag. The zipper rasped shut. He'd had enough excitement today to last the next ten years, at least. "Guess not."

Botine attempted to blow a smoke ring. "Didn't think I'd ever be investigating another dead prisoner in Chandler County.

Not with you and Reed in charge now."

Wonder what Botine would say if he knew their primary, albeit unknown, suspect was a Chandler County cop? A cop Tick himself had helped choose. Cursing, he ground his cigarette out in his empty foam coffee cup.

Botine gestured toward the ceiling. "I thought y'all were going to install cameras for this room."

"They've been ordered. County commission won't cut a check for them—said they were an unnecessary expense."

Cookie snorted. "Bet you ten bucks someone's here tomorrow, installing them."

Botine leaned against the wall, his casual posture not fooling Tick for a minute. "So who was down here, anyway?"

Cookie hooked his thumbs in his belt. "I walked through about thirty, maybe forty minutes before we found him. Roger had been down here, but he takes the front desk when Lydia goes to lunch. Could've been half a dozen deputies in and out the back door."

"Where were you?" Botine waved his cigarette at Tick.

"Tallahassee. Running down a lead."

"Can anybody verify that?"

"Agent Caitlin Falconetti, FBI."

"Agent Falconetti. I had the pleasure of talking with her this morning about some lab work you all are waiting on." His expression indicated it was anything but. "Was Schaefer here?"

Cookie shrugged. "Except for earlier this morning when he went out to Mrs. Milson's place. Her car was missing again."

Botine grinned. "Where'd she park it this time?"

"Behind her garage."

"You said earlier Chris Parker went with you to bring Butler in. Where is he now?"

"Home, probably. It's his split shift. He left around eleven."

Botine added his cigarette butt to Tick's coffee cup. "Well, let me go check in with Stan. Talk to you boys later."

Cookie watched him go. "We are so screwed."

"Oh, yeah." Maybe the FBI would take him back. A long undercover assignment in Podunk, Mississippi didn't sound so bad right about now.

Frustrated, Caitlin stepped out of the car and glared at the oil pooling beneath it.

She slammed the car door, muttering curses that would have horrified her grandfather. The car was dead, her cell phone was MIA and she was on a deserted rural highway.

Even in the middle of the day, the Georgia sun bright overhead, the scenario was terrifying. She didn't want to think about what it had been like at night.

Sharon had to have been scared out of her mind.

Caitlin put her hands on her hips and cursed the car again. At her waist, the holstered nine-millimeter SIG was a reassuring weight.

Unlike Sharon Ingler, she wasn't defenseless.

A thin trickle of perspiration ran down her spine, her blouse clinging to the dampness. Nearly an hour since the car shuddered and died. She wanted to think that sooner or later Tick would come looking for her.

"You're talking about the man with absolutely no sense of time," she muttered, using the sound of her own voice for reassurance. Arms crossed over her chest, she leaned against the car and eyed the highway. No traffic, in broad daylight, in almost an hour. A house lay a mile up the road, she remembered it, and she could understand the compulsion to start walking toward the nearest people.

She shivered in spite of the glaring heat. She understood the impulse, but she wouldn't give in to it. The distance was nothing—she ran far more than that on a regular basis. The isolation was everything. And she could just imagine Tick's reaction if she did set out on foot and he happened upon the empty car. The worry would drive him berserk. She loved him too much to do that to him.

She closed her eyes on a long, slow exhale. She loved him.

That was something else he needed to know.

She needed to give him the words. She killed the next fifteen minutes indulging in fantasies of the best way to do just that, imagining his response. The following fifteen minutes she spent devising ways to punish him for not noticing that she'd been MIA for an hour and a half. If he was shooting the bull with Cookie while she sweltered, she would handcuff his ass to the bed, tease him to within an inch of his life, and leave him there until she was good and ready to put him out of his misery.

Considering she couldn't keep her hands off his long, lean frame, about five minutes max.

She brushed her hair back, eyeing the heat mirages on the blacktop. A vehicle topped the hill, coming into sight before the rumble of the engine reached her ears. It slowed to a stop behind her rental, and she tensed, not pushing away from the car. She unsnapped her holster, resting her hand lightly on the butt of the semiautomatic.

She didn't relax, even when she recognized the driver. He stepped out of the car and began walking toward her. "Having a little trouble, Agent Falconetti?"

Sitting against the wall, Tick studied the patrol schedule from the night Sharon Ingler disappeared. Something was off, but he just couldn't figure out what it was—like having a popcorn kernel stuck between two molars and being unable to wiggle it free. The sensation drove him crazy.

Peace and quiet to think would probably help. He glared at the commotion brewing around him. The coroner had finally arrived, and Butler's body had been removed. The jail complex still crawled with GBI agents, and he'd given the same answers to the same questions to four different agents, not counting Will Botine. They made it very clear who was in charge and the sense of powerlessness grated.

Desperate to get something done, he'd pulled the patrol schedules for the last two months and sent Roger for the dispatch tapes and unit videos. There had to be something here that would lead him to the son of a bitch hiding among them.

"Here." Cookie handed him a fresh cup of coffee and slid to the floor next to him, grunting. "Find anything?"

"No. Not a damn thing." Tick leaned his head back, sipping the hot, bitter brew with caution. Four cups of coffee and a half a pack of cigarettes on a now-empty stomach were coming back to haunt him. Acid gnawed at his gut, the burn spreading into his chest. His eyes drifted closed.

"Hey, where is Falconetti, anyway?"

"She went to check her voice mail at the hotel. She should be back anytime now." Reluctantly, he opened his eyes and glanced at his watch, unease skittering along his nerves. Two hours. More than two hours. The trip to her hotel and back should have taken fifteen minutes at the most.

Setting his coffee aside, he jerked his cell from his belt and dialed. Phone at his ear, he rolled to his feet, brushing dust from his slacks. Her voice mail picked up immediately, her husky voice cool and professional as she directed the caller to leave a message.

"Cait, it's Tick. We've got a problem at the jail. Call me."

Cookie stood. "Tick. You just left a message on a cell phone she can't find."

"Ah, damn it." He dialed the hotel's number, asked for her room extension and listened to the phone ring until the message center picked up there. He shook his head, worry joining the coffee and nicotine gnawing at his gut. "She was just going to the hotel and back."

Cookie shrugged. "Maybe she stopped off somewhere, went to lunch or something."

"I've got a bad feeling about this, Cookie."

"No, you've just got it bad, period."

"Not you, too."

"Hey, I say go for it, man. It'll be fun to watch her make you toe the line. And if you think about it, the idea of this bastard being a cop makes a sick kind of sense. Falconetti and I talked about it...you know, who would a woman trust enough to get out of a disabled vehicle."

"What did she say?"

"That she wouldn't get out of the car for anyone."

"Sounds like Cait." He jerked a hand through his hair. Where the hell was she? "I'm going to look for her. Not like I'm needed around here—"

"Well." Stanton joined them, his face haggard. "An hour and a half of investigating, and the GBI has ascertained that we have a dead prisoner on our hands."

Cookie grinned. "Careful, Stan, your superiority complex is showing."

Stanton turned to Tick. "Ray's at the front desk, screaming for a statement. You want to talk to him?"

Tick fixed him with a baleful glare. "You think I'm capable of putting more than two words together?"

"Damn it, Tick, I don't need this right now. Just go give him a statement."

Botine jogged down the stairs. "Damn, Reed, your day keeps getting better and better."

With a quiet curse, Stanton rolled his eyes skyward. "What now?"

"State trooper located an abandoned rental car out on Highway 19 a few minutes ago."

Stanton shrugged. "So? We probably get a couple of abandoned cars a week."

"Well, this one happens to have a dead female FBI agent in it."

A red haze exploded behind Tick's eyes. Hands at Botine's neck, he slammed him into the wall. "What did you say? What the hell did you just say?"

"Calvert, what the fuck!"

"Stop it." Stanton's arm came across his chest, attempting to break his hold on Botine and push him away at the same time. Tick ignored him, horror and grief and a desperate disbelief pulsing through his brain.

Oh, God, no, it wasn't...it couldn't be...not...he couldn't lose her, too...

"What did you say?" He pushed Botine against the wall again, and Stanton's arm tightened on his chest and shoulders, thumb pressing hard into the nerve point behind his clavicle. Numbness took his body, knees buckling, giving Stanton the leverage to drag him away from Botine and pin him against the opposite wall.

He closed his eyes, a scream pushing up in his throat. No. She couldn't be dead. He couldn't take it. He could not bear it...not this.

Absolute silence blanketed the room. Botine's voice emerged choked with fury and pain. "Reed, what the hell?"

"They're old friends. They were at Quantico together." Stanton supported Tick against the wall—his own knees didn't want to bear his weight.

"He was doing her on the side." Schaefer's muttered words coincided with Stanton's.

Snarling, Tick lunged at him, breaking Stanton's startled hold. "Son of a bitch—"

He hit the solid wall of Cookie's chest, preventing him from wrapping his hands around Schaefer's throat as well. Strong fingers grasped his wrist, pushing his arm up behind his back, shoving him against the wall again. The physical discomfort didn't come close to the agony crushing his chest. Shit, he couldn't breathe, couldn't think, couldn't...

"Come on, Tick, calm down."

Calm down? Was he crazy?

Cookie released his arm, keeping him restrained by pressing his shoulder into the wall, Stanton's hand pinning his other shoulder. Stanton growled next to his ear. "I don't want to throw you in a cell, but I will if I have to."

"I don't think that's such a good idea, Stan. The last guy we put in there is dead."

"Shut up, Cookie."

The fury drained, swallowed by the shock and anguish. His lungs wouldn't work, first heaving, then seeming to stop altogether. "Cookie, my God...Mark, she can't be dead. She just can't be..."

Heavy fingers tightened on his shoulder in sympathy. "I'm sorry, Tick."

His eyes closed once more. How could she be dead? How could everything be gone, just like that? His throat shut against the animal sob of despair welling within.

Stanton's voice, from a distance. "What happened?"

"Car's on the southbound side of 19." Botine sounded less outraged. "Trooper on site mentioned multiple gunshot wounds. I was going to see if you and Tick wanted to ride out that way with me, but—"

"I'm going." Tick opened his eyes.

Stanton shook his head. "No."

"I need to see her, Stan. I'm going, with or without you." His voice was thick, clogged with pain. "I have to."

Outside, the sun gleamed off the white marble courthouse, the sky clear of clouds after the morning's storm. Stanton refused to let him drive and Tick stared at the ordinary busyness of life going on in Coney as the town flashed by: a group of kids gathered in front of the First Baptist church, two young mothers pushed baby strollers, the parking lot at Debbie's Main Street Café filled with cars.

Ordinary. Everything seemed perfectly ordinary, so this had to be a mistake. It had to be because he couldn't get by without her.

This was nothing more than a nightmare, another of those weird dreams...

The two southbound lanes of Highway 19 were a sea of blue—blue and silver state patrol units, pulsing blue lights, blue uniforms. Tick leaned against Stanton's Explorer, eyeing the traffic crawling in the northbound lanes, steeling himself for what was to come. He still couldn't get his mind around the fact she was gone.

He'd thought standing on the tarmac, watching the small plane flip, roll and burn with his father aboard, was the worst thing he could ever experience. He was wrong—this was much, much worse.

"Tick?" Stanton watched him with sympathetic eyes. He'd tried several times to talk on the way over, but Tick froze him out, refusing to be drawn into conversation.

He blew out a harsh breath, running a hand through his hair. "Let's go."

The blue sea parted, letting them pass without comment. This case would be county turf, although the state patrol was first on scene. Chris was already here, Cookie was en route. They'd left Schaefer in charge of the jail, along with what had to be half of the state's GBI agents. Tick didn't care who worked this case. Jurisdiction didn't matter anymore.

Everything that mattered was gone.

An ambulance and the coroner's hearse blocked his view of

the car, but he could see the body bag lying on the ground, open and waiting. His heart jerked. Oh, God. It was real—this was really happening, and he wasn't going to wake up screaming and sweating to find it was all just a bad dream. He walked in a living nightmare, worse than anything the night could dream up.

A state patrol sergeant stepped in front of them, tapping the edge of his campaign hat in a one-fingered salute. "Stanton. Hell of a scene, isn't it? Tick, you look like shit. You sick?"

"What have you got?" Stanton's voice was the quietest Tick had ever heard it.

"Caucasian female, early thirties. Shot multiple times. Looks like a small caliber, maybe a .32 or .380."

"She was shot in the car?"

"Driver's window is rolled down. Her seat belt is undone, but her service piece is still holstered. Doubt she even knew what hit her until it was too late. FBI credentials were in her lap."

Nausea pitched in Tick's stomach. "So you're sure it's her?"

The trooper shrugged and glanced at the evidence bag in his hand, containing a familiar black credentials folder. The shield winked in the sunlight. "Says it right here, in black and white. Federal Bureau of Investigation. Special Agent Bocaccio, Gina Anne."

Bocaccio?

"It's not her." A weak, shaky laugh escaped him. He collapsed against the nearest squad car, knees bent, elbows on his thighs, head in his hands. Relief left him limp and boneless, wrung out. "Sweet Jesus, it's not her."

"What's with him?" Chris Parker's voice floated over Tick's head. The caffeine and nicotine conspired with the emotional merry-go-round, nausea clutching at his throat. He concentrated on breathing, forcing down the queasiness.

"He thought it was Falconetti."

"I just saw her over at Lawson Automotive when I picked up my unit. They towed her rental car in—the line to the oil cooler busted. She's been stranded out on 112 for almost three hours, and she's fit to be tied, too."

"I'll bet." Stanton nudged Tick's foot with his. "Tick, who's Bocaccio? What's she doing here?"

The question penetrated the fog still gripping his brain. "She's Cait's partner, a computer expert. Cait asked her to run down some leads—"

"Bocaccio?" Chris's voice was a surprised yelp. "That's who's in the car? Hell, I talked to her this morning. I took a message for Falconetti. Tick, I taped it to your door—didn't you get it?"

Tick glanced up, shaking his head. He straightened, his legs still unsteady. "What did she say?"

Chris frowned. "Not much. She couldn't get Falconetti at the hotel and wanted to let Falconetti know she was on her way down. Said to tell her that she'd found something she wanted to show her in person."

That message, taped to his office door where every person in the department could see it, had signed Bocaccio's death warrant. He wanted to be sorry and later he would be, but right now...right now, all that mattered was the fact that Caitlin was still alive, still with him. Damn if he'd wait any longer to tell her how he felt.

Stanton nodded toward the car. "Sergeant, I don't suppose there's a laptop in the car? Any files?"

"Yeah, right. Not even her cell phone. Nothing but her and the ID."

Tick and Stanton exchanged a look. "Took the purse, took the computer, but left the gun. Rules out our friendly local drug dealers."

The handheld radio attached to the trooper's belt squawked. "Excuse me a minute."

"He killed her, Stanton. She'd found something, and he killed her to keep it quiet. Same with Bobby Gene Butler—he knew something, and the son of a bitch killed him to stop him from talking."

Chris tugged off his cap and scratched the top of his head. "Bobby Gene Butler is dead? When did that happen?"

"Couple hours ago. He hung himself in holding."

Chris grimaced. "Yeah. Sure he did. And you hate fishing.

You're thinking Bobby Gene's related to what happened with Bocaccio?"

"Unfortunately." Stanton shot them a warning look. "We don't need to talk about this here. Cookie'll be here in a few minutes—we'll let him work this one. Chris, you help him. Damn it, we've got to notify the FBI."

"I'll do that." Tick passed a hand over his eyes. He was going to have to tell Caitlin that Bocaccio was dead, and he'd gotten the impression the two women were close friends as well as partners. Dread dragged at him. "Chris, let me have the keys to your unit. I'll leave it in the lot at the station."

"Thanks." Caitlin smiled, accepting the keys Keith Lawson proffered. The young man had not only stopped alongside the highway where'd she'd been stranded, but he'd radioed his father's wrecker service, arranged to have her car towed and then gone out to the rental company to pick up another vehicle for her. He might possess a juvenile record a mile long, but he had his good points.

He walked outside with her to the rental car. "Agent Falconetti? You said I should tell you anything I remembered about Amy, even if it didn't seem important."

She pushed her sunglasses up into her hair so she could meet his gaze. "I did. Did you remember something?"

"Yeah. A couple of things. I been thinking about it a lot. When I fixed her car? The vehicle she hit was white. There was paint embedded in the dent on her car. And when I called her to let her know it was ready, I could hear this guy in the background. I couldn't hear what he said because there was a dog barking. Sounded like a big one, too."

"Could you hear any other noises? Music or people or traffic? Anything at all?"

"No." His shoulders slumped further. "Maybe. I don't know. I wasn't paying attention. I didn't know it would be important."

"It's all right." She tapped a finger against her lips. "Was she calling you from her cell?"

"Yeah."

"Remember what date? Morning, afternoon, night?"

"A couple of days before she went missing." He shrugged. "Why?"

"Because it might give us a lead." She jotted herself a note on the rental paperwork. Cookie had gotten a rush from simply trying to ping her cell phone. She'd let him have a run at triangulating Amy's cell call so they could possibly match it against estimated patrol car movements. "Did you call from here, from home, your cell?"

"Here." He looked at her askance, like he couldn't quite figure out how any of this was going to help.

"Okay." She tucked the note in her back pocket. "Thanks again, Keith. For everything."

He waved as she pulled out of the parking lot. She adjusted the rearview mirror. The car was a twin to the disabled one and she wondered if the rental company had purchased anything but beige Chevrolets.

Three hours stranded doing nothing. The loss of time irritated her and she made a mental list of things to do as she drove—call about their evidence reports again, check in with Gina on the insurance claims and background checks, teach Tick what a damn watch was.

A Chandler County patrol car flashed by her, headed in the opposite direction. She glanced at the mirror again, in time to see brake lights flare before the driver executed a textbook example of a J-turn. Blue lights blazed, headlights sparking in an alternating pattern.

Her gaze flew to the speedometer. Fifty-seven. Not enough to justify that display. She pulled to the shoulder and killed the engine. Jerking her credentials from her pocket, she stepped from the car, spoiling for a fight.

She hoped it was Troy Lee, the young deputy with peach fuzz on his chin who kept eyeing her ass. She felt like grinding someone's professional ego into the dust.

The unit slid to a stop behind her car. She started toward it, noting it was the county's K-9 unit. The door opened, and Tick stepped from the car, hair mussed, jacket and tie gone, collar undone, sleeves rolled up.

She smiled, feral satisfaction curling through her.

Oh, even better.

She met him at the patrol car. "You know that thing on your wrist? It's called a watch—"

"Oh God, Cait." He reached for her, fingers warm against her skin, and jerked her into his arms. Her irritation receded, swallowed by the first brush of his long body along hers. He buried his face in her hair, his hands roving her back, caressing, touching everywhere. A long exhale shuddered through him.

With her face pressed to his throat, she took a deep breath, layers of smell filling her senses—soap, starch, coffee, cigarette smoke.

Tick.

"Calvert." She wrapped her arms around his neck and sighed into him. Being this close to him felt oh, so good. "I love you."

His breathing trembled against her temple, and he lifted his head, his eyes dark and fierce. He caught her lips with his.

Engulfed in a crushing embrace, his mouth on hers, kissing her, devouring her, she could do little but hang on. He slid his long-fingered hands to her hips, pulling her into him, and she opened her mouth to him, their tongues engaged in a fierce duel. Any remaining annoyance dissipated under a rush of love and desire.

He groaned and backed her against the patrol car, his body heavy against her. She sank her fingers into his thick hair, tugging. Yanking her blouse free from her slacks, he eased his palms up and down her ribcage, touch warm on her bare skin. She moaned her approval into his mouth.

She kissed him deeper, tasting the tang of cigarettes and coffee. Gripping his hair, she pulled his head back. "You've been smoking."

The words left her lips on a gasp as his mouth found her neck, suckling, biting lightly, the tip of his tongue soothing over the spot. She pressed closer, needing to be nearer.

"I love you." He rasped the words near her ear. "I love you, Falconetti, and I'm not letting you go again."

The declaration imbued her with a bubbling joy. "Are you asking or telling me?"

"Telling you."

She pressed open kisses to the column of his throat, his skin salty against her tongue. "There you go, rushing—"

"I don't care. I don't care if you move here or if I go to Virginia with you—it doesn't matter. I will not go through another day like today."

His words penetrated the hot haze of need holding her captive and with reality came the realization he was shaking in her arms. Tangling her hands in his hair again, she tugged his head up, looking into his pale face. "Calvert, what are you talking about?"

He cupped her chin, smoothing her cheekbones. "I thought you were dead, that he'd gotten to you, and I couldn't bear it. I believed you were *dead.*"

Anguish darkened his eyes, his voice a choked whisper. She stroked his temple, a soothing, tender touch. "I'm fine. The car broke down."

He rested his face against her hair. "I can't lose you again. Do you hear me, Cait? Never again."

She caressed his nape, a touch designed to comfort rather than arouse. "You won't."

He sighed, an unsteady exhale, and she felt some of the tension leave his body. They stood in a simple embrace, and Caitlin rubbed her face against his neck, listening to his breathing return to normal. God, she loved this man.

She closed her eyes, massaging his neck and shoulders in light, soothing circles. He relaxed further against her. Her nose brushed his jaw, his scent saturating her senses. "Calvert?"

"Hmmm?"

"Why did you think he'd gotten to me?" The muscles under her hands jumped, tensed. He heaved a rough breath and pulled away.

"Butler's dead."

Surprise jerked through her. "What?"

"Cookie found him hanging in the holding cell a couple of hours ago."

No wonder he hadn't thought to come looking for her. She could imagine the chaos taking place at the jail. "Oh, God. He killed Butler to keep us from talking to him."

"Yeah. I think so."

"He'll do whatever he has to in order to maintain control of the situation." The realization terrified her with its implications. And he had the ultimate advantage—they didn't have a clue who he was. "He thinks he's losing control. Oh, Tick, this is not good."

"Cait." She glanced up at him, startled by the stark worry darkening his eyes. "Gina Bocaccio called the department this morning when she couldn't get in touch with you. She was on her way down here to show you something she'd found."

"That sounds like Gina. She's impulsive—"

The words stopped in her throat. He'd thought she was dead. Something had led him to believe that. She stepped away from him, horror's clammy hand grabbing her spine. "You thought I was dead. Something happened and you thought it was me. But it wasn't, was it? He—"

"I'm sorry, precious." He stepped forward, reached for her, but she knocked his hands away.

"It was Gina, wasn't it? He got to her." Even the whisper hurt her throat, tight with a sudden rush of tears. Not Gina— not Gina with her laughing brown eyes and wicked sense of humor. Not Gina, who had helped keep her sane, who had bullied and cajoled her back to a semblance of real life.

He nodded, drawing her into his arms. She shook her head, pushing at him, and his hold tightened.

He rested his brow against hers. "I am so sorry—"

"How?"

"Precious, don't."

One clenched fist pummeled his chest before she shoved him away. "Damn you, tell me how!"

"She was shot, in her rental car at close range. She died instantly."

"Oh, God." An anguished moan clawed its way out of her. She sagged against the vehicle, his arms coming around her again. This time, she clutched at him, seeking protection from the sobs attacking her body. "Oh, God."

He didn't lie and whisper that it was all right. He didn't speak at all. He wrapped her close, rocking her against him.

When the tears finally eased, she pulled away, everything—grief, pain, love—frozen in a hard knot of ice in her stomach. She drew in a deep breath and shored up her defenses. "Is she in Moultrie?"

Brushing her damp hair from her face, he nodded. "The bureau is sending two agents from the Atlanta field office—"

"I want to see her."

"I don't think that's a good idea. She...I just don't think you should."

She straightened her blouse and tucked it in again, easing away from him. Her knees trembled, but she stiffened them. "She's in that damned morgue because I asked for her help."

"Don't." He gazed at her with dark tortured eyes, concern softening the lines of his face. "This isn't your fault."

"Like hell." Her laugh was harsh, rusty. "I don't care if you come or not, but I'm going to see her. She's my *partner*, Tick."

She walked away, leaving him standing by the unit. His frustrated oath rang in her ears, followed by the crunch of his footsteps on the loose gravel beside the blacktop.

When she reached her car, he laid a gentle hand on her arm, and she turned on him. "Don't."

"Of course I'm coming." He cradled her face in his hands. "Don't you get it by now, Cait? There is no more going it alone. We're in this together, all the way."

Chapter Thirteen

White paint. Barking dog.

Caitlin added the items to Amy Gillabeaux's section of the dry-erase board. Two new columns occupied the end of the board—Bobby Gene Butler and Gina Bocaccio.

"Getting anywhere?" Tick set a cup of fresh coffee on the table, sipping his own.

She shrugged and continued writing, this time under Kimberly Johnson's name, filling in the results the GBI lab had faxed. Canine hair—results inconclusive, but most likely German Shepherd or Belgian Malinois. Green fiber—cotton polyester blend, but no luck on matching the manufacturer yet.

With a weary sigh, she capped the marker and dropped it in the tray. Her eyes burned, a combination of fatigue and grief. She lifted the cup, aware of Tick's concerned gaze, thankful for his steady presence. There was no way she'd have gotten through the horror of viewing Gina's body without him.

"Frazier has a couple of agents tracing Gina's research." Speaking hurt her throat, and the words emerged sounding painful and raw. "It may take a few days, but he thinks they'll turn up whatever she'd found."

He leaned a hip against the table. "You and Bocaccio were close."

Fresh tears burned the backs of her eyes, and she shoved them down ruthlessly. "Yes, we were. After Fuller, when I was ready to go back to work and I just couldn't face trying to live alone, she showed up and bullied me into moving in with her."

Not smiling, he smoothed a finger along her cheek. "Somehow, I can't imagine anyone bullying you into anything."

"You didn't know Gina. It was really hard to say no to her. But she'd do anything for someone she cared about." She wanted to succumb to the tears, to turn into him and let his solid embrace and easy drawl make the hurt fade, at least for a while.

Schaefer rapped on the open door. "Hey, Cookie and I are walking down to the diner. Y'all want to come?"

Tick glanced at her, then turned to Schaefer. "No, you two go on. Take your time."

"Want us to bring anything back?"

She pushed away from the table and turned her back on the younger investigator, looking for the file that held Amy's phone records. "We're fine."

She caught Schaefer's shrug from the corner of her eye. His and Cookie's footsteps faded down the hall. Tick tossed his coffee cup toward the trashcan, missed and went to pick it up. "You don't like him, do you?"

"He's...arrogant, under that demeanor of his. Given a choice, I'd take Cookie any day."

He shuddered. "Don't let him hear you say that. He'd put a spin on that statement that would make my skin crawl."

She smiled, the humor a welcome, though peculiar experience after the day they'd had. "I said I'd take Cookie over Schaefer, not over you."

"I'm glad to hear that." He pulled a chair from the table, spun it around and straddled it. One long finger tapped the phone records. "I thought Jeff finished those after we left."

"He didn't." She examined him. Weariness tugged at his features, but she resisted the wave of tenderness, the urge to reach for him. Time for that later, when they were alone. She rested her chin on her hand. "You did the right thing, you know."

A tiny frown pulled his brows downward. "What?"

"Leaving the bureau. Taking this job. You belong here. You believe in this."

"I'd give it up, go back to the bureau, if you wanted me to." His voice dropped with intensity. "I'd do anything for you."

And she was too tired to even think of sorting that out right now. Time for that later, too. Frowning, she stretched out to brush at his shoulder, grayish-brown hairs clinging to the fabric of his shirt. "What is that? And where did it come from?"

"I drove Chris's unit, remember?" He grimaced at his shoulder and blew out an exasperated breath. "That damn dog is still shedding his winter coat, and the hair gets on everything..."

The words died, his gaze locked on hers. They glanced at the board, then back at each other. Tick shook his head. "No."

She lifted an eyebrow at his adamant tone. "Tell me why not."

He squinted at the board, still shaking his head. "Chris is...not capable of cruelty."

"He's a cop. We're all capable of cruelty to some extent. It's part of the personality."

"Slapping the cuffs on a perp too tight? Sure. But not deliberate cruelty. Not *this*." He drummed the crime scene photo lying on top of Kimberly Johnson's file, a shot of Amy Gillabeaux's battered body, the stab wounds gaping.

"You said you didn't know him well."

"I know enough. This is the same guy who cried the night we had to take a five-year-old to the ER after his father raped him. Chris was the first one of us on scene when the mama called it in. He used the dog to calm the boy down, hell, even rode in the ambulance with him. I'm telling you, Cait, it's not him. Guys like that don't do shit like this."

"Then tell me who." Her voice was quiet as she laid another photo out, and another. "Who *is* capable of this and this...and Gina."

"I don't know." His dark eyes glinted with anger, hurt and frustration. "I just don't know. You think I don't walk through this place and look at every guy I work with, wondering if he's the one? Hell, I've even looked at Stanton funny—"

"Somehow, I don't think it's Reed."

"Well, that's nice to know. I figured I'd be at the top of your list." Stanton's tense voice held a wry note. He placed a typewritten list of names in front of Tick. "And we can cross these off the list of suspects in Bobby Gene's death anyway. GBI checked out their alibis."

Caitlin scribbled a note next to a highlighted entry on the phone records. "Chris Parker was picking up his unit from Lawson Automotive while I was there. Any particular reason?"

Stanton shrugged, a quizzical expression crossing his face as Tick dropped his head into his hands. "Somebody backed into it. Lawson pulled the dent and repainted the quarter panel. Why?"

Tick lifted his head, pinching the bridge of his nose. "Department business card. Kimberly Johnson's body had canine hair on it. White patrol unit with a dent. Keith Lawson repaired a dent to Amy Gillabeaux's car that had white paint embedded in it."

"Parker?" Stanton's tone lowered to a hissed whisper. "You think it's *Chris*?"

Tick glanced at the patrol records in front of him. "He was scheduled for duty the nights Ingler, Gillabeaux and Johnson disappeared."

"Who're we talking about?" Cookie strolled into the room, bearing a grease-stained white paper bag. Schaefer followed, sucking on a milkshake.

Stanton and Tick exchanged a glance. Tick jumped to his feet to pull the door closed. With a weary sigh, Stanton waved the two investigators to empty chairs. "Chris Parker."

"Can't see it." Cookie laughed. "Chris? Come on."

"He fits Falconetti's profile." Schaefer shrugged. "His age is right. He's smart, socially competent, has a casual girlfriend, lives alone. His mother ran off when he was a kid, so I bet there's a ton of those maternal issues Falconetti insists our guy has. I say we bring him in and talk to him."

Tick paced, rubbing the back of his neck. Caitlin watched him. Something didn't feel right, but she couldn't pin it down. His shoulders heaved with a sigh. "What if we're wrong? It gets out in the county that we brought him in, and he's ruined."

If Chris Parker was Gina's murderer, his reputation was the least of her concerns, but she understood Tick's reservations. Even a taint of suspicion could ruin a man and what they had was circumstantial.

"Then don't bring him in tonight," she suggested. "Put someone outside his place. We'll look at the patrol tapes, go over the dispatch transcripts, and we can talk to him in the morning. We may find something specific you want to ask him about."

Stanton and Tick exchanged another glance, and Stanton nodded. "Sounds like a plan. Cookie, you're on call. Jeff, you're on surveillance. Chris Parker doesn't make a move that you don't know about."

Stanton consulted his watch as Cookie and Schaefer strolled out. "You're going to be late if you don't get a move on. It's ten to six now."

Tick covered his eyes with one hand and groaned. "Lord, I forgot it was Tuesday."

Stanton moved to the door. "You've had a rough day," he said, with a sardonic glance at Caitlin. She returned his scornful look with a cool little smile before he walked out.

Tick lowered his hand. "I've got to go. Tuesday's my night to teach the crisis center's self-defense class, and it's too late to cancel. You want to come with me? You can hang out with Tori."

The grief was still close to the surface, and she wasn't sure she could pull off pleasant socializing tonight. "I think I'll take the tapes and go to the hotel. I really need a shower."

He stood, fishing his keys from his pocket and pulling his extra house key from the ring. "I don't want you alone tonight."

"I'm a big girl. I'm used to being alone."

"Yeah, but tonight you don't have to be. Let me have my way in this. Let me be there for you. Get your stuff for the night, go to my place, make yourself at home. I'll sleep on the couch if you want me to."

"Thank you, but no." She ran a finger over the key's outline. "I'd much rather be in your arms."

"That I can arrange." He nodded, a light glowing in his dark, serious gaze. Leaning forward, he dropped a brief kiss on her lips. "I've got to go because if I'm late, my little sister will make my life a living hell. I'll be home soon."

Home. The word shimmered through her with unspoken promises.

She pointed at the cardboard box of videotapes and

dispatch transcripts. "Take your time. I have plenty to keep me occupied."

Tick surveyed the crowd of women packed into the women's center's meeting room. The classes were usually full, but since dead women seemed to be turning up every couple of days in Chandler County, the class enrollment was at overload. Women of all ages and backgrounds filled the chairs—girls just out of high school, matrons his mother's age, clerks, teachers, soccer moms. All there for the same reason.

Fear. The fact they needed to be afraid angered him, renewing his determination to find the son of a bitch menacing his county. He couldn't picture Chris Parker as that threat. Chris had been with him the night Sharon Ingler disappeared. They'd worked the scene together and searched the nearby woods in the dark, calling Sharon's name until their voices were hoarse. Could Parker have killed her, dumped the body, and acted as if nothing had happened when he returned?

Not Chris.

Tick just didn't see it.

Low conversation buzzed around the room, much of it focused on Amy and Sharon. News of Gina Bocaccio's death made the rounds as well, fueling the anxiety. If even a highly trained FBI agent had become a victim, what chance did they have?

Clearing his throat, he strode to the front of the room. He introduced himself and welcomed the women, all the while trying to exude a competent, reassuring attitude. He launched the class with basic background information and general safety tips. Tonight would be all discussion; Jeff would pick up the physical techniques on Thursday.

When he opened the floor for questions, the class bombarded him. "Most importantly, if you're in a parking lot, in your driveway, if an attacker is trying to get you into his car or yours, do whatever you have to do to prevent that from happening. If you're in your car, and you're approached, stay in the car, doors locked, windows up."

A petite blonde on the front row raised her hand. "What if it's someone I know?"

He shook his head. "Doesn't matter. Do not exit that car. The moment you do, you're vulnerable."

"Yeah, like Sharon." He recognized the redhead next to the blonde as one of Sharon and Amy's classmates. She fixed him with a challenging look. "So, what if it's a cop?"

"Don't exit the car. Leave your engine running. You can lower the window enough to slide your license and insurance card out to him. Ask him to radio for backup. We can have another unit dispatched anywhere in the county within minutes. If he refuses, you drive away, straight to the sheriff's office or the nearest business. Again, don't get out of the car. Lean on the horn until someone comes out."

With the abundance of questions, the class ran twenty minutes past the scheduled conclusion time. The women drifted out in pairs or small groups, never alone, and several stayed after to ask further questions. Once the room emptied, he walked down the hall to Tori's office. "You ready?"

She shut down her computer. "I guess."

A vase, overflowing with pink roses, graced the corner of her desk. He fingered the edge of one blossom. "Who are these from?"

Like he had to ask.

She rummaged in her purse for her keys, a smile playing around her mouth. "Jeff."

First she brought the guy to Sunday dinner, now he was sending her flowers. And they'd been out, what? Three or four times. Holy hell, Schaefer was moving fast. After the last couple of days, Tick didn't like it one bit. "You're serious about him, aren't you?"

With an impish glint in her eyes, she reached up and tweaked his nose. "Wouldn't you like to know?"

"Tori." He reminded himself that she was supposed to be one of his joys.

"I like him. He likes me. We're taking things really slowly, but, yes, I could see this relationship going places." Stacking a couple of folders in the basket at the corner of her desk, she fixed him with a wry look. "I thought you liked him."

"Tori, I...hell, I've seen a side of him lately I don't like."

She shut off the lights and nudged him with her elbow. "Yeah, he told me ya'll got into it last night."

"He told you about that?"

With a shrug, she pulled her office door closed and locked it. "He just said you were in a bad mood and when he tried to talk to you about it, you bit his head off."

Son of a bitch. Nice how Schaefer had twisted that to his advantage.

Tick opened his mouth to ask if Schaefer had mentioned how close he'd come to having Tick wring his neck earlier and closed it. Already, Tori was regarding him with a familiar stubborn tilt to her chin.

"I want you to rethink seeing him, Tor."

"Meaning you're laying down a dictate that I shouldn't go out with him again, because you don't approve." She rolled her eyes at him. "I hate that about you, you know. I don't want you running my life."

"I don't run your life. I try to look out for you."

"Oh, please. If you keep telling whoppers like that, lightning will strike you." She pushed the front door open, let him precede her, and set the alarm before joining him on the sidewalk. "Of course, I must be crazy for dating a cop. I always swore I wouldn't. He broke our date tonight. Said he had something to do. Secret cop stuff."

Yeah. Like watching Chris Parker.

"I suppose you want me to say I'm sorry about that."

"No, because we both know you'd be lying." She leaned her head against his arm. "I think I'll call Layla and see if she wants to go get a drink. And don't you dare say anything—I'm well over twenty-one."

"Yeah, you are. Just be careful. Listen, I've got to go—"

"Cait waiting for you?"

"Yeah." The idea of her, waiting for him, sent a warm glow through him, despite the day's events.

"How is she?" Tori wrapped her arms over her midriff. "She has to be devastated, Tick."

"She is." Moultrie had been hard. He understood her compulsion to see Gina but wished he'd been able to spare her that. Silent tears had come in the autopsy lab, but outside in his truck, she'd wept into his neck, clinging to him as the sobs shook her. "She's holding it together, but I know it's hard."

"Take care of her. She'll need that from you right now." Tori tucked her hair behind her ear. "She's got that whole strong, capable woman thing going on and doesn't like to appear vulnerable. Don't push but be there, be what she needs."

"Thanks." He took her keys, unlocking and opening the door. "Tori?"

She slid behind the wheel of the Miata and reached for her keys. "Yes?"

He held on to her key ring until she looked at him and he had her full attention. "Promise me you'll think about what I said about Jeff."

Her shoulders slumped under a heavy sigh. "I promise. Now go take care of Cait."

The cold water washed over Caitlin's head, sending little shockwaves along her skin. She'd tried working once she'd reached Tick's, but her concentration was shot. Finally, in desperation, she'd stripped off and headed for the bathroom in the hopes that a brisk shower would focus her.

She wished she could wash away the visions of Gina's death from her mind, make herself forget her partner, her *friend*, was dead.

She rested her forehead against the smooth tile of the shower and let the water flow over her. She was exhausted, spent, with no more tears to shed.

"Cait?" Tick's voice penetrated the sound of rushing water. "Are you all right?"

"Yes." She didn't move. Physically, she was fine. Emotionally? She felt like someone had taken her apart over the past few days and put her back together haphazardly, with a few pieces missing.

Seconds later, the shower door opened and he stepped inside. At the first touch of the icy water, he jumped and muttered an oath.

"Precious?" He touched her shoulder, swept the wet hair

from her cheek.

She released a shuddery sigh and turned into his solid form. He held her, kissing her temple, cheek, jaw. Keeping one arm around her, he reached out to adjust the water until it washed over them in a warm, comforting fall.

Without speaking, he rubbed at her back and shoulders, up her nape and under her hair. She relaxed into him, resting her face on his chest, relishing the way he cherished her. He snagged the soap from a shelf and massaged a foamy lather over her skin. The water flowed, washing the suds and stress from her body, rinsing down the drain. She closed her eyes. With the soap, his scent surrounded her, permeating her. The steady warmth of his body, the reality of him against her, and the rhythmic motion of his touch were hypnotic, entrancing.

"Tick," she breathed, "I want this over. I want him locked up, where he can never do this again."

"I know." He slid his arm around her waist and nuzzled behind her ear before kissing the corner of her mouth. "Me, too."

He shut off the water, droplets pattering to the tile floor. He backed out of the cubicle, wrapped a towel about his hips and pulled her with him to stand on the fluffy rug. With another thick bath sheet, he wiped the water from her skin, rubbed at her damp hair. Using the terrycloth for leverage, he tugged her to him.

"You need some sleep." He brushed his lips against hers. "And probably some food. Why don't you lie down for a little while?"

"Hmm." Soothed by the ministrations, she tipped into him, resting her mouth against his throat. She could melt, right here, could hold on to him forever, right here. "I still have patrol tapes to watch."

"Later." With one smooth movement, he swung her into his arms and carried her through to the bedroom. "Sleep first. Twenty-minute power nap while I walk down to the dock and check the feeder. Then I'll fix us something to eat and we'll watch them together."

He settled her on the bed and pulled away to don a pair of faded jeans and a T-shirt.

"Tick, I'm not going to be able to sleep." She examined the ceiling and fingered the edge of the soft bath sheet wrapped around her body. She was afraid to close her eyes, knew what images would linger on her lids if she did.

His dark gaze solemn, he leaned over her, a hand planted beside each hip, and kissed her. "Rest."

"I'll try."

She did attempt to sleep, but despite her physically relaxed state, her mind refused to cooperate. After ten minutes of staring at the ceiling, she pulled on jeans and a soft cotton T-shirt and popped the first of the patrol tapes into the bedroom VCR.

Minutes later, Caitlin tucked her feet under her on the bed, watching for the third time the film of the night Sharon Ingler disappeared. Something wasn't right. The video came from Chris Parker's unit and the audio wasn't anything to write home about with the dog whining and snuffling in the foreground.

"...it's been moved. I'm telling you, I saw it at the twenty-three mark."

On the screen, Tick listened as Parker explained. An unwilling smile tugged at her lips while she watched him. He leaned a hand on the roof of the car, and she groaned at the unthinking gesture. He wasn't wearing gloves—no wonder his fingerprints had been found.

Her gaze riveted on the screen, she watched Schaefer, who stood off to the side, arms crossed over his chest, wearing his customary serious expression. On screen, Tick and Parker walked away from the car, flashlight beams bobbing into the woods. Schaefer remained with the disabled vehicle, maintaining his distance from it.

A nervous shiver running along her arms, she slid off the bed and closer to the television. With the remote, she rewound, watching. Parker explained. Tick leaned on the car. They walked into the woods, leaving Schaefer behind. They returned as Bobby Gene Butler pulled up in his wrecker. He stepped out, adjusting his belt. Tick and Schaefer conferred, then Schaefer sauntered to his car, driving away.

"Oh, my God," she whispered, staring. She backed away

from the television and cast a wild look around for her shoes and holster. She had to find Tick.

Chapter Fourteen

A flick of Tick's experienced wrist sent the sparkling lure flying over the murky water. The spangled spinner winked once in the dusky twilight before disappearing beneath the surface with a soft plop. He reeled it in with slow, deliberate motions, pausing, leading to the left with the rod tip.

With Caitlin resting, he hadn't been able to resist picking up his rod from the dock. Fishing soothed him better than nicotine and he needed that tonight.

Lifting the lure from the water, he let it dangle a moment before sending it out over the waters of the blue hole again. A huge granddaddy bass lurked around his dock in the late evening and he indulged in a routine battle of wills with the animal. Again tonight, he'd failed in that battle.

He'd also failed in trying to find some peace. Too much bounced around in his head—all the what-ifs about their baby and their future, the aftershocks from the day's events, Caitlin's suspicions where Chris was concerned, the fear he'd seen in those women's faces earlier at the women's center, remnants of the rage he felt toward Benjamin Fuller.

Not to mention the all-out urge he had to kick Jeff Schaefer's ass. The boy had torn it with him today, with that crack about his screwing Caitlin on the side. Tori's displeasure or no, Tick intended to have a man-to-man talk with him real soon about the level of respect he'd show her.

Wonder if he could convince Del to talk to Tori? Sometimes she was more inclined to listen to Del's calm, quiet reason.

The lure snagged on an underwater tree and a violent curse escaped him. While he jerked the rod up, he spun the reel, tugging hard. The line snapped and the distinctive sound of his reel stripping sent more anger than it should coursing through him. Another curse ripped across the still evening air.

His reel was dead and his favorite spinner had just disappeared into the depths of the Flint River. Freakin' perfect.

Pine straw crackled on the path behind him, followed by Caitlin's strained voice. "Tick? Are you down here?"

"Yeah." So much for taking care of her. He picked up his rod and pulled out his pocketknife to cut off the excess line. She skidded to a stop on the dock, her hair falling in damp disarray about her face, T-shirt hitching over the top of her holster. "Aren't you supposed to be asleep?"

"He didn't—"

"You're worn out, precious." Pocketing his knife, he walked by her to his tackle box.

She grabbed his arm, pulling him back to face her. "I know who he is!"

"What—"

"Catch anything?" Behind Tick, at the edge of the tree line, Jeff Schaefer's smooth voice cut through the still air. Tick went rigid, every cop instinct he had screaming. Shit, this was not good. "Because it looks like I did."

With swift, practiced ease, Caitlin drew her gun, and Tick registered her grim expression at the same instant Schaefer chambered a round with an audible click. Tick half-turned, trying his damnedest to place himself between her and Schaefer's weapon without blocking her own aim.

"Drop it, Schaefer." Caitlin's throat moved with a hard swallow, but otherwise, she remained the picture of cool bureau competence.

Schaefer laughed and time slowed in a surreal crawl. Moving to stand at the top of the dock, Schaefer held a gun in an easy, two-handed grip, a second semiautomatic tucked in the waistband of his slacks. Hell, not just any automatic, either. Tick's Glock. Sick anger pounding through him, Tick remembered leaving it and his badge on the island before going to find Caitlin.

The son of a bitch had *his* gun.

Adrenaline and aggression surged through Tick. His body screamed at him to rush the other man; his training and intuition whispered terse warnings to stay still.

"You drop it, Falconetti." Smug triumph colored Schaefer's words. "Don't make it difficult. I can do him now as well as later."

"Won't that screw up your plan?" The hint of challenge in Caitlin's tone sent unease skittering down Tick's spine.

"Not really." Schaefer moved a hand to rest on the butt of Tick's Glock. Hooked over his belt, handcuffs gleamed next to it. "Murder-suicides are messy anyway. If you won't drop the gun, I'll just say he had already killed you when I got here, and I had no choice but to shoot him when he turned on me. A quicker death for you, a little less fun for me, but it works."

"Just one problem with that, Jeff." Tick tried to keep his voice level. "The forensics won't support—"

"Fuck the forensics. Think I can't handle that?"

"No one's going to believe I hurt her." Ingrained training tingled to life, overriding the anger and fear. He needed Schaefer distracted, on the defensive. Schaefer kept glancing between them, gaze bouncing from Caitlin to Tick and back again. He didn't appear nervous, but if they could break his concentration enough, Caitlin would have the opening she needed. "You hear me? *No one* will believe it. Not Cookie. Not Tori. Not Stan. Not anyone."

"They'll believe what I tell them to. You were already out of control today, after you got in my face last night. Hell, you attacked Botine today. If you'd go after the local head of the GBI, who knows what you'd do? So maybe she"—he cast an insulting, narrow-eyed look in Caitlin's direction—"rejected you again tonight. It got ugly and you killed her. Better yet, she discovered you were the murderer and you killed her to cover your tracks."

"You believe it. You believe if you say it, it's true and you can do this," Caitlin said, and from his peripheral vision, Tick saw her shift to her right.

Schaefer's stance tightened. "Try it, Falconetti, and I'll put a bullet in him. I can do it, too, before you can put one in me. Are you willing to watch him die first?"

Caitlin didn't reply and Schaefer relaxed, a sneer curling his lip.

"I win. Drop the gun, Falconetti."

Caitlin paused several silent moments before she eased farther to the right, lowered her gleaming SIG nine millimeter, and moved to lay it on the dock.

Tick tensed, checking the instinct to reach for her. "Sweet Jesus, Cait, don't do this."

Schaefer moved onto the dock. Tick took a step backward, to his left, away from the line of fire. Schaefer glared at him, his malevolence concentrated solely on Tick. "Don't move again."

Tick sensed the movement before he glimpsed it. In a smooth motion, Caitlin lifted her gun and fired. The rapid succession of blasts echoed in the still air. Schaefer jerked with the impact. The muzzle flashes sparked and more shots rang out before burning pain exploded in Tick's consciousness.

Continue firing until the threat is eliminated.

The words she'd not only heard as a recruit, but had repeated over and over to her own trainees, reverberated through Caitlin's brain. She emptied the gun in a matter of seconds.

Her ears buzzed with the overwhelming noise, sensation sizzling over her scalp.

Schaefer didn't fall with the first bullet. Scrambling backward, he got off four wild shots before his gun clattered to the wooden dock and his body slumped against the railing.

Aware of the rush of water and a whip-o-will calling, still gripping her SIG, she approached Schaefer's motionless body and checked for a pulse, finding it weak and uneven.

Her hand came away stained red.

She stared at the blood with a weird sense of detachment and rubbed her hand down her leg, trying to shake the sensation she walked in mud a foot thick.

Tick.

She spun toward the river. He'd dropped with the first shots, and he rolled to his feet, movements clumsy and disjointed.

"Are you okay?" Her palms prickled and stung, as if a million gnats crawled under her skin. Pain pulsed in her head, flashes of light and black dots squirming at her peripheral vision.

"No." His voice was a thick rasp and he clutched at his right side, blood spilling over his fingers.

"You're bleeding." The words sounded cold and uninterested to her own ears and he glanced at her oddly, his expression tight with pain.

Tick opened his mouth to reply, his face paling. Spinning, he leaned over the railing, retching until only dry heaves shook his lean body. When the spasms had passed, he rested his forehead on the wood and groaned.

She lifted a hand to push her hair back, surprised at its wild trembling. Schaefer moaned, and the training rushed back, full-force. *Secure the scene.* She moved his gun out of reach and pulled the handcuffs from his waistband. Ignoring his hoarse grunt of pain, she rolled him to his stomach and cuffed him. *Call for backup.* She reached automatically for her cell phone.

Damn.

"I have to call for help." She tried to swallow, her mouth dry and filled with a strange metallic taste. Tick had slumped to a kneeling position, still holding his side, head bent. She paused, torn between love and duty. "I don't want to leave you."

"Be fine. Just go."

She ran for the house and dialed with shaking hands. It took her long, agonizing seconds to convince the dispatcher she wasn't joking.

Time crawled. She sprinted back to the dock and sidestepped the pool of blood spreading from Schaefer's prone body. Aware of the screech of tires on blacktop, the spray of gravel, car doors slamming and familiar male voices raised in alarm, she knelt by Tick. Eyes closed, he clutched at his chest, breathing labored, blood trickling over his fingers with each gasp.

"Oh, God," she whispered, looking around for anything to stem that flow of red. Nothing. She covered his fingers with hers, pressing, still holding her gun with her right hand. He winced and she gulped back a sob. "It's going to be all right,

Tick. I swear. Hold on, okay?"

He opened his eyes, the dark depths cloudy with pain and confusion. "Holding on to you."

"I'm right here." She rested her cheek against his, the warm ooze of his blood stealing her breath. "Don't you dare die, Calvert. Do you hear me? I need you. I'm not letting you go."

"Not going anywhere." His labored gasp puffed along her neck. "Too...damn stubborn. Stuck with me now."

Footsteps vaulted onto the dock, stopping short. Behind her, Cookie swore.

"What the hell happened?" Stanton's voice shook. He hit his knees beside them, yanking his shirt over his head, leaving him in khakis and an undershirt.

"Son...of a bitch shot me," Tick wheezed, his fingers contracting under hers. "Shit, can't breathe, Stan."

"Let me see." Stanton took Caitlin's wrist in a firm grip and moved her hand to the side. Blood spurted over Tick's fingers.

Fear erupted in her brain. "God, Reed, keep the pressure on—"

"Cookie, help me here." Stanton pushed Tick's hand aside and bunched his shirt over the wound. "Take care of her."

"Come on. Stan's got him." Cookie hooked a hand around her elbow and lifted her to her feet, taking her SIG. "You don't look so good, Falconetti."

"I'm fine." She inhaled hard, her knees quivering. Tick's eyes closed, his lashes casting long shadows on a too-pale face, uneven breaths coming in harsh gurgles. "Be careful with him, Reed—"

"Tick? Stay with me. Come on, partner." Stanton tapped his jaw. Tick grunted.

She rubbed her arms, trying to dispel the awful cold. The blood smeared over her skin turned her stomach and she shuddered. More commotion ensued as other officers arrived. Paramedics rushed onto the dock, one going to Schaefer, the other to Tick.

Caitlin glanced at Schaefer's inert body. She should feel something. Guilt. Worry. Anything but this vast, yawning nothing.

Cookie pulled her away, up the path. She struggled to remove her arm from his firm hold. "Cookie, wait, not—"

"Cait, he's in good hands. Harrell's the best EMT I've ever seen. He'll take care of him, I promise. I want to make sure you're okay."

"He didn't touch the car." She pushed the words past numb lips.

Cookie looked at her, gray eyes sharp with worry. "What?"

"Schaefer. In the patrol film, Tick touched the car. Schaefer never did, but his prints were on the car. And he was in the gas station right before Kimberly Johnson came in." A sob racked her chest, and she couldn't stop shaking. "God, Cookie, he killed Gina. She's *dead*."

Her voice rose on the word and he wrapped an arm around her shoulders, leading her toward the patrol cars lining Tick's driveway, lights whirling in the semidarkness. "Come on, Falconetti."

Tears spilled over her lashes. If she'd put it together sooner, Gina might still be alive. Tick wouldn't be shot and possibly bleeding out. *I wasn't ready yet. I shouldn't have come—I should have told ADIC Frazier that—if I had, Gina...oh, God, Gina, I'm sorry.*

At his unmarked unit, Cookie draped his duty jacket over her shoulders and eased her onto the passenger seat. "Can you tell me what happened?"

Beyond his shoulder, her gaze lingered on what she could see of the scene below, Schaefer being lifted onto a stretcher, paramedics assessing Tick's injury while Stanton knelt beside him. Gina was dead, and Tick could have died. The air left her lungs in a harsh sigh. Tell him what happened?

"I screwed up."

Moisture dripped down her neck, and she swiped at it. Cookie swore, and she stared at her hand, the wetness of her blood mingled with Schaefer's and Tick's.

Still cursing, Cookie pushed her hair aside. "Did you hit your head?"

She tried to remember. "No."

A harried expression on his face, he pressed a handkerchief

to her scalp. "Hey, Troy Lee! I need a medical kit. Damn it, Falconetti, don't you dare faint on me."

Her vision blurred and she blinked, scoffing at him. "I've never fainted in my life, Cook, and I don't plan to start now—"

"Oh, shit." His voice rang in her ears as everything tunneled to black.

Cʒ

Caitlin leaned her head against the pea-green wall, sending pain shooting through the stitches in her scalp. She had a deep hotline graze, courtesy of one of Schaefer's wild shots, but she welcomed the discomfort, which drew her attention momentarily from the icy knot of worry and fear gripping her throat. Recounting the night's events over and over again, for Stanton and Cookie, the GBI and then the two FBI agents dispatched from the Atlanta field office, had driven the numb detachment from her mind and emotions. In its place was a stark dread that Tick would die.

The waiting area outside the surgical unit overflowed with people—Tick's family and friends along with what looked like the entire Chandler County Sheriff's Department. The deputies huddled in small groups, their faces shocked, voices low. Tori and Tick's brothers sat with their mother, whispering reassurances. Caitlin had spoken to them earlier, before being separated and questioned again by agents Hatcher and Jackson.

She stared at the double doors marked *No Admittance*, wondering what was happening on the other side. She knew Tick had blacked out before the paramedics had even loaded him into the ambulance. Upon arriving at the hospital, he'd gone from trauma to surgery within minutes. More than three hours had crawled by since.

Somewhere behind those doors, doctors also fought to save Jeff Schaefer's life. She couldn't care less one way or the other. He'd taken Gina's life and he'd tried to take Tick's. She shivered, closing her eyes.

Tick couldn't die. He couldn't.

Please don't let him die. Please.

The simple prayer echoed through her mind. *He won't. He's too strong, too stubborn. He has too many people who need him.*

She needed him. And he was always there when needed.

"How's the head?"

She glanced up at Stanton. Her fingers fluttered over the neat row of stitches under her hair. The local had worn off, and the ibuprofen tablets she'd swallowed dry earlier did little to deaden the ache. "Fine, thanks."

He proffered a paper cup. "Out of a vending machine, but at least it's caffeine."

"Thank you." She rolled the hot cup between her hands, gaze straying to those double doors again.

"I just talked to Cookie. He and Troy Lee executed the search warrants on Jeff's house. Kimberly Johnson's driver's license was in his dresser drawer, along with Sharon Ingler's class ring. Nothing of Vontressa's yet, except her cell phone." He passed a hand over the back of his neck. "All of their phones, actually. And yours, too."

"Souvenirs." She sipped the strong coffee and grimaced at the sour taste. "To help him pull up the memories later."

"They're still looking. No telling what else they'll find." He cleared his throat and darted a look around the crowd. "You know Tick's going to be okay."

She swallowed the fear. "Of course he is."

"He's too damned stubborn not to be." A weak grin curved Stanton's mouth, although his eyes remained bleak and serious.

"Reed, you're a lousy liar." She crossed her arms over her chest, still balancing the cup in one hand. "You're just as worried about him as I am."

"Yeah. Did you know the GBI has a profiling section?"

The abrupt change of subject startled her. Wariness curled through her. "No, I didn't."

"Botine says one of the older guys is retiring in a couple of months. They'll be looking for someone to fill that position. Bet they'd love to see your resume."

"Gee, Reed, is this an olive branch?"

He sighed, hands braced on his hips. "You could call it

that. I have the feeling if Tick gets his way, you and I will see a lot more of each other."

Agent Hatcher approached, saving her from having to reply. "I hate to interrupt, but there were a couple of questions I forgot to ask earlier. Falconetti, do you mind if we step outside? It'll only take a few minutes."

She couldn't imagine what he hadn't already asked at least twice. Smothering the urge to tell him what he could do with his questions, she gave him a cool smile. "Of course."

His "couple of questions" turned out to be another thirty-minute review of the evening's events. Since Quantico, she'd heard horror stories of being the subject of an inquiry by the FBI's Office of Professional Responsibility. The stories were true in one sense—the investigation was more stressful than the actual shooting situation.

"I think that's about it." Hatcher closed his pocket notebook with a snap. "If there's anything else, I'll call."

Caitlin watched him walk to the hospital's parking lot. She wrapped her arms about her midriff, drawing in a long breath of the moist, warm air. Eyes closed, she pulled up memories of Tick's smile, his voice, his touch.

Please, please be okay. I can't lose you, too.

Footsteps clattered on the wide brick steps behind her. "Falconetti?"

At Stanton's voice, she turned, searching his face, her heart jerking at the lines spreading out from his hazel eyes. He looked tired, worried, grim. "Is he—"

"The doctor's sent word that he'll be out to talk with the family shortly."

She sagged with relief, but the tension rushed right back in. Talk with the family? Was that good, bad, what?

He swung a hand toward the doors. "Let's go."

The doctor was entering the waiting area as they arrived. With her first glimpse of his grim expression, Caitlin's heart stuttered and fell. A warm clasp on her hand startled her and she turned to find Tori beside her, a reassuring smile on her pretty face. The younger woman slipped an arm about her waist and squeezed.

"That's Jay Mackey," Tori whispered. "He's the ER trauma specialist and he's a great doctor."

"Mrs. Lenora?" Dr. Mackey strode toward Tick's mother. She rose, one of Tick's brothers on either side. The doctor gave her a gentle smile. "The surgical team is closing now. The bullet's removed, but we had to take a small section of his lower right lung. That lung had collapsed—that's why he couldn't breathe earlier."

Lenora covered her heart with one hand, a whispered prayer of thanks slipping past her lips. Caitlin didn't relax, her gaze on the doctor's face. There was too much stress in his expression, a stiffness that sent a sick apprehension through her.

"We..." Dr. Mackey's Adam's apple bobbed with a harsh swallow and he cleared his throat. "We had some complications during the surgery."

"Complications?" The brother closest to Caitlin spoke, his face sharpening with worry. "What kind of complications?"

"Apparently, Tick suffered an allergic reaction to one of the anesthetics. The surgical draping tends to camouflage the first signs of that, as it did with him in this case. Our first warning was when he experienced tachycardia, an increased heart rate. While we were trying to stabilize that, he started having bronchial spasms, which increased the bleeding from the original wound."

"Oh, Lord," Tori murmured, her grasp on Caitlin's hand tightening.

Dr. Mackey propped his hands on his hips, dropped his head for a moment and took a deep breath. "The renewed bleeding, combined with the blood loss he'd already experienced, put him into shock. We were worried about the possibility of circulatory collapse and cardiac arrest, but thank God we were able to stabilize him before that happened."

Lenora nodded, her face dazed, her grip on her sons' arms seeming excruciatingly tight. Caitlin concentrated on breathing and keeping her legs under her, since her knees seemed determined to turn to a weak, quivering mess. Tori pulled her tighter, closer, and Caitlin held on, thankful.

"He should be in recovery in a few minutes." Mackey was

speaking again. "He'll be there at least a couple of hours, then we'll move him to surgical intensive care. Once he's in recovery, Mrs. Lenora, you can see him for a few minutes. Other than that, we're going to restrict access to him until he's in SICU."

"It's all right," Tori whispered near Caitlin's ear and rested her forehead against Caitlin's temple. "He's okay, Cait. He's okay."

Caitlin nodded, aware now of the silent tears slipping down her face to match Tori's. She wrapped her own fingers tighter around Tori's hand. She couldn't speak, couldn't force any words past the throbbing lump in her throat.

She wanted to see him, to touch him, so badly she ached with it, but for now knowing he was okay would have to be enough.

A crushing weight pushed on his chest. A bruising pain thudded through him with his pulse, and every breath sent sharp agony racing across his chest. His teeth chattered with the most incredible cold he'd ever experienced. He tried to open his eyes and failed, the lids too heavy. He listened to the murmuring of a male voice, the deep tones throbbing through his head. For a moment, he allowed the darkness to tug at him again.

A soft, familiar touch on his cheek pulled him from the depths. A hand lifted his, pressing his fingers against a damp face. Aware of his mother's voice, he struggled to open his eyes again, to push words out through dry, cracked lips. "Mama, don't cry. S'okay now. Don't cry..."

Before the night was over, Caitlin went two more rounds with the agents from the Office of Professional Responsibility. Exhausted and with her professional patience gone, she less-than-politely informed Agent Hatcher what he could do if he had any further questions and went in search of Tori. Once Caitlin's fatigued mind had processed the shock and anguish of Tick's shooting, the agonizing reality of Tori's situation had started to sink in.

She found the younger woman in the dimness of the hospital's chapel, sitting in the third pew from the rear, head bent, forehead resting on the back of the bench before her. Caitlin slipped into the cushioned seat beside her and rested a hesitant hand on her shoulder.

"He tried to talk to me about Jeff earlier and I wouldn't listen." Tori released a shivery sigh and straightened, her eyes dry, features pinched with hurt and distress. "You know what his first words to me will be, don't you?"

Caitlin didn't have to ask who "he" was or guess what Tick's sister thought those words would be. She reached out and with a tentative touch smoothed Tori's hair behind her ear. "No, they won't. He loves you too much."

Tori pressed trembling fingertips to her eyelids. "Cait, this is bad."

She could only imagine. She slid an arm around Tori's slender shoulders and squeezed.

"I *dated* him. I was thinking about a future with him, kinda hazily, but still. I took him home to my mama." Another long shuddery breath that shook her entire body. "I let him kiss me, let him...Lord, I need a shower."

Caitlin laid her head against hers. "I'm sorry, Tori. I really am."

"Yeah, me, too." A self-deprecating, near-hysterical giggle rose between them. "Oh, this is going to be good. First, I had 'rape victim' tattooed on my forehead. Now, I get to add 'dated a serial killer'. Bet the old biddy committee will have fun with that."

"Oh, Tori, don't do this to yourself. Please."

"I am never dating again. Do you hear me? Never. Again."

The familiar sounds of a leather gunbelt creaking and handcuffs clinking came from behind them followed by the clearing of a male throat. Tori tensed in Caitlin's easy embrace.

"I'm sorry for interrupting." Cookie eased into the row behind them. Tori didn't look around, her head bent once more, but Caitlin shifted to face him. His sturdy countenance was drawn and tight. His sharp gaze, dulled by weariness and worry, darted to the back of Tori's head before he met Caitlin's.

"Stan says they just moved him from recovery to the ICU." He spoke in a hushed tone. "Family can see him there."

Tori nodded but didn't lift her head. Caitlin took her hand.

"There's an ADIC Frazier calling the station, looking for you, Falconetti. Wants you back in Quantico for debriefing tomorrow..." He glanced at his watch. "Well, I'd guess that would be today."

Leave now? There was no way. "I'm not going."

Cookie's eyebrows rose. Tori looked up and moistened her lips. "They'll censure you for that, won't they?"

"Probably." Caitlin lifted a shoulder in an offhand shrug. "I don't care. I'm not leaving him."

A soft smile crept over Tori's face, for a moment chasing the awful blankness from her eyes.

"Hot da—" Cookie darted a look at the altar. "Dang."

The second time Tick surfaced from the darkness, daylight peeked in between horizontal blinds. A steady beeping registered in his consciousness. A weird metallic taste wrapped around his tongue, his mouth cottony. The pressure in his chest remained to a lesser extent. Turning his head, he eyed the IV line running from above the bed to his hand, aware of more tubing invading his nose.

"Hey." His brother Del leaned over him, smiling. "About time you woke up."

His body lagged in obeying his brain's commands, like a movie where the sound track didn't fit with the movements of the actor's mouth. Drugs. He lifted his hand for a moment to stare at the needle. "Mouth's...dry."

"I'll bet." Del moved away and returned with a foam cup. "Ice chips. All you get until they know you're not going to be nauseous. Open up. I've had lots of experience feeding these things to Barbara."

Cool heaven melted on his tongue. He touched the vinyl tube at his nose, the effort exhausting already shaky muscles.

"Don't mess with that." Del eased his hand back down. "They're giving you oxygen until your lung reinflates."

His eyes slid closed despite his efforts to keep them open. The darkness sucked at his body again. With a burst of will, he lifted weighted lids. "Cait?"

"Come on, Tick, you need to rest."

"Need...see her."

"Okay. I'll find her."

Minutes or hours could have passed. He drifted somewhere between the dark and reality until a cool touch smoothed his jaw. He forced his eyes open.

A haunted green gaze looked down at him. With her hair secured in a disheveled knot, she appeared weary and troubled. Her unsmiling mouth trembled, and he lifted a hand, wanting to brush a finger over her lips.

"Hey."

She bit her bottom lip. "Hey, yourself."

He struggled to catch his breath between words. "Wanted to see you."

Her teeth worried her lip again, her eyes closing. "You scared me, Calvert."

"Really know you love me now." He tried to chuckle and regretted it, his chest seizing up with pain.

"What?"

"S'many bureau regs you broke to save my sorry ass, you have to."

"Oh, you don't know the half of it." Twin tears slipped from beneath her lashes.

"Don't cry. S'all right." Black dots swirled at the edges of his vision. "Ever'thing's okay. Love you."

"I know. Sleep now. You need to rest."

"Be here?"

"Yes. Of course."

Unwilling, he allowed the drugged exhaustion to pull him under once more.

A heavy rain, courtesy of an early evening thunderstorm, pattered harsh fingers against the windows. Feet tucked under her, Caitlin curled into a vinyl armchair with Jeff Schaefer's journal balanced on her lap.

Tick slept, much as he had for the last twenty-four hours, the strong painkillers keeping him sedated. The comforting regularity of his heart and oxygen monitors provided a soft beeping in the background, but even joined with the rain, they couldn't drown out the gurgling of the lung catheter.

Caitlin hated the wet, slushy sound with a shuddering aversion, but it wasn't going to run her from the room, anymore than the nurses had been able to earlier. When he'd awakened and asked for her, when she'd finally been able to touch him and see for herself he was all right, she'd promised him she'd stay. And except for a roundtrip flight out for Gina's funeral, it was a promise she intended to keep.

She stroked the back of his hand, the skin warm. He was right. Now, everything was okay, would be okay. Schaefer hadn't gotten the victory he'd been so smugly confident would be his.

Once more, she focused her attention on Schaefer's forceful handwriting. She had no intention of doing a jailhouse interview with the son of a bitch, but the record of his thoughts and plans and actions provided glimpses of the man lurking beneath the earnest façade.

The first one was too easy. The second was over too fast. Sharon, though, she was a rush. Listening to Calvert and Parker search for her, knowing they'd never even fucking think to look at me was even sweeter.

Caitlin fingered the page corner. He'd passed his pre-employment polygraph with flying colors then written of the administrator with derisive scorn. The same contempt nuanced the printed history of his time with the sheriff's department, his interactions with Tick and Cookie, with her.

Killing Amy was almost like killing my mother and for a while it relieved some of the anger. But this FBI bitch? She's too cool, too watchful. She could almost, almost be my equal. Getting the better of her could be interesting. Wonder what it would be like to hear her scream?

And Calvert's so obsessed with her. Wonder what it would be like to make him watch her die?

Arrogant bastard. She snapped the plain notebook shut, anger trembling through her.

In his sleep, Tick made a soft, indefinable sound, somewhere between a pained grunt and a smothered snore.

Caitlin cast the journal aside and unfolded stiff limbs. She leaned over him, tracing the lines of his much-adored features.

Bending closer, she kissed his cheek, slightly stubbled now, and let the familiar scent of him fill her.

"I love you," she murmured near his ear. "Always, Calvert, no matter what. We're in this together, all the way."

The door whispered open and she looked up as Cookie slipped into the room. His concerned gaze darted to Tick's face.

"How is he?"

She stroked her thumb over the inside of Tick's wrist, careful to avoid the IV line. "Good, I think."

He closed the door and moved to stand on the other side of the bed. A slight frown dragging at his brows, he studied her. "How are you?"

With her palm pressed to Tick's forearm, she let his warmth seep into her. "Better."

"I'm sorry, Falconetti...you know, about Bocaccio."

The lingering desolation of that loss flooded through her. "So am I. Want to hear the most ironic thing, Cookie?"

He clasped his hands, leaning on the bedrail. "Sure."

"Gina didn't come here because she'd found something on Schaefer." A completely humorless laugh escaped Caitlin's lips. "It was you, an old missing-persons case from when you worked in Florida. You flag as a possible suspect."

Cookie's lashes fell but he didn't say anything.

"She died for *nothing*. He killed her for nothing." Caitlin sifted her hair away from her face. "My God, he was so twisted, Cookie...I've been reading his journal. Have you looked at that thing?"

"No." On a harsh sigh, Cookie opened his eyes. "We've been taking Butler's place apart, trying to make a connection between him and Schaefer."

"It's in the journal. Butler moved Sharon's car. Schaefer wrote about it, how he used Butler, manipulated him. The same way he did Amy."

"And Tori." Cookie's voice hardened.

"Yes. I'm worried about her. She—" Caitlin cut off the

sentence. Probably Cookie wasn't the person to share this with, her concern over the way Tori seemed to be withdrawing into herself, the way her sparkling personality had dimmed overnight. Caitlin glanced at Tick's face, the lines of pain apparent even in his drugged sleep. "I wish I'd killed the bastard."

"Yeah. Me, too."

She passed a hand over her eyes. "I can't remember the last time I was this tired."

"Not sleeping for a week will do that to you. If I get out of here, will you at least try to take a nap?"

She smiled at his gruff concern. "Maybe."

"Which means no, you won't. Stubborn as he is, aren't you?" Cookie's impish grin appeared momentarily. "Damn, he's gonna have a long, hard row to hoe with you. I can't wait to watch."

"Good night, Cookie."

He chuckled and headed for the door. He stopped, one hand on the lever. "Hey, Falconetti. Told you y'all would be good together."

Disjointed dreams came, of Caitlin's gentle touch on his face and her husky voice whispering that she loved him. He surfaced through layers of darkness, wanting to hang onto the dream as long as possible. Something tickled his nose and he brushed it away, his arm still leaden.

The tickle returned and he dashed at it again, the movement sending sharp pain racing across his chest. Familiar male laughter penetrated the haze. "Come on, Lamar Eugene, wake up."

"Leave him alone and let him rest, Ash." Stanton spoke somewhere over his head.

He opened his eyes to find them on either side of the bed, Stanton eyeing the monitors and Ash twirling a feathered fishing lure in his hand. "Hey."

Stanton appraised him with a critical gaze. "You look better."

"Better than what?" He groaned, pressing the heel of his

hand into his eyes, grateful that he felt more alert, but aware of every ache in his body now. He ran an exploratory hand across his chest. "I feel like hell."

Stanton shot him a wry look. "I wonder why? It wouldn't have anything to do with getting shot in the chest."

Ash chuckled. "They cut the dosage on your pain meds."

Tick glanced at the window, the blinds closed. Fingers of deep golden light slid between the slats. "What time is it? Hell, what day is it?"

"It's Thursday night, a little after eight," Stanton replied, checking his watch.

Tick stared at him. "Thursday? I've been out of it for two days?"

Stanton nodded, dropping into the vinyl chair by the bed. "Pretty much. You've come around a few times. You spoke to your mom, to Del. The doctor said you woke up long enough to cuss him out when they removed the lung catheter earlier today."

"Lord, I'm glad I don't remember that." He rubbed a hand over his throat. "I'm dying of thirst."

Ash filled a foam cup with ice water from the pitcher by the bed and dropped a straw in. To Tick's disgust, he couldn't keep the cup steady, and Ash had to hold it for him.

Ash set it aside. "At least you weren't throwing up from the anesthesia. When I had my appendix out, I was sick as a dog for a week afterward."

"Nah, he did that at the scene," Cookie drawled, strolling into the room. He tossed a packet of saltine crackers on the bed, smirking. "Thought you might need those."

"Funny." Tick grimaced and struggled to sit up, Ash helping him. Pain arced across his chest and he gasped, pausing a moment to catch his breath. "Where's Cait?"

Cookie hooked his thumbs in his gun belt. "She said something about her and Troy Lee taking your truck and boat and heading to Key West."

Tick cast his gaze heavenward. "Shouldn't you be out arresting someone?"

"She flew out to New York this morning for Bocaccio's

funeral." Stanton leaned forward, hands clasped loosely between his knees. Vinyl creaked and cloth rustled as he stood. "We should go and let you get some rest."

Tick wanted to point out that he'd been asleep for two days, but with pain still rolling through him, he wouldn't be good company either. Opening his eyes, he grinned, a half-hearted effort. "Thanks for coming."

"I'll catch up to y'all." Cookie waited for the others to clear the room. He cleared his throat, his gray gaze solemn for once. "So, you okay?"

"Yeah." He'd be better if Caitlin were around, wanted to see her now that he was actually coherent. Images from that standoff on the dock flickered in his head and a shudder moved through him, spreading darts of agony over his torso. Damn, that situation could have so easily gone the other way.

"Tick, it's over, man. Don't dwell on it. You'll make yourself crazy."

"So what about Schaefer?" Tick wasn't sure how many of Caitlin's bullets the son of a bitch had actually taken, but there'd been a hell of a lot of blood spilling from him.

"He's alive. Barely." Cookie's grim tone indicated he wished it otherwise. "Still in ICU, still pretty touch and go, according to the docs."

Tick nodded. "And Cait?"

"It's been tough, but she can deal." A familiar evil glint appeared in Cookie's eyes. "Quit worrying. She couldn't miss that funeral but she'll be back tonight. Has a hot date with Troy Lee."

"You can get out now."

"Later, man." At the door, Cookie stopped and glanced back. "Hey, Tick."

"Yeah?"

"Falconetti says Tori's having a tough time. When you talk to her...make sure you take it easy with her."

"I will." Remorse pulsed in him. Damn it, he hadn't kept Tori safe from the bastard, either.

As his partner left, Tick let his lids slide closed once more. He felt like hell, but a rush of hope and promise deluged him, despite the lingering worry and regret.

He had his Caitlin back. For good.

Chapter Fifteen

His chest was on fire, burning along the healing incision. Tick shifted on the hard courtroom bench. He probably should have listened to his doctor and taken another week off, but the emptiness of his house was driving him crazy, the department was understaffed and no way would he miss this.

Plus, if everything went right, he'd be taking the long weekend to kick back and relax.

Lawyer at his side, Schaefer, still pale and weak, sat in a wheelchair before Judge Virgil Holton. Pain twisted his expression, but no sympathy rose in Tick. Schaefer deserved to hurt, deserved everything he got, for what he'd done to those girls, what he'd planned to do to Caitlin. Those plans, outlined in the journals Cookie had found hidden in Schaefer's closet, gave Tick nightmares. Shooting them quickly had been far from the guy's final plan. Schaefer had seen Caitlin as a challenge and Tick as inferior, and making Tick watch her slow death was to have been the ultimate victory.

He'd written of the other murders, of Butler's help in disposing of the cars, with the arrogance of a man who believed himself invincible. He'd drawn Butler in after Sharon's disappearance, when he'd returned to Sharon's car after killing her and found Butler there. Between threats and Butler's own greed, Schaefer had convinced him to remain quiet.

Tick was glad Caitlin had shot the son of a bitch. Too bad she hadn't killed him and saved the state the cost of a trial.

"The state requests remand, Your Honor." From his position in the side gallery, Tick could see the contemptuous sideways glance Tom McMillian slid in Schaefer's direction.

"Considering Mr. Schaefer's current physical condition, flight is unlikely, Your Honor." Autry Holton clutched the edge of the defense podium, and even at this distance, the white tension surrounding her knuckles was visible. Having to mount this defense had to be difficult for her—she'd known the victims, her father was the judge and she was sleeping with the sheriff. Or had been. After the fierce argument Tick had caught the tail end of the night before, he was guessing whatever Stanton and Autry had going between them was gone.

Autry leaned forward. "And the state's case is largely circumstantial."

"The state requests the court consider the heinous nature of the crimes, Your Honor. Mr. Schaefer murdered five young women as well as a witness and attempted to kill two law enforcement officers, including a federal agent. He remains a suspect in the murder of another federal agent."

Autry turned a cool look on McMillian. "Allegedly murdered. As for Agent Bocaccio's death, the state has absolutely no evidence pointing to his involvement. And the GBI report on Investigator Calvert's shooting isn't complete yet. My client may be cleared of wrongdoing in that incident."

Beside Tick, Stanton made a disbelieving sound in his throat. Tick could empathize. Autry was really reaching here.

Virgil Holton lifted quizzical eyebrows at his daughter. "Mr. Schaefer is remanded without bail."

Autry recovered quickly, as though she'd never expected to win. "Your Honor, under the circumstances, I request Mr. Schaefer be housed in a facility other than the Chandler County Jail."

Virgil gave a quick nod. "Remanded to the Haynes County Jail while awaiting trial. Any objections, Mr. McMillian?"

McMillian was already gathering his materials. "None, Your Honor."

The bailiff moved forward to collect Schaefer, and Virgil rose from the bench. Autry stepped across the aisle to hand a folded document to McMillian.

"Bet it's a motion to suppress the fingerprint evidence on that bag y'all brought back from Tallahassee," Stanton whispered, cynical disdain coating his words. "She'll swear it was illegally obtained."

Tick rose and reached for his suit jacket. His side pulled with the movement, the area around his gunshot wound still tender, and he winced. "And Virgil will toss the motion out. Nothing illegal about it, but she has to try. She's just doing her job, Stan."

Stanton straightened his tie. "You can't really agree with her doing this. He tried to kill you, Tick, damn near succeeded, too, and she's defending him."

Ignoring for a moment the pain in his side, Tick shrugged. "She's a defense attorney. That's what she does."

"What if she gets him off?"

"She won't." Tick eased toward the door. "Not with everything we have, plus my testimony. Not to mention Cait's."

Simply saying her name gave him a thrill, much the way having her voice wash over him when he picked up the phone did. Holy hell, he was so far gone it wasn't even funny. He'd told her so the night before when she'd called after deplaning in Texas. She was stopping over to see her grandfather and had tried to talk Tick into joining her. Since her last case—a kidnapping and murder in Oregon—had kept them apart for weeks, he'd been hard put to tell her no.

Hopefully, surprising her would make up for the very real disappointment in that beautifully husky voice.

He stopped on the wide marble steps outside and shook out a cigarette. Stanton scowled. "What the hell are you doing?"

His lighter flared, heating his fingers. "Don't start, Stan."

"Didn't Jay tell you...oh, hell, why am I bothering? You're just going to do what you want to anyway."

Tick inhaled, the nicotine seeping into him, steadying his nerves. Actually seeing Schaefer had the banked sense of fury bleeding through him.

"What time is your flight tomorrow?"

Anticipation shivered over him, leaving a different form of tension in its wake. "Eight o'clock. I'm going on to Atlanta this afternoon. There's something I need to do."

The door whooshed open behind them. "Stanton," Autry said, her pretty voice tight. "Could I speak with you a moment?"

Tick could feel the hesitation before Stanton cleared his throat. "Yeah. Give me a minute, though."

Stanton exhaled roughly. "Try to get some rest, Tick. You still look like hell. And have a good time."

Have a good time? Considering the bureau had kept Caitlin from him for almost three weeks, he had every intention of doing so.

CR

He was definitely lost.

Tick frowned at the map and driving directions Cookie had printed off the Internet for him. Two-point-one miles east. If he followed this, he'd end up...

He looked at the end of the dead-end street that widened into a parking lot, beyond which water glittered under the morning sun.

In the Gulf of Mexico.

That definitely wasn't Court Avenue.

"Damn it." He pulled into the next driveway to turn around. Give him a plain old-fashioned atlas any day. Impatience danced under his skin. He'd waited days, weeks, to see her and the little delays standing in his way were driving him nuts.

He pulled into the first business he came to, a sprawling shack-like structure labeled The Rooster's Nest. The white gravel parking lot sat nearly empty, holding one SUV, an unmarked police unit and a wicked-looking black Jaguar XKR. When he stepped from the rental car and headed for the building, a warm breeze saturated with ocean and carrying the cry of gulls washed over him.

"Beyond tipsy. She'll be hung over this morning. And I thought the old man would stroke out." The taller of two men descending the creaking wooden steps spoke. Both in their late thirties, one wore a green sheriff's uniform, the other sported impeccable navy slacks and a fine white shirt, expensive sunglasses hiding his eyes. He was the one speaking, his voice even and cultured. "It was actually rather nice. Like old times."

"I bet." The cop caught Tick's gaze, spotted the Internet

map and grinned. "You know, those are—"

"Shit. Figured that out."

"Exactly." The cop laughed. Tick shifted to get a better look at the guy in shades. Something about the man whispered of intense watchfulness and had all of his law-enforcement instincts coming to life. "Where are you going?"

"137 Court Avenue."

The cop studied him, his gaze sharp and assessing. "The Cavanaugh house?"

"He's here to see Cait," Sunglasses said, sizing him up. Tick knew that look. He'd turned it on every guy who'd ever gotten within five feet of Tori.

Tick nodded. "Vince."

Sunglasses jerked his chin at him. "Calvert."

Deadpan, the cop looked between them. "Should I call for backup?"

"No." Vince continued to watch him. "His intentions are honorable. That's why he's here. The question is, will she say yes?"

The arrogance didn't sit well with Tick. He stiffened, his chest aching again, but damn if he would rub at it. "She will."

The cop snorted. "You're sure of yourself."

Tick ignored him, still focused on Vince. "But what makes you so sure of yourself?"

"You'd be surprised what I know, hot shot." Vince discarded the sunglasses, green eyes glowing in his tanned face. "For example, I know you made a little detour on your way here. I know in your pocket is a small blue box from Tiffany's in Atlanta and in that box is a one-carat solitaire in a classic platinum setting. I know you spent a little more than the prerequisite two months' salary on said ring. I also know you charged it to your American Express, which you pay off in full every month and have never been late on. I know you're planning to propose to my only sister and unfortunately, I know she's going to say yes, which means I'll be stuck with you for the next fifty years or so. Anything else?"

"Yeah. You know how to get from here to 137 Court Avenue?"

Vince chuckled, a glimmer of respect appearing for the first time in his dark green eyes. "Come on."

He'd only been two blocks away. Tick shook his head at the irony, unable to resist an anticipatory grin as he followed Vince's sleek Jag around a sharp curve. The street opened into a neighborhood filled with massive old homes. Vince pulled into the circular drive before a red brick three-story, its white trim gleaming under the morning sun. Tick braked behind the other car. The foundation was high, and globular topiaries in varying sizes marched up the wide front stairs.

With one foot on the bottom step, Vince flipped through his keys. "I want you to understand this upfront. She's the only item of true value in my life and I've already watched one man try to destroy her. If you hurt her, break her heart, hell, make her shed a goddamn tear, I'll have you killed and your body dumped so deep in the Mexican desert that only future archaeologists will find you. Just so we're clear on that."

Was he supposed to be intimidated? "I'll make sure my buddies at the FBI know to look your way first if anything ever happens to me."

Seemingly satisfied now that he'd expressed himself, Vince jogged up the steps, swung the large oak door open and waved Tick through a vestibule that flowed into a larger, more formal foyer. Mingled scents of oil soap and fresh flowers sank into Tick's consciousness.

Vince tossed his keys on a large silver tray atop a side table. His expensive loafers whispered over glistening hardwood floors as they passed through the living room.

Framed photographs in varying sizes lined the cream-colored walls of the hallway off the living room. Following Vince, Tick stopped, intrigued. He smiled at the pictorial history of Caitlin's life, her memories and accomplishments. One included the same woman from the oil portrait over the fireplace, older, but her lined face still lovely, with a much younger Caitlin at her side. They stood on a rocky landscape, a deep blue-green ocean shimmering behind them.

Vince touched the frame. "Greece, when Cait was eighteen, the year before Grandmother died." He tapped another. "College commencement ceremony."

Tick recognized her graduation from Quantico. He smiled

over a candid shot in which, clad in formal riding garb, she grinned at the camera. In another, she stood on the staircase from the foyer, in a simple black gown. The next snapshot depicted her among a bevy of laughing young women in light summer clothes, on a green lawn holding croquet mallets. Beside it, a more recent shot of Caitlin and Vince dressed casually in jeans and white shirts, seated on the house's front steps, a fat beagle grinning by her feet.

In each, she appeared happy and secure, her eyes clear and unshadowed.

Something was missing.

Taking a step back, he studied the photographs as a whole and frowned as realization sank in. "Where's her childhood?"

Vince's face hardened. "She didn't have one. My father saw to that."

He spun, stalking down the hall. With a last glance at the photos, Tick trailed him into a massive gourmet kitchen where sunlight splashed on Mexican tile floors. A radio played, filling the room with soft strains of jazz and blues.

A round, petite woman in her sixties cast a long-suffering look in Vince's direction as they entered the room. "About time *you* got home."

"Good morning, Isabel." Vince swept her into a hug, his tall frame swamping hers, and plopped a kiss on the side of her neck. She waved him away with a swat, all the while eyeing Tick.

He was being sized up again, measured, gauged.

Isabel added a glass of milk to the tray on the counter and studied Tick. "So this is the one."

He wasn't sure if that was positive or negative. Vince settled on a stool and slanted a mocking glance at Tick. "This is the one. Izzy, Tick Calvert. Calvert, Isabel Covas."

Tick leaned forward to offer the woman his hand. "Ma'am."

She grasped his hand in both of hers, her deep brown gaze locked on his a moment. Definitely sizing him up.

"She's the heartbeat of the place," Vince said, drawing their attention. A slow charming smile slid over his sharply angled face. "Not to mention the woman who ruined me for all others."

"You." Isabel rolled her eyes and made a clucking sound, still holding Tick's hand. "You will never change."

"Would you have me any other way?" Vince jerked a thumb toward the second set of stairs leading out of the kitchen. "Where's Cait?"

Ignoring him, Isabel gave Tick one last look and released him. She pointed a bony finger in Tick's direction. *"He* is a good boy. I can tell."

One of Vince's eyebrows rose in an askance expression. "From two minutes and a handshake?"

"Unlike you." Isabel turned the finger on Vince, her eyes narrowed to slits. *"Tu...tu eres el nino del Diablo."*

Tick swallowed a laugh at Vince's outraged expression.

"Your grandfather has been looking for you, Vincent. He wants to play golf today and says do not keep him waiting." She lifted the tray. An affectionate smile softened her face. "Miss Caitlin is on the patio by the pool."

She waltzed up the stairs.

"Miss Caitlin." Vince shook his head and went to the tall cabinets to pull down a tray. "You see how this is? Some things never change. She's the favorite and I'm the spawn of Satan." He paused in the act of transferring a coffee carafe to the tray. "Actually, that describes Father pretty well. Izzy might be on to something there."

Tick ignored him, his gaze bouncing around the room.

He was waiting for me in the kitchen.

Caitlin's tear-clogged voice echoed in his head and sent a frisson of ice trickling over him. This was the room where everything had changed, where he'd lost his child and almost lost Caitlin. His nape prickled and he looked around to find Vince watching him with unreadable eyes and a viciously hard expression.

"There. She's herself in the rest of the house but she still can't come in here." Vince jerked his chin toward the tiled floor between the massive island and the staircase. His face hardened further, bordering on murderous. "I should have killed the son of a bitch that night when I had the chance."

Tick nodded, a completely male understanding flowing

between them before Vince lifted the tray bearing coffee, orange juice and an array of muffins and fruit. Tick opened the French door for him.

Outside, Tick found himself enveloped by a humid heat tempered by a brisk sea-scented breeze. After the episode in the kitchen, some of his edginess had returned, the healing incision at his ribcage pulsing. He'd had enough now; he needed to see Caitlin.

The flagstone patio wrapped around the side and back of the house, steps leading to a large turquoise pool shimmering under the bright morning sun.

Tick paused on the bottom step, recognition and anticipation flaring in him, followed by the sense of homecoming and rightness he associated with being in Caitlin's presence.

Clad in a brown crochet tankini, she reclined on a lounger. A pair of sunglasses rested atop her head, and with her eyes closed, she tilted her face up to the sun.

Vince held a finger to his lips, a devilish glint in his eyes. He set the tray on a glass-topped table and adjusted the umbrella. "Well, good morning, Angel Face."

Her face twisted at his words, but she didn't open her eyes. "No loud talking."

Her husky voice shivered over him and Tick eased down the final step and to the pool apron. He took advantage of the opportunity to study her, drinking in her presence after their enforced separation. The swimsuit concealed her abdomen and the scars, except for a glimpse of skin at her waist, but revealed the toned length of her legs. She relaxed deeper into the cushion, wiggling crimson-tipped toes as she did so.

"Ah, did someone overindulge a little last night?" A distinct bite entered Vince's voice, an absolute warning Tick didn't miss. The guy didn't like him even looking in Caitlin's direction.

An ironic smile tipped the corners of her mouth. "I can't keep up with our cousins anymore. I think I had one Sunrise too many."

"I have a surprise for you, sister mine." Vince pulled out a chair, the legs squawking a bit on the stone.

"If it's not six-foot-three, lean, dark and handsome with a

wicked southern drawl, I'm not interested."

"Him?" Vince settled into a chair, crossed one leg over the other and adjusted the crease in his slacks. He poured a cup of coffee. "Forget about him. I have it on good authority he's off on a fishing trip with some little blonde."

"Nice try, Vinnie." She waved a dismissive hand. "Talked to him yesterday. I know exactly where he is."

"And where's that?"

She lifted her little finger and made a twirling motion around it with her other hand. "Right here."

Tick swallowed a surprised laugh. He eased up behind the chaise, planted a palm on either side of the frame and leaned forward, his face directly over hers. "Really."

Her eyes flew open and he saw the surprised joy bloom in the green depths as her lips parted on his name. An answering pleasure sparked in him. She straightened, winced, touched her forehead, and subsided. "Ouch."

Tick chuckled and bowed closer over her to murmur, "Think I'm whipped, do you, precious?"

She opened her eyes again, giving him a glimpse of the need and desire he knew belonged solely to him. "I think you're mine."

"No think about it." He tilted forward. "I'm definitely yours."

She reached for him, linked her hands behind his neck, pulled him down. With the first touch of her lips on his, everything disappeared but her. He let himself sink into the kiss, making a lazy exploration of the sweet darkness of her mouth, the way kissing her upside down changed the feel of it.

Dear holy hell, he'd missed her.

A whole new set of fantasies kicked off in his head, of nibbling down her throat to the line of her cleavage above the swimsuit and lower...

"I'm still sitting here, you know." Vince's voice was hard, terse.

Caitlin sighed into Tick's mouth and he lifted his head enough to focus on her eyes.

"I'd tell him to go away," she whispered, "but he'd just ignore me. He's obstinate like that."

He stroked a soft caress along her cheek. "There's always later."

She eased to a sitting position and he straightened. She rose and slipped her arm about his waist, hugging him to her as she moved toward the table. "I thought you couldn't get away."

He tugged out a chair for her. "I blackmailed Stan into giving me time off. Told him he could give me the comp time or pay me the overtime the department owes me. His choice."

Once he settled in his own chair, she clung to his hand and leaned toward him. "I'm glad you're here."

"So am I." His gaze dropped to her lips, still damp and a little swollen from his kiss. "Go away, Vince."

"Gladly." Vince pushed up from the chair. "This is turning my stomach."

His footsteps clattered up the steps and disappeared. Tick hooked a hand around Caitlin's neck and pulled her mouth back to his.

She loved having him here.

Warmed by his presence, Caitlin relaxed, sipping a cup of coffee and picking at one of Isabel's incredibly moist muffins. Even the mild pounding in her head was receding.

"We're lucky we didn't miss each other," she said, trailing her fingers along his arm. The last few weeks had been too long; she couldn't stop touching him, couldn't stop looking at him, couldn't get enough of him. "I've been trying to get an afternoon flight out to Atlanta all morning. Everything's booked for the holiday."

He chuckled, not lifting his head or opening his eyes. He lounged in the chair next to her, sprawling almost, in what appeared to be boneless relaxation. Popping another bite of lemon poppy-seed muffin in her mouth, she studied him. He still looked tired, a little pale under his tan, and she was sure the chest wound continued to bother him, even though he assured her it was healing. He was putting on weight, though, the pounds he really hadn't needed to lose slowly easing back onto his long frame.

She stroked her thumb across his wrist. "You've been

pulling doubles again, haven't you?"

He gave a humming exhale under her touch, a sound of pure male satisfaction. "Monroe's daddy suffered a heart attack and Anderson's wife had her baby. Someone had to cover them."

"You work too hard." She slipped her caress to the sensitive inside of his arm.

He opened one eye. "That's funny, coming from you."

"Mmm." She tickled his inner elbow, smoothed his biceps, and he shifted under her fingers, a smile flirting about his mouth. "We both need some R and R. A little playtime."

His lashes lifted, his dark gaze serious. "Oregon was bad, wasn't it?"

She caught her breath and nodded. They'd talked nightly while she'd been away, sometimes more than once, but she hadn't shared the details of that case with him. Hadn't wanted to expose him to the horrors. "Oregon was worse than bad."

He caught her hand, lifted it, pressed a kiss to her palm. "I'm sorry."

"It's better now." How to explain that being here helped her lose the memories?

"This is—"

"Calvert, do you golf?" Vince dropped a file folder on the table between them. "Happy birthday, Angel Face."

"My birthday isn't until October." Caitlin eyed the folder with caution. If it contained what she thought it did, just maybe she'd never speak to him again.

Vince ignored her. "Do you golf?"

"Do I know how? Sure." Tick shook his head. "Am I any good? Hell, no."

"Fantastic." Vince helped himself to the last bite of Caitlin's muffin. "Troupe hates to lose. The two of you have a twelve-fifteen tee time, so we need to get moving."

Caitlin glanced up, still fingering the edge of the file. Annoyance shivered through her. She wasn't ready to share him yet. "Wait a minute—"

"Don't argue, Angel Face. The old man wants to talk with him."

"He hears you call him 'old man' and you'll be disinherited for life."

"What else is new?" Vince tilted his head and fixed Tick with an inquiring look. "Calvert? Come on so you can explain your intentions."

Tick glared at him once and pushed up from the chair. He leaned down and whispered a kiss across her mouth. "We have plenty of time, precious. I'll see you."

Caitlin watched them walk away, happiness tugging at her. Yes, they had plenty of time. With a sigh, she flipped open the folder, sure she'd be looking at a damn prenuptial agreement.

Her breath strangled in her throat. It did contain legal papers, financially endowing a trust at a high school in Brooklyn, New York. A trust to fund the Gina Bocaccio Memorial Scholarship, providing a four-year college scholarship to a deserving student planning to pursue a career in law or its enforcement.

A sudden rush of tears pricked at her eyelids and she blinked them away.

Even the overprotective ass had his good points.

∽

The driver hit the ball with a solid *thwack*, the impact shivering up Tick's arms. The small white sphere veered sharply to the left. He shook his head. Troupe Cavanaugh had no fear of losing to him.

Not that the older man seemed to have any interest in winning or losing today. He'd spent the last seventeen holes drawing out details about Tick's life, his law-enforcement career, his family and his finances.

Why he didn't just ask Vince the All-Knowing was beyond Tick.

Except as soon as they'd arrived at the golf course, Vince had escaped to the clubhouse, a polished young blonde clinging to his arm.

Troupe, who seemed at least two decades younger than his eighty-odd years, lined up his next shot. He squinted down the fairway then eyed the ball and drew back for the swing. "You do intend to marry her."

The firm words were not a question. "Yes, sir, I do. As soon as possible."

Troupe dropped his club into the bag and shouldered it, walking toward the hole. "I'm sure Vincent has already threatened you."

An indulgent, resigned affection colored the statement. Tick chuckled, falling into step beside him. "Yes, sir, he did. Quite thoroughly."

Troupe gave a curt nod. "He loves her dearly, as she does him, although it's hard to tell sometimes when they're hurling obscenities at one another. Shift your right hand up, loosen your elbow."

Tick looked at Caitlin's grandfather over his shoulder and obeyed. This time, the ball sailed straight, landing on the putting green.

"Normally, I would be a stickler for a long engagement so that all the proprieties could be observed." With a sharp swoosh, Troupe sent his ball flying. It bounced twice and plopped into the hole. "However, I think the two of you may have waited long enough already." He focused a stern look on Tick. "You will take care with her."

"I have every aim to do so."

"The situation with my daughter and Caitlin's father...I should have done a better job at protecting her." Troupe didn't make it plain which "her" he referred to—Caitlin or her mother. Tick wasn't sure the old man didn't mean both of them. "And after Katherine, my daughter, died, I should have listened to my wife and done more to extricate Caitlin from that man's custody. I assumed because she was away at school that the situation was under control. I was wrong."

His chest tight, Tick leaned on the golf bag and waited.

Troupe turned fierce blue eyes in his direction. "I failed to protect her from Nicholas Falconetti's emotional machinations, and I believe, young man, that you have already had to pay part of the price for my failure. She does not love without total trust and she does not give that trust easily, unless she has reason to feel utterly safe. I think the fact that she loves you speaks volumes."

ᗉ

During the too-warm evening, dinner guests descended on the Cavanaugh household: a couple of Troupe's political cronies, a handful of Vince's business associates and their wives. Amused, Tick watched Caitlin play the perfect hostess, a polished role that didn't disappear until the visitors did.

If he'd thought he get her to himself then, he'd been wrong. Two of her cousins and an old friend came calling, and they sat in the less-formal sitting room on the second floor, chatting and laughing.

It didn't take Tick long to figure out who these people were.

They were the ones who made her feel safe. The ones she trusted enough to love.

He'd realized, too, as she'd introduced him around and perched on the arm of his chair, her fingers playing with the edge of his hair, sending pleasurable thrills along his spine, that she was enfolding him within that group.

Any lingering doubt he'd had that she'd say yes evaporated, like mist on the river under a rising Georgia sun.

Once this second round of guests departed, he captured her hand in his just after she closed the front door and leaned against it with a laughing exhale. "Oh my God, Tick, I didn't think we'd ever get this house empty."

He chuckled, reveling in the sensation of finally being alone with her. Damn, she was beautiful, soft and casual, in faded jeans and a yellow halter-top sweater. He was ready to wrap himself around her and never let go.

She tilted her head toward the French doors, sliding her fingers down his wrist. "Do you want to take a walk on the beach?"

"Sounds good." A few minutes later, having snagged a thin blanket from the pool house, she led him down a pathway. Laughing, they tugged off their shoes and Tick dug his toes in, relishing the residual warmth from the day's sun. Waves crashed on the beach, a steady rhythm with a muted roar.

Linda Winfree

Caitlin spread the blanket, dropped her shoes on it as an anchor and turned toward the water with an audible sigh. Tick stepped up behind her and wrapped his arms about her waist. He nuzzled the side of her neck, inhaling her unique scent blended with the tang of salt and sea. A warm glow of contentment flushed through his body.

She laid her arms over his, letting her head fall back to rest against his shoulder. He tightened his embrace, soaking her in, drinking in the bubbling joy he felt within her, a joy he knew all too well because she engendered the same emotion in him.

Sometimes our greatest joys come out of our greatest pain.

"I love you," he murmured against her ear, his mother's wisdom flowing through him. He'd found his greatest joy, the woman right here in his arms.

"Mmm, I love you, too." She shifted against him, leaning into his caress.

He trailed a line of soft kisses across her jaw. The past with its hurts and pain and doubt washed away, leaving behind the only real thing that mattered, the way she felt in his arms, the way he felt in hers. He sighed against her temple, loving her.

"Ask me, Lamar Eugene." Laughter and joy sparkled in her low voice. "Ask me so I can say yes."

"Marry me," he whispered. "Live with me, love me, be my wife. Let me take care of you, stand by you, be your husband. Give me forever with you."

"Yes." She turned in his arms and pressed her fingers to his chin. "*Yes.*"

The last she murmured against his mouth, and he caught the glimmer of tears before he kissed her, cradling her face, sipping at her lips.

Her fingertip drifted over his chin down to his collarbone, the smooth warmth of the caress sending a shiver down his spine. "I want everything with you, Calvert."

"Oh, precious, you've got it."

She buried her face against his throat, arms about his waist. "I've been told your mother loves big weddings."

"She does. And she's been waiting to marry me off forever." Her mouth moved against him, in what he knew was that

314

wonderful, beautiful smile.

"Has Troupe already told you he believes in long engagements?"

"He let me off the hook there, thank the good Lord. I'd go crazy."

"You know big weddings can take up to a year to plan."

"I'm not that patient."

"Neither am I." She ran an easy touch along his jaw. "Small wedding, three months tops. Or six. No more than nine."

"Three."

"Three." A soft glow warmed her eyes. "We get married here, *right* here."

"Right here? On the beach?"

"Yes, small ceremony, with Troupe officiating, and we let your mother plan a huge reception for Georgia."

"Deal." He curved his hand around her shoulder, rubbing at the smooth bare skin. Actually, he liked the idea of marrying her here. "You feel safe here, don't you, precious?"

"Yes." She leaned up to kiss him, holding on to him. He pressed his face against her throat and wrapped her close. "Exactly the way I feel with you."

About the Author

How does a high school English teacher end up plotting murders? She uses her experiences as a cop's wife to become a writer of romantic suspense! Linda Winfree lives in a quintessential small Georgia town with her husband and two children. By day, she teaches American Literature, advises the student government and coaches the drama team; by night she pens sultry books full of murder and mayhem.

To learn more about Linda and her books, visit her website at www.lindawinfree.com or join her Yahoo newsletter group at http://groups.yahoo.com/group/linda_winfree. Linda loves hearing from readers. Feel free to drop her an email at linda_winfree@yahoo.com.

When a member of the CIA's premiere counter terrorism unit discovers the woman he loves is a suspected terrorist, he'll go to any lengths to uncover the truth.

Long Road Home
© 2007 Sharon Long

Jules Trehan disappeared without a trace three years ago much to the dismay of her parents and Manuel Ramirez. A counter terrorism specialist, Manny has utilized every agency resource in his attempt to discover what happened to Jules, to no avail.

As suddenly as she disappeared, Jules reappears in a small Colorado town. Injured in an explosion, she's hospitalized, and Manny rushes to her side, determined not to ever let her go again.

But Jules has one last job to do or Manny's life will be forfeit. A mission she must complete, even if it means betraying the only man she's ever loved.

Available now in ebook and print from Samhain Publishing.

*Someone wants a secret to stay buried—even
if it means murder.*

For the Love of Jazz
© 2007 Shiloh Walker

Since waking up in a hospital at age eighteen, accused of
driving the car that killed his best friend, Jazz McNeil has lived
with a guilty heart. Now, more than a decade later, he has
returned to his hometown to raise his daughter and to uncover
the truth about what happened that fateful summer. And gaze
into the eyes of the girl whose life he shattered.

Though Anne-Marie Kincaid was told that Jazz was
responsible for her brother's death all those years ago, she has
never quite believed it. The facts don't quite fit; they never did.
All she knows is, she still feels loved and safe when she's with
Jazz, and that he misses her brother just as much as she.

And since he returned home, people have started dying.

Available now in ebook from Samhain Publishing.

*Reunited by their teenage son's possible involvement in a
murder...old passions and new needs
are destined to explode.*

His Ordinary Life
© *2007 Linda Winfree*

Book 2 of the Hearts of the South series.

Del Calvert has spent his life in quiet desperation, trying to meet everyone's expectations and feeling like he never quite measured up. From his teens, Barb was everything he wanted and needed, but knowing he wasn't enough for her drove him out of the marriage.

Barbara Calvert is afraid to need anyone—especially the soon-to-be ex-husband she still loves. She's reluctant to fall under his seductive spell of love and security once more.

But when their son's secrets threaten his life, everything changes. Del must help his son as unseen and threatening forces move ever closer, putting the entire family at risk. And along the way, he hopes to convince Barbara to give him one more chance to win back the wonderful, ordinary life he didn't appreciate until it was gone.

Available now in ebook and print from Samhain Publishing.

GREAT
cheap
fun

Discover eBooks!

THE FASTEST WAY TO GET THE HOTTEST NAMES

Get your favorite authors on your favorite reader, long before they're
out in print! Ebooks from Samhain go wherever you go, and work with
whatever you carry—Palm, PDF, Mobi, and more.

samhain
publishing
Ltd

LaVergne, TN USA
20 October 2009
161416LV00006B/17/P